MEN AT WAR

BOOK FOUR

THE FIGHTING AGENTS

ALEX BALDWIN

PUBLISHED BY POCKET BOOKS NEW YORK

Distributed in Canada by PaperJacks Ltd., a Licensee of the trademarks of Simon & Schuster, Inc.

This novel is a work of fiction. Names, characters, places and incidents are either the product of the author's imagination or are used fictitiously. Any resemblance to actual events or locales or persons, living or dead, is entirely coincidental.

Another *Original* publication of POCKET BOOKS

POCKET BOOKS, a division of Simon & Schuster, Inc.
1230 Avenue of the Americas, New York, N.Y. 10020
In Canada distributed by PaperJacks Ltd.,
330 Steelcase Road, Markham, Ontario

ISBN: 0-671-60758-8

First Pocket Books printing January 1987

10 9 8 7 6 5 4 3 2 1

Printed in Canada

THEY WERE AN ELITE COVERT STRIKE FORCE, TAKING THE WAR BEHIND ENEMY LINES!

JAMES WHITTAKER: With a movie star turned agent, Whittaker heads for the Pacific in a submarine—loaded down with weapons, supplies and gold.

CHARITY HOCHE: On the surface she was a G.I. pin-up. But Donovan sends her to England on a vital mission—and she's got the toughness and the smarts to see it through.

WENDEL W. FERTIG: the U.S. had abandoned the islands to the Japanese, but Fertig proclaims himself Brigadier General—to lead the resistance in the Philippines.

RICHARD CANIDY: The war is getting into his blood. Now he's moving fast and hard to free agent Fulmar from a Hungarian jail—or make sure his friend is dead.

HENRY DARMSTADTER: An unspectacular pilot, but an uncommon hero. Now he's in the hands of Canidy and company, flying into the heart of Nazi territory on one of the most dangerous missions of the war.

MEN AT WAR series by Alex Baldwin

#1: The Last Heroes
#2: The Secret Warriors
#3: The Soldier Spies
#4: The Fighting Agents

Published by POCKET BOOKS

Prologue

SINCE GENERAL DOUGLAS MacArthur's departure for Australia from the Fortress of Corregidor in Manila Bay was in compliance with a direct order from President and Commander-in-Chief Franklin Delano Roosevelt, it was the General's belief that the move was nothing more than a transfer of his headquarters. He believed, in other words, that the battered, outnumbered, starving U.S. and Philippine troops in the Philippine Islands would remain under his command.

He believed specifically that Lieutenant General Jonathan M. Wainwright, a tall, skinny cavalryman who had been his deputy, would, as regulations and custom prescribed, remain under his orders.

General MacArthur's last order to Wainwright—on the small wooden wharf at Corregidor just before MacArthur, his wife, his son, and a small staff boarded the boats that would take them away—was verbal: He told Wainwright to "hold on." Wainwright understood this to mean that he was forbidden to surrender.

Since he had been promised reinforcement and resupply of his beleaguered forces by Roosevelt himself, MacArthur believed that so long as the Fortress of Corregidor held out, Roosevelt would be forced to make good on his promise of reinforcement. The island of Luzon, including the capital city of Manila, had fallen to the Japanese. But there were upward of 20,000 reasonably healthy, reasonably well-supplied troops under Major General William Sharp on the island of Mindanao. That force, MacArthur believed, could serve as the nucleus for the recapture of Luzon, once reinforcements came.

MacArthur accepted the possibility that Corregidor might fall. But if that should happen, he believed that Wainwright should move his three-starred, red general's flag and the other colors to Mindanao, assume command of General Sharp's troops, and continue the fight.

Before MacArthur reached Brisbane, however, traveling first by PT boat[1] and then by B-17 aircraft, General Wainwright began to receive orders directly from Washington, from General George Catlett Marshall, the Chief of Staff.

General MacArthur and General Marshall were not friends. For instance, some time before the war when Marshall was a colonel at Fort Benning, MacArthur, then Chief of Staff of the Army, had officially described Marshall as unfit for command of a unit larger than a regiment. Several such incidents did not bring the two closer.

It was made clear to General Wainwright by the War Department that he was no longer subject to General MacArthur's orders, and that the conduct of resistance in the Philippines was entirely his own responsibility.

Without MacArthur's knowledge or consent, the decision had already been made by President Roosevelt, acting with the advice of General Marshall and Brigadier General Dwight D. Eisenhower (who had once served as MacArthur's deputy in the Philippines), that not only was reinforcement of the Philippines impossible—given the relative capabilities of the United States and Imperial Japanese navies—but that the first priority in the war was the conflict against the Germans in North Africa and Europe.

On May 1, 1942, there were 13,000 American and Philippine troops (on a three-eighths ratio) in the granite tunnels of Corregidor Island. These included a large number of wounded and all the nurses evacuated from Luzon in order to spare them rape at the hands of the Japanese. That day, Japanese artillery fired 16,000 rounds at Corregidor, one heavy shell landing every five seconds. And that many shells were fired the next day. And the next day. And the next.

---

[1]Patrol Torpedo: Small, wooden craft powered by Cadillac automobile engines.

On the night of May 5, 1942, when it became evident to General Wainwright that the Japanese were about to make an assault on the fortress, he radioed General Sharp and other commanders elsewhere in the Philippines, releasing them from his command.

Although most of the heavy coast artillery cannon on the island had already been destroyed by Japanese artillery, there were enough smaller cannon and automatic weapons still available to Wainwright's forces so that Japanese losses in the assault were severe. But the Japanese were both determined and courageous, and a foothold was gained.

The fall of Corregidor was no longer in doubt.

There was nothing to be gained by further resistance. In fact, further resistance would have meant that the Japanese would have trained cannon at the mouth of Malinta Tunnel. These would have swept the tunnel clean of nurses and wounded and the rest of the garrison as effectively as a hose washing down a drainage pipe.

Wainwright sent his aide, carrying a white flag, and a staff officer, to treat with the enemy.

Soon after that, General Wainwright met with his counterpart, Lieutenant General Masaharu Homma, on the porch of a small, bullet-pocked frame house on Luzon. The shaven-headed Homma, although he spoke fluent English,[2] addressed Wainwright through an interpreter.

Homma was not interested in the surrender of Corregidor. He demanded the absolute, unconditional surrender of all American troops in the Philippine Islands. If General Wainwright were not prepared to offer absolute surrender of all U.S. Forces, he would resume tactical operations. By this, he clearly meant wiping out the Corregidor garrison.

Accompanied by a Japanese lieutenant named Kano, who had been educated in New Jersey, General Wainwright was taken in a captured Cadillac to the studios of radio station KZRH in Manila. There, he broadcast a message to all commanders of all U.S. military and naval forces in the

[2]He had been an observer with the British Expeditionary Force in France, 1917; Japanese Resident Officer in India, 1925; and Military Attaché in London, 1930.

Philippines. As senior U.S. officer in the Philippines, he ordered all American Forces to immediately suspend hostile action and to make all preparations to surrender to the Imperial Japanese Army.

Not all Americans chose to obey General Wainwright's final order.

One

1

Headquarters, Mindanao-Visayan Force
United States Forces in the Philippines
28 December 1942

BRIGADIER GENERAL WENDELL W. Fertig, Commanding, Mindanao-Visayan Force, wore two items not commonly seen on general officers of the U.S. Army, a goatee with mustache and a cone-shaped, woven-reed hat perched at a cocky angle on his head. From this dangled what looked like a native bracelet.

General Fertig, a trim, red-haired man of forty-one, was not a professional soldier. He had not gone to West Point; but rather, he had entered the military service of the United States just over a year before, directly commissioned as Lieutenant Colonel, Corps of Engineers, U.S. Army Reserve. The U.S. Army in the Philippines had been delighted to have the services of an experienced civil engineer, in particular one who was familiar with the Philippines. When he had entered the Army, Fertig had sent his wife and family to safety in Colorado.

From the time of the Japanese invasion until the surrender ordered by General Wainwright on May 5, 1942, Lt. Col. Fertig had been primarily involved in the demolition—usually by explosive—of roads, bridges, and tunnels, supply and petrol dumps, and other facilities to deny their use to the enemy. Many of the facilities he destroyed he had built before the war.

On May 5, 1942, Lt. Colonel Fertig willfully and with full knowledge of the consequences elected to disobey the lawful order of his military superior, Lt. General Jonathan Wainwright, to immediately cease hostile action against the Imperial Japanese Army and to make all preparations to surrender.

He went instead into the mountains of Mindanao, with every intention of waging what hostile action he could against the Japanese. With him at the beginning were Captain Charles Hedges, another newly commissioned reserve officer of the Army, Chief Petty Officer Ellwood Orfett, USN, and Private Robert Ball, USA.

Things did not go well at first for the little group. To avoid Japanese capture, they had to live in the jungle, eating what they could find there. Or else they ate the native food Moro tribesmen furnished them every now and again—at the risk of their lives.

Once, they watched from the jungle as a long line of American prisoners—their officers bareheaded and with their arms tied behind them—were moved to a prison camp.

Although they encountered some yet-to-surrender Philippine troops, there was no rush to Fertig's colors. Most of the Filipinos, in and out of uniform, sadly suggested to them that the war was over and that the only logical course for the ragtag quartet to follow was to surrender.

But Fertig, if personally modest, had a somewhat grand notion of the role he could play in the war. He kept a diary, which has survived, and in it, in a rice paddy near Moray, he wrote:

"I am called on to lead a resistance movement against an implacable enemy under conditions that make victory barely possible. . . . But I feel . . . my course is charted and that only success lies at the end of the trail. . . . If we are to win only part of the time and gain a little each time, in the end we will be successful."

Lt. Colonel Fertig gave a good deal of thought to the reluctance of the Filipinos and other Americans who had not surrendered to join him. He finally concluded that this was because they quite naturally thought he was simply one more middle-level brass hat, one more American civilian temporarily commissioned into the Army.

They would, on the other hand, follow a real soldier, he realized. He improved on this: If there were a general officer who announced himself as the official representative of the United States and Philippine governments, that individual would command the respect of everybody.

On October 1, 1942, on the back of a Delinquent Tax Notice, Fertig wrote a proclamation in pencil and nailed it to a tree:

Office of the Commanding General United States Forces
In the Philippines
Mindanao-Visayan Force in the Field
1 October 1942

PROCLAMATION

1. By virtue of the power invested in me, the undersigned, as senior representative of the United States Government and the Philippine Commonwealth, herewith assumes command.
2. A state of martial law is declared for the duration of the war.

By Order of the Commanding General:
Wendell W. Fertig, Brigadier General,
USA, Commanding

DISTRIBUTION:
1. To all commanding officers, USFIP 2. To all Provincial Governors 3. To all Provincial Officials 4. To all Justice of Peace Courts 5. File

A Moro silversmith hammered out two five-pointed stars—the rank insignia of a brigadier general—from silver dollars, and Fertig pinned them to his collar points.

It was likely, Fertig knew, that his proclamation would be blown by the wind from the tree before anyone saw it. Or if it stayed on the tree (the distribution list, for instance, was a bluff; the delinquent tax form was the only sheet of paper he had), that whoever read it would either laugh or conclude there was a crazy American running loose.

But two days later, as the quartet was walking along the beach beside a Mindanao jungle, ready to rush in and hide if Japanese soldiers appeared, a wiry little Moro wearing vestiges of a uniform and carrying a Model 1917 Enfield U.S. Army rifle stepped into view. And then others appeared, until there were almost two hundred of them.

The wiry little Moro saluted crisply and in the best English he could manage informed General Fertig that he and his men were at the General's orders, and with respect, could he suggest they go into the jungle, for there were Japanese just a short distance down the beach.

Soon other Filipinos appeared, as well as other Americans who had decided to take their chances in the mountains and the jungles rather than enter Japanese captivity. No one seemed to question the stars on Fertig's collar points; they all seemed happy to be able to place themselves under the orders of someone who knew what he was doing.

A reasonably safe headquarters was established. Though it was not defensible, it was in a location that would be invisible from the air and difficult to locate on the ground. And even if located, it would be very difficult to surround. If Japanese appeared, Fertig and his forces would be able to vanish into the mountains before the Japanese got close.

Remaining free was the first priority.

The second priority, as Fertig saw it, was to make his presence known to others who had not surrendered and who could join his forces; to the Japanese, who would be obliged to tie down forces on a ratio of at least seven to one in order to look for and contain him; and to the U.S. Army.

There were risks involved in making the U.S. Army aware of what he was doing. For one thing, he simply might be ordered to surrender. He thus decided that if such an order came, he would not acknowledge it. For another, the U.S. Army was likely to frown both on his self-promotion to Brigadier General and on the authority he had vested in himself to take command of Mindanao and proclaim martial law.

Fertig decided that these risks had to be taken. There was simply no way he could arm a guerrilla force as large as he envisioned by stealing arms from the Japanese. And the only possible source of arms was the U.S. Army, which could either make airdrops or possibly send a submarine. And then on top of that, just about as important as arms was medicine, especially quinine. And the only possible source of medicine was the Army.

But what he really needed most of all was money. Not greenbacks. Gold. Preferably twenty-dollar gold coins. Lots of twenty-dollar gold coins. With them he could pay his troops, which would lend sorely needed credence to Brigadier General Fertig and his authority. And he could buy food and possibly medicine, and make gifts to Moro chieftains and others who could thereby be persuaded to help him.

There was one major problem with informing the U.S. Army of the existence of the Mindanao-Visayan Force of United States Forces in the Philippines: Headquarters, USFIP, had no radio. And if it could somehow get hold of a radio, it had no generator to power it. And if USFIP came into possession of a radio and a generator, and could somehow begin to transmit, there was a very good possibility that the U.S. Army Signal Corps radio operators in the States would not reply. They would presume that the Japanese were playing games with them, because any message from legitimate American Forces would be encrypted, that is, sent in code.

Acting on the authority he had invested in himself, Fertig commissioned Chief Petty Officer Orfett and Private Ball as Second Lieutenants. Lieutenant Orfett was put in charge of a deserted coconut-oil mill. Coconut oil could be sold or bartered. Lieutenant Ball was appointed Signal Officer, USFIP, and ordered to establish communications with the U.S. Army in Australia. He was to use his own judgment in determining how this could be best accomplished.

Lieutenant Ball appointed as his chief radio operator a Filipino high school boy by the name of Gerardo Almendres. Almendres, before war came, had completed slightly more than half of a correspondence course in radiotelephony. Using the correspondence course schematic diagrams as a guide, Almendres set about building a shortwave transmitter. Most of his parts came from the sound system of a motion picture projector that had been buried to keep it out of Japanese hands.

A boatload of recruits from Luzon arrived. It comprised the remnants of a Philippine Scout Explosive Ordnance

Disposal Detachment: six master sergeants, one of them an American. With them they had an American captain who had deserted USAFFE[1] and taken to the jungles, rather than face certain capture on Corregidor.

The Captain, Horace B. Buchanan, USMA '34, a slight, balding man showing signs of malnutrition, provided the second item necessary to establish communication with the U.S. Army in Australia. It was a small metal box bearing a brass identification tag on which was stamped:

SECRET

DEVICE, CRYPTOGRAPHIC, M94 SERIAL NUMBER 145.
IT IS ABSOLUTELY FORBIDDEN TO REMOVE THIS DEVICE FROM
ITS ASSIGNED SECURE CRYPTOGRAPHIC FACILITY

SECRET

General Fertig had never seen one before. He found it fascinating.

It consisted of twenty-five aluminum disks. Each disk was about the size of a silver dollar and just a little thicker. The disks were stacked together and laid on their edges, so they could rotate independently on an axle. The stack of disks was about five inches long. On the outside of each disk there was printed an alphabet, sometimes A,B,C in proper sequence and sometimes with the characters in a random order.

"How does it work?" Fertig asked.

Captain Buchanan showed him.

Each of the disks was rotated until they all spelled out, horizontally on the "encrypt-decrypt line" the first twenty-five characters of the message they were to transmit. That left the other lines spelling out gibberish.

Cryptographic facilities were furnished a TOP SECRET document, known as the SOI (Signal Operating Instructions). Among other things, the SOI prescribed the use of another horizontal line, called the "genatrix" for use on a particular

[1]U.S. Army Forces, Far East, was the official designation of MacArthur's Philippine Force.

day. The gibberish on the genatrix line was what was sent over the air.

Actually, Buchanan explained, the SOI provided for a number of genatrix lines, for messages usually were far longer than twenty-five characters. The genatrix lines were selected at random. One day, for example, Lines 02,13,18,21,07 and so on were selected, and Lines 24,04,16,09,09 and so on, the next.

When the message was received, all the decrypt operator had to do was consult his SOI for that day's genatrix lines. He would then set the first twenty-five characters of the gibberish received on that genatrix line on his Device, Cryptographic, M94, and the decrypted message would appear on the encrypt-decrypt line. He would then move to the next prescribed genatrix line and repeat the process until the entire message had been decrypted.

The forehead of the red-goateed brigadier general creased thoughtfully.

Buchanan read his mind.

"In an emergency, Sir," Buchanan said, "in the absence of an SOI, there is an emergency procedure. A code block . . ."

"A what?" Fertig asked.

"A five-character group of letters, Sir," Buchanan explained, "is included as the third block of the five five-character blocks in the first twenty-five characters. That alerts the decrypt operator to the absence of an SOI."

"And then what?"

"First, there is a standard emergency genatrix line sequence. The message will then be decrypted. The receiving station will then attempt to determine the legitimacy of the sender by other means."

"Such as?"

"His name, for one thing. Then the maiden name of his wife's mother, the name of his high school principal, or his children. Personal data that would not be available to the enemy."

General Fertig nodded.

"You are a very clever fellow, Buchanan," Fertig said. "You are herewith appointed Cryptographic Officer for United States Forces in the Philippines."

That left two connected problems. The first was to get Gerardo Almendres's International Correspondence School transmitter-receiver up and running. That would require electrical power, and that translated to mean a generator would be required.

Buchanan had no idea how that could be handled, but both he and Lt. Ball suggested that perhaps Master Sergeant George Withers might be of help. Withers was the NCOIC (Non-Commissioned Officer in Charge) of the Explosive Ordnance Disposal Detachment on whose boat Buchanan had escaped from Luzon. He was a competent fellow; Master Sergeants of the Regular U.S. Army are almost by definition highly knowledgeable and resourceful. He had, after all, managed to acquire and hide the boat and bring his detachment safely to Mindanao on it.

Master Sergeant Withers was summoned.

He was obviously uncomfortable, and after some gentle prodding, General Fertig got him to blurt out:

"The truth of the matter is, General, I'm not sure I'm a master sergeant."

"Would you care to explain that, Sergeant?"

Withers explained that he had been a staff sergeant[2] assigned to an Army Ammunition Depot on Luzon when he had been suddenly transferred to a Philippine Scout Explosive Ordnance Disposal Detachment.

"There was fifteen Scouts, General . . . we lost ten before we finally got out. Anyway, Sir, two of them was Technical Sergeants. They didn't know nothing about explosives, they'd come out of the 26th Cavalry with Lieutenant Whittaker when it got all shot up and was disbanded."

"Lieutenant Whittaker? A cavalry officer? Was he killed, too?" General Fertig asked.

"No, Sir, and he wasn't a cavalry officer, either. He was a fighter pilot. They put him in the cavalry after they ran out of airplanes, and then they put him to work blowing things up when the 26th Cavalry got all shot up and they butchered

[2]There were then seven enlisted grades: Private, Private First Class, Corporal, Sergeant, Staff Sergeant, Technical Sergeant—and First Sergeant/Master Sergeant.

their horses for rations. He was a fucking artist with TNT . . ."

"What happened to him?"

"I don't know," Withers said. "The brass on Corregidor sent for him. That's where we got Capt. Buchanan. He was sent to fetch Lieutenant Whittaker, and he talked Lieutenant Whittaker into letting him come with us."

It made sense, Fertig thought, *that a demolitions expert . . . "a fucking artist with TNT" . . . would be summoned to Corregidor to practice his art just before the fortress fell. Poor bastard, if he wasn't dead, he was now in a prison camp. With a little bit of luck, he could be here, and free. USFIP could use a fucking artist with TNT.*

"You were telling me, Sergeant," General Fertig said. "About your rank."

"Yes, Sir. Well, Lieutenant Whittaker thought that since I knew about explosives, and the Scouts didn't, it would be awkward with two of the Scouts outranking me, so he said, right when I first reported to him, that I had been promoted to Master Sergeant. I'm not sure he had the authority to do that, Sir. I wasn't even on the Technical Sergeant promotion list."

Sgt. Withers looked at General Fertig for the general's reaction. His face bore the look of a man who has made a complete confession of his sins and has prepared himself for whatever Fate is about to send his way.

"Sergeant Withers," General Fertig said. "You may consider that your promotion in the field, by my authority, has been confirmed and is now a matter of record."

"Yes, Sir," Sgt. Withers said. "Thank you, General."

"The reason I asked you in here, Sergeant," General Fertig said, "is to ask for your thoughts on a problem we have. We have need of a source of electrical power."

"What for, Sir?"

"To power our radio transmitter."

Withers hardly hesitated.

"There's a diesel on the boat . . ."

"We sank the boat."

"We sunk it before on Luzon," Withers said, undaunted. "The engine's sealed. I'll take my Scouts down there and get it."

"And how will you get it up here?"

"We'll steal a carabao[3] and make a travois . . . like the Indians had? . . . No problem, General."

"The sooner the better, Sergeant," General Fertig said.

2

Naval Communications Facility
Mare Island Navy Yard
San Francisco, California
5 January 1943

The Radioman Second looked to be about seventeen years old. He was small and slight, and his light brown hair was cropped close to his skull. He wore government issue metal-framed glasses, and his earphones made his head look very small.

But he was good at his trade, capable of transcribing the International Morse Code coming over his Hallicrafters receiver far faster than it was being sent. He had time, in other words, to read what he was typing instead of just serving as a human link in the transmission process.

He raised one hand over his head to signal his superior while with the other, with practiced skill, he took the sheet of paper in his typewriter out and fed a fresh sheet.

The Lieutenant junior grade who came to his station looked very much like the Radioman Second, except that he was perhaps four years older and just a little heavier. But he was slight, too, and wore glasses and looked very young.

He took the sheet of yellow paper from the Radioman Second and read it:

MFS FOR US FORCES AUSTRALIA
MFS FOR US FORCES AUSTRALIA
ACNOW BRTSS DXSYT QRSHJ ERASH

[3]This is the water buffalo, the most important domesticated animal of the region.

POFTP QOPOQ CHTFS SDHST ALITS
CGHRZ QMSGL QROTX VABCG LSTYE
ACNOW BRTSS DXSYT QRSHJ ERASH
POFTP QOPOQ CHTFS SDHST ALITS
CGHRZ QMSGL QROTX VABCG LSTYE
MFS STANDING BY FOR US FORCES AUSTRALIA
MFS STANDING BY FOR US FORCES AUSTRALIA

"What the hell is this?"

"Look at the third block," the Radioman Second said.

"What about it?"

"It was the emergency code, no SOI, when the Army was still using the old M94,"[4] the Radioman Second said.

"Who's MFS?" the j.g. asked.

"No such station," the Radioman Second said.

"What do you think?"

"I think it's the Japs playing games," the Radioman said.

"Well, what the hell, I'll send it over to the Presidio," the j.g. said. "Maybe they've still got an M94 around someplace."

"You don't think I should give them a call back?"

"They weren't trying to reach us, they were calling Australia. Let Australia call them back."

3

The National Institute of Health Building Washington, D.C. 10 January 1943

Motor Machinist's Mate First Class Charles D. Staley, USN, in compliance with his orders, presented himself at the National Institute of Health building.

Five weeks before, Staley had been running the tune-up shop at the Great Lakes Naval Training Center motor pool,

[4]Use of Device, Cryptographic, M94 was discontinued by the U.S. Army when it had become apparent that at least one of the devices had fallen into the hands of the Japanese.

outside Chicago. It was a hell of a thing for a first class petty officer with eighteen years service to be doing with a war on; but Staley was a Yangtze River Patrol sailor, and he had learned that Yangtze River Patrol sailors who had managed to make it back to the States—instead of either getting killed or captured in the Philippines—seemed to get dumb billets like that. The Navy didn't seem to know what to do with them, so it gave them billets like running a motor pool, shit that had to be done but had little to do with ships or fighting a war.

And then the Personnel Chief had called him in, and said there was a levy down from BuPers[5] for someone with his rate, who had been a China Sailor, and who was unmarried. The Personnel Chief said he had to volunteer, for the billet was "classified and hazardous." Reasoning that anything had to be better than cleaning carburetors, Staley volunteered.

Five days later his orders came through. For the first time in his service, Staley was flown somewhere in a Navy airplane. He was flown to Anacostia Naval Air Station in Washington, where a civilian driving a Plymouth station wagon met him and took him to a large country estate in Virginia about 40 miles from Washington. Some very rich guy's house . . . there was a mansion, and a stable, and a swimming pool, set on 240 acres in the middle of nowhere . . . had been taken over by the government for the duration.

A real hardnosed civilian sonofabitch named Eldon C. Baker had given him and ten other guys a short speech, saying the purpose of the training they were about to undergo was to determine if they met the standards of the OSS. Staley didn't know what the hell the OSS was, but he'd been in the service long enough to know when to ask questions and when not to ask questions, and this was one of the times not to ask questions.

Baker, as if he had been reading his mind, almost immediately made that official. This was not a summer camp, Baker said, where you made friends for life. You were not to ask questions about the backgrounds, including girl friends and families, of other trainees, and if a trainee asked you ques-

[5]Navy Bureau of Personnel.

tions that did not directly concern what was going on at the school, you would report that immediately to one of the cadre. If you reported it, the trainee who had asked the questions would be immediately "relieved" (which Staley understood to mean thrown out on his ass) and if you didn't report it, *you* would be relieved.

They would be restricted to the camp, Mr. Baker told them, for the length of the course, or unless "sooner relieved for cause."

The training itself had been part boot camp—running around and learning about small arms; and part how to fight like a Shanghai pimp, in other words with a knife, or by sticking your thumbs into a guy's eyes, or kicking him in the balls; and part how to blow things up; and part how to be a radio operator. Staley hadn't had any trouble with any of it, but some of the other guys had had a hell of a time, and although they had said as little as possible about themselves, Staley had been able to figure out that most of the other guys were college guys, and he would have laid three to one that at least three of them were officers. Of the twelve guys who started, six made it through. Three got thrown out, one broke his leg climbing up the side of a barn, and two just quit.

Some Army full-bull colonel, a silver-haired Irishman wearing the blue-starred ribbon of the Medal of Honor (the first one Staley had ever seen actually being worn) came to the estate just before they were through with the course and shook their hands; Staley was able to figure out from that that whatever was going on involved more than one service.

Two days before, the cadre had loaded them all in station wagons, taken them to Washington, and handed them $300 and a list of "recommended civilian clothing." Staley had bought two suits, six shirts, a pair of shoes, and some neckties.

The night before, one at a time, Baker had called everybody in and given them their orders, which they were not to discuss with anyone else. Staley didn't know what to make of his. He was ordered to report in civilian clothing to The National Institute of Health, in Washington, D.C.

They had brought him there in one of the station wagons.

There was a receptionist in the lobby, and a couple of cops.

He went to the receptionist, not sure what to do about his orders. They were stamped SECRET, and you don't go around showing SECRET orders to every dame behind a plate-glass window with a hole in it.

"I was told to report here," Staley said, when she finally looked at him.

"May I have your name, Sir?" she asked.

When he gave it to her, she looked at a typewritten list, and then handed him a cardboard badge with VISITOR printed on it, and an alligator clip on the back of it so that he could pin it to the lapel of his new suit. Then she called one of the cops over.

"Would you take Mr. Staley to Chief Ellis, please?" she said.

The cop smiled, and made a "come with me" gesture with his hand. Staley followed him to an elevator, and they rode up in it and then went down a corridor until they came to a door with a little sign reading "Director." Inside that door was an office with a couple of women clerks pushing typewriters, and an older woman who was obviously in charge. And a door with another sign reading "Director" on it.

"This is Mr. Staley," the cop said.

"The Chief expects him," the gray-haired woman said, with a smile. Then she looked at Staley. "Go on in," she said.

Staley stopped at the door, and conditioned by long habit of the proper way to report to a commanding officer, knocked and waited to be told to enter.

"Come in," a male voice called.

There was another office beyond that door, furnished with a large, glistening desk, a red leather couch, and two red leather chairs. Sitting at the desk, sidewards, so he could rest his feet on the open lower drawer of the desk, was a Chief Boatswain's Mate, USN, smoking a cigar and reading a newspaper.

"Whaddayasay, Staley?" the Chief said. "Getting any, lately?"

It took a moment before Staley was sure who the Chief was, then he said, "Jesus H. Christ! Ellis!"

Ellis swung around in his high-backed chair and pushed a lever on an intercom box.

"Could somebody bring us some coffee?" he asked. Then he turned to Staley and gestured toward the red leather couch. "Sit down," he said. "Take a load off."

Chief Boatswain's Mate J.R. Ellis, USN, was wearing a brand-new uniform. There were twenty-four years' worth of hash marks[6] on the sleeve. The uniform was his Christmas present to himself. It was custom-made. He had had custom-made uniforms before, but in China, when he'd been with the Yangtze River Patrol. But he hadn't been a Chief then, and custom-made uniforms cost a hell of a lot less in China than they did in the States. Chief Ellis had figured, what the hell, he had never even expected that he would make Chief, why the hell not get a stateside custom-made uniform. He could afford it.

The last time Staley had seen Ellis had been in Shanghai, and Ellis had been right on the edge of getting busted from Bosun's Mate First and maybe even getting his ass kicked out of the Navy. Ellis had been on the *Panay* when the Japs sank it.[7] After he'd swum away from the burning *Panay*, Ellis just hadn't given much of a damn for anything. Staley understood that: How the hell could you take pride in being a sailor if your government didn't do a goddamn thing to the goddamn Japs after they sank a U.S. Man-of-War and killed a lot of sailors while they were at it?

But he had never expected to see Ellis as a Chief, and certainly not in a billet where he was obviously some kind of a big wheel.

One of the typists came in with two cups of coffee, in nice cups and saucers, not mugs.

"There's cream and sugar," she said, smiling at Staley, "but Chief Ellis never uses what he calls 'canned cow.'"

"Black's just fine, Ma'am," Staley said.

When she left, curiosity got the better of him.

"What the hell is going on around here, Ellis?" he asked.

"I've been trying to figure out how to tell you that," Ellis said. "I guess the quickest way is the chain of command."

---

[6]Diagonal bars, each signifying four years of service.

[7]The USS *Panay*, a gunship of the Yangtze River Patrol, was attacked and sunk by Japanese aircraft near Wuhu, in Southern Anhwei, on December 12, 1937, almost four years before the Japanese attack on Pearl Harbor.

"Huh?"

"Tell me about the chain of command."

Staley looked at him in confusion. Ellis was obviously dead serious.

"Tell me," Ellis repeated.

"Well," Staley said, "I'm first class, and you're a chief, so I report to you, and you report to some officer, and he reports to some senior officer, and it works its way to the top, all the way, I suppose, to the Chief of Naval Operations."

"All the way to the President," Ellis corrected him. "The Chief of Naval Operations reports to the Chairman of the Joint Chiefs of Staff, and *he* reports to the President, who is Commander-in-Chief."

"So?" Staley said.

"The way it is here," Ellis said, "is that you report to me, and I report to the Colonel . . . you met him, he was out to look things over in Virginia . . ."

"The guy with the Medal of Honor?"

"Colonel William J. Donovan," Ellis said. "I work for him, and he works for the President. I mean, directly. He gets his orders from the President. Nobody else can tell him what to do."

Staley said, "No shit?"

"You're going to have to learn to watch your language around here, Charley," Ellis said, almost primly.

"Sorry," Staley said. "Where do I fit in around here?"

"You're going to be the Colonel's driver," Ellis said. "And don't look down your nose at it. There's more to it than driving a car."

"Such as?"

"There's a lot of people would like to see him dead, for one thing. Your first job is to see that don't happen."

"Like a bodyguard, you mean? Is that what all that crap in Virginia was for?"

Ellis nodded, but then explained. "Baker got to the Colonel," he said. "Everybody who comes into the OSS gets run through that school. For a while, I thought they were going to make me go."

"What exactly is this 'O.S.S.'?"

"It stands for 'Office of Strategic Services,'" Ellis said.

"It's sort of like the FBI and ONI (Office of Naval Intelligence) put together, plus Errol Flynn in one of them war movies where he parachutes behind enemy lines and takes on the whole Jap Army by himself."

"Give me a for example," Staley said.

"The school was supposed to teach you Rule One around here," Ellis said. "You don't ask questions. If they figure you should know something, they'll tell you. You ask the wrong questions around here, and you'll wind up counting snowballs on Attu."

"Can I ask what you do around here?" Staley asked.

"I'm on the books as 'Special Assistant to the Director,'" Ellis said. "What that means is that I do everything and anything that makes life easier for him, and keeps him from wasting his time. And what you're going to do is help me do that."

"Plus being a bodyguard, you said," Staley said.

"We don't talk about that," Ellis said. "He's got bodyguards, mostly ex-FBI guys and ex-Secret Service guys. And he ducks away from them whenever he can. *That's* when you cover him. Get the picture?"

Staley nodded. "I get the feeling you get along pretty good with him."

"I never met anybody smarter or nicer," Ellis said, flatly. "Or who works harder."

"How come I got this job?"

"The Colonel came in here about two weeks ago," Ellis said, "and found me working about midnight. And he said, 'I thought I told you to get some help.' And he sounded like he meant it. So I asked myself, do I want some FBI guy who looks down his nose at a sailor, and is going to be pissed when he has to take orders from me? And unless I could think of something else, that's what was going to happen. So I called the Navy, BuPers, and told them to find me ex-China Sailors in the States."

"You *told* the Navy?" Staley asked.

Ellis, grunting, took a small leather wallet from his hip pocket and handed it to Staley.

"It means what it says on there," he said. "You carry one of those things, everybody in the government, civilian agencies, as well as the military, has got to give you what you ask for. If they don't like it, they can bitch, later, after they give you what you ask for."

"Jesus Christ!" Staley said, and handed the OSS credentials back.

"You're going to get one of those," Ellis said. "You fuck up with it, Charley, we'll send you someplace that'll make Portsmouth[8] look like heaven. And no second chances. You read me?"

"Loud and clear, Chief," Staley said.

"You're also going to get a badge and credentials saying you're a Deputy U.S. Marshal. That's in case anybody asks why you're carrying a gun. You try to get by with that. I mean you don't show the OSS credentials until you don't have any other choice. You understand?"

Staley nodded.

"Same thing applies to the Marshal's credentials, fuck up with them once, and you're finished."

"OK, OK," Staley said.

"So like I was saying, the Navy found you in Great Lakes, and I remembered that we always got along pretty good, and that you weren't as dumb as you look, so I told them to see if you would volunteer. And you did. And you got through the school all right, and here you are."

"Yeah," Staley said. "Here I am."

"You can walk out of here right now, Charley," Ellis said. "I'll get you any billet you want in the Navy. But if you stay, you're here for good. And there's liable to be more to it before we're done than driving the Colonel's Buick."

He looked at Staley and waited for a response.

"I'm in, Chief," Staley said.

Ellis nodded and then dialed one of the three telephones on his desk.

"I'm sending a guy named Staley down there," he said. "Get him credentials, and take him by the arms room and get him a .45 and a shoulder holster, and then take him over to the house."

He hung the phone up.

"You'll get a rations and quarters allowance from the

[8]The U.S. Navy Prison is at Portsmouth, R.I.

Navy," Ellis said. "And a rations and quarters allowance from us, otherwise you would wind up sleeping on a park bench and starving. Until you can find someplace to live, we'll put you up in the garage at the house."

"The house?"

"It's a mansion over in Rock Creek we have," Ellis explained. "There's a couple of apartments over the garage. Nice. Get yourself settled, and then come back here in the morning. I probably shouldn't have to tell you this, but I will. There's two women at the house. They're absolutely Off Limits."

"Got it," Staley said.

"You fixed all right for money?" Ellis asked.

"Fine."

Ellis pushed a lever on the intercom.

"Will you have somebody take Staley to the photolab, please?" he said, and then gestured for Staley to leave.

Ellis was pleased with the way things had turned out with Staley. It had been a risk, recruiting him. But he'd done well in the school (That sonofabitch Baker had even been impressed; he'd called and said he had a job for Staley if what he was going to do in Washington was "relatively unimportant") and now that Ellis had talked to him, he thought he could handle what was expected of him here, and, very important, that he would get along with The Colonel. He hadn't been worried about how Staley would get along with Captain Peter Douglass, Sr., USN, Donovan's deputy (a Navy petty officer and a Navy officer would understand each other); but the Colonel might have been a problem.

Colonel "Wild Bill" Donovan had been one hell of a soldier in his day. He'd won the Medal of Honor in France with the "Fighting 69th," the National Guard regiment from New York City. Between wars, he'd been a rich and powerful lawyer in New York City and Washington. He had little patience for people he decided were fools. But Staley was no fool. The way he'd handled himself at the school, and the way he acted now had proved that. He would fit in.

Ellis thought of his responsibilities—now to be shared with Staley and maybe even a couple of others, if he could find the right men—rather simply: It was his job to make things easier for The Colonel. Sometimes that meant he would fry up ham and eggs in the kitchen of the Colonel's Georgetown town house. And sometimes it meant that he went around the world with the Colonel, serving as bodyguard and confidant and sort of private secretary and transportation officer. You name it, he did it.

And he got to learn a lot. He was *supposed* to read everything the Colonel read, so that if he had to do something for the Colonel, the Colonel wouldn't have to waste his time explaining things. Some of the stuff he had to read was really pretty dull, but sometimes it was interesting. So far as he had been able to figure out, there was only one secret the Colonel knew that he didn't. Ellis had concluded that Captain Douglass knew that secret, because when Ellis had started getting nosey, Douglass got his back up.

That secret had something to do with what an Army Brigadier General named Leslie Groves was doing at a secret base in the Tennessee mountains with something called uranium. That's what he'd asked Captain Douglass, "What's uranium?"

That's what had gotten Douglass's back up.

"Now hear this clearly, Chief. You don't ask that question. You don't mention the word 'uranium' to me, or to Colonel Donovan, and certainly not to anyone else. You understand that?"

"Aye, aye, Sir."

Ellis was confident that when the time came, he would find out what uranium was, and what General Groves was doing with it.

Some of the interesting things that came with the job had nothing to do with secrets.

What he had been doing when Staley had reported in, for example. He had been reading the *Mainichi.* He didn't think there were very many other people who got to do that. The *Mainichi* was the English language newspaper published in Tokyo. The edition he had in his hands was only ten days old. Ellis wondered how the hell they managed to get one in ten days halfway around the world from the Jap capital. But they did. And they did it regularly.

It was full of bullshit, of course.

For example, there was a story in the *Mainichi* today that troops under some Jap general with an unpronounceable name had destroyed the headquarters of Major General Fertig on Mindanao, killed General Fertig, and sent the rest of his troops running off to the mountains to starve.

The reason Ellis knew the story was pure bullshit was because he had been at a briefing in the situation room when guerrilla activity in the Philippines had been discussed. A full-bull colonel—a guy who had gotten out of the Philippines with MacArthur and then had been sent to Washington as a liaison officer and who should know what he was talking about—had said that while there was a chance that small units of a dozen or so men, could evade Japanese capture for as long as several months, there was no possibility of organized "militarily significant" guerrilla activity in the Philippines.

And there was no General Fertig. Ellis had checked that out himself. The only guy named Fertig in the Philippines was a light colonel, a reserve officer reliably reported to have blown himself up taking down a bridge.

According to the *Mainichi,* this non-existent general had at least a regiment; which the Japs wiped out to the last man at least once a week.

The messenger appeared in Chief Ellis's office, with the distribution. The messenger was an Army warrant officer in civilian clothes. There was no love lost between them. The warrant officer naturally wondered how come he was wandering around the halls of the National Institute of Health, delivering the mail like a PFC clerk, while this swab-jockey got to sit around with his feet on a desk reading a newspaper.

Ellis signed his name twenty-seven times, acknowledging receipt of twenty-seven TOP SECRET documents, each of which had to be accounted for separately, and then signed twice more for a batch of SECRET, and CONFIDENTIAL, Files.

When the messenger had gone, he scanned the titles of the TOP SECRET documents. He recognized every one of them. They had been here before. Then he read the titles of the SECRET documents and scanned through the half dozen he had not seen before. Finally, he turned to the CONFIDENTIAL titles, saw nothing of interest except the regular OF POSSIBLE INTEREST memorandum, which Ellis thought of as the "What-the-Hell-Is-This List."

This was a compilation of intelligence data that didn't fit into any of the established categories. A report that the

Germans had bought a ferryboat in Spain, for example. Or that the Italian gendarmerie had lost another battle against the Mafia in Sicily. It had come to someone's attention in one of the intelligence agencies. He hadn't known what to do with it, but maybe somebody else could make something of it. When that happened, it was circulated on the OF POSSIBLE INTEREST memorandum.

Ellis read it faithfully. And his eyebrows went up when he came to item six:

> 6. The Presidio of San Francisco has received from Mare Island Communications Facility an encrypted message transmitted by an unknown station operating in the 20-meter band. The message was encrypted using an apparently captured M94 encryption device.
>
> The message was addressed to "U.S. Forces in Australia."
>
> The decrypted message follows: We Have the Hot Poop from the Hot Yanks in the Phils. Fertig Brig Gen
>
> The station identified itself with the call letters MFS and reported itself standing by.
>
> Comment: There is no station with call letters MFS. There is no General officer in the USA or USMC by the name of Fertig. This is therefore presumed to be a Japanese subterfuge. No attempt to contact the calling station has been made.

Chief Ellis called the Office of the Adjutant General in the Pentagon, where he ascertained that there was no confirmed report of the death of Lt. Colonel Wendell W. Fertig, or that he had been captured. His status was missing and presumed dead. He got the name and telephone number of Colonel Fertig's next of kin, Mrs. Mary Fertig, his wife, in Golden, Colorado.

And then he took a red grease pencil and drew a box around Item 6 on the What-the-Hell-Is-This List, tore that sheet from the file, and moved it to the top of the stack of TOP SECRET documents. Then he carefully scissored the clipping about the glorious victory of Japanese forces over Major General Fertig from the *Mainichi* and stapled that to the What-the-Hell-Is-This List.

Twenty minutes later, Colonel William Donovan marched into the office, his face betraying that the morning session at the White House had been difficult.

"I would kill for a cup of coffee," he greeted Ellis as he walked past his desk.

When Ellis carried the coffee into the office, Donovan was dangling the page torn from the What-the-Hell-Is-This List between his thumb and forefinger.

"What the hell is this?" he asked.

"I think it's interesting," Ellis said.

"You want to try to call that station back?" Donovan asked.

Ellis nodded.

"Have it done," Colonel Donovan ordered.

"Colonel, things get lost in proper channels," Ellis said.

Donovan considered that a moment.

"Meaning you want to go out to California?"

"I could be back in three days," Ellis said. "Before it got there through channels."

"You have a gut feeling, Chief?" Donovan asked.

"Yes, Sir, you could put it that way."

"OK," Donovan said.

Chief Ellis called the Chief at Flight Operations at Anacostia Naval Air Station, on the other side of the District of Columbia.

"Hey, Chief, how they hanging? This is Chief Ellis."

"How's my favorite China Sailor? What are you trying to beat me out of today?"

"I need a seat for somebody very important on the next plane to Mare Island."

"Is he self-important, or just very important?"

"Actually, he's a pretty good guy."

"Reason I ask, is I got a half dozen torpedo bombers being ferried from Baltimore to load on a carrier at Mare Island. If this guy's not too ritzy to ride in a torpedo bomber . . ."

"From Anacostia or Baltimore?"

"Here. They're picking up people here. That's how I know about it."

"When?"

"How soon can he get here?"

"He's on his way."

4

United States Navy Base, Mare Island
San Francisco, California
12 January 1943

The Radioman Second had only seen the Base Commander once before, and then he had been riding by in his Navy gray Packard Clipper with its three-starred Vice Admiral's plate.

And now, here he was, in the radio room, looking right at him.

"Stand at ease, Son," the admiral said, almost kindly. "This is Chief Ellis, and he wants to ask you some questions."

"You picked up a message from somebody calling themselves MFS, right?"

"That's right, Chief."

"You heard them again?"

"They're on every day, for ten, sometimes twenty minutes," the Radioman Second said. "They were on, oh, hell, twenty minutes ago."

"See if you can raise them," Ellis said.

The Vice Admiral's eyes went up, but he said nothing. He had seen the card signed by the Chairman of the Joint Chiefs of Staff.

"Go on," Ellis repeated. "See if you can raise them."

The Radioman Second turned to his key and moved it quickly.

"I sent 'KSF calling MFS,'" he replied.

"I read code," Ellis said, not arrogantly.

There was no immediate reply.

The Radioman Second tapped his key again. When the transmitter was activated, the receiver was automatically shut down. When he turned the transmitter to standby, the receiver was issuing a series of dots and dashes.

The Radioman Second, without thinking, tapped it out on his typewriter. The Vice Admiral leaned over to read: MFS STANDING BY FOR KSF

"Send this," Ellis said, and handed the radioman a sheet of paper, on which was written, in pencil:

KSF TO MFS SEND ENCRYPTED FOLLOWING FIRST NAME OF FERTIG SECOND NEXT OF KIN NAME AND DATE OF BIRTH KSF BY

"Send it twice, and then wait," Ellis said. "If he's using one of these things, it'll take him a minute."

He held up a Device, Cryptographic, M94. He'd had a hell of a time finding one and had annoyed the Presidio of San Francisco no end by requisitioning theirs.

Five minutes later, MFS came back on the air.

MFS TO KSF QEWRG SJTRE SDIQN SPIID CVKQJ MFS BY

Ellis took as long to work the Device, Cryptographic, M94.

"Send 'We are ready for your traffic,'" he ordered, and then corrected himself. "No, send, 'Welcome to the net, we are ready for your traffic.'"

Then, without asking permission, Chief Ellis picked up the telephone and told the Navy operator to get him Mrs. Mary Fertig in Golden, Colorado.

The telephone operator said that no long distance calls could be placed without the authority of the Communications Officer and an authorization number.

"I'm going to need an authorization number," Ellis said to the communications officer.

The admiral motioned for Ellis to hand him the telephone.

"This is Admiral Sendy," he said to the telephone. "Put the call through."

In Golden, Colorado, Mrs. Mary Fertig answered her telephone.

"Ma'am," Ellis said. "This is Chief Ellis. You remember me?"

Of course, she remembered him. He had telephoned late the night before and said he couldn't tell her why he wanted to know, but could she give him the full name and date of birth of her oldest child? He had waked her up, and she hadn't been thinking too clearly, so she had given it to him. Later, she had worried about it. There were all kinds of nuts and sick people running loose.

"Yes, I remember you, Chief," Mrs. Fertig said, somewhat warily. "What do you want now?"

"Ma'am," the salty old Chief Bosun's Mate said, "we're in contact with your husband. I thought maybe you'd want to say something to him."

"Where is he?" she asked, very softly.

"Somewhere in the Philippines, that's all we know," Ellis said. Then he said, "Wait a minute."

The Radioman Second had handed him a brief decrypted message.

FOR MRS FERTIG QUOTE PINEAPPLES FOR BREAKFAST LOVE END QUOTE

Ellis read it over the telephone.

It took Mrs. Fertig a moment to reply, and then, when she spoke, it was with an audible effort to control her voice.

"My husband, Chief Ellis," she said, "is on the island of Mindanao. We used to go there to play golf at the course on the Dole Plantation. And we ate pineapples for breakfast."

Two

1

Shepheard's Hotel
Cairo, Egypt
23 January 1943

CAPTAIN JAMES M.B. Whittaker, U.S. Army Air Corps, was twenty-five years old. He was tall, big-boned, and graceful, with large, dark eyes. He was wearing a superbly tailored pink-and-green uniform and Half Wellington boots. The uniform and the boots had both come from Savile Row in London. The boots had cost just about as much money as the Air Corps paid Captain Whittaker each month, and the uniform had cost a little more than the boots.

Whittaker had never considered what the uniform and boots had cost. Mostly because he really had no idea how much money he had. Whatever his civilian income was, it was more than he could spend. There was a lawyer in New York who looked after his affairs and saw to it that there was always a comfortable balance in his Hanover Trust checking account.

This is not to suggest that Whittaker was simply a rich young man who happened to be in uniform. There were silver pilot's wings on the breast of his green blouse. He was checked-out (qualified to fly) in fighter, bomber and transport aircraft. Beneath the wings were ribbons representing the award of the Silver Star; the Distinguished Flying Cross; several lesser awards for valor; and brightly colored ribbons indicating that he had had overseas service in both the European and Pacific Theaters of Operation.

At the moment, Captain James M.B. Whittaker, Harvard University '39, was solemnly considering what he believed to be irrefutable evidence that he was a miserable, amoral, good-for-nothing sonofabitch.

This solemn consideration sometimes came upon him when he'd taken a drink or two more than he should have. When he had a load on (and he had been drinking, more or less steadily, for the last three days), truth raised its ugly head, and he could see things with a painful clarity.

He had started drinking before he'd boarded the MATS (Military Air Transport Service) C-54 at London's Croydon Airfield.

Taking leave of Liz Stanfield had been very painful. He loved Liz and she loved him, and there were certain problems with that. For one thing, Elizabeth Alexandra Mary, Captain WRAC (Women's Royal Army Corps), The Duchess Stanfield, a pale-skinned, splendidly bosomed, lithe woman in her middle thirties, was not really free to love him. There was a husband, Wing Commander The Duke Stanfield, RAF. He was down somewhere, "missing in action," the poor sonofabitch.

Only a miserable, amoral, good-for-nothing sonofabitch, such as himself, Capt. Whittaker reasoned, would carry on the way he had with a married woman whose husband was missing in action, and a fellow airman to boot. That was really low and rotten.

And it wasn't as if he was free, either. He was in love himself. Her name was Cynthia Chenowith, and he had loved her from the time he was thirteen and she was eighteen, and he had gotten a look at her boobs as she hauled herself out of his Uncle Chesty's swimming pool at the winter place in Palm Beach.

It didn't matter that Cynthia professed not to love him (that was the age difference, he had concluded): *he* loved her. And a man who loves a woman with his entire soul, who wants to spend the rest of his life with her, caring for her, making babies, is not supposed to go around fucking married women. Unless, of course, he is a miserable good-for-nothing sonofabitch.

Capt. Whittaker had had the foresight to bring with him on

the MATS C-54 three quart bottles of single malt Scotch whiskey. Half of one had gotten him to Casablanca, and the other half had sustained him from Casablanca to Cairo.

Since he had been in Cairo, he'd worked his way through all of the second bottle and one quarter of the third. The airplane was broken. The pilot had told Capt. Whittaker, as a courtesy to a fellow flyer, that he'd lost oil pressure on Number Three and had no intention of taking off again until they had replaced—rather than repaired—the faulty pump. One was being flown in from England. When it had been installed, they would continue on their flight, which would ultimately terminate in Brisbane, Australia.

Until the airplane was repaired, there was a good deal to see and do in Cairo.

Madame Jeanine d'Autrey-Lascal—who was thirty, tall for a French woman, blond, blue-eyed, and who saw no need to wear a brassiere—leaned close to Capt. Whittaker and laid her hand on his.

Madame d'Autrey-Lascal had been left behind in Cairo when her husband, who had been Managing Director of the Banc d'Egypte et Nord Afrique, had gone off to fight with the Free French under General Charles de Gaulle. She had been in the bank lobby when Capt. Whittaker had appeared to change money and to see if the bank, with which his family's firm had had a long relationship, could do something about getting him into a decent hotel. He had spent the previous night in the transient officers' quarters at the airfield and really didn't want to do that again.

They had been introduced quite properly, after which it had seemed to Madame d'Autrey-Lascal simply the courteous thing to do to offer to drive him to Shepheard's Hotel. The bank would call in as many favors as it could to get him accommodation in Shepheard's. No promises. The place was always jammed.

The assistant manager who greeted them said that he would try to find something. No promises. But perhaps if the Captain would not mind waiting for a bit in the bar . . .

It had seemed to Madame d'Autrey-Lascal that simple courtesy dictated that she not just leave him stranded high and dry in the bar at Shepheard's. If the bank's influence could not get him into Shepheard's, then something else would have to be arranged.

Capt. Whittaker spoke French, which was unexpected of an American, and they chatted pleasantly. She told him that her husband was off with General de Gaulle, and he told her a story about de Gaulle that it took her a moment to understand. It seemed that General de Gaulle had declined an invitation to visit with President Roosevelt, on the grounds that it was too long a walk.

But finally she understood and laughed, and then he told her about London. She hadn't been in London since 1939, and she found what he told her very interesting.

By the time they had had three drinks from his bottle of single malt Scotch whiskey, it occurred to Madame d'Autrey-Lascal that it didn't look as though the assistant manager was going to be able to find a room for him in Shepheard's (and if he did, it would be little more than a closet), and that there was absolutely no reason she couldn't put him up overnight, or for a day or two, at her house.

The first time she suggested this, Capt. Whittaker smiled at her (and she noticed his fine, even teeth) and told her that she was very kind, but he wouldn't think of imposing.

She told him it would be no imposition at all; the house was large, and at the moment empty, for her children were spending the night with friends.

He repeated that he wouldn't think of imposing. And then he lapsed into silence, broken only when she laid her hand on his.

"Sorry," Whittaker said. "I was thousands of miles away."

"Thousands of miles away, you would probably have a hotel room," Madame Jeanine d'Autrey-Lascal said. "Here, you don't. I think you are very sweet for not wanting to impose on me, and very foolish for not believing me when I say it will not be an imposition."

He turned his hand over and caught hers in it.

"And you are very kind to a lonely traveler," he said.

And I knew the moment I saw you in the bank manager's office that you had an itch in your britches, and miserable, amoral, no-good sonofabitch that I am, given half a chance, that I would wind up scratching it.

"You have such sad eyes," Madame d'Autrey-Lascal said, very softly, as she looked into them.

And then, finally, she reclaimed her hand and stood up.

"Shall we go?" she asked.

Whittaker followed her out of the crowded bar. As they walked across the lobby, she took his arm.

2

OSS Station
Cairo Savoy Hotel, Opera Square
24 January 1943

The Chief, Cairo Station, was Ernest J. Wilkins, 36, a roly-poly man whose face darkened considerably whenever he was upset. He was upset now, and smart enough to know that he was. Before speaking, he went to his window and looked out at the statue of Ibrahim, sitting on his horse in the middle of Opera Square. And then he looked at the Opera building itself, until he was sure he had his temper under control.

Then he turned and faced the three men standing in front of his desk. They were his deputy, his administrative officer, and his liaison officer to the British.

"Well, where the hell could he be?" he asked.

"I think," his administrative officer said, "that we can no longer overlook the possibility of foul play."

"Horseshit," Wilkins snapped. "If anything had happened to him, we would have heard it by now. And since nobody knew he was coming, how the hell could they get anything like that going so quick?"

His administrative officer had no response to that and said nothing. Wilkins had hoped that he would say something, so that he could jump his ass.

Wilkins lost his temper again.

"Jesus Christ," he flared. "Do you realize how goddamned inept this makes us look?" He saw the message on his desk and picked it up and read it aloud:

URGENT OFFICE OF THE DIRECTOR WASHINGTON CAIRO FOR WILKINS INTERCEPT CAPTAIN JAMES M.B. WHITTAKER ENROUTE LONDON TO BRISBANE VIA MATS FLIGHT 216 STOP REDIRECT WASHINGTON FIRST AVAILABLE AIR TRANSPORT STOP ADVISE COMPLIANCE AND ETA WASHINGTON STOP DONOVAN

"You'll notice," Wilkins said, "that it's signed 'Donovan.' Not 'Douglass,' or 'Chenowith' or even 'Ellis for Donovan.' 'Donovan' himself, goddamnit. And what he's asked us to do isn't going to be written up in a history of intelligence triumphs of the Second World War. All Colonel Donovan asks is that we find some Air Corps Captain that he knows is on a MATS flight and send the sonofabitch to Washington."

"Skipper," his deputy said to Wilkins (in deference to Wilkins's pre-OSS service as a Naval officer), "I'll lay even money he's off somewhere getting his ashes hauled."

"Where, for Christ's sake? In the bushes in Al Ezbekia Park, no doubt? For three goddamn days? He's not in a hotel, we know that. And he's not with any high-class whore, or we'd know that, too . . . and goddamn, I found it embarrassing to have to call the Egyptian cops and ask them to check their whores for him . . ."

He stopped, and looked out the window at Opera Square again.

"The Chrysler here?" he asked, reasonably calmly, when he turned around a moment later.

"Yes, Sir," his deputy said.

"Nobody stole the wheels? The driver is present and sober?"

"Yes, Sir."

"I'll be back," Wilkins said, and headed for the door.

"Going to the airport, Sir?"

Wilkins glared at what he considered to be a stupid question.

"I'll lay even money he'll show up for the flight, Skipper," his deputy said reassuringly.

"And if he doesn't? What if he got tired of waiting for them to fix the engine and hitchhiked a ride to Brisbane? That MATS flight isn't the only plane headed in that direction. How the hell am I going to say anything to Donovan without looking like a horse's ass?"

With an effort, Wilkins kept from slamming the door after him.

The 1941 Chrysler Imperial was equipped with the very latest in automotive transmission technology. This was called "Fluid Drive." In theory, it eliminated the need to shift gears. In practice, it didn't work, the result being that it crawled away from a stop. The Chrysler was, Wilkins decided on the way from Opera Square to the airfield, northeast of Cairo, probably the worst possible automobile in the world for Cairo traffic, less practical than a water buffalo pulling a wooden-wheeled cart.

At the MATS Terminal, he sought out the Military Police captain in charge of security, showed him his OSS identification, and said that it was absolutely essential that he locate one Captain Whittaker, James M.B., USAAC.

Ten minutes later, three Military Police brought Captain Whittaker and a strikingly beautiful woman to the MP captain's office. A flyboy, Wilkins decided somewhat sourly. A good one, to judge by the DFC. He wondered what the OSS wanted from a flyboy.

"This gentleman wishes to see you, Captain," the MP captain said.

Whittaker smiled.

"As long as it won't take long," Whittaker said, with a smile. "They're loading my plane."

"You won't be making that flight, Captain," Wilkins said.

"Says who?"

"Says me."

"And who are you?"

"That's not really important," Wilkins said. "You'll have to take my word for it. You're coming with me."

Whittaker looked at him with amusement in his eyes, his left eyebrow cocked quizzically.

"That just won't wash," Whittaker said.

Wilkins took his OSS identity card and held it out.

Captain Whittaker fumbled in his pockets and came out with a nearly identical card and held it out. Wilkins saw that there were two differences in the cards. His own card bore the serial number 1109 and was signed "FOR THE CHAIRMAN, THE JOINT CHIEFS OF STAFF" by Captain Peter Douglass, Sr., USN. Whittaker's card bore the serial number 29 and was signed by

Colonel W.J. Donovan, GSC, USA. Obviously, this handsome flyboy had been in the OSS almost from the beginning.

"What is all this, mon cher?" the Frenchwoman asked, softly, in French.

"Nothing at all," Whittaker replied, in French, and then looked at Wilkins, waiting for an explanation.

Wilkins handed him the radiogram from Donovan.

"I'll be damned," Whittaker said. "When's my plane?"

"Tomorrow," Wilkins said. "At 0915. You had a seat on this morning's flight, but you missed it."

"It appears," Whittaker said to the Frenchwoman in French, "that we're going to have to climb the Great Pyramid again."

She blushed attractively.

"There are quarters available, if you've checked out of your hotel," Wilkins said.

"That's very kind of you, Sir," Whittaker said. "But that won't be necessary. I'll be staying with a friend."

The Frenchwoman blushed attractively again.

"War is hell, isn't it?" Whittaker, smiling broadly, asked Mr. Wilkins.

3

Virginia Highway 234 near Washington, D.C.
25 January 1943

There were four men in the 1942 black Buick Roadmaster, riding in silence.

There had been a little snow, but the road was clear, and the illuminated needle of the speedometer pointed just past seventy miles per hour. There was virtually no traffic on the road, not even the glow of distant headlights over the gentle hills before them.

When the flashing red signal lantern suddenly appeared in the road before them, Chief Ellis was startled. But, even as the driver started stabbing at the brakes, Ellis reached under the seat and came out with a Thompson machine-pistol.[1]

In the back seat, Colonel William J. Donovan looked up from the document he was reading. Ellis had rigged a really nice reading light on a flexible shaft. The light turned automobile rides into work sessions rather than wastes of time.

"What is it?" Captain Peter Douglass asked.

"Dunno," Ellis replied, and then, almost immediately, "it's the fucking cops!"

"How fast were we going?" Donovan asked, calmly.

"About seventy, Sir," Staley, the driver, said.

Staley was in civilian clothing. Ellis was in uniform, except for his brimmed chief's cap, which was on the seat beside him. But in his blue, insignia-less overcoat, he appeared at casual glance to be a portly, ruddy-faced civilian.

Ellis shoved the Thompson back under the front seat as the driver pulled onto the shoulder.

The Virginia state trooper, in a stiff-brimmed hat, swaggered up to the car.

"May I see your license and registration, please, Sir?" he asked, with ritual courtesy.

They were handed over.

"Sir, are you Charles D. Staley, of this Q Street, Northwest, address, in the District?"

"Yes, Sir," the driver said.

"And this vehicle is the property of . . ." He paused to examine the registration with his flashlight. ". . . W.J. Donovan?"

"Yes, it is."

"Does Mr. Donovan know you are driving his vehicle?"

"I'm Donovan," Donovan said. The trooper flashed his light in Donovan's face.

"Yes, Sir," he said. He returned his attention to the driver. "Sir, you went through a speed detection area. You were clocked, over a measured quarter mile, at 73.6 miles per hour."

"I didn't realize I was going that fast," the driver said.

---

[1]A Thompson .45 caliber submachine gun, equipped with two hand grips, but without a shoulder stock.

"Two state troopers will testify that you were, Sir," the trooper said. "I'm going to have to issue you a citation. You will be charged with reckless driving. The law is that any speed twenty miles in excess of the posted speed limit is considered reckless driving. Are you aware, Sir, that in order to conserve gasoline and rubber for the war effort, the speed limit across the nation is now thirty-five miles per hour?"

"I heard about that," the driver said, drily.

"If you are found guilty in a court of law . . . the place and time of your required appearance will be on the citation I am about to give you . . . your local ration board will be notified of this violation. You have a C sticker[2] which means that you agreed in writing to make a genuine effort to conserve the gasoline authorized for you. I think you will agree that driving seventy-three-point-six miles per hour does not conserve fuel."

"I was in sort of a hurry," the driver said.

"So are our boys in uniform," the state trooper said. "In a hurry to get the war over. And personally, I think we should do all we can to help them."

"Ellis!" Donovan warned softly.

"Can I go now?" the driver said, taking the citation.

"Yes, Sir," the state trooper said, and marched off.

The driver cranked up the window.

"Sorry about that, Colonel," he said.

"Hell, I told you to step on it," Donovan said. "Ellis, give him money to pay the fine. If there are any other complications, let Captain Douglass know."

"Yes, Sir," Ellis said.

"And as soon as we're over the next hill," Donovan said, "step on it."

Twenty minutes later, the Buick was in the Rock Creek section of the District of Columbia, moving down Q Street, Northwest. They came to an estate surrounded by an eight-foot-high brick wall. The driver switched from low beam to high beam and back again, and a moment later turned off Q Street, stopping the Buick with its nose against a heavy, solid gate in the wall.

A muscular man in civilian clothing stepped out of the

[2]There were four categories of ration stickers: A,B,C, and X.

shadows and walked to the car. The driver turned the interior lights on for a moment, and then off again.

The muscular man touched the brim of his snap-brim hat. A moment later, the double gate swung inward. As soon as the car was inside, the gates closed after it.

"Ellis," Donovan said, "I hate to make you an orderly, but it would save us a lot of time if you went by my house and packed a bag. And get your own while you're at it. Then we can go from here to Union Station."

"Yes, Sir."

"The Secret Service sent over the passes?" Donovan asked.

"I'll check on that, too, Sir," Ellis said.

"I don't want to find myself waving bye-bye on the platform as the President goes off to Georgia by himself," Donovan said.

"No, Sir, I'll see we're aboard the train," Ellis said.

Donovan and Douglass got out of the car and entered the turn-of-the-century mansion through the kitchen door. The kitchen was enormous and furnished with restaurant-size stoves and refrigerators.

A tall young woman with blond hair hanging to her shoulders came into the room. She wore a simple black dress, a single string of pearls, and just above her right nipple a miniature pair of pilot's wings. Captain Douglass's eyes betrayed a moment's surprise and special interest in the wings. He was sure he knew their source: His wife had an identical pair, sent from London by their son. What seemed like last week, their son had seemed an eager-eyed West Point Cadet; and now, at twenty-five, he was a lieutenant colonel. His son also liked this girl very much.

"Good evening," Charity Hoche said, with a radiant smile. Her accent betrayed her origins: Charity Hoche was raised on a twenty-acre estate in Wallingford, which was one of the plusher suburbs of Philadelphia, and educated at Bryn Mawr.

"Hello, Charity," Donovan said. "Mr. Hoover here?"

"No, Sir," she said. "And no calls, either. From him."

"Time and J. Edgar Hoover wait for no man," Donovan said. "What are we going to feed him?"

"Capon," she said. "And wild rice."

"Good," Donovan chuckled. "Eating chicken with a knife

and fork is not one of J. Edgar's strong points. He always makes me feel he'd rather eat one with his hands. After biting off the head, of course."

"And," Charity said, "a very nice Chateau de Long Chablis, '35."

"Where the hell did we get that?" Donovan asked.

"Actually, I brought it from home," Charity said. "I knew this was important."

"And you wanted to butter up the boss, too," Donovan said.

"Guilty," Charity said, with a smile.

"I might decide to keep you here for your father's cellar," Donovan said.

"As opposed to what?" Douglass asked.

"Charity wants to go to England," Donovan said. "I can't imagine why."

Charity chuckled deep in her throat.

A very sexual young woman, Captain Douglass thought. Not quite what he had hoped for Peter Douglass, Jr. . . . He wanted for Doug a girl just like the girl who had married dear old dad when he'd been an ensign fresh from Annapolis. Not this Main Line socialite who was used to spending more money on her clothing than Doug (even as an Air Corps Lieutenant Colonel drawing flight pay) made in a year. And who, according to the FBI's CBI (Complete Background Investigation) on her was a long way from having any claim to a virginal white bridal dress.

He was really worried, he thought, that Charity looked on Doug as this year's chic catch, a dashing hero, rather than as someone whose life she would share.

"There have been some cables from London," Charity said. "Nothing important, except that Fulmar and Fine have left for Lisbon. And there's one from Cairo, with Jimmy Whittaker's ETA."

"Good," Donovan said. "I wasn't sure we could catch him."

"Apparently, they had some trouble finding him," Charity said. "The cable said that he had not checked in with them, which is why he wasn't on an earlier plane."

"I wonder what her name was?" Donovan chuckled.

"Jeanine d'Autrey-Lascal," Charity furnished. "Her husband ran a bank there before the war, and is now with General de Gaulle."

"Wilkins sent that, too?" Donovan chuckled. "Thorough, isn't he?"

"Wilkins described her as Jimmy's 'good friend,'" Charity said.

"Pilots do get around, don't they, Charity?" Donovan teased.

"Until they're finally forced to land," Charity said. "What goes up, they say, has to come down. Eventually, if they're lucky, a Delilah comes into their lives."

"As in Samson-and?" Donovan chuckled. "You're planning on giving young Douglass a haircut?"

"I don't really think that's what Delilah did to Samson," Charity said. "But if that's what it takes . . ."

Both Donovan and Douglass laughed, but Douglass's laughter seemed a little strained. If he had correctly understood Charity, and he was afraid he had, she had as much as said that she was going to drain Doug sexually to the point where straying would be physically impossible.

A buzzer buzzed four times.

"The Director has arrived," Charity said. "Are you going to meet him outside, or would it be better if we all prostrated ourselves in the entrance foyer?"

Donovan laughed heartily. He genuinely enjoyed Charity Hoche.

"Let's meet him outside and bring him in through the kitchen," Donovan said.

They went back to the cobblestone driveway which separated the mansion from the stable—still so-called although it had been converted to a five-car garage—as a Cadillac limousine, bristling with shortwave radio antennae, rolled majestically in.

There were two neatly dressed young men in the front seat, one of whom jumped out to open the door the instant the car stopped.

J. Edgar Hoover, the director of the Federal Bureau of Investigation, got out.

"Hello, Edgar," Donovan said. "I'm glad you could find the time."

"It's always a pleasure, Bill," Hoover said, firmly shaking his hand. He nodded curtly to Captain Douglass. "Douglass," he said.

"Mr. Director," Douglass said.

"And you know Miss Hoche, I believe, Edgar?"

Hoover beamed.

"How nice to see you, my dear," he said. "And how is your father?" Before Charity could open her mouth, he went on, "You be sure to give both your mother and father my kindest regards."

"Of course," Charity said.

"Would you like a little belt, Edgar?" Donovan asked. "Or would you rather go right in to dinner?"

"This is one of those days when I would dearly like a little taste," Hoover said, "and just don't have the time."

"Well, we'll give you a raincheck," Donovan said. "I'm trying to be very nice to you, Edgar."

"That sounds as if you want something," Hoover said, jovially, as they entered the house through the kitchen.

"Actually," Donovan said, "I was hoping you might have a contact with the state police in Virginia."

"I can probably help," Hoover said. "What is it you need?"

"You know somebody that can fix a speeding ticket?" Donovan asked.

Hoover looked at him in genuine surprise.

"Seventy-three-point-six in a thirty-five mile zone," Donovan said, straight-faced. "The cop said that we'd probably lose our C ration sticker, too."

Hoover smiled.

"Darn you, Bill," he said. "You really had me going there for a minute."

"Oh, Edgar, you know better than that. I'd never ask you to fix a speeding ticket."

"You didn't really get one, did you?" Hoover asked.

"Less than an hour ago," Donovan said. "On the way here. But don't worry about it, Edgar. I'm going to ask the boss for a Presidential pardon."

Hoover's smile was now strained.

"As soon as we get our business out of the way, Edgar, we're headed for Warm Springs," Donovan said. "On his way down there, Franklin's always in a very good mood. *He'll* take care of the speeding ticket, I'm sure."

Hoover marched ahead of him toward the dining room. He knew the way.

Donovan glanced at Charity Hoche. She smiled and gave him a nod of approval. He had put Hoover off balance, and with consummate skill that Charity appreciated. First, by the suggestion of an insult: that the nation's ranking law enforcement officer, Mr. G-Man himself, would fix a speeding ticket, and then with the announcement that he was going to Warm Springs with President Roosevelt (whom he was privileged to call by his first name) on a trip on which Hoover had obviously not been invited.

There were very few people who could discomfit J. Edgar Hoover. Donovan, Charity thought, could play him like a violin.

The table was set for three.

Charity waited until they were seated, and then started to leave.

"I'll serve now, if that would be all right," she said.

"Fine," Donovan said, and then, as if he had just thought of it, 'oh, Charity, there was one more cable from London, a personal to me from Stevens."

"Something I should know about?"

"I want you to get it decoded," Donovan said. "The message is 'Katharine Hepburn's Fine by Me.'"

She smiled at him. It needed no decoding. Donovan had apparently cabled Lt. Colonel Ed Stevens, Deputy Chief of London Station, asking how he felt about Charity's being transferred there. Making light of her Main Line Philadelphia accent, Charity was known as "Katharine Hepburn," after the actress.

"Oh, Uncle Bill," Charity blurted, and ran to him and kissed him wetly on the cheek. "*Thank* you!"

"Serve dinner, Miss Hoche," Donovan said. "The Director looks hungry."

Hoover did not turn over his glass when a middle-aged Negro maid produced the bottle of Chateau de Long '35.

Donovan interpreted this as a good sign; that Hoover had not come to this meeting with a litany of OSS offenses against the FBI.

The relationship between the Director of the FBI and the Director of the OSS was complex. When a new broom had been needed to sweep out the scandal-ridden Federal Office of Investigation, the post had been offered to Donovan, both because of his public image as a war hero of untainted honesty, and because of his political influence. He had declined, and taken some effort to see that the job went to J. Edgar Hoover, then a young Justice Department lawyer. When the FBI was established in 1935, Hoover—again with Donovan's support—was named its first director.

By the time Donovan returned to public service, shortly before the war, as the $1.00 per annum Coordinator of Information, the predecessor organization to the OSS, Hoover had become a highly respected fixture in Washington, very nearly above criticism.

The FBI was without question the most efficient law enforcement agency the nation had ever known, and the credit was clearly Hoover's.

And when the idea of a super-agency to sit atop all the other governmental intelligence agencies came up, Hoover perhaps naturally presumed that it would fall under the FBI. He was bitterly disappointed when that role was given to the Office of the Coordinator of Information, and his old friend and mentor Bill Donovan was named as its head.

Hoover was a skilled political infighter with many friends on Capitol Hill and within Roosevelt's inner circle. He did not simply roll over and play dead. He got President Roosevelt to agree that the FBI should retain its intelligence and counterintelligence roles, not only within the United States, but in Latin and South America as well. And he got Roosevelt to keep Bill Donovan's agents in South America under his own control by claiming the right to "coordinate" all their activities. Clearly, he could not coordinate their activities unless they made frequent and detailed reports of their activities to the FBI.

Donovan, because he acknowledged the battle as lost, or perhaps because Latin and South America were low in his priorities, gave Hoover his way. Not completely, of course, but he paid lip service to the notion that Hoover had been given North and South America as his area of operations.

Hoover saw Donovan for what he was: a highly competent

man with a sense of morality and patriotism that was close to his own—and a good friend. But he also saw Donovan as someone who was challenging his (the FBI's) authority in all things concerned with espionage. And this was especially galling because Donovan had the same access to the President's ear that Hoover did. Despite their sharp political and ideological differences, Donovan and Roosevelt had been friends since they had been students at the Columbia School of Law.

And, with consummate skill, Roosevelt played games with them—Hoover and Donovan—sometimes pitting one against the other, and other times assuring one that the other regarded him as the greatest patriot and most efficient employee on the government payroll.

And both Hoover and Donovan understood that the most dangerous thing that could happen to either was to force Roosevelt to choose between them. As confident of their own ability and their own influence with Roosevelt, as they each were, neither was assured that the other would ever be asked for his resignation.

Tonight, with nothing specific on the agenda, they exchanged tidbits. Hoover told Donovan and Douglass what his agents had uncovered in Latin and South America. Donovan heard nothing he thought was very important. Much of what Hoover told him, he had heard before.

Hoover, only half joking, said that he was on the edge of doubling his security force at Oak Ridge, Tennessee, where the refining of uranium was getting under way in a top-secret plant. He would use half the force, he said, to keep the Germans from finding out what was going on, and the other half to keep the scientists—fifty percent of whom, he said, were "pinkos"—from passing what they knew and were learning to the Soviets. There was no question in his mind, Hoover said, that the scientist in charge, J. Robert Oppenheimer, was as left of center as Vladimir Lenin.

"And it's delicate, you know, Bill, with The Boss," Hoover said. "If he has one flaw in his political judgment, it has to do with the Russians. He thinks Joe Stalin is sort of the Russian senator from Georgia. And that he can buy him off with a dam or a highway."

Donovan laughed.

"You think there's a genuine danger of somebody actually spilling the beans to the Russians?" he asked.

"Not so long as I'm in charge of security," Hoover said. "Instead of, for example, Henry Wallace."

He said it with a smile, but Donovan understood that Hoover regarded the Vice President and several of the people around him as bona fide threats to the one great secret of the war: that the United States was engaged in building a bomb which would use as its explosive force nuclear energy, a force—presuming theory could be turned into practice—which would give one 5,000-pound bomb the destructive force of 20,000 tons of TNT.

"Henry doesn't know about Oak Ridge," Donovan said. "And the President tells me he has no intention of telling him."

"Franklin Roosevelt has been known to change his mind to fit the circumstances of the moment," Hoover said, adding, drily, "I'm surprised you haven't noticed."

Donovan chuckled appreciatively.

"On the subject of Oak Ridge, Edgar," Donovan said, "there's something coming up . . ."

"Oh?" Hoover interrupted.

"We are going to try to bring some German scientists here," Donovan said.

"You mean, get them out of Germany?" Hoover asked, surprised. "Can you do that?"

"In the next couple of days," Donovan said, "we're going to make sort of a trial run." He waited for Hoover to interrupt him again, and when he didn't, went on. "The first man we're going to bring out is a metallurgist . . ."

Now Hoover obliged him, "Why a metallurgist?"

"I've told you about the German flying bombs, and jet-propulsion engines," Donovan said. "I finally managed to convince the President that they pose a real threat, no matter what the Air Corps says, to our plans for the massive bombing of Germany. I have permission to do what I can to at least slow down the production of jet-propulsion and rocket engines. Both require special metal alloys and special techniques to machine the special alloys. The idea is that when we find out what kind of special metal and what kind of special techniques are required for the necessary machining, we will just put those locations on the top of the bombing priority list."

Hoover grunted, then asked, "What's this got to do with Groves's[3] bomb? With Oak Ridge?"

"If we succeed in getting the metallurgist safely out, and see how much attention the Germans pay to his disappearance, we'll start bringing out the mathematicians and physicists we need . . . or whose services we don't want the Germans to have."

"And if they catch you bringing out the metallurgist, the Germans won't connect it with the Manhattan Project?" Hoover asked.

"Precisely," Donovan said. "If we get to the point where we do bring nuclear people out, once they get to this country, they'll be your responsibility, protecting them at either Oak Ridge or White Sands. I thought perhaps, presuming we get the metallurgist out, you might want to use him as sort of a dry run yourself."

"You keep saying 'if' and 'presuming' you can get him out," Hoover said. "There's some question in your mind that you will? Or do you believe the operation won't work?"

"We have high hopes, of course," Donovan said, and went on to explain that the OSS had set up a new escape route "pipeline," which ran through Hungary and Yugoslavia, for the sole purpose of getting the "special category" people out of Germany. The normal, in-place pipelines took people off the European continent through Holland and France to England.

Hoover displayed a deep curiosity in the details of the new pipeline, and Donovan explained the operation to him, wondering if the FBI Director's curiosity was professional or personal. Hoover, he knew, liked to think of himself as an agent rather than an administrator. Donovan suspected that Hoover was vicariously crossing the border from Germany into Hungary, and then walking out of Yugoslavia in the company of Yugoslavian partisans.

---

[3]Brigadier General Leslie Groves, USA, an Army engineer, had been placed in charge of the atomic bomb project, which bore the code name, "Manhattan Project."

When the explanation was finally over, Hoover grunted, and then looked at Captain Douglass.

"You don't seem to have much to say, Douglass," he said.

"I ask Pete to sit in on the more important meetings, Edgar, so I don't have to spend time repeating to him what was said."

"I was thinking along those lines myself," Hoover said. "That it's going to take me some time to repeat all this to Colson."[4]

"If Clyde was cleared for the Manhattan Project," Donovan said, "I'd be the first to say bring him along."

"Clyde knows about the Manhattan Project," Hoover said. "He's my Deputy."

Donovan was not surprised that Hoover had made Colson privy to the secrets of the Manhattan Project, but he was surprised that Hoover had admitted it so openly to him. Colson, like Vice President Wallace, was not on the short list of people authorized to access to information concerning the atomic bomb.

"Then you should have brought him with you, Edgar," Donovan said. "Clyde's an old pal. He doesn't need a formal invitation to break bread with us."

Hoover, Donovan realized, had just put him on a spot. Should he run, as he was supposed to, to Roosevelt and tattle that the head of the FBI had taken it upon himself to breach security? If he did, would it turn out that Hoover had gotten permission from Roosevelt to tell Colson? Which would make him look the fool. And if he didn't go, would Roosevelt find out, and be justifiably angry that he had known and said nothing?

He decided that this was one of those rare instances where it was necessary to be very open with Hoover.

"Edgar, does Roosevelt know you've decided it was necessary to brief Clyde?"

"No," Hoover said, and met his eyes. "Are you going to tell him?"

"Certainly," Donovan said. "I've been hearing rumors

[4]Clyde Colson was Deputy Director of the FBI, and Hoover's closest friend. They shared a house.

about Clyde. He's supposed to be about as pinko as Henry Wallace."

Hoover laughed, but his smile was strained.

I'll let you worry about whether or not I'm going to tell Roosevelt, Donovan thought. *That hand went to me. Another proof of the theory that when you really don't know what to do, try telling the truth.*

Hoover looked at his wristwatch and stood up.

"I had no idea how late it is," he said.

"I'll walk you to your car, Edgar," Donovan said.

4

Union Station
Washington, D.C.
30 January 1943

Staley had no trouble picking Capt. James M.B. Whittaker out of the crowd of people walking away from the train, although many of them were in uniform, and almost a dozen of those in uniform were captains of the U.S. Army Air Corps.

"Look for a guy who looks like an Air Corps recruiting poster," Chief Ellis had told him. "Tall, good-looking, and either the sloppiest officer you ever saw, or the sharpest. Depends on how he feels right then."

Capt. Whittaker, Staley concluded, had decided to be sharp. He was wearing a perfectly tailored pink-and-green uniform, and he was in the process of putting on a camel's-hair short coat when Staley spotted him. His brimmed cap had the 50-mission crush, an affectation of a fighter pilot, but except for that, he looked as if he had just walked out of a clothing store window.

Staley intercepted him, catching himself just before he started to salute. He was not quite used to wearing civilian clothes and acting like a civilian.

"Captain Whittaker?"

"Guilty," Whittaker said, smiling at him.

"I'm standing in for Chief Ellis, Sir," Staley said. "Let me give you a hand with your gear."

"Since you're foolish enough to volunteer," Whittaker said, "you can have the heavy one. Where's Ellis?"

"He's in Georgia, Sir," Staley said.

"With the Colonel? And our commander in chief?"

"Yes, Sir," Staley said, wondering how Whittaker could have known that.

When they were in the Buick, Whittaker said, "Well, I appreciate you meeting me, but I could have taken a cab."

"To Virginia?" Staley blurted. Ellis had told him that Whittaker was rich, that, in fact, he owned the house on Q Street, but the notion of taking a 40-mile taxi ride startled him.

"Virginia? I'm talking about Q Street."

"Sir, I'm supposed to take you to Virginia," Staley said.

"I'm going to the house on Q Street," Whittaker said, firmly. "If that makes it awkward for you, just drop me at the next corner. I'll catch a cab, and we'll say you couldn't find me at Union Station."

"They expect you in Virginia," Staley protested.

"In a word, fuck 'em," Whittaker said, then, quickly. "Right over there, there's a cab."

"I'll take you to the house," Staley said. "Nobody said anything about me making you go to Virginia. But if you tell them I told you . . ."

"I'll cover you," Whittaker said. "You know what goes on in Virginia, I suppose? They do all sorts of obscene things out there, like push-ups and running for miles before they have breakfast."

Staley laughed. "I went through it."

"Then you must know a prick by the name of Eldon C. Baker," Whittaker said, "which is another reason I'm not going to Virginia."

"I know him," Staley said.

When they got to the house on Q Street, Northwest, the guard would not pass the Buick through the gate until Whittaker showed him his credentials.

And when they walked into the kitchen, Charity Hoche, in her bathrobe, was waiting for them.

"You're not supposed to be here, Jimmy," she said.

"Jesus, and I was hoping for something along the lines of 'Welcome Home, Jimmy.' "

"They expect you in Virginia," Charity said.

"I hope they're not holding their breath," Whittaker said. "Aren't you going to ask me about Doug?"

"How's Doug?"

"Bearing up rather well, considering," he said.

"Bearing up rather well considering what?"

"That he's the official stud for the London area Red Cross girls," Whittaker said. "Some of them are real man-eaters."

"Damn you," she said.

"Actually, the last time I saw him, he was staring moodily off into space, muttering Browning sonnets," Whittaker said. " 'How do I love Charity? Let me count the ways . . . I love her . . .' "

"That's better," Charity said. "I'm going over there. I found out a couple of days ago."

"Well, that should certainly change his social life," Whittaker said, and then he asked the question that had been on his mind since he first saw Charity.

"Where's the regular house mother?"

"Cynthia's at the place in Virginia," Charity said.

"What's she doing there?"

"Going through the course," Charity said.

"What course?"

"The regular course," Charity said.

"What the hell is that all about?" he asked.

"What do you think?" Charity asked.

The notion that Cynthia was undergoing training to become an agent was so preposterous that he didn't pursue it.

"I'll go out there in the morning," he said. "Is my car here?"

"It is, but I'm not sure they allow you to have a car out there," Charity said.

"I'll take my chances," he said. "Now, if you will give me some whiskey to drink, I'll brief you on the competition you're going to face when you get to England. And just for the record, Charity, I came here over the very strenuous objections of this gentleman."

"Staley's my name, Captain," Staley said, and offered his hand. Staley liked Whittaker. Ellis had said he would. He himself hadn't been so sure. Officers are officers. But there was something about this guy that made him special.

"Over the strenuous objections of Mr. Staley," Whittaker said. "And now can I have some booze?"

He woke early, his body clock confused by the distances he'd covered, and aware that sometime around two in the afternoon, he would get very sleepy. Worse, he thought, his mind would be dulled. And he wanted to be sharp when he saw Cynthia.

He took a shower in the large, tiled, two-headed shower where legend had it that Chesley Haywood Whittaker, his Uncle "Chesty," had died of a stroke. The truth was that Chesty Whittaker had died in the saddle, on Pearl Harbor Day, and that Chief Ellis had manhandled the body over here so that it could be "found" in his own shower rather than in the bed of a young woman, the daughter of a college classmate, with whom he had had a two-year affair. The young woman's name was Cynthia Chenowith.

Only a few people knew what had really happened: Wild Bill Donovan—who had been Chesty's lifelong crony and with whom he had flown to Washington when Donovan had been summoned to the White House—knew. And Captain Douglass knew. And Chief Ellis. And Dick Canidy, Whittaker's school chum and now Number Three man in London for the OSS. And of course, Jimmy Whittaker knew. He didn't think Cynthia knew he knew, and that was the way he wanted to keep it. It didn't matter to him, he told himself—and most of the time, he believed, it didn't.

But he thought about it in the shower, and he thought about it when he backed the Packard out of the garage. The 1941 Packard 280 convertible coupe had been Chesty's. Presumably, Chesty and Cynthia had been in it together on many happy occasions. He didn't think they had made the beast with two backs in the back seat, but it was reasonable to presume that they had held hands, and kissed, and that sort of thing.

Despite the cold, when he was out of The District, he pulled to the side of the road and put the roof down. He had the heater going full blast, and he left the windows up, and it was really rather pleasant.

A quarter of a mile off the state highway into the Virginia

property, well out of sight of the highway, a guard post had been erected, and Whittaker learned that Charity had been right about the car. They expected him, but not at the wheel of a car.

"I really don't know what the hell to say," the guard, wearing the uniform of a member of the National Park Service Police said. "I got your name on the list, Captain, but as a trainee, and trainees can't have private cars."

"But as I've shown you, I'm not a trainee," Whittaker said. "Look, call Baker and tell him I'm here, and driving a car."

The guard went into his little shack and a moment later came out again, and said, "Mr. Baker says come right to his office, Captain. It's in the main house. You can't miss it."

The road wound through a stand of pine trees, and as he was coming out of it, he passed a group of twelve or fifteen trainees taking a run. They were carrying, in front of them, at "Port Arms," Springfield Model 1903 caliber .30-06 rifles, not that it was expected they would ever use one, but to make the physical conditioning a little tougher.

He slowed down, and glanced out the side window at them as he passed them. And saw Cynthia Chenowith. She had her hair hidden under a GI fatigue habit, and the truth was that he saw her breasts flopping around under her fatigue jacket and marveled at that for a moment before he recognized her.

"Oh, shit!" he said with great disgust, and then stepped on the accelerator.

Eldon Baker's office was in what had been the breakfast room of the mansion, a rather small room whose floor-length doors opened onto a flagstone patio, and beyond that to a flat grassy area that Whittaker remembered as having been a putting green.

Baker was sitting behind a government-issue gray metal desk when Whittaker walked in. He was a pudgy-faced man in his thirties. He was wearing fatigues, but where an officer would have worn the insignia of his rank and branch of service, there was a square insignia embroidered in blue: a triangle within the square, and the letters "U.S." It was the insignia worn by civilian experts attached to the U.S. Army in the field. Baker had been a State Department intelligence officer before joining the OSS, where he was listed on the OSS Table of Organization as "Chief, Recruitment and

Training." So far as Whittaker knew, he had never been in the service.

"Well, hello, Jim," Baker said. "We rather expected you last night."

"You look very military, Eldon," Whittaker said. "Am I expected to salute?"

"We don't salute around here," Baker said. "Neither do we wear insignia of rank or branch of service."

"Can I ask you a question?" Whittaker asked.

"What are you doing here? Well, that's very simple. You haven't gone through the course and . . ."

"What is Cynthia Chenowith doing running around in fatigues and carrying a Springfield?"

"Isn't that self-evident? She's going through the course. And doing rather well. Frankly, much better than I expected she would."

"To what end?" Whittaker asked.

"Again, isn't that self-evident?"

"You're out of your fucking mind, Eldon," Whittaker said, matter-of-factly. "What the hell is the matter with you?"

"I had hoped that our relationship would be amicable," Baker said. "You're making that difficult."

"Are you telling me you seriously propose to send that girl out operationally?" Whittaker asked.

"Nothing specific at the moment, but when the opportunity presents itself . . ."

"And Bill Donovan's going along with that insane notion?"

"Obviously, it has Colonel Donovan's approval," Baker said. "And, as obviously, it's really none of your business, is it?"

"I'm making it my business," Whittaker said.

"Have you some explanation for not coming here as you were directed to do?" Baker said. "You will notice I have changed the subject."

"I don't have to explain anything to you, Eldon," Whittaker said. "I don't work for you. I don't even know what I'm doing in the States."

There was more, Whittaker thought, than simple chemistry to explain why he had disliked Eldon Baker from the moment he had met him. He could prepare a long list of Things-Wrong-with-Eldon-Baker, headed by Baker's ruthlessness, and running down to such items as pompous, overbearing, and the compleat bureaucrat, but it was the chemistry primarily responsible for the inevitable verbal flare-ups whenever they were together.

Baker now chose to tolerate Whittaker.

"There's a mission envisioned for you," he said.

"What kind of a mission?"

Baker ignored the question.

"Prior to which it has been decided that you will go through the course."

"Decided by whom?"

"It's OSS policy," Baker said, "that everybody will go through the school."

"You're weaseling," Whittaker said. "Donovan doesn't know you expect me to go through this school of yours for spies, does he? You were just going to tell me that's the 'way it is.' Screw you, Eldon. That won't work. Canidy told me that Donovan told him that neither one of us had to do this. For Christ's sake, I was *running* the school in England."

"You have no training in infiltration by rubber boat from a submarine," Baker said. "Obviously, it was not my intention to send you through the whole course . . ."

"Oh?"

"And actually, I had planned to ask you to teach a few hours. I thought it would really get and keep the men's attention if they understood they were being taught by someone who had been operational."

"If that's a bone you're throwing, gnaw on it yourself," Whittaker said. He started out of the room, and then turned and stopped at the door. "I'm going back to Washington," he said. "And it's going to take Wild Bill himself to order me back here. And then I may not come."

"Obviously, there's no purpose in debating this with you," Baker said.

When he went outside the building, determined to find Cynthia, Whittaker saw her immediately. In the time it had taken him to go through the confrontation with Baker, her group of trainees had run from where he had seen them on the road to the mansion.

Presumably, he decided, they had run all the way. Cynthia and another woman, both of them red-faced and heaving from the exertion, were sitting on the ground, their backs against a wall.

He walked over to her. She looked up at him, but said nothing.

One of the senior trainees walked quickly up to him. He was tall and muscular and very handsome, and looked somehow familiar to Whittaker.

"May I help you, Sir?" he asked.

"Take a walk," Whittaker said. He met Cynthia's eyes. "What the hell do you think you're doing?"

"What does it look like?" she replied.

"Jesus Christ, if it wasn't so stupid, it would be funny," he said.

"Jimmy, why don't you just turn around and walk away from here?" Cynthia asked.

Instead, he reached down, and grabbed her wrist and jerked her to her feet.

"What do you think you're doing?" she snapped.

He kissed her, moving so quickly there was no time for her to avert her face, and so surprising her that it was a moment before she twisted free.

One of the trainees laughed and applauded.

"What was that all about?" Cynthia said, seeming torn between outrage and tears. "Why did you do that?"

"Two reasons," he said. "To remind you that you're a woman. And because I love you."

"Damn you!" Cynthia said, fighting an infuriating urge to cry.

"Now, just a minute here!" the senior trainee said.

"Greg, don't!" Cynthia called quickly. "He's crazy. He'll kill you!"

The trainee looked at him warily and with great interest.

"Relax," Whittaker said. "I'm a lover, not a fighter." Then, feeling very pleased with himself, he walked over to the Packard, and got in, and started it up.

Three

1

Headquarters, 344th Fighter Group
Atcham Army Air Corps Station, England
31 January 1943

RANK HATH ITS privileges. In this case that meant that the commanding officer of the 344th Fighter Group was driven in a jeep from the final briefing to the revetment where his aircraft was parked. The other pilots rode jammed together in the backs of trucks.

The commanding officer of the 344th Fighter Group, Eighth United States Air Force, was Lieutenant Colonel Peter ("Doug") Douglass, Jr., USMA '39, a slight pleasant-appearing officer who looked, until you saw his eyes, much too young to be either a fighter group commander or a lieutenant colonel. He was in fact twenty-five years old.

He was wearing a horsehide A-2 jacket, which had a zipper front and knit cuffs. On its back was painted the flag of the Republic of China and a legend in Chinese stating that the wearer had come to China to fight the Japanese invader, and that a reward in gold would be paid for his safe return in case he fell from the sky.

Doug Douglass had been a member of the American Volunteer Group in China and Burma, a "Flying Tiger," one of a small group of pilots who, before the United States had entered the war, were recruited from the Army Air Corps, the Marines, and the Navy to fly Curtiss P-40 fighters against the Japanese. On the nose of his P-38F there were painted ten small Japanese flags, called "meatballs," each signifying a

Japanese kill. There were also painted six Swastikas, representing the kills of six German aircraft, and the representation of a submarine.

While attacking the German submarine pens at Saint-Lazare, then-Major Douglass had attempted to skip-bomb a 500-pound aerial bomb into the mouth of the pens. He hadn't made it. But his bomb had struck, literally by accident, a U-Boat tied to a wharf just outside the mouth of the pen. It had penetrated the hull in the forward torpedo room, and what was known as a "sympathetic explosion" had occurred. The explosives in the bomb and in God-alone-knew-how-many torpedos had combined, and the submarine had simply disappeared, leaving few recognizable pieces.

Douglass and his group had been accompanied on the mission by photoreconnaissance aircraft, and there was a motion picture record of the 500-pound bombs dropping from Douglass's wings, and of one of them striking the submarine, and of large chunks of the submarine hull floating lazily through the air. There was no question about it, mistakes counted, it was a confirmed kill.

Newly promoted Lieutenant Colonel Douglass had given in to the "suggestion" by his division commander that he paint a submarine on the nose of his P-38F not because he considered it a victory, but because it signified that he had been on the Saint-Lazare raid. He had lost 40% of his aircraft—and his pilots—on that raid.

A story made the rounds that after the raid, Douglass had walked into Eighth Air Force Headquarters and decked the Plans & Training officer who had ordered the mission. And that the bloody nose he'd given the chair-warmer had given the brass a choice between court-martialing a West Pointer who was a triple ace or promoting him, and they'd opted in favor of the promotion.

Today, there was with him in the jeep as it made its way down the parking ramp at Atcham another pilot wearing an identical A-2 jacket with the Chinese flag and calligraphy painted on its back. He was taller and heavier than Douglass, and, at twenty-six, a year older. His name was Richard Canidy, and he had been Lt. Col. Douglass's squadron leader in the Flying Tigers.

He was not a member of the 344th Fighter Group, nor,

despite the gold leaves of a major pinned to his A-2 jacket epaulets, even an officer of the Army Air Corps. Canidy (BS, Aeronautical Engineering, MIT '38) had first been recruited from his duty as a Lieutenant Junior Grade, USNR, Instructor Pilot to be a Flying Tiger, and from the Flying Tigers to be a "Technical Consultant" to the Office of the Coordinator of Information.

The Office of the Coordinator of Information had been redesignated the Office of Strategic Services, and Canidy was now Officer in Charge, Whitbey House Station, OSS-England, which made him the third ranking OSS officer in England. Civilians, in a military environment, attract attention. But little attention is paid, particularly at the upper levels of the military hierarchy, to majors. It had been arranged with the Army Air Corps to issue "Technical Consultant Canidy" an AGO card[1] identifying him as a major, and to insure that if inquiries were made at Eighth Air Force or SHAEF (Supreme Headquarters, Allied Expeditionary Force) there would be a record of a Canidy, Major Richard M., USAAC.

Canidy was not supposed to be flying with the 344th Fighter Group on this mission. Indeed, if either he or Lt. Col. Douglass had asked their superiors for permission for him to come along, the request would have been denied.

Douglass wasn't sure why Canidy wanted to go. He guessed that it had something to do with Jimmy Whittaker getting his ass shipped to Australia, and with Eric Fulmar and Stanley Fine having disappeared suddenly from Whitbey House, destination and purpose unspecified. Canidy's old gang, with the exception of Lt. Commander Eddie Bitter, USN (another ex-Flying Tiger), and of course Douglass himself, had been broken up. A deal like that, being with your buddies, was of course too good to last.

Once, at Whitbey House, Douglass with most of a quart of Scotch in him, had looked at the others with a sudden wave of warmth: *They were good guys, the best, and they were his buddies; he would never so long as he lived, have better friends.* And then he had made what had seemed in his

---

[1]The plastic covered identity card issued to all commissioned officers by the Adjutant General's Office.

condition to be a profound philosophical observation: *"War, like politics, makes strange bedfellows."*

The undisputed leader of the gang, the best natural commander Douglass had ever seen—and the test had been combat—was Canidy. And Canidy was not, like Douglass (West Point) and Bitter (Annapolis), a professional warrior, but almost the antithesis, an MIT-trained aeronautical engineer who made no secret that he found most of the traditions sacred to the professional military hilarious.

The wise man, the philosopher so to speak, of the gang was Captain Stanley S. Fine, a tall ascetic Jew, who had been a Hollywood lawyer before he had been recruited for the OSS from command of a B-17 Squadron. If closing with the enemy and killing him with bare hands was the ultimate description of a warrior, then the gang's most ferocious members were unlikely warriors. Eric Fulmar was the son of a movie star and a German industrialist, and Jimmy Whittaker was a wealthy socialite who addressed the President of the United States as "Uncle Franklin."

Douglass knew that if coincidence had thrown these men together in any normal military organization, and if, improbably, they had become buddies there, any commanding officer with enough sense to find his ass with both hands would have broken up the gang and transferred them as far from each other as possible—as awesome threats to "good military order and discipline."

But they weren't in any normal military organization. They were in the Office of Strategic Services.

Lt. Col. Douglass knew more about the OSS than he had any right to know. He wasn't even supposed to know about Whitbey House, much less spend most of his free time in the requisitioned mansion, the ancestral home of the Dukes of Stanfield. But he was a special case. Not only had he been Dick Canidy's wingman in the Flying Tigers, but his father was Captain Peter Douglass, Sr., deputy director of the OSS, Colonel Wild Bill Donovan's Number Two.

David Bruce, Chief of London Station, and his deputy, Lt. Col. Ed Stevens, simply ignored Douglass's illegal presence at Whitbey House when they saw him there. Canidy and the others didn't talk about what they were doing in Douglass's presence, or tried hard not to, but it was difficult to remember all the time that Douglass didn't have the Need-to-Know, and things slipped out.

When Canidy had hinted that he wouldn't mind getting checked out in the P-38F, Douglass had known that the next inevitable step would be for him to go along on a mission. But it would have been difficult to tell his old squadron commander, on whose wing he had first experienced aerial combat, that that was against regulations and therefore impossible. It would have been difficult if he had wanted to say "no," and he didn't want to say no.

He was the Group Commander, and no one asked questions when they saw him personally showing an Air Corps major around a P-38F, or when he scheduled a couple of P-38Fs for training flights and went along with the major.

If Dick dumped a P-38F while he was learning, Douglass decided, he would just say that he was flying it. That would work unless Canidy killed himself, in which case it wouldn't matter. That fear turned out to have been academic. Canidy hadn't had any trouble with the P-38F. He was a good pilot, and an experienced one. He had several thousand hours in the air. Many of Douglass's pilots had less than two hundred fifty.

When the jeep stopped in front of the revetment in which waited the P-38F that Canidy would fly today, and Canidy started to get out, Douglass touched his arm.

"I'll fly your wing, if you like, Skipper," he said.

Canidy smiled at him, touched by the gesture.

"I'm just going along for the ride, thank you, *Colonel,*" he said.

Douglass nodded and motioned for the driver to continue.

Canidy walked into the revetment. The crew chief, a young technical sergeant, threw him a casual salute.

"Good morning, Major," he said.

"Morning," Canidy said. "You've wound both rubber bands, I presume?"

"Yes, Sir," the crew chief said.

Canidy, with the crew chief trailing him, walked around the airplane, making the pre-flight check. He found nothing wrong and nodded his approval of the aircraft's condition.

They walked back to the nose of the aircraft, where the crew chief held out a sheepskin flying jacket to Canidy, and then when Canidy had put his arms into it, steadied him as he pulled sheepskin trousers over his uniform trousers.

Canidy started to climb the ladder to the cockpit, which sat between the twin engines. And for the first time he saw what was painted on the nose. The Flying Tiger's shark's jaw, and "Dick Canidy," in flowing script, and beneath it five meatballs.

"That was very nice of you, Sergeant," Canidy said. "Thank you very much."

"The colonel thought you'd like it, Major," the crew chief said. "He was your squadron CO in the Flying Tigers, wasn't he?"

"Right," Canidy said. It was not the time for historical accuracy.

He climbed into the cockpit. The crew chief climbed the ladder after him, carrying sheepskin boots. Canidy, not without difficulty, put them on, and then the crew chief helped him with the parachute straps, and finally handed him the leather helmet and oxygen mask, with its built-in microphone.

"Go get a couple, Major," the crew chief said. "God go with you."

Canidy smiled and nodded.

The crew chief climbed down the ladder, and then removed it from where it hooked on the cockpit. Another crew member, as Canidy ran the controls through their limits, rolled up a fire extinguisher. Then he and the crew chief looked up at the cockpit, waiting for Canidy's next order.

Canidy looked down and saw they were ready for him.

This is not the smartest thing I have ever done, Canidy thought. *I know better. Only a goddamn fool goes off voluntarily into the wild blue yonder, from which he stands a good chance indeed of dying in flames.*

The alternative was sitting around Whitbey House going nuts. Christ only knew what Donovan had in mind for Jimmy Whittaker. And at this moment, Eric Fulmar was somewhere in Germany wearing the uniform of an SS-Obersturmführer (First Lieutenant). If the SS caught him in that, they would be inspired to see that his death was preceded by their most imaginative interrogation techniques.

It was either this—which by stretching a point could be

considered flying a reconnaissance mission himself that otherwise the Air Corps would have to make. Or drink. Or go nuts.

He flipped the Main Power Buss on, and then adjusted the richness control of the left engine. He looked down from the cockpit.

"Clear!" he called.

"Clear, Sir," the crew chief called back.

Canidy leaned forward and held the "ENGINE START LEFT" toggle switch against the pressure of its spring.

The left engine began to grind, and the prop began to turn, very slowly. Then the engine caught for a moment, bucked and spit. The prop became a silver blur.

There had been time to think. He was just along for the ride. He was riding Douglass's wing, throttled back at 25,000 feet so as not to outrun the bomber stream of B-17Es at 23,000 feet. Douglass had the responsibility for the flock of sheep. All Canidy had to do was maintain his position relative to Doug.

The first thing he thought was that this was where he really belonged. He was a pilot, and a good one, a combat-experienced pilot. And also an aeronautical engineer. He knew what he was doing here. He should have fought this war as a pilot.

But other thoughts intruded. Experience was relative to somebody else's experience. Relatively speaking, he was an old-timer in the intelligence business, not because he'd done so much, but because hardly anybody else had done anything at all. The Americans, as the British were so fond of pointing out whenever they found the opportunity, were virgins in the intelligence business.

There had been a cartoon one time on the bulletin board at MIT in Cambridge: "Last Weak I Cudn't Even Spell 'Enginnear' And Now I Are One."

There should be one on his corkboard in his office, he thought: "Last Year, I Didn't Even Know What An Action Officer Was, But Look At Me Now!"

And I am now possessed of knowledge, he thought, *that would scare the shit out of those guys in the bombers. They have been told so often—by people who believe what they are saying—that the "box" tactic (which provided a theoretically impenetrable fire zone of .50 caliber machine-gun fire) is going to keep them safe from harm that they tend to believe it.*

They question what they are told, of course. They're smart enough to figure out—or have learned from experience—that German fighters will get past the fighter escort and then penetrate the box. But they hope that the fighter escorts will grow more skilled and the .50 caliber fire zones will be refined so that things will get better, not worse, and that all they will really have to worry about is flak.

I know that the Germans have flight-tested fighter aircraft propelled not by airscrews, but by jets of hot air. I know that these aircraft will fly two or three hundred miles per hour faster than our fighters, which means the Germans will be able to just about ignore our fighter escorts. And I know that the best aerial gunner in the world isn't going to be able to hit a small fighter approaching at closing speeds[2] *over 800 mph.*

And I know that unless we can stop the Germans from getting their jet fighters operational, there is going to be an unbelievable blood bath up here.

It is for that reason that I can intellectually, if not emotionally, justify sending Eric Fulmar into Germany. If we can find out from the guy he's bringing out what the Germans need to build their jet engines, maybe we can bomb their factories out of existence before they can start turning out engines. In the cold, emotionless logic of my profession, that justifies dispatching an agent, even running the risk that if he is caught, the Sicherheitsdienst will begin his interrogation by peeling the skin from his wang, before they get down to serious business.

"Dawn Patrol Leader," Douglass's voice came over the air-to-air. "Dawn Patrol Two. We just crossed the German border."

Under the black rubber oxygen mask that covered the lower half of his face, Canidy smiled. What seemed like a very long time ago, when he and Doug had been assigned to fly patrols at first light looking for Japanese bombers on their way to attack Chungking, they had, feeling very clever about it, chosen "Dawn Patrol" as their air-to-air identity. Errol

---

[2]The sum of the velocities of two approaching aircraft: The closing speed of aircraft headed north at 250 mph and south at 350 mph is 600 mph.

Flynn had recently played a heroic fighter pilot in a movie with that name.

"If you see Eric, wave," Canidy said to his microphone. He immediately thought, *Now, that wasn't too smart, was it?*

"No shit?" Douglass replied. This time Canidy didn't reply.

Five minutes later, Douglass came on the air again.

"Blue Group Leader. We have what looks like two squadrons of ME-109s at ten o'clock. Baker and Charley flights, hold your positions. Able will engage. Able, follow me."

Canidy looked for the German fighters, and found them, maybe twenty-five black specks in a nose-down attitude, obviously intending to strike the bomber stream from behind and above.

The Germans preferred to attack from above, preferably from above and to the rear, but from above. Diving at the P-38Fs on their way to the bomber stream beneath would give the Messerschmidts a considerable advantage. With the American fighters between the B-17s and the Germans, the B-17 gunners would have their fields of fire restricted unless they wanted to run the risk of hitting the P-38Fs. And with just a little bit of luck, machine gun and cannon fire directed at the P-38Fs might strike one of the bombers beyond them.

Canidy waited until Douglass was out of the way, then tested his guns (he had tested them over the English channel, but it was better to test them again than to find himself nose up against a Messerschmidt with a bad solenoid[3] and no guns) and then pushed the nose up and to the left and stayed on Douglass's wing.

He felt his hands sweating inside his gloves, and knew that it was a manifestation of fear.

The attacking Messerschmidts split into two groups, one to continue the attack on the bomber stream, the other to engage the American fighters. The tactic had obviously been preplanned.

The P-38Fs had not been able to gain much speed from the time they left their original position to rise to the attack, but the Germans were running with their needles on the DO NOT EXCEED red line, and the closing speed was greater

---

[3]The electromagnetic device which triggered the machine guns.

than Canidy expected. He was sure that his three-second burst had missed the Messerschmidt he had aimed at.

Turning outside of Douglass, he felt the world grow red, and then almost black, as the centrifugal forces of the turn drained the blood from his head.

The twin 1325-horsepower Allison engines, with their throttles shoved forward to FULL EMERGENCY MILITARY POWER indent were screaming. Full Emergency Military Power was hell on fuel consumption, and cut deeply into the operational life of engines, but the extra power, when needed, was worth the cost. When they came out of the 360-degree turn, they were running a little faster than the Messerschmidts. They gained on them slowly and followed them through the bomber stream.

The tracers from the bombers' guns seemed to fill the sky; there was a real possibility that he would be hit, and that prospect was frightening. But the fear was overcome by what Canidy, very privately, thought of as the animal urge to kill. Man—because he fancied himself civilized—liked to pretend he entered combat reluctantly. And he prepared for combat reluctantly. But once he was in it, he was far less removed from the savage than he liked to believe. He wallowed in the prospect of killing the enemy.

The pair of Messerschmidts he and Douglass were chasing pulled out of their dives. To be sure of a killing burst from his battery of eight .50 caliber Brownings (the mark, Canidy thought approvingly, of the experienced fighter pilot; "don't shoot until you can see the whites of their eyes"), Douglass, who had crept ever closer to the German before him, was taken by surprise. His P-38F could not respond in time, and he had lost his opportunity to fire.

Canidy was two hundred yards behind him. Without thinking of what he was doing, he moved the nose of his P38-F from the Messerschmidt he had been following to the one that had gotten away from Doug. The plane vibrated for a moment from the recoil of eight heavy machine guns, and then he aimed at the first plane, this time firing a three-second burst.

---

[4]Machine gun belts were loaded with various "mixes" of ball, incendiary and tracer cartridges, most commonly with one tracer cartridge in each five rounds.

He saw his tracer stream[4] move from just in front of the Messerschmidt to the engine cowling, and then to the left wing. There was a hint of orange, and then the wing tank exploded.

Canidy pulled up abruptly and looked around for the other fighter. He couldn't find it for a moment, and then he saw it, smoke pouring from its engine nacelle as it spun toward the cloud cover below. He looked for a parachute but didn't see one.

And then Douglass was on his wing.

"Two more," Douglass's voice came over the air-to-air. "How the hell are we going to explain that?"

"That'll make seventeen for you, won't it, Colonel?" Canidy replied.

"Bullshit!" Douglass said, and then switched frequencies. "Blue Group Able, this is Blue Group Leader. Form on me in Position A."

The P-38Fs scattered all over the sky began to turn and to resume their original protective positions over the B-17 stream.

Canidy reached inside his sheepskin jacket, and then inside his uniform jacket and came out with a MAP, US ARMY CORPS OF ENGINEERS: GERMANY.

It wasn't an aerial navigation chart, but rather one intended for use by ground troops. It could also be used by a pilot who intended to navigate by flying close enough to the ground and following roads and rivers. Canidy had taken it with him to the final briefing, and copied the course the bomber stream would fly. Once they had joined the bomber stream, over a known location, it was not difficult to plot from that position and time where the head of the bomber stream would be at a given time.

It wasn't precise, but Canidy had had experience in China navigating with a lot less. He looked at his watch, and then scrawled some arithmetic computations on the map. He put a check mark on the map. The way he had it figured, the lead aircraft of the bomber stream was now passing over a relatively unpopulated area of Germany, southeast of Dortmund. He made some more marks on the map, and then touched his air-to-air microphone switch.

"Dawn Patrol Two," he called.

"Go ahead," Douglass replied a moment later.

"There's something I want to see," Canidy said.

"Say again?"

"I say again, I'm going to have a look at something I want to see," Canidy said. "I'll be back in about two zero minutes."

"Dick, are you all right?" Douglass asked, the concern in his voice clear even over the clipped tones of the radio.

"Affirmative," Canidy said.

"Permission to leave the formation is denied," Douglass said.

Canidy ignored him. He dropped the nose of the P-38F and headed East. He knew that Douglass could not simply ignore his responsibilities as fighter escort commander; so Douglass would not follow him.

Canidy dropped through the bomber stream, more than a little surprised that at least one gunner didn't get excited and take a shot at him. In a P-51 or a P-47, that probably would have happened. But the twin-engine, twin tail boom shape of the P-38F was distinctive. There was no German plane that looked even remotely like it.

When he passed through 11,000 feet, he took the oxygen mask from his face, and rubbed the marks it had made on his cheeks and nose, and under his chin. He loosened the snaps of the sheepskin jacket. It was cold, but not nearly as bitter cold as it had been at 25,000 feet, nearly five miles up.

He dropped to 2,000 feet and trimmed it up to cruise at 300 miles per hour. If the air were still, that would have moved him across the ground at five miles per minute. The air wasn't still, of course, but it still helped to have that stored in the back of his mind. He was making, roughly, a mile every twelve seconds.

His chronometer showed that he had left the formation thirteen minutes before when he found what he was looking for. The River Eder had been dammed near Bad Wildungen, making a lake with a distinctive shape. He passed east of it, far enough so that if there was antiaircraft protecting the dam, he would not be in its range.

He reset the second counter on the chronometer.

Almost exactly six minutes later, which would put him thirty miles from the dam, he spotted what had to be the River Lahn. Right, he thought, where it should be.

He banked sharply to follow the river south, and dropped even lower toward the ground. He would be very vulnerable if he was attacked from behind and above. He was counting on not being detected until he had seen what he had come looking for. He was also counting on the probability that whatever Germans were airborne would be directing their efforts toward the bomber stream and its escorts, rather than trying to look for one lone fighter on the deck.

He saw first the medieval castle on the hill in Marburg, and then he dropped his eyes just ahead of him and to the right.

And there it was, the Marburg Werke of Fulmar Elektrische GmbH.

He retarded his throttle and extended the flaps, and when it was safe, lowered his wheels. Technically, lowering the gear was a sign of surrender. But in order to surrender, there had to be someone to surrender to, and there was no German in sight. He lowered his wheels to slow the P-38F down. He wanted as good a look as he could get.

He passed so low and so slow that he thought he could see surprise on the faces of the workmen who were erecting fences and framework for camouflage netting around and over the new, square, windowless concrete block building.

And then he was past it. He shoved the throttle ahead and retracted his gear and flaps and pulled back on the stick.

He wondered if Eric was down there and could hear, or perhaps even see, the American fighter as it climbed steeply into the sky.

He hadn't seen anything of great significance. And he wasn't even sure that the Germans really intended to use the Marburg facility's electric furnaces to make the special alloy steel parts for their jet-propulsion engines. But it was important that he have a look for himself. Now that he'd done so, he was glad that he had—even if his fund of knowledge was not appreciably greater than it had been.

The odds were that he would be responsible for mounting a mission against that particular factory. He wanted to know what would certainly cost American lives looked like. And he would now be in a position to recommend the path attackers would take. Having been there, he was now an expert.

As he came out of a cloud layer at 15,000 feet, he saw the bomber stream above him. When he reached 20,000 feet, .50 caliber tracers from several of the bombers began to arc in his direction.

That was bad, but worse would follow. There was a mob instinct. *If the guy in the next plane is firing at that airplane, maybe he can see something I can't, like Maltese crosses on the wings. Why take a chance?*

Canidy put the P-38F into a steep dive away from the bomber stream, to get out of range, and when he felt safe, he went to 23,000 feet and caught up with the fighter escort. He got there just as a swarm of Messerschmidts based near Frankfurt began their attack, and the fighter formations broke up to repel it. He didn't find Douglass until long after the bombing run, when they were headed home.

When he pulled beside him, Douglass took off his glove so there would be no question but that he was giving Canidy the international aviation hand signal known as "The Finger."

The commanding officer of the 344th Fighter Group went on the air-to-air.

"You goddamn sonofabitch," he said. "I was worried about you."

2

East Railway Station
Budapest, Hungary
1145 Hours 31 January 1943

When the Opel Admiral[5] was found parked in the reserved area of the East Railway Station, it quite naturally caused a certain curiosity among the Gestapo agents assigned to the station.

For one thing, there were few Admirals around anywhere, and possession of one was a symbol of power and authority.

[5]Because of its connection with General Motors, the line of automobiles produced by Adam Opel GmbH paralleled that of GM. The Admiral was the Opel counterpart to the Cadillac.

This one, moreover, bore Berlin license plates, a CD (Corps diplomatique) plate, and affixed to the Berlin license tag where the tax sticker was supposed to go, a sticker signifying that taxes had been waived because the automobile was in the service of the German Reich, and specifically in the service of the SS-SD.[6]

Obviously, whoever had parked the car was someone of high importance. The question was just who he was.

First things first. Josef Hamm, the ranking Gestapo agent, ordered that the Hungarian railway police be "requested" to station a railway policeman to watch the car. If there was one thing known for sure, it was that, whoever the high official was, he would not be at all pleased to return to his car and find that someone had taken a key or a coin and run it along the fenders and doors. There had been a good deal of that, lately. A number of Hungarians took offense at the Hungarian-German alliance generally, and at the large (and growing) presence of German troops and SS in Budapest specifically, and expressed their displeasure in small, nasty ways.

Then Hamm called the security officer at the German embassy, and asked who the car belonged to.

"It probably belongs to von Heurten-Mitnitz," the security officer said. "That would explain the SD sticker, and he's the type to have an Admiral."

"Who's von Heurten-Mitnitz?"

"Helmut von Heurten-Mitnitz," the security officer said. "He's the new first secretary."

"How does he rate an SD sticker?"

"Because when he's bored with wearing striped pants, he can wear the uniform of a Brigadeführer SS-SD," the security officer said. "You could say that von Heurten-Mitnitz is a very influential man. His brother is a great friend of the Führer. If you'd like, I can check the license plate number by teletype with Berlin."

"How long would that take?"

"Thirty, forty minutes," the security officer said.

"I'll call you back in an hour," Josef Hamm said. "Thank you, Karl."

---

[6]Schutzstaffel Sicherheitsdienst: The Secret Service of the SS.

When he called back, Hamm was told that von Heurten-Mitnitz did not own the Admiral. It was owned by Standartenführer (Colonel) Johann Müller, of the SS-SD.

"Do you think he knows von Heurten-Mitnitz is driving it?"

"I think if it was stolen, Josef," the security officer said sarcastically, "they probably would have said something. Müller is with the Führer at Wolf's Lair.[7] Nobody takes a personal car there. So maybe he loaned it to von Heurten-Mitnitz."

"Have you seen this von Heurten-Mitnitz? What's he look like?"

"Tall, thin, sharp-featured. Classy dresser. If you're thinking, Josef, of asking von Heurten-Mitnitz what he's doing with Müller's car, I wouldn't."

"I'm thinking of finding the new First Secretary when he comes back and telling him that if he will be so good, when he leaves his car at the station, as to tell us, we will do our very best to make sure some Hungarian doesn't piss on his engine or write a dirty word on the hood with a pocketknife."

The security officer chuckled. "You're learning, Josef," he said, and then hung up.

Josef Hamm and two of his men were waiting at the end of the platform when the 1705 from Vienna pulled in. The two men positioned themselves at opposite ends of the three first-class cars, and, when one of them spotted a "tall, sharp-featured, classy dresser" getting off, he signaled to Josef Hamm by taking off his hat and waving it over his head, as if waving at someone who had come to meet him at the train.

Hamm saw that Helmut von Heurten-Mitnitz was indeed a classy dresser. He wore a gray homburg and an overcoat with a fur collar. With him were three people, an Obersturmführer-SS and a man and woman who looked like father and daughter.

When they had almost reached the police checkpoint at the end of the platform, Hamm walked around it and up to von Heurten-Mitnitz.

[7]Hitler's secret command post at Rastenburg.

"Heil Hitler!" Hamm said, giving a quick, straight-armed salute. Von Heurten-Mitnitz made a casual wave in return.

"Herr Brigadeführer von Heurten-Mitnitz?" Hamm asked.

"Yes," von Heurten-Mitnitz said, but did not smile.

"Josef Hamm at your service, Herr Brigadeführer," he said. "I have the honor to command the Railway Detachment, Gestapo District Budapest."

"What can I do for you, Herr Hamm?" von Heurten-Mitnitz asked, obviously annoyed to be detained.

"First, let me get you past the checkpoint," Hamm said.

"This officer and these people are with me," von Heurten-Mitnitz said.

The young SS officer raised his hand in a sloppy salute.

"Make way for the Brigadeführer and his party!" Hamm called out as he led them to and past the checkpoint.

"Very kind of you," von Heurten-Mitnitz mumbled. "Now, what's on your mind?"

"Herr Brigadeführer," Hamm began, "if you would be so kind as to notify one of my men whenever you park your car here at the station . . ."

"Why would I want to do that?" von Heurten-Mitnitz interrupted.

". . . then I can make sure that no one bothers it while you are gone."

Helmut von Heurten-Mitnitz looked at Hamm without speaking, but a raised eyebrow asked, What the hell are you talking about?

"There have been unfortunate incidents, Herr Brigadeführer," Hamm explained, "where cars have been . . . *defiled* . . . by unsavory elements among the Budapest population. Paint scratched. Worse."

Von Heurten-Mitnitz seemed to consider this a moment, and then he smiled.

"I believe I am beginning to understand," he said. "You saw my car parked, and took the trouble to find out whose it was, and then to meet me. How very obliging of you, Herr Hamm! I am most grateful."

"It was my pleasure, Herr Brigadeführer," Hamm said.

"You can do me one other courtesy," von Heurten-Mitnitz said. "Please do not use my SS rank when addressing me. The less well known it is in Budapest the better, if you take my meaning. I also hold the rank of Minister."

"That was thoughtless of me, Herr Minister," Hamm said. "I beg the Herr Minister's pardon."

"Don't be silly, my dear Hamm," von Heurten-Mitnitz said. "How could you have known?"

"Is there any other way in which I can help the Herr Minister?" Hamm said.

"I can't think of one," von Heurten-Mitnitz said, after a moment's hesitation. He offered his hand. "I am touched by your courtesy, Herr Hamm, and impressed with your thoroughness. I shall tell the Ambassador what you've done for me."

They were by then standing beside the Admiral. Hamm opened both doors, and after the father-and-daughter had gotten into the back seat, closed them. The young SS officer walked around the rear of the car and slipped in beside von Heurten-Mitnitz. Hamm gave another salute, which von Heurten-Mitnitz returned casually, and with a smile, and then Hamm stood back as von Heurten-Mitnitz backed the Admiral out of its parking space.

All things considered, Hamm thought, *I handled that rather well.*

When they were a few yards from the station, the tall, gray-haired man in the back seat spoke. "My God, when he stopped you, I thought I was going to faint."

"You really don't faint when you're frightened, Professor," the young SS officer said. "Fear causes adrenaline to flow, and that increases, not decreases, the flow of blood to the brain. Shutting off blood to the brain is what makes you faint."

"Oh, my God!" the young woman in the back seat said, with infinite disgust.

Helmut von Heurten-Mitnitz chuckled.

"How very American," he said.

The young SS officer carried an identification card which identified him as Obersturmführer-SS Baron von Fulmar, of the personal staff of the Reichsführer-SS. It was a forgery, a very good one. In a safe at Whitbey House, Kent, there was a bona fide identity card issued by the Adjutant General's

Office, U.S. Army, identifying him as FULMAR, Eric, 1st Lt., Infantry, Army of the United States.

"Where are we going?" the gray-haired man asked. He was Professor Doktor Friedrich Dyer, until two days before of the Metallurgy Department, College of Physics, the University of Marburg. His name was now being circulated over SS-SD and police teletypes. He was being sought for questioning regarding the murder of SS Hauptsturmführer (Captain) Wilhelm Peis. The teletype message said that he was probably accompanied by his daughter Gisella, that it was possible that they would try to flee the country, and that authorities in ports along the English Channel should consequently be on special alert.

"To Batthyany Palace," von Heurten-Mitnitz said. "It's on Holy Trinity Square. Not far from here."

"And what happens there?" Professor Dyer asked.

"I don't know about anybody else," Fulmar said. "But I intend to go to work on a bottle of brandy."

"That's not what I meant," Professor Dyer snapped.

"You'll be told what you have to know, Professor," Fulmar said, "when you have to know it. The less you know, the better. I thought I'd made that plain."

Professor Dyer exhaled audibly and slumped against his seat. His daughter flashed a look of contempt at the back of Fulmar's head, and shook her own head in resignation.

Batthyany Palace, directly across Holy Trinity Square from St. Matthias's Church, had been built at approximately the same time (1775-77) as the royal castle (1715-70) atop Castle Hill. Twelve-foot statues of bare-chested men on the facade appeared to be carrying the upper stories on their shoulders, earning the admiration of ten-foot, large-bosomed granite women twined around pillars at each of three identical double doors.

The door at the left was a fake. The center door opened into the entrance foyer of the palace, and the door at the right was the carriage entrance. Von Heurten-Mitnitz turned off the square and stopped the Admiral with its nose against the right door and blew the horn. A moment later, one by one, the double doors opened. He drove through, and the doors closed after him.

Beatrice, Countess Batthyany and Baroness von Steighofen, was standing in a vestibule waiting for them. She was a tall, generously built woman in her early thirties. She was wearing a sable coat that reached nearly to her ankles and a matching sable hat under which a good deal of dark red hair was visible. Von Heurten-Mitnitz drove past her into a courtyard, turned around, and returned to the vestibule, where he stopped.

The Countess went to the rear door and pulled it open.

"I'm the Countess Batthyany," she said. "Won't you please come in?"

Professor Dyer and his daughter got out of the car and, following the direction indicated by the Countess's outstretched hand, walked into the building. The Countess turned to smile at Fulmar. "And you must be dear cousin Eric," she said, drily. "How nice to finally meet you."

Fulmar laughed. "Hello," he said.

She turned to Von Heurten-Mitnitz, who had walked around the front of the car.

"I see everything turned out all right," she said.

"The Gestapo man at the station personally led us past the checkpoint," he said.

"Oooh," she said. "I suppose you could use a drink."

"I could," Fulmar said.

She turned to look at him again.

"You look like Manny," she said. "You even sound like him. That terrible Hessian dialect."

He chuckled.

"Let's hope you are luckier," the Countess said, as she started into the house.

"Let's hope there's some of his clothing here, and that it fits," Fulmar said. "Particularly shoes."

She turned and looked at him again, this time appraisingly.

"You're a little larger than Manny was," she said. "But there should be something. I gather you want to get out of that uniform?"

"They're looking for an Obersturmführer who looks like me," Fulmar said. "There was a Gestapo agent at the border who thought he had found him."

"That close?" she asked.

"I think it's been smoothed over," von Heurten-Mitnitz said. "It was close, but I think it . . . is smoothed over."

The Countess considered what he had said, and nodded her head.

Heating the enormous old palace had under the best of circumstances always been difficult. Now, without adequate supplies of coal, it had proved impossible. It wasn't as if she didn't have coal. There were half a dozen coal mines running around the clock on Batthyany property, and she could have all the coal she wanted. The problem was getting the coal from the mines to Batthyany Palace. That required trucks, and she had been allocated one truckload per month. She didn't always get that, and even when she did, one truckload was nowhere near enough to heat the palace.

She didn't even bother to try to heat the entire lower floor of the palace, nor the two upper floors. They had been shut off with rather ugly and really not very effective wooden barriers over the stairwells. Only the first floor[8] was occupied. The Countess was living in a five-room apartment overlooking Holy Trinity Square, but she often thought she might as well be living in the basement for all she got to look at the square. Most of the floor-to-ceiling windows had been timbered over to preserve the heat from the tall, porcelain-covered stoves in the corners of the rooms. The two windows (leading to the balcony over the square and the garden in the rear that were not covered over with timber were covered with seldom-opened drapes.

The Dyers, not knowing where to go and looking uncomfortable, waited for the others to catch up with them at the foot of what had been the servants' stairway to the first floor. The Countess went up ahead of them. They came out in the large, elegantly furnished sitting room overlooking the square.

Fulmar immediately sat down on a fragile-looking gilded wood Louis XIV sofa and began to pull his black leather boots off.

The Countess looked askance at him, but von Heurten-Mitnitz sensed there was something wrong.

"Something wrong with your feet?" he asked.

---

[8]In America, the second floor.

"These goddamned boots are four sizes too small," Fulmar said. "I soaked them with water, but it didn't help a whole hell of a lot."

When he had the boots off, he pulled a stocking off and holding his foot in his lap, examined it carefully.

"Goddamn, look at that!" he said. The skin was rubbed raw, and was bleeding in several places.

The Countess walked to the sofa, dropped to her knees, and took the foot in her hand.

"How did you manage to walk?" she asked.

"Why, Cousin," Fulmar said, "I simply considered the alternative."

"You'll have to soak that in brine," she said. "It's the only thing that will help."

"By brine, you mean salt in water?" he asked, and she nodded.

"Before we do that, I would like a very large cognac," he said, and pulled off the other sock. The other foot was worse. The blood from the sore spots had flowed more copiously, and when it had dried, it had glued the sock to the wounds. He swore as he pulled the stocking off.

The Countess walked to a cabinet and returned with a large crystal brandy snifter.

"I'll heat some water," she said. "And make a brine."

"And pickle my feet," Fulmar said, drily. "Thank you, Cousin, ever so much."

"Why do you call her 'cousin'?" Professor Dyer asked.

"We are, by marriage," the Countess said. "My late husband and Eric are, or were, cousins."

"Your late husband?" the professor asked.

"The Professor tends to ask a lot of questions," Fulmar said, mockingly.

"My husband, the late Oberstleutnant (Lieutenant Colonel) Baron Manfried von Steighofen, fell for his fatherland on the Eastern front," the Countess said drily.

"And you're doing this?" the professor asked.

"It's one of the reasons I'm doing 'this,' my dear Herr Professor," the Countess said.

"And the other?" Fulmar asked.

"Is it important?"

"I'm curious," Fulmar said. "If I were in your shoes, I would be rooting for the Germans."

"If I thought they had a chance to win, I probably would be," she said, matter-of-factly. "But they won't win. Which means that the Communists will come to Budapest. If they don't shoot me, I'll find myself walking the square outside asking strangers if they're looking for a good time."

"Beatrice!" von Heurten-Mitnitz exclaimed.

"Face facts, my dear Helmut," the Countess said.

"The flaw in your logic," Fulmar said, "is that you are helping the Russians to come here."

"In which case, I can only hope that you and Helmut will still be alive and in a position to tell the Commissar what a fearless antifascist I was," she said. "There's a small chance that would keep them from shooting me out of hand." There was a moment's silence, and then she went on. "What I'm really hoping for is that there will be a *coup d'état* by people like Helmut against the Bavarian corporal, and in time for whoever takes over to sue for an armistice. If there's an armistice, perhaps I won't lose everything."

"Huh," Fulmar grunted.

"And what has motivated you, my dear Eric," the Countess said, "to do what you're doing?"

It was a moment before he replied. "Sometimes I really wonder," he said.

The Countess nodded, and then turned to Gisella Dyer.

"Would you help me, please?" she said. "I made a gulyás, and if you would help serve it, I'll heat some water to 'pickle' Eric's feet."

The sting of the warm salt water on his feet was not as painful as Eric Fulmar had expected, and he wondered if this was because he was partially anesthetized by the Countess's brandy, or whether his feet were beyond hurting. The gulyás was delicious, and he decided that was because it was delicious and not because of the cognac—or because they'd had little to eat save lard and dark bread sandwiches since leaving Marburg an der Lahn.

Von Heurten-Mitnitz waited until they were finished and Fulmar was pouring a little brandy to improve his small, strong cup of coffee, and then he said:

"I think it would be best if I knew precisely what has happened since you entered Germany, Eric."

"A synopsis would be that everything that could go wrong, did," Fulmar said.

"What about the Gestapo agent? Did you have to kill him?"

"I killed him when he opened the luggage that had been left on the train for me," Fulmar said, matter-of-factly, "and found the Obersturmführer's uniform. And then the boots didn't fit."

Von Heurten-Mitnitz nodded. "And in Marburg, was what happened there necessary?"

"Yes, of course it was," Fulmar said, impatiently. "I don't like scrambling people's brains."

"You could learn some delicacy," the Countess said.

"We are not in a delicate business, Cousin," Fulmar said.

"But that's it? There's nothing else I don't know about?" von Heurten-Mitnitz asked.

Fulmar's hesitation was obvious.

"What else?" von Heurten-Mitnitz persisted.

"I was recognized on the train," he said. "Before I got to Frankfurt. On the way to Marburg."

"By whom?"

There was another perceptible hesitation.

"Christ, I really hate to tell you," he said. "I don't want you playing games with her."

"I think I have to know," von Heurten-Mitnitz said.

"Fuck you," Fulmar said. "You have to know what I goddamn well decide to tell you."

Von Heurten-Mitnitz stiffened. He was not used to being talked to like that. But he kept control of himself.

"Someone you knew when you were at Marburg?" he asked, reasonably. And then when Fulmar remained silent, he added, "I don't want to sound melodramatic, but I will be here when you are safe in England."

"Tell him, Eric," the Countess said. "As you pointed out, we are not in a delicate business."

"I don't want you trying to use her, you understand me? Her, or her father."

"Who recognized you?" von Heurten-Mitnitz persisted, gently.

"Elizabeth von Handleman-Bitburg," Fulmar said.

Von Heurten-Mitnitz's eyebrows went up. The Countess looked at him with a question in her eyes.

"Generaloberst[9] von Handleman-Bitburg's daughter?" von Heurten-Mitnitz asked.

Fulmar nodded.

"Possibly it's meaningless," von Heurten-Mitnitz said. "She met a young Obersturmführer whom she had once known. Was there any reason you think she was suspicious?"

"Her father had told her that I was seen in Morocco in an American uniform," Fulmar said. "She knew."

"And what do you think she will tell her father?" von Heurten-Mitnitz asked.

"Nothing," Fulmar said. "She won't tell him a thing."

"I wish I shared your confidence," von Heurten-Mitnitz said.

"The only reason I'm telling you this," Fulmar said, "is because I don't want you to protect your ass by taking her out."

"Telling me what?"

"We spent the night together," Fulmar said. "OK? Get the picture?"

"Yes, I think I do," von Heurten-Mitnitz said.

"If anything happens to her," Fulmar said. "I will . . ."

"Don't be childish," von Heurten-Mitnitz said.

"I was about to say something childish," Fulmar said. "Like I will come back here and kill you myself. But I won't have to do that. All I'll have to do is make sure the Sicherheitsdienst finds out about you."

"My God!" von Heurten-Mitnitz said.

"I made a mistake in telling you," Fulmar said.

"No, you didn't, Eric," the Countess said. She walked to von Heurten-Mitnitz and put her arm in his, and then stood on her tiptoes and kissed his cheek. "Helmut understands that even in the midst of this insanity, people fall in love."

Fulmar looked through them, and then chuckled.

"Well, I'll be goddamned," he said. "The Merry Widow in the flesh."

---

[9]Colonel General; the equivalent of a U.S. Army full (four-star) General.

Four

1

The Maylaybalay-Kibawe Highway
Island of Mindanao
Commonwealth of the Philippines
4 February 1943

THE MOUNTAINOUS CENTER of the island of Mindanao is virtually inaccessible by motor vehicle, and accessible by foot only with great difficulty. It was for that reason that Brigadier General Wendell Fertig Commanding, U.S. Forces in the Philippines, had elected to place his headquarters and the bulk of his force in the mountains: the Japs had a hell of a hard time getting in there, and when they tried it, he was always notified in plenty of time to plan his defensive strategy.

Almost without exception, that strategy was to evacuate his headquarters and, from positions in the mountainous jungle nearby, observe how close the Japanese had come to finding it.

So far, they had failed, although on occasion they had come across outposts or villages where he had stationed small detachments of his guerrilla force. That was, he knew, a somewhat grandiose manner of describing the six, or eight, or a dozen armed men living in those villages and earning their support from the villagers by working in the fields.

When the Japanese had proof (or strongly suspected) that a village was harboring guerrillas, they burned it to the ground. They would have shot the village leaders, had they caught them, but the villagers—men, women, and children, as well as the guerrillas—invariably found safety in the surrounding jungle when Japanese appeared.

Pour encourager les autres, the elders of several villages that had not been housing guerrillas had been shot, and their villages burned down by the Japanese. The result of this had been to increase the number of natives willing to support U.S. Forces in the Philippines. The remaining men would have been happy to enlist in USFIP, but Fertig had neither food to feed them nor arms with which to equip them.

The Japanese had quickly learned, too, that their expeditions into the mountains were very expensive—and did little good. They were almost always engaged by Fertig's guerrillas. Not in pitched battles, not even in situations that could be considered an armed engagement. Although Fertig liked to think that he was doing to the Japanese what the Minute Men had done to the English on their way back from Concord—causing them serious harm by attacking their formations with accurate rifle fire from the surrounding forests—all he was really able to do was harass the Japanese patrols.

When it was absolutely safe to do so (in the sense that there was a sure escape route into the impenetrable jungle), and when there was an absolutely sure target, two or three or half a dozen shots would ring out from the jungle, and one or two or three sweating Japanese soldiers marching along a trail would be killed or wounded.

With some exceptions (there were some guerrillas who had as much as one hundred rounds of ammunition, which they were unwilling to share), most of Fertig's troops had no more than twenty-five rounds of ammunition for their Model 1917 Enfield .30-06 caliber rifles, or their Arisaka 7.7 mm caliber captured Japanese rifles, or their Winchester or Savage hunting rifles, or their Browning and Remington shotguns.

Fertig's guerrillas were not equipped to engage Japanese forces in battle.

Before long, the Japanese, who were not fools, had for all practical purposes abandoned their expeditions into the mountains. Fertig wasn't posing any bona fide military threat to their occupation. He was contained. And they could live with him until such time as the Filipinos came to understand that it was in their best interest to cooperate with the Japanese, to enter willingly into the Japanese Greater Co-

Prosperity Sphere. At that point, they would stop feeding and supporting Fertig's guerrillas, and the threat would be over.

The Japanese had turned to winning the hearts and minds of the people. Propaganda detachments, protected by company-sized detachments of riflemen, began to visit villages on the periphery of Fertig's mountainous jungle area of operations. The propaganda detachments carried with them 16-mm motion picture projectors and generators, and gifts of food and candy. They would set up a screen and show Charlie Chaplin and Bugs Bunny motion pictures, along with newsreels of the fall of Singapore, and of Lieutenant General Jonathan Wainwright surrendering to General Homma, and of long lines of American soldiers—hands in the air in surrender—entering Japanese captivity.

And then there would be a speech, or speeches, most often by Filipinos already convinced that the future of the Philippine people lay with their Japanese brothers. The speeches would invariably contain sarcastic references to General Fertig and his so-called U.S. Forces in the Philippines.

Where were they? If they hadn't already died of starvation, hiding out like rats in the jungle, why weren't they attacking the Japanese?

General Fertig was aware of the problem, and aware that it had to be dealt with. With some reluctance, he had concluded that the only way to deal with it was by doing exactly what he believed he was probably incapable of doing: engaging a Japanese company-strength unit in a battle. A battle, in which there would be a winner and a loser, not just a dozen shots fired from concealment in the jungle.

The Japanese cooperated in two ways that helped Fertig's plans. First, they were methodical. Their propaganda detachments had a schedule. And Fertig obtained a copy of it from a Filipino woman who had been employed by the Japanese as a typist. Secondly, when it had become apparent to the Japanese that Fertig was unwilling to attack the propaganda detachment convoys, they had grown a little careless.

When the first convoys had gone out, fully expecting to be attacked, they had moved slowly and with great caution. They had sent a point ahead and they were prepared to fight at any moment. Now, as a general rule of thumb, the troops in the trucks did their best to sleep when they were on the road.

Their officers indulged them, for they believed that if Fertig were going to attack, he would do so at night. The way to preclude that was to establish a strong perimeter guard. That required the use of wide-awake soldiers. It was better that the troops get what sleep they could when they could, so they would be wide-awake guards at night.

Two highways cross the main portion of the island of Mindanao, both running north-south, one to the west of the mountains, the other to the east. There is no highway running east-west through the mountains. The terrain is difficult, construction would be practically impossible, and there was no economic justification to build such highways.

The place Fertig picked for the attack on the convoy was almost exactly equidistant between Maylaybalay and Kibawe on the highway that crosses Mindanao to the west of the mountains. The nearest Japanese reinforcements would be twenty-three miles north in Maylaybalay, or twenty-one miles south in Kibawe. In one possible scenario (where one of the trucks would escape the ambush and run for help), it would be anywhere from an hour and a half to two hours before Japanese reinforcements could reach the ambush location.

In another—and much worse—possible scenario, they would not be able to totally overwhelm the Japanese in twenty minutes. In that scenario, the Japanese troops would be equipped with both machine guns and mortars. If they were not able to knock out the mortars and machine guns in the first minute or two of the ambush, overwhelming the Japanese would be difficult and time-consuming.

And overwhelming the Japanese quickly was absolutely necessary. The initial attack would consume a great percentage of available ammunition, including the entire stock (fourteen) of fragmentation hand grenades. Fertig's only possible source of resupply was from the bodies of vanquished Japanese. There would be no question of breaking off the attack and making for the mountains. And the longer it took to overwhelm the Japanese, the more time they would have to defend themselves, which meant the more ammunition they would expend, and the less there would be for the guerrillas to capture.

There were other problems, of course. For one thing, statistically (and this was not a reflection on the Filipinos' loyalty generally) he had to assume that several of his troops were in Japanese service. A father, or a wife, or a child was in Japanese "protection," with the understanding that as soon as proof came of the "loyalty" of the guerrilla the father or wife or child would be released. Loyalty could be proved by getting word to the Japanese of where and when there would be an ambush of Japanese forces, or where and when Fertig or one of his senior officers could be found.

It was not black and white. The same guerrilla who would decide that his greater loyalty lay to his family, and that therefore he should let the Japanese know where they could find Fertig, could more often than not be counted upon to be willing to lay his life on the line sniping at a Japanese patrol.

What this situation required was keeping secret the actual place and time of the planned attack until virtually the last minute, so that the guerrilla with a member of his family in Japanese "protection" would not have the opportunity to communicate with the Japanese.

To assemble the 120-150 man force he considered the optimum for the ambush of the propaganda detachment, therefore, Fertig had to pick several sites within two hours' march of the ambush site. In the event, he picked five different sites, then sent word by runner to various guerrilla cells (numbering in the aggregate just over two hundred men) to assemble into five larger groups at the designated sites.

His experience had taught him that about sixty percent of the guerrillas summoned would appear at the designated site at the proper time.

Five hours before the propaganda detachment and its company of guards was scheduled to reach the ambush site, a second group of runners was sent to the five assembly areas, bearing orders for the men to come to the final assembly point. From the moment the runners reached the five sites, it was presumed that anyone leaving intended to betray the troops to the Japanese. If someone ran and it was impossible to capture him, the operation would be called off, and the guerrillas would disperse. If someone ran and was caught, he would be beheaded. Beheading with a heavy, razor-sharp machete was supposed to be more or less painless, and it did not expend ammunition.

One hour before the Japanese were to pass the ambush site, the last group of guerrillas arrived. No one had disappeared, or tried to. The force now totaled 136 men; and two of the guerrillas, formerly Philippine Scouts, had brought with them BARs[1] and seven loaded magazines.

Fertig was of two minds about using the BARs. They were splendid weapons, and God knew his troops needed something to counter the Japanese Namimba machine guns the guards would certainly have. But he had only 70 rounds per gun—three and a half magazines. And every round that ripped through the BARs with such speed could be fired one at a time from an Enfield in sniping fire, where the kill-per-cartridge rate was so much more effective.

In the end, he decided that the more fire expended at the beginning of the assault, the sooner the Japanese would be overwhelmed, and thus the more ammunition could be taken from their bodies.

Fertig then explained the tactics of the attack, which were very simple.

The force would be divided into two elements, with two-thirds of the force close to one side of the road. From there a devastating fire could be delivered at close range. The second element, commanded by Fertig and consisting of the remaining third of the force, with both BARs and ten of the fourteen fragmentation grenades, would be on the opposite side of the road.

On signal, which was when Fertig and a former Philippine Scout opened fire with their Enfield rifles on the driver of the first vehicle in the convoy, the smaller force would bring BAR fire to bear on the trucks carrying the troops. Other riflemen would disable the last truck in the convoy, preferably by killing its driver.

At this point, Fertig authorized the throwing of one—only —fragmentation grenade at each troop-carrying truck.

The Japanese convoy would thus be immobilized, and it was to be hoped that many, if not most, of the truck-borne troops would be killed before they exited the trucks.

Some, of course, would survive. Most, Fertig believed,

[1]Browning Automatic Rifles, in essence a light .30-06 caliber machine gun, utilizing 20-round magazines.

would exit toward the ditch and forest opposite the direction from which they had been attacked.

They would then present themselves as targets to the bulk of the ambush force. Meanwhile, the third of the force which had opened the attack would rapidly divide itself in half, half going to the head of the convoy, and half to the tail. This would get them out of the line of fire of the larger ambush force and leave them in a position to fire upon any Japanese from the sides.

Fertig did his best to impress upon his men the absolute necessity of aimed fire. They were dangerously short of ammunition, and there was absolutely no excuse for a guerrilla to fall from a bullet fired by another guerrilla.

Everyone seemed to accept his reasoning. But Fertig knew that even the most phlegmatic of people got excited once the crack of small-arms fire filled the air. And by no stretch of the imagination could his force be called at all phlegmatic.

In the engagement that followed, the Ambush Force of United States Forces in the Philippines, Brigadier General W.W. Fertig Commanding, triumphed over the 1104th Army Information Detachment and Company 3, 505th Infantry Regiment of the Imperial Japanese Army. There were no Japanese survivors.

USFIP suffered eleven dead (including the Philippine Scout who had opened the engagement at General Fertig's side, and of whom he had been extraordinarily fond) and thirty-six wounded. Of the thirty-six wounded, twenty would subsequently die. USFIP had virtually no medical supplies.

The Japanese, once they overcame their initial surprise, had fought gallantly and well. It was more than half an hour before the last of them had died for his Emperor. By the time the engagement was over, the Japanese had expended a large part of their ammunition.

On balance, USFIP had more weapons after the ambush than before, including two 60-mm mortars and sixty rounds for them, several Nambu pistols, nearly two hundred Arisaka rifles, and one Namimba machine gun. Countering this increase was the expenditure of .30-06 ammunition and hand grenades. An Enfield or a BAR without .30-06 ammunition is simply a finely machined piece of steel, not a weapon. And the Japanese had expended all of their hand grenades before they were overwhelmed, the last dozen of them as instruments of suicide.

Just before he disappeared back into the jungle, General Fertig took a last look at the carnage on the highway.

The Japanese, if for no other reason than to save face, would rush reinforcements up here. Patrols would be sent into the jungle.

There would be an opportunity for other ambushes, perhaps not as overwhelmingly successful as this one, but successful enough to kill many Japanese, to force the Japanese to expend fuel and manpower on one patrol after another—and to lose face.

There was a caveat. To conduct other ambushes, he would need ammunition. He had come out of the ambush with only marginally greater stocks of ammunition than he had going in, and that was for the Japanese Arisaka rifles, not the Enfields and the BARs.

He turned and entered the jungle. He would now go back into hiding.

How the hell can I wage a war if they won't supply me with what I need? Supply me with what I need? The sonsofbitches won't even talk to me!

2

The House on Q Street, N.W.
Washington, D.C.
4 February 1943

Chief Ellis found Captain James M.B. Whittaker in the billiards room in the basement. There were two tables in the darkly paneled room: a standard English billiards table, and a somewhat smaller pocket billiards table. Whittaker was alone at the smaller table.

"Anchors aweigh, Chief," Whittaker said, looking up from the table when he saw Ellis. He had carefully arranged balls at the lip of each of the pockets on the table. What he was trying to do was sink as many of them as he could with one shot.

Ellis waited until he had made the shot (sinking four of the six balls) before replying.

"I hear you've been a bad boy again, Captain Whittaker," Ellis said.

"Was Baker waiting for you when you got back?" Whittaker asked, and then, before Ellis could reply, he asked, "Who's your friend?"

Ellis had with him a Navy whitehat, a small man made to look even smaller by his waist-length Navy blue peacoat. He wore round-framed GI glasses. He looked, Whittaker thought, like a Sea Scout.

"Radioman Second Joe Garvey, say hello to Captain Jim Whittaker," Ellis said.

The sailor snatched off his white hat and came to attention.

"How do you do, Sir?" he asked.

"Poorly, now that you ask," Whittaker said, smiling at him. "Didn't your mother warn you to avoid evil companions when you joined the Navy?"

Then he saw that his joke had fallen flat and that the young sailor was uncomfortable, not amused. Whittaker came quickly around the pool table and, smiling, offered his hand.

"Hello, Garvey," he said. "If you're with Chief Ellis, you must be somebody special. I'm happy to meet you."

Garvey shook his hand and smiled uneasily.

"You ever know somebody named Fertig?" Ellis asked.

Whittaker thought it over. "There is a faint tinkle of the bell of memory," he said.

"In the Philippines?"

"I put that together," Whittaker said, "but that's as far as it goes. Is there some reason I should know him?"

"He's still in the Philippines," Ellis said.

"Poor sonofabitch," Whittaker said.

"Garvey's been talking to him on the radio," Ellis said.

Whittaker's face lit up with curiosity.

"He's in the mountains of Mindanao," Ellis said. "He says there's an Army sergeant named Withers with him."

"I knew a guy named Withers over there," Whittaker said.

"You want to find out if it's the same one?" Ellis said.

"I don't think this is just idle curiosity on your part," Whittaker said.

Ellis shrugged.

"How could we do that?" Whittaker asked.

"You got time to take a ride over to the Navy commo facility in Virginia?" Ellis asked.

"You're starting to act like Captain Douglass," Whittaker said. "You answer questions with another question."

"Well, I don't 'manifest a belligerent and uncooperative attitude,'" Ellis said.

"Is that what that sonofabitch said?" Whittaker asked.

"There was more," Ellis said. "There was something about 'subjecting a trainee to a humiliating public display of affection.' Two pages, single spaced."

"Has the Colonel seen it?" Whittaker asked.

"Not yet," Ellis said. "I intercepted it. I can lose it, but Baker's going to expect some kind of a reply, so you better start thinking about that. And about the fact that The Colonel thinks you're in Virginia running around in the woods."

"Hmmm," Whittaker said, considering that.

"You want to take a run over to Virginia?" Ellis asked.

"Nothing would give me greater pleasure," Whittaker said. He turned to put the pool cue in its rack. "We'll have lunch on the way," he said. "I want to go to that three-for-a-quarter hamburger place."

"White Castle?" Ellis asked, incredulously.

"White Castle," Whittaker confirmed happily. "And eat a dollar's worth, with a large fries and a Dr. Pepper."

"Maybe Baker's right," Ellis said. "He says he thinks you may be crazy."

"In that case, you can buy your own hamburgers," Whittaker said, as he took his tunic from a bentwood coat rack.

An hour and a half later, a lieutenant commander signed them into his log, and then took them past a Marine MP guarding access to a gray painted steel door with "RADIO ROOM POSITIVELY NO UNAUTHORIZED VISITORS" painted on it.

The officer on watch, a young lieutenant j.g. with a blond crew cut, got up from his desk and walked to meet them.

"These people wish to use one of your transmitters," the lieutenant commander said. "They have their own operator."

"Sir?" the j.g. asked, not sure he had heard correctly.

"We'd like to use that Collins, Lieutenant," Chief Ellis

said, nodding his head toward one of a row of transmitters lining the wall.

The j.g. looked at the lieutenant commander for instructions. Strange people coming into the transmitter room was unusual; it was absolutely out of the lieutenant's experience that they should be given access to the equipment.

"Do it, Mr. Fenway," the lieutenant commander said.

"Aye, aye, Sir," the j.g. said, and motioned Garvey to follow him. He led him to a small cubicle holding a telegrapher's key, a typewriter, and a control panel. Garvey, still wearing his peacoat, pulled up a chair and reached for a set of earphones.

He tapped the key tentatively, and then adjusted set screws on its base, and tried it again. He rolled paper into the typewriter, and then tuned both the receiver and the transmitter.

Then he started to tap the key.

Ellis and Whittaker walked and stood behind him, and looked over his shoulder.

"All they've got is an old M94," Ellis said. "There's no sense even trying to encrypt. We're talking in the clear."

"I have no idea what you're talking about," Whittaker said.

"It's a coding device," Ellis explained. "But we have to presume the Japs got at least one of them."

"Oh," Whittaker said.

"When we raise them, you're going to have to think of some way to find out if this Withers guy is the one you were with, and do it so the Japs will be as confused as possible."

"Ask him if he still has the watch," Whittaker said. "Call him Sergeant Boomboom. Sign it, Polo."

Garvey's fingers flew over the typewriter keys. It was an automatic reaction to what he had heard in his earphones. Ellis and Whittaker looked at what he had typed:

MFS FOR KGS BY

"Send, 'For Sergeant Boomboom,'" Ellis ordered, "'Have you got the watch Signed Polo.'"

Garvey tapped the message out with his key.

"What's with the watch?" Ellis asked.

"I gave him my watch, just before I left," Whittaker said. There was a long wait before Garvey started typing again.

MFS FOR KGS AFFIRMATIVE WHERE POLO MFS BY

"Send 'Polo Washington,'" Whittaker ordered. "'Where Scarface.'"

MFS FOR KGS SCARFACE EVERYBODY HERE MFS BY

"Send 'Send Third Letter Scarface Last Name,'" Whittaker ordered.

MFS FOR KGS VVVVVVVVVVVVVVVV MSF BY

"Send 'Glad You All Made It,'" Whittaker said.

MFS FOR KGS FOR POLO FROM SCARFACE VAYA CON DIOS MFS BY

"Send," Whittaker began, and then his voice broke, and when Ellis turned to look at him, he saw tears running down his cheeks. "Send," Whittaker went on, "'Hold On. The 26th Will Ride Again. God Bless You All. Polo.'"

MFS FOR KGS MFS OUT

Captain James M.B. Whittaker, rather loudly, blew his nose. When he spoke, he had his voice under control.

"'Scarface' is Master Sergeant Victor Alvarez, late of the 26th Cavalry, Philippine Scouts. He was in the habit of calling Sergeant Withers 'Sergeant BoomBoom' because Withers blew things up."

"Clandestine station in the Philippines?" the lieutenant commander asked. Whittaker nodded. "Poor bastards!"

"Thank you for your assistance, Commander," Whittaker said, formally. "Let's get out of here, Ellis."

When they got in the Buick Roadmaster, Ellis reached into the glove compartment and came out with a pint bottle of Old Overholt. He handed it to Whittaker.

"Good for the sinuses," he said.

"I wish I had gone with you to Warm Springs, Ellis," Whittaker said, tensely. "It would have given me a chance to ask Uncle Franklin why the hell we have abandoned those guys."

"I suppose that's why The Colonel wanted you to run around in the woods in Virginia," Ellis said. "Every time you tell off your Uncle Franklin, he has to pick up the pieces."

"And what, exactly, he plans to do about it," Whittaker said.

"You might as well hear this now," Ellis said. "They asked for money. There is Army brass, both here and in Australia, who are against it, because they think the Japs are using those people . . . what The Colonel calls 'turned agents.'"

"How much did they ask for?" Whittaker asked.

Ellis thought it was a strange question, but told him.

"A million, in gold, gold coins, for openers."

"They say what for?"

"We're talking in the clear, Captain," Ellis said. "You can't expect them to offer details."

"When can I get to see The Colonel?" Whittaker asked.

"He said that I should go to Virginia and pick you up and see if we could raise MFS," Ellis said. "I think he wanted to see if you thought they were being controlled by the Japs. To answer your question, Captain, that's where we're going now."

3

Office of Strategic Services
The National Institute of Health Building
Washington, D.C.
4 February 1943

Colonel William J. Donovan was in civilian clothing: a well-cut, double-breasted Glen plaid suit, a crisp white shirt, and a red-and-blue finely patterned necktie. He looked, Whittaker thought, like a successful lawyer about to sue Chrysler or DuPont for a lot of money.

When Whittaker entered the office, Donovan walked around his desk with his hand extended, and then the handshake gave way to a quick embrace.

"Good to see you, Jimmy," he said. "How did you find the place in Virginia?"

"I'd been there before," Jimmy said. "And Staley drew a map. No problem."

"Why do I suspect you purposely misunderstood me?" Donovan asked.

"You mean 'what did I think of the place?'"

Donovan nodded.

"Baker and I crossed swords again," Whittaker said. "He seems to feel I 'manifested a belligerent and uncooperative attitude.' I also 'subjected a trainee to public humiliation.'"

"Oh, Jimmy," Donovan said, both angry and resigned. "What the hell was that all about?"

"Well, the belligerent and uncooperative attitude is something that seems to happen when I get in the same room with Baker," Whittaker said. "It seems to be contagious. Canidy has the same thing happen to him."

"We're talking about you, not Dick Canidy," Donovan said. "What happened with the trainee? What was he doing so wrong you felt you had to humiliate him?"

"Her," Whittaker corrected him. "I kissed *her."*

"Cynthia?" Donovan asked. Whittaker nodded. "I don't know why I'm smiling," Donovan added. "I'm sure she didn't think it was funny. You'll notice that I am assuming she didn't want to be kissed."

"That girl doesn't know what she wants," Whittaker said. "For example, she has some absurd notion that she wants to go operational. When I saw her, she was all dressed up in fatigues and carrying a Springfield at port arms. I found her irresistible. I wonder what a psychiatrist would make of that?"

"You made your peace with Baker?" Donovan asked.

"I left," Whittaker said. "He's probably still mad."

"You left?" Donovan asked, confused. "You mean, when Ellis came for you?"

"I left about thirty minutes after I got there," Whittaker said. "I've been at the house."

"I left orders that you were to be taken out there," Donovan said, coldly.

"Staley told me," Whittaker said. "He was pretty insistent."

Donovan looked at him coldly, waiting for a further explanation.

"I could offer some excuse, like I would probably have broken Baker's arms if I stayed, but the real reason I left was that Baker was acting as if he was controlling me."

"That's what he's paid to do," Donovan said sharply.

"I don't know what you've got planned for me, why I'm here and not in Australia, but if it means that Baker is my control, you're going to have to get yourself another boy."

"You can be a real pain in the ass, sometimes, Jim," Donovan said. "And this is one of them. Just who the hell do you think you're talking to?"

Whittaker's reply came a long moment later.

"I know I'm talking to the head of the OSS," he said. "Not Uncle Bill, who used to bounce me on his knee. I'm not asking for any special treatment. I don't know what my alternatives are, but whatever they are, I'll take them, rather than go anywhere with him as my control."

Donovan glared at him.

"You have a reason for feeling that way, I presume?"

"There are two kinds of controls," Whittaker said. "Both profess great sadness when somebody gets bagged. One kind means it. Baker is the other kind. Baker is too willing to accept risks with somebody else's life. He sees 'the big picture' much too clearly."

They locked eyes for a moment, and then Donovan asked, "Did Ellis mention anything about dinner tonight?"

The question surprised Whittaker.

"No," he said. "He didn't." Then he thought a moment. "Don't tell me I'm to have dinner with Baker?"

"Not with Baker," Donovan said. And then, when he was sure in his own mind that Ellis hadn't said anything about the dinner and that Whittaker in fact did not know, he added, "With the President."

"Oh?" Whittaker said.

"There will be no repetition, nothing remotely resembling

a repetition, of what happened the last time you had dinner with him," Donovan said.

"I was a little crazy the last time," Whittaker said. "And I don't want to find myself locked up in a loony bin again."

"You take my point," Donovan said, evenly.

Whittaker nodded. "Is dinner his idea, or yours?" he asked.

"His idea," Donovan said. "But when I told him you were in Washington, I was pretty sure he'd want to see you."

"You're being devious again," Whittaker said.

"Trust me, Jimmy," Donovan said, smiling.

"*You,* I trust," Whittaker said.

"Ellis has some dossiers, and some other material, I want you to look at," Donovan said. "By the time you're finished, I should be finished here; and we can go over to the house."

The President of the United States traveled from 1600 Pennsylvania to Embassy Row in a four-car convoy: there was a District of Columbia police car with flashing red lights; then a black Chevrolet full of Secret Service agents; a 1939 Packard limousine (not *the* Presidential limousine); and finally another Chevrolet packed with Secret Service agents.

The gate in the wall was already open when the convoy arrived. The police car and the tailing Secret Service car pulled to the curb and stopped. The lead Secret Service car and the Packard drove through the gate, which closed immediately after them.

When the two cars stopped, two burly Secret Service agents half-trotted to the limousine. One of them reached in and swung the President's feet outward. Then he hauled him from the car and erect. Then he and the other agent, with an ease born of practice, made a cradle of their locked arms and carried him to and up the kitchen stairs. By the time they got there, a third Secret Service agent had taken a collapsible wheelchair from the trunk of the Chevrolet, trotted with it to the kitchen, and had it unfolded and waiting when the President was carried to it.

"One of you," the President of the United States said, "smells of something that didn't come out of an after-shave bottle. 'My Sin?'"

The burly Secret Service agent now pushing the wheelchair chuckled.

"No comment, Mr. President," he said.

The other agent trotted ahead and pushed open doors until he reached the double sliding doors to the library, both of which he slid open.

"Is this the place with the booze?" the President asked as he was rolled in.

Donovan and Whittaker, who had been sitting on identical couches at right angles to a carved sandstone fireplace, stood up.

"Good evening, Mr. President," Donovan said.

"That'll be all, Casey," the President said. "If I need it, The Colonel can push me around."

The Secret Service agent left the room, closing the double doors carefully behind him.

"Well, Jimmy," the President said. "You look a hell of a lot better than the last time I saw you."

"Good whiskey and fast women, Uncle Frank," Whittaker said.

He went to Roosevelt and offered his hand. Roosevelt ignored it. He gripped his arms with both hands, and with strength that always surprised Whittaker forced his body down so that his face was level with Roosevelt's. Roosevelt studied him intently for a moment, and then, nodding his head in approval, let him go.

"Chesty would be very proud of you," the President said. "I am."

He let that sink in a moment, and then changed the tone. "I had a letter from Jimmy," he said. "You know about Jimmy?"[2]

"Somebody talked him into joining the Marines," Whittaker said. "I thought he was smarter than that."

Roosevelt laughed heartily.

"I think he was taken with the uniform," he said. "Anyway, he asked about you."

"Give him my regards," Whittaker said.

Donovan handed the President a martini glass.

---

[2]James Roosevelt, the President's eldest son, was commissioned in the USMC. He was second in command of the Marine Raiders in the Pacific.

"I think you'll like that, Franklin," he said. "Basically, it's frozen gin."

Roosevelt sipped the martini and nodded his approval.

Roosevelt asked about England, first generally, and then specifically about David Bruce, the OSS Chief of Station in London, and finally about Canidy.

"Your friend Canidy's all right?"

"Just fine," Whittaker said.

"I'm sorry that Bill and I can't tell you why, Jimmy," Roosevelt said, "but that Congo mission the two of you flew was of great importance."

"I thought it probably was of enormous importance," Whittaker said.

"Why did you think that?" Roosevelt asked. His famous smile was just perceptibly strained.

"The airplane Canidy and I flew was a brand-new C-46, fitted out like the Taj Mahal, and intended to fly Navy brass around the Pacific."

"Nothing is too good for our boys in the OSS," Roosevelt joked, exchanging a quick glance with Donovan.

The mission, ordered by Roosevelt himself, had been to bring ten tons of bagged ore from Kolwezi in the Katanga Province of the Belgian Congo. Only four people, the President: Donovan; Capt. Peter Douglass, Donovan's deputy; and Brig. General Leslie R. Groves, director of something called "The Manhattan Project" knew that the ore was uraninite. The Manhattan Project was intended, in the great secret of the Second World War, to refine the uraninite into uranium 235, and from uranium 235 to construct a bomb, an "atomic bomb" which would have the explosive equivalent of 20,000 tons of TNT.

Roosevelt's, and Donovan's, great fear was that the Germans, among whose scientists were some of the greatest physicists in the world, and who were known to be conducting their own nuclear research, would learn of the American effort and increase their own research effort. Whoever could produce the first nuclear weapons would win the war.

"Canidy," Donovan said very quickly, to shut off any possibility that Whittaker—now that he'd made his little joke—might ask why it was of great importance and that the

President just might tell him, "shot down two German fighters, Messerschmidts, near Dortmund three days ago."

"Good for him!" the President said, pleased to change the subject.

"Bad for him," Donovan said. "He's not supposed to be flying missions as a fighter pilot."

"He must have had his reasons," Whittaker said, loyally.

"You and Dick always have your reasons," Donovan said, drily.

"Come on, Bill," the President said. "You're just jealous. I'm sure that you would rather be in the field with a regiment than doing what you're doing."

"I do what I'm told," Donovan said. "And I naively expect people who work for me to do what they're told."

"Did I hear a subtle reprimand?" Whittaker asked. "Or is that just my guilty conscience?"

"Well, Jimmy, what have you been doing that you shouldn't?" Roosevelt asked.

Donovan walked to Roosevelt and topped off the President's martini from a heavy crystal mixer.

"Not doing what he should have been doing, Franklin," Donovan said.

"What was that?" Whittaker asked.

"Learning how to get into a rubber boat from a submarine," Donovan said.

"Why would I want to do that?" Whittaker asked.

"Scheduled Pan American service to the Philippines has been temporarily suspended," Donovan said. "A submarine's the only way we know to get you into the Philippines."

"Is that where I'm going?" Whittaker asked.

"That hasn't been decided yet," the President said coldly. "Whether you or anybody else is going into the Philippines."

"Now that you mention it, Uncle Frank, . . ." Whittaker said.

"I don't think I'm going to like it, Jim," Roosevelt said. "But finish that."

"Why have we abandoned the people in the Philippines?" Whittaker asked.

"What makes you think we have?" Roosevelt replied, just a little indignantly. He was not used to having his decisions questioned by anyone. "There was simply no way to reinforce MacArthur before the Japanese overwhelmed him, and there is simply no way, at this time, that we can consider an invasion. It's just too far away, and we just don't have the logistical capability."

"I'm talking about the guerrillas," Whittaker said. "The people who haven't quit. The ones in the mountains."

It was a moment before Roosevelt replied.

"I was about to say, Jim, that you are emotionally involved, and that unfortunately I can't always do what my emotions tell me I should. But then it occurred to me that you have a greater right to be emotionally involved than most people. So I will not change the subject. The answer to your question is that the best advice I can get is that there are no guerrillas. I tend to place faith in that advice, because it comes to me from Douglas MacArthur and George Marshall, and it is the first thing I can think of that they have agreed upon since 1935."

"There are at least ten guerrillas, Uncle Frank," Whittaker said.

"How can you possibly know that?"

"I talked to them on the radio this afternoon," Whittaker said.

"You did?"

"I did," Whittaker said.

Roosevelt looked at Donovan.

"You arranged that, Bill? He's talking about this self-appointed general . . . what's the name?"

"Fertig," Donovan said.

"Fertig," Roosevelt repeated. "Jim," he said, kindly, "it is the opinion of everybody but Bill Donovan that the Japanese, for whatever reason, are using prisoners, attempting something. Most likely, that they hope to get us to send them a million dollars in gold by submarine. Whereupon, they will take the million dollars and sink the submarine."

"Uncle Frank, I talked on the radio this afternoon with two of *my* men."

"What do you mean, 'your' men?"

"When MacArthur ordered me from Luzon to Corregidor, I gave my wristwatch to my sergeant, a guy named George

Withers. And I told him when Luzon fell, he should make his way, him and the Philippine Scouts I had, to Mindanao. I talked to him and to one of the Philippine Scouts this afternoon. They're on Mindanao and waiting for help."

"And they said what their Japanese captors told them to say."

"There is no way the Japanese could know what they used to call me and I used to call them," Whittaker said. "They're on Mindanao, and they're free, and God damn it, we have a duty to help them."

"You mean, send them the million dollars?"

"And a radio, and quinine, and ammunition," Whittaker said.

"They have a radio," Roosevelt said. "You talked to them."

"They need an encryption device," Whittaker said. "So the Japs won't be able to listen in."

"Bill?" the President asked.

"We need to send somebody in there who can separate fact from fantasy, and then come out armed with facts on which further decisions can be made," Donovan said. "The basic fact of guerrilla warfare is that one guerrilla can tie down at least seven troops . . ."

"So you keep telling me," Roosevelt said. "And you think Jimmy is the man to go to the Philippines, have a look around, and then come out?"

"Yes," Donovan said.

"And since the Japanese are listening to the guerrilla radio, and since there is no way we can code what we are sending, how do you propose to let the people in the Philippines know where and when he's coming? With the Japanese listening in, I mean?"

"We're working on that, Franklin," Donovan said.

"The translation of which is, 'we hope to think of something'?"

Donovan didn't reply.

"And you're willing to put your neck in the noose again, Jimmy?" Roosevelt asked.

"Being very coldblooded about it," Whittaker said, "I seem to be the round peg for that round hole."

"You already escaped once from the Philippines," Roosevelt said. "How often do you think you can do that?"

"I hear that Jimmy nearly got himself blown away on Makin Island," Whittaker replied.

"'Blown away?'" Roosevelt said. "Interesting euphemism." It was obvious that he was making his decision.

"All right," he said, finally. "Do it. I'll avoid telling George Marshall as long as I can. And I don't think we should tell Douglas MacArthur until you come out."

"Thank you, Mr. President," Donovan said.

Roosevelt was not through. "And come out you will, Jimmy. You understand that? You will go in there, and have a look around, and come out. You may consider that a direct order."

"I suppose that means I'll have to go freeze my ass learning how to get into a rubber boat from a submarine?" Whittaker asked.

Roosevelt and Donovan chuckled.

"Now we get down to price," Whittaker said. "I have a price."

"Everybody else seems to," Roosevelt said, drily. "What's yours?"

"Cynthia Chenowith is my control," Whittaker said. "Reporting directly to Colonel Donovan."

"I think I see a hook in there," Roosevelt said. "What's all that about?"

"Cynthia was the control for the Kolwezi operation," Whittaker said.

"Cynthia is going through the agents' course," Donovan said. "That runs against Jimmy's notions of the proper role of women."

Roosevelt chuckled. "Mine, too," he said. "Eleanor, maybe. But Cynthia?"

Whittaker laughed.

"That would be your decision, of course, Bill," the President said.

"OK," Donovan said. "You win, Jimmy. I think she'll be furious, Jimmy, but that's your worry."

"She'll be alive," Whittaker said simply. "I would much rather have her pissed and alive than happy, heroic and dead."

"Are you getting hungry, Franklin?" Donovan asked. "Or would you rather have some more frozen gin?"

"Why does it have to be either/or?" Roosevelt asked, holding his glass up to be refilled.

Donovan pushed the servant call button twice, and then went to refill Roosevelt's glass.

4

OSS London Station Berkeley Square
London, England
5 February 1943

Helene B. Dancy, Captain, WAC (Women's Army Corps), U.S. Army, administrative assistant to London Chief of Station David Bruce, was of two minds about Richard Canidy. When she didn't see him for a while, she began to mirror her boss's opinion of him: that Canidy wasn't a team player, that he was often doing things (going off with Capt. Douglass's son as a fighter pilot was the most recent example) that brought into question the wisdom of his having as much authority and autonomy as he did.

But when she was with him, most of her disapproval seemed to vanish. It was absurd to think that anything could happen between them (Helene B. Dancy, had been commissioned in the WAC from her job as Executive Secretary to the Senior Vice President for Real Estate, the Prudential Insurance Company, thirty-six hours before she turned thirty-eight and became ineligible because of her age), but she privately admitted that Richard Canidy was the most desirable male she had ever seen. And when she'd been with The Rock, she'd seen a large number of desirable men.

She thought you could tell a lot about a man by his eyes, and when she looked into Canidy's eyes, she saw gentleness and strength and compassion. And when she did that, she felt about nineteen years old.

"Good morning, Dancy," Canidy greeted her. "What's the latest fire from the dragon's mouth all about?"

"Good morning, Major Canidy," Capt. Dancy said.

"Well, have I done something new, or he is still mad from the last time?"

"You really did put him on a spot with the Air Corps, Major," Capt. Dancy said.

"I know," Canidy said, smiling at her (she thought he had very nice teeth, which gave him a very nice smile), "white is black, up is down, and I am supposed to apologize for taking a shot at the bad guys."

There is, Capt. Helene Dancy thought, *a certain undeniable logic to what he says. You'd think they'd want to give him a medal for shooting down enemy planes, not be furious with him.*

"Major Canidy," she said chastisingly.

"I let all the pretty girls call me 'Dick,'" he said.

"You are impossible," she said. "This is supposed to be a military organization."

Canidy's face registered great surprise.

"You're kidding!" he said.

"Mr. Bruce is down in crypto," she said. "You are to wait."

"And you're not going to tell me what I've done wrong, are you, Dancy?"

"No," she said, unable to resist smiling back at him. "But it may have something to do with this."

She opened her drawer and took from it a TOP SECRET cover sheet.[3]

As he took it from her, she said, softly, "If it doesn't come up, it would probably be better if you didn't mention I'd shown you that."

Canidy raised the cover sheet and read the partially decrypted message. Even if the Germans intercepted the message and succeeded in decrypting the text, they would not know the meaning of the code words.

EXLAX FOUR PROCEEDING ALL WELL YACHTSMAN

"Speaking to you both as your military superior, Captain,"

---

[3]A page-sized sheet of cardboard imprinted in red with the words TOP SECRET at top and bottom, and with a border of red lines. It was used to cover TOP SECRET documents, which were stapled or paper-clipped under it.

Canidy said, "and as someone you *know* has the Need-to-Know, have there been any developments in the Balkans I should know about?"

Shaking her head and smiling, Capt. Dancy said, "You have it in your hand."

"Well, now you're off the hook with the dragon," Canidy said. "I *asked* you for this. You had no choice but to give it to me."

She smiled at him. She thought that was nice of him.

"Have you got a copy of the OPPLAN (Operations Plan) here, or am I going to have to root around in the basement?"

Capt. Dancy walked to a sturdy safe from which, quite unnecessarily, for the door was ajar, hung a sign reading "OPEN" and took from it a manila folder with TOP SECRET stamped on it.

Canidy unfolded a map. On it was drawn in grease pencil Eric Fulmar's route into Germany, and his escape route. Along it were marked, in Roman numerals, the stages of the route. There was a I at Marburg an der Lahn, in Germany. There was a II beside Vienna on the map, and a III beside Budapest. The fourth leg of the route ended at Pécs, in southwest Hungary.

Pécs was the site of the Batthyany family coal mines. Most of the coal in Hungary is low grade "brown" coal. The mines at Pécs produced a high-grade anthracite which for hundreds of years had contributed to the Batthyany wealth. Now it was of value because one of the heavy, multiwheeled Tatra trucks which had carried bagged anthracite to Budapest (including, through the influence of Helmut von Heurten-Mitnitz, some to Batthyany Palace) had returned to Pécs with Eric Fulmar and Professor Dyer and his daughter concealed in a box under a stack of coal bags.

Professor Dyer was a physicist. There was a tenuous connection between physics the science and physics as in laxative. Hence, "Ex-Lax." In the planning stages of the operation, when they were picking code names, David Bruce had reluctantly admitted that the Germans would probably be baffled by references to a laxative, although he privately thought Canidy's suggestion was one more indication that Canidy was not as serious as he should be.

"Yachtsman" was an OSS agent in Hungary. He was a first-generation American from Hamtramck, Michigan, who had learned Hungarian from his mother. Equipped with the appropriate forged identity documents, he was employed with relatives as a deckhand on a Danube River barge. It permitted him to move around the country and when necessary to disappear from the barge for a couple of hours, or days.

Completely decoded, Yachtsman's message meant that Fulmar and the Dyers had made it from Budapest safely to Pécs, and were proceeding to V. This leg of the route was by barge. "Ex-Lax" would travel down the barge canal built under the auspices of Emperor Franz Josef of Austro-Hungary to transport coal from Pécs to the Danube.

The barge canal crossed the border between Hungary and Croatia (Yugoslavia) in a sparsely populated region near Beli Manastir, and joined the Danube at Batina. Shortly before reaching Bačka Palanka, where the Danube turned east toward Belgrade in another desolate unpopulated area, there would be a signal (in response to lights arranged in a special way on the barge) from the western shore of the Danube.

The barge would then move close enough to the bank for Fulmar and the Dyers to jump off and pass into the hands of "Postman," the senior (of four) OSS agents with the guerrilla forces of Colonel Draža Mihajlović, late of the Royal Yugoslav Army.

Canidy had a little trouble with the bland assurances by radio of Postman (an American of Yugoslavian parentage who had literally been a mail carrier in the States) that this leg of the trip could be safely and conveniently accomplished by truck. According to Postman, the trucks (and the diesel fuel to run them) had been captured by Mihajlović from the Germans, and the Colonel's warning system was so effective that he ran them up and down forest and mountain roads of Croatia and Bosnia and Hercegovina on regular supply and transport missions as if the Germans weren't there and actively looking for him.

VI was the town of Metković on the Neretva River, fifteen miles from Neretljanski Kanal, a sheltered, natural body of water which opened onto the Adriatic Sea. At Metković, "Ex-Lax" would be turned over to an agent of the British

SOE[4] who would arrange for their transport by fishing boat to the island of Vis, VII. The SOE agent's code name, "Saint Peter" was another Canidy suggestion to which David Bruce had somewhat uneasily agreed.

Vis was entirely in British hands, though the Germans, who made periodic sweeps of the island, did not suspect it. There was a hidden wharf, onto which supplies could be offloaded from submarines for trans-shipment to the mainland. And, between two hills, there was a 4,900-foot runway. A stream flowing across the field seemed to entirely discount the notion that the long valley could be used as a landing strip. But the stream had been altered. There was a twenty-yard-wide stretch where the water was only a foot deep. To observers both on the ground and in the air, it looked for all intents and purposes to be just an area of turbulent water.

Exlax will be transported from VII to Cairo, Malta, or such other final destination as the circumstances at the time dictate by U.S. aircraft. In the event this is impossible, Exlax will be evacuated from VII by Royal Navy submarine on a space-available basis.

"You look deep in thought, Richard," David Bruce said, as he came into the office, trailed by Lt. Col. Edmund T. Stevens, his deputy. Bruce and Stevens were tall and erect and well-tailored. There was a West Point ring on Stevens's hand. He had resigned from the Army before the war and had been in England when the war broke out, running his wife's food and wine import-export business.

"Either of you ever collect stamps when you were kids?" Canidy asked. "Ever have any from Bosnia-Hercegovina?"

"I don't really recall," Bruce said, impatiently.

"They had some that were triangular," Canidy said, "that intrigued me."

"I remember those," Col. Stevens said.

"Come on in, Richard," Bruce said. "I fear we are about to have another of our arguments."

"What have I done now?" Canidy asked, folding the map and handing it to Capt. Dancy.

---

[4]Special Operations Executive, roughly the British equivalent of the OSS.

"I presume you have the Yachtsman message?" Bruce asked, after he'd taken a look at the folder.

"Captain Dancy gave it to me with great reluctance," Canidy said, "only after I threatened to write her name and phone number in phone booths in pubs all over town."

"Major Canidy," Capt. Dancy said, "you're impossible." But she was smiling.

Bruce closed his office door after they were inside.

"It isn't what you've done . . . unless, of course, there's something I don't know about yet . . . it's what you are planning to do."

"What would that be?"

"Go to Vis to pick up 'Ex-Lax' yourself," Bruce said.

"Have you made up your mind about that, or are you open to my reasoning?"

"I'm always willing to listen," Bruce said, with a smile, "even when you make it difficult. But this, you should be forewarned, is coloring my thinking."

He took a sheet of yellow foolscap from his desk drawer and handed it to Canidy.

ROUTINE FROM OSS WASH DC FOR OSS LONDON PERSONAL BRUCE PLEASE RELAY CANIDY QUOTE CONGRATULATIONS ON DOUBLE KILL UNQUOTE STOP PRESUME HE HAD REASONS FOR BEING WHERE HE WAS STOP REGARDS STOP DONOVAN

"Looks like he's giving me the benefit of the doubt," Canidy said. "In my experience, the Colonel is not at all subtle. That message could just as easily have read, 'Ground the sonofabitch.' "

Stevens chuckled, earning himself a dirty look from Bruce.

"Grounding you might make sense, Richard," Stevens said. "From this side of the desk, perceptions are a little different."

"The arguments I made are still valid. And to refresh your memory they were (a) that the Air Corps is already bitching about our photorecon missions; and (b) that laying on a mission we would have had to fight over would have called unwanted attention to the Fulmar Werke."

"So are my counter-arguments that you're pretty far up in the scheme of things for us to lose you if you get shot down,"

Bruce said. "But that's over. What you have to do now is convince me there are reasons why we should not just tell the Eighth Air Force what we need, and have them do it. Or even why it is necessary to bring 'Ex-Lax' out by air at all. Why shouldn't they come out on a British submarine?"

"Arrogance," Canidy said.

"I beg your pardon? My arrogance, or yours?" Bruce asked.

"Mine," Canidy chuckled. "I want to take a good look at the field on Vis myself," Canidy said. "I arrogantly don't trust anybody else's enthusiastic opinion of how good it is. I don't want to lose 'Ex-Lax,' or whoever we bring out later, at stop VII because of pilot error. I want to make that landing and takeoff by myself, so I can tell somebody else how to do it."

The look on Bruce's face, Canidy thought, was not one of acceptance, but he thought Stevens understood.

"I can also argue," Canidy continued, "that we don't want to involve the English in this operation any more than we have to. If we start demanding space on their submarines, they are going to want justification."

He stopped again and looked at Bruce. After a moment, Bruce made a "give me more" gesture with his hand.

"We have the B-25," Canidy said, "already rigged for this sort of passenger-haul mission, with auxiliary fuel tanks, and even seats. If we ask the Air Corps, they're going to have to modify one of their aircraft, and they will naturally ask questions."

"Unless we let them use our B-25," Bruce said.

"I was afraid you'd think of that," Canidy said. "And I'm prepared. I think we would have trouble getting it back from them. If they get their hands on it, David, they're liable to remember it's on loan. Think 'lawn mower,' as in borrowed from next-door neighbor."

Bruce shook his head.

"And for a crew?"

"I thought about asking for an Eighth Air Force volunteer," Canidy said. "If he turns out OK, we can draft him, permanently. If he doesn't, we send him back."

"Just a co-pilot?" Stevens asked.

"No," Canidy said. "Before we sent him to Switzerland, I was planning to take Stanley Fine. And then, before we sent him to Australia, I was going to take Jimmy Whittaker. Now, I think Dolan."

Bruce's eyebrows rose again.

"Why Dolan?" he asked.

"He's an old pilot . . ." Canidy began.

"That's what I mean," Bruce interrupted reasonably.

Chief Aviation Motor Machinist's Mate (formerly, until physically disqualified, Chief Aviation Pilot) John B. Dolan, USN, had, after twenty-six years of service, retired from the Navy to go to Burma and China with the Flying Tigers as a maintenance officer. Afterward, he had managed to acquire a reserve commission in the Navy as a Lieutenant Commander and had been sent by the Navy to England as the aviation maintenance officer for Operation Aphrodite.[5]

Eisenhower, his patience with Air Corps-Navy squabbling exhausted, had turned Project Aphrodite over to the OSS. Dolan had been delighted. Canidy had been put in charge of the project, and he had known Canidy at the Pensacola, Florida, Naval Air Station when they had both been in the American Volunteer Group. Dolan had correctly guessed that Canidy would not watch his every move the way the Air and Navy brass had been doing.

"We intrepid birdmen have a saying," Canidy said. " 'There are old pilots, and there are bold pilots, but there are no old, bold pilots.' "

"Very interesting," David Bruce said.

Colonel Stevens gave in to the temptation, "And where, Richard, would you say that profound observation leaves you?" he asked, innocently.

"Why, I thought you knew, Colonel," Canidy said, smiling broadly, "that I intend to be a very old pilot."

"Not the way you're going, you're not," Stevens said. "But, OK, Richard, you have . . . just barely . . . made your point."

---

[5]The code name for an attempt to convert worn-out B-17 aircraft into radio-controlled flying bombs, to be used against the German submarine pens at Saint-Lazare, which had proven immune to attack by conventional aerial bombardment.

"I presume Commander Dolan is physically up to it?" Bruce asked. "Specifically, that he's had a recent flight physical?"

"It's in his records," Canidy said. "Look for yourself."

"I just might," Bruce said.

There was a Report of Physical Examination (Flight) in Lt. Commander Dolan's records. Canidy did not think that David Bruce would notice the astonishing similarity between the handwriting of Commander A.J. Franklin, Medical Corps, USNR, who had signed the examination, and that of Lt. Commander John B. Dolan, USNR.

Canidy intended to see that the old sailor didn't overexert himself on the flight. But he really wanted the old "Flying Chief" with his 8,000-plus hours in the air with him, heart condition or not. Experience was far more valuable than youth and health on a flight like this.

"It just makes sense for me to go," Canidy argued. "It accomplishes what has to be done with the least fuss."

Bruce studied him thoughtfully for a moment, and then asked, "Ed?"

"You will take good care of Commander Dolan, won't you, Dick?" Stevens asked, and when Canidy looked at him, Canidy knew that he knew who had signed Dolan's flight physical.

"It'll be the other way around, Colonel," Canidy said.

"I think we should defer to Dick's judgment," Stevens said.

"So be it," Bruce said, resignedly.

Canidy thanked Stevens with a slight nod of his head. Stevens responded with a slight shrug of his shoulders. The message was clear. He had meant what he had said about deferring to Canidy's judgment.

Canidy stopped by Capt. Dancy's desk on his way out.

"Would you ask the Air Corps to furnish us with short- and long-term weather forecasts for from here to Casablanca, and from Casa to Malta, and from Malta to the Adriatic, starting right now?" he asked.

"I was afraid you'd talk him into it," she said. "You want them here, or do you want me to send them out to Whitbey House with the courier?"

"Send them to Dolan," Canidy said.

"Will he know what they're for?"

"He will after I tell him," Canidy said. "I'm going out there now."

"I thought you would be staying in London," she said.

"No reason for me to do that," Canidy said.

"Yes, there is," Capt. Dancy said. "She's back. She called earlier."

"You didn't tell me," Canidy said. It was more of a question than a reprimand.

"She said that she would be at Broadcast House until half past five, and after that at her apartment, if I happened to see you," Capt. Dancy said.

Sometimes, Capt. Dancy realized, she was just a little jealous of Ann Chambers, for being young and pretty, and for being able to light up Dick Canidy's eyes at the mere mention of her. And sometimes, like now, she felt like Canidy's sister or for that matter like his mother, happy that he had a nice, decent girl.

"You will call in when you decide where you're going to spend the night?" Capt. Dancy asked.

"Yeah, sure," Canidy said. Then he suddenly leaned across Capt. Dancy's desk and kissed her on the forehead.

"Major Canidy," Capt. Dancy said. "You're impossible."

5

Woburn Mansions, Woburn Square
London, England
5 February 1943

Before the war, the private park in the center of Woburn Square had been an area of manicured lawns and flower beds and curving walks beneath ancient trees, all surrounded by a neat fence. Now, only the fence and the trees were left. A bomb shelter had been excavated, and several corrugated sheds had been erected by the Fire Protection Service to store firefighting equipment.

It had been needed. There were ugly gaps in the rows of limestone-faced houses where German bombs had landed.

There had been twenty-four entrances on all four sides of Woburn Square in 1940. Now there were fourteen.

16, Woburn Mansions had not been hit, although the limestone facade had been darkened by the furious fires that had raged down the street on both sides; and there was plywood nailed over what once had been beveled glass windows in the entrance door.

But inside, it was much as it had always been, a quietly elegant building holding five large, floor-sized apartments. The basement apartment and the one on the top floor were smaller than the three main apartments, but they all had large, high-ceilinged rooms and central heating, which was an uncommon luxury.

The first floor flat, which would have been the second floor flat in America, was occupied by Miss Ann Chambers. Technically, it was assigned to the Chambers News Service and intended to house all Chambers News Service female employees in London. The SHAEF Billeting Officer had been informed that the Chambers News Service ultimately planned to have six to eight female employees with correspondent status stationed in London. That would effectively fill the three bedrooms with the regulation two officer-equivalent persons per room.

The SHAEF Billeting Officer had not been told the truth, the whole truth, and nothing but the truth, which was that the Chambers News Service had no plans at all to station any additional female correspondents in London. Brandon Chambers, Chairman of the Board of the Chambers Publishing Company, did not believe that women should go to war as correspondents or anything else. The rule was bent only in the case of his daughter, and that was not really nepotism. Rather, Brandon Chambers had believed his daughter when she told him that either he send her to London as a war correspondent, or she would go to work for Gardiner Cowles (the publisher of, among other things, LOOK magazine), with whom he had carried on a running feud for twenty years, and who was just the kind of a sonofabitch to give Ann a job just because he knew it would annoy her father.

Ann Chambers had had the London Bureau Chief tell the Billeting Officer the story of the five to seven soon-to-arrive female accredited correspondents not because she was the spoiled daughter of a very rich man who considered herself entitled to private quarters (in fact the other two bedrooms were more often than not occupied by roomless journalists of both sexes), but because Ann intended to share her own bed, whenever possible, with Richard Canidy, and she didn't want anybody around when that might happen.

If she had a permanent roommate, or roommates, it would not have been possible, for example, to do what she and Richard Canidy were doing now, which was recovering from an enthusiastic, wholly satisfying roll in the hay (actually a roll on a dozen large pillows covered with Chinese silk) at quarter to six in the evening before the fireplace in the sitting room.

"I don't suppose," Ann said, her face against his chest, "that I will have to ask if you have been a good boy while I was gone, will I?"

"If you don't ask, I won't have to lie about it," Canidy said.

"You bastard!" she said, and jerked a hair from his chest.

"Two can play at that game," he warned.

"And you would, too," she said, shifting her midsection to avoid his searching hand. She failed.

"You've heard the expression, 'by the short hairs'?" he asked.

"Let go," she said. "I'll be good."

"Who wants good?" he asked.

"Wicked?" she asked.

"You got it," he said, and let her go.

She got to her feet and walked out of the room, with an exaggerated shake of her tail. In a moment she was back. She tossed him a dressing gown, and shrugged into a sheepskin high altitude flyer's jacket. It was far too large for her, but it was warm.

"You look like you should be painted on the fuselage of a B-17," Canidy said. "'Dick's Delight' or something like that."

"Is that a compliment or a complaint?" she asked.

"Compliment," he said.

"You like me to wear it because when I bend over you can see my fanny," she said.

"And everything else," he said. "That's why you wear it, to excite me."

"So what else is new?" Ann said.

"You're about to get a roommate," he said.

"You'll be spending some time in London?"

"No," he said. "As a matter of fact, I've got a little trip to make. I'll be gone a week or ten days."

"Where are you going?" she asked, quickly, softly.

"You're not curious about your roommate?" he asked, ignoring the question.

"Where are you going, Dick?" she insisted.

"Come on, Annie," he said. "You know the rules."

"To hell with the rules, and don't call me 'Annie,'" she said.

"Yes, Ma'am."

"After Fulmar?" Ann asked.

"Who?"

She dropped to her knees on the pillows beside him.

"He's all right, isn't he?" she challenged. "I know you . . ."

"And I know you, as Moses said to the slave girl."

"And if he wasn't, you'd be miserable. And if you didn't know, you'd be all tense. You're relaxed and making jokes, and that means that you've heard something good."

"That's not why I'm relaxed, as Samson said to Delilah," Canidy said. "But, yeah, Honey, he's all right. I was a little worried, but the rough part of what he was doing is over."

"Oh, Baby, I'm happy for you," she said.

"And you're not curious about your roommate?"

"I don't know what you're talking about," she said. "I don't have roommates. If I had a roommate, I couldn't greet you at the door wearing nothing but a sheepskin jacket and a smile. So I don't want a roommate. Get the idea?"

"What about good ol' Chastity?"

"Charity," she corrected him automatically. Then "Charity? She's coming here?"

"In the next couple of days," Canidy said. "What I was thinking was that maybe you could take a couple of days off."

"For what purpose?" she asked, suspiciously.

"So she could stay here with Doug Douglass," Canidy said.

"If she moved in here, I'd never get rid of her," Ann said. "How long is she going to be in London, anyway?"

"Permanently," he said.

"Then no, period," Ann said. "Charity cannot stay here. She would move in, and I wouldn't have the heart to throw her out, and that would be the end of us making love on the pillows."

"In that case, screw her," Canidy said. "Your logic is irrefutable."

She threw herself at him and nibbled his ear.

"You keep that up, you know what's going to happen," he said.

"I hope, I hope, I hope," Ann said. Then she said, "Damn, I'm glad Eric's all right. I love you when you're like this."

"Like what?"

"Happy and horny," Ann said. "Where is he?"

"Ah, come on, Mata Hari," he said.

"I was just trying to find out how long you'd be gone, and where you'll be going."

"Eric at this very moment is somewhere on the European land mass, riding down a forest road between towering pines," he said. "That tell you anything?"

"No," she said, "And I don't really mean to pry."

"I know," he said.

Eric Fulmar, at that very moment, was walking down a basement corridor in the municipal jail in Pécs, Hungary. He was handcuffed to Professor Friedrich Dyer, and both of them wore chain hobbles.

A Black Guard guard[6] stopped them by a cell, unlocked the handcuffs, and pushed Professor Dyer inside. Then he pushed Fulmar into motion again, until he came to the next cell door. He retrieved his handcuffs, and then pushed Fulmar into the cell.

[6]An SS-like organization owing its allegiance to Admiral Horthy, the Regent of Hungary.

Five

1

OSS Virginia Station
5 February 1943

CYNTHIA CHENOWITH HAD elected to skip the evening meal. When she had finished her bath, she would dine on Ritz crackers and canned Vienna sausages and Nescafé from the PX store. The Vienna sausages tasted like soap and would more than likely give her indigestion, and boiling water for the Nescafé (indeed, possessing an electric hot plate) was a specific violation of Station Regulations for trainees, but she desperately needed a bath, and she didn't want to go to supper, or for that matter to leave the privacy of her room.

His name was Horace G. Hammersmith. It had been impossible in the case of Lt. Horace G. Hammersmith, Signal Corps, U.S. Army, to obey either the spirit or the letter of the regulation that forbade any interest in, or discussion of, the private life of fellow trainees. Horace Hammersmith was also known as Greg Hammer, and Greg Hammer was a movie star in private life. He wasn't up there with Clark Gable or Tyrone Power, but his rough-hewn face, his astonishingly golden wavy hair, and his football player's build had left no question in any of the trainees' minds from the moment they first saw him that Lt. Horace G. Hammersmith was *really him!*

And from the moment Lt. Hammersmith had seen Miss Chenowith, he had made it plain that he found her fascinating. At first, Cynthia had thought it was simply a case of movie-staritis. Without arrogance, as a simple statement of fact, she realized that she was the best looking of the half dozen women at Virginia Station. As a movie star accustomed to the adoration of his female fans, Cynthia reasoned, Hammersmith had come to believe that the pick of the herd, or the pride, or the flock, or whatever word fitted the half dozen women at Virginia Station, was his.

His Training Group had begun training six weeks before Cynthia's. The way the school was set up (before she had come to Virginia Station as a trainee, Cynthia had read Eldon Baker's training syllabus), incoming trainees were placed under the supervision of trainees who had finished their training and were awaiting assignment. The announced purpose was to spare the training staff the mundane work of seeing to the issue of equipment, the first painful hours of calisthenics, the explanation of the rules, and so on. The real reason was so that the training staff could judge how well the "senior" trainees dealt with subordinates—to see if they could inspire cooperation. There was no place on an operational OSS team for someone who antagonized, intentionally or otherwise, the others on the team.

Lt. Horace G. Hammersmith had been as good and as natural a leader of his peers at Virginia Station as Greg Hammer had been a leader in the movies. Despite herself, Cynthia had come to like him. And she found that her first snap judgment of him had been almost entirely wrong. She had found Hammersmith to be really shy, rather than being arrogant. And she learned that, rather than being awed with himself as a movie star, he thought the whole movie business was rather funny.

Over the weeks, she had learned that he was an electrical engineer who had been sent to Los Angeles by the Murray Hill Laboratories of the Bell Telephone Company to supervise the installation of a recording studio at Continental Studios.

"Lana Turner," he told her one afternoon while they were taking a five-minute break on a ten-mile run, "was discovered in Schwab's Drug Store. I was discovered having dinner with a vice president of Continental Studios, Stan Fine, at the Villa Friscati."

"Stanley Fine?" she asked, genuinely surprised.

"Uh huh," he said.

"We're not supposed to be talking about our private lives, you know," she said.

"I know," he said, "and I also know you know Stan."

Then he'd looked at his watch, and the five-minute break was over, and he'd jumped to his feet and blown his whistle, and they'd resumed the ten-mile run. That night, at supper, he had sat down beside her and resumed the conversation where he'd broken it off.

"Over a steak, which Bell Labs was paying for, I was explaining to Stanley why it was going to cost Continental Studios a bunch of money more than they expected to get what they wanted, when this fat little baldheaded man walked up to the table and said, in an accent you could cut with a knife, 'So tell me, Stanley, who's your friend? And vy I haven't zeen any film?' "

"Max Liebermann," Cynthia said, laughing at Hammersmith's apt mimicry of the founder and chairman of the board of Continental Studios.

"Right," Hammersmith said. "But I didn't know who he was. So Stanley said, 'Uncle Max, he's the engineer from Bell Telephone.' "

" 'What I vant to know is can he ride a horz?' Max said," Hammersmith went on. " 'If he can ride a horz, I tink he's Major Porter. We god a hell uf a problem wit dat, Stanley, if I god to tell you.' "

By then, Cynthia was giggling at the mimicry.

"It didn't take much to corrupt me," Hammersmith had gone on. "All it took to get me before the cameras was as much by the week, on a year's contract, as Bell Labs was paying me by the month. And luckily, I could ride a 'horz.' "

"I saw 'Cavalry Raid,' " Cynthia said. "You were very good."

"That's because my only lines were 'Yes, Sir,' and 'Sound the Charge!' " Hammersmith said. "Anyway, Stan and I became pals. And he got me into this, and he wrote me a letter saying if I got to Washington and desperately needed a place to stay, I should call a Miss Cynthia Chenowith and say I was a friend of his. Unless there is another Cynthia Chenowith?"

Horace G. Hammersmith had not so much as touched

her hand, except in the line of duty. But neither had he for long taken his eyes off her whenever they were around each other.

And now he was going. He was going operational. She wondered where, and doing what. And she just wasn't up to spending his last night here with him. In the morning, she would have breakfast with him, and maybe even go to the station wagon with him, and kiss his cheek.

But she didn't want to see him tonight. Tonight, there would be just too much of a temptation to give him what he wanted, even if he didn't ask for it. She didn't want him to go operational with her on his mind. She didn't love him, but she really liked him, and she was almost sure he thought he was falling in love with her. Whatever they were going to have him doing, the one thing he didn't need was her on his mind any more than she already was.

The bathtub was full. So when Cynthia sensed the water was cooling, she had to let water out before filling it again with hot water. She bent her left leg, in order to get a good look at her foot, and then vigorously rubbed away a layer or two on the calluses. Then she repeated the operation on the right foot.

And finally she stepped out of the tub and toweled herself dry. Then she took the towel and wiped the condensation from the full-length mirror on the door and examined herself in it.

She "made muscles," as she had seen men do, and was surprised—and not sure whether she was pleased or disappointed—that she could see no development in her biceps. With all the push-ups and pull-ups she'd done, she had expected some.

She had bruised, ugly blue areas, in several places. The largest area was in her right shoulder, from the recoil of the Springfield rifle, and the Garand rifle, and the Winchester shotgun, and the Thompson submachine gun she had fired on the range. She had fallen twice on the obstacle course. There was a bruised area on her lower stomach, a souvenir of an encounter with a peeled log when she had tripped running up an obstacle, and another on her right leg, just above her knee. She had earned that battle stripe just by stumbling, exhausted, and landing on the goddamned Springfield.

Finally, there was a raw spot on the web of her right hand, where the Colt .45 automatic pistol had "bitten" her.

She dried that spot very carefully with a wad of toilet tissue and then applied Merthiolate and a Band-Aid. And then she took a Large Economy Size tube of Ben-Gay and applied it liberally to all the bruised areas.

If Greg should come up here, she thought, *I will smell like the men's locker room, and maybe that will dampen his ardor.*

Still naked, she washed and dried her hair, wrapped her head in a towel, and then finally put on what she considered a grossly unfeminine set of pajamas. They were from the PX, too. Flannel, with a particularly ugly red and brown pattern. She put a bathrobe over the pajamas, examined herself a final time in the mirror, stuck her tongue out at herself, and then went into her bedroom.

She sat down at a government issue gray metal desk, which was conspicuously ugly in comparison to the rest of the furniture, turned on the desk lamp, and took a brown-paper-bound book from a rack. The book was entitled, "U.S. Field Manual, FM 21-10, The Law of Land Warfare." There would be a written examination to make sure the trainees knew what the Hague and Geneva Conventions had had to say about where the line was between a soldier (who was entitled to treatment as a prisoner of war), a partisan, and a spy. Under the law of land warfare, a spy could be shot.

Cynthia had serious doubts that either the Germans or the Japanese were going to pay much attention to the fine print, but the course was a part of the curriculum, and she had to pass it to graduate. And she was determined to graduate.

Thirty minutes later, just after she had opened a can of Vienna sausages and was trying without much success to get one of the tightly packed little obscenities out of the can, there was a knock at her door.

She didn't respond. If it was Horace G. Hammersmith and she didn't respond to his knock, he might take the hint and go away.

But after a moment, there was another knock, this time far more demanding.

"Who is it?"

"Eldon Baker."

"Come on in," Cynthia called.

Baker entered the room.

"Studying," Cynthia said, unnecessarily.

She saw that Baker had seen the hot plate and the jar of Nescafé and wondered if he would turn her in. He knew that she had a close relationship with Colonel Donovan and Captain Douglass; the other training personnel did not.

"Have you got a minute so that we can talk?" Baker asked.

"I should study, Eldon," she said, "but sure."

"Don't worry about the examination," he said, as he closed the door. "You won't be taking it."

"Oh?"

"I have just had a telephone call from Chief Ellis," Baker said. "You are to go to Washington to the house on Q Street with the station wagon in the morning."

"Oh?" she repeated.

"You will take your things with you," Baker said. "According to the Chief, you will not be coming back. At least as a trainee."

"What's this all about?" Cynthia asked.

She was sure she knew.

Oh, goddamn you, Jimmy!

"Chief Ellis did not elect to tell me," Baker said. "But I think we can both make an educated guess, can't we?"

"Whittaker?" Cynthia asked.

"Doesn't it seem that way to you?" Baker said. "I can't tell you how annoyed this makes me."

"Why should it bother you? He's not offering you his unasked-for male protection."

"After some thought," Baker said, "after Captain Whittaker's visit, I decided I could not overlook it. That, in other words, I had to make an official issue of it."

"I don't think I quite follow you," Cynthia said.

"In addition to what he did to you," Baker said, "he had a run-in with me. He was insubordinate. Technically, I suppose, he's AWOL. He was ordered to report here for training. He decided, on his own, that he'd really rather not do that. I wrote a letter reporting what had transpired to Colonel Donovan."

Cynthia wondered why that bothered her, why she felt a

surprising flash of anger. Baker was right. Jimmy Whittaker was an Air Corps officer. Officers do what they are told to do. And there was absolutely no excuse for his having kissed her the way he had, making a fool of her in front of the others.

"It would appear that the rules which apply to everyone else in the OSS, myself included, do not apply to Captain Whittaker."

"We don't know that's what's happened," she said.

"I felt sure that Colonel Donovan would understand my motives in making an official report of what happened," Baker said. "That, rather than trying to get Whittaker in trouble, my concern was for the overall discipline of the organization. I felt confident he would understand that it was not a personality clash between Captain Whittaker and myself, but rather an impersonal incident in which an agent willfully disobeyed his superior, with the result that the authority of the Director of Training was seriously undermined."

He waited for her to respond to that, and then, when she did not, went on, "Obviously, I was wrong. The only response to my letter was the telephone call just now. When Whittaker left here, after telling me that I was 'out of my mind' for having you in the school, he said that he was going to see The Colonel. I had the impression he meant both about his coming here, and about you."

"He's known Colonel Donovan all his life," Cynthia said softly.

"And so have you," Baker said.

Cynthia looked at him.

"You want me to go to Colonel Donovan?" she asked.

"I thought you might consider it," Baker said. "For what a fraternal organization would call 'the good of the order.'"

"I'm going to see Colonel Donovan," Cynthia said. "I intend to graduate from this school."

"I thought perhaps you could make it clear to him why this whole sequence of events is so distressing to me," Baker said.

Cynthia's mind was rushing ahead.

"If I'm to go to Washington in the morning," she said, "what do I do about turning in my equipment, settling things?"

"I'll take care of that for you myself," Baker said.

2

It had taken a long time for Cynthia to go to sleep, and she had gone to sleep angry.

And she had awakened still angry, and had grown angrier with the realization that there was not going to be time to pack and dress and eat breakfast, too, and that she was just going to have to miss breakfast.

There was a small silver lining to the black cloud, she thought. It would be the first time that Greg had seen her dressed up in anything fancier than a skirt and a sweater, or wearing any makeup except a faint touch of lipstick. She had a moment to enjoy that before thinking that it probably would be better if he didn't get to see her that way. It would fuel what she suspected he felt for her.

When she carried her luggage downstairs, he was in the entrance foyer. It was the first time she had seen him dressed up, too. He was in his pink-and-green lieutenant's uniform, wearing his new silver parachutist's wings.

He smiled when he saw her.

"Baker said you would be going to Washington," he said. "He didn't say why, and he didn't tell me how pretty you are in your civilian clothing."

"Good morning, Greg," she said.

She wondered what his destination was, and when they had passed the checkpoint, she asked him.

"I don't know," he said.

Cynthia leaned forward and asked the driver, "Where are you taking Lieutenant Hammersmith?"

"The house on Q Street," the driver replied. "He's to see Chief Ellis."

"What's the 'house on Q Street'?" Greg Hammersmith asked.

"It's a mansion near Rock Creek Park," she said. "We use it as both a safe house, and sort of a hotel for transients."

"You've been there before, I gather."

"I used to run it," she said.

"And am I permitted to ask where you're going?" he asked.

"I'm going there, too," she said.

"And am I permitted to ask why?"

"No," she said. "I'm sorry."

"Then, in the short time remaining to us, Miss Chenowith . . ." he began.

"Don't, Greg," she said. "Please don't . . ."

"What I was going to say, you have apparently figured out all by yourself," he said.

She looked at him and met his eyes, and then averted her eyes, and avoided looking at him on the rest of the way to Washington.

When she walked into the kitchen, she asked the cook if Chief Ellis was around.

"In the dining room with Captain Whittaker," the cook replied.

"Come on, Greg," Cynthia said, aware that her temper was up and not caring.

Captain Whittaker and Chief Ellis were eating either a late breakfast or an early lunch. They were having eggs with their steaks, she saw, so it had to be breakfast.

"I think you know Miss Chenowith, Chief," Whittaker said, when he saw her. "Otherwise known as 'Superwoman.' And I don't know the name of the gentleman with her, but he is the one who almost came to her aid when I publicly humiliated her."

"Damn you!" Cynthia flared.

"My name is Hammersmith," Greg said coldly.

"'My name is Hammersmith, *Sir,*'" Whittaker said. "We try very hard to observe the military amenities around here, don't we, Chief?"

"Yes, Sir," Ellis said. "That we do, Sir."

"Sit down, Cynthia," Whittaker said. "Take a load off. Have a bite to eat. We have several hours to kill."

Glowering at him, she walked to the head of the table and stabbed the call button on the floor with her toe.

"For a moment, there, I thought she was going to slug me with her purse," Whittaker said. "Didn't it look that way to you?"

"You sonofabitch," Cynthia said.

"Nice to see you, too, Miss Chenowith," Whittaker said.

The cook appeared.

"Yes, Ma'am?"

"I'd like some breakfast," Cynthia said. "Greg, are you hungry?"

"I missed breakfast," he said.

"Bring us, please, the same thing they had," Cynthia said.

"You may sit down, Lieutenant," Whittaker said.

Lieutenant Hammersmith didn't move.

"I'll rephrase," Whittaker said. "Sit down, Lieutenant."

"Damn you, play your games with me, but leave Greg alone."

"'Greg'?" Whittaker parroted mockingly. "Wonder-woman to the rescue of 'Greg'?"

"You really are a bastard, Jimmy," she said.

"You miss the point, Cynthia," Whittaker said. "The one thing I demand of my subordinates when I'm off saving the world for democracy is what they call instant, cheerful obedience."

"What is that supposed to mean?" Cynthia flared.

"I'm about to go into the Philippines," Whittaker said. "If the lieutenant here is half the radio wizard Douglass tells me he is, and if I'm convinced he'll take orders, he's going with me."

"That's operational information," Cynthia flared. "That's top secret. I'm going to tell Colonel Donovan you've been running off at the mouth again, and Ellis, damn you, too, you're my witness."

"Oh, you've got the Need-to-Know, Cynthia," Whittaker said. "You're the control."

She looked at him and saw in his eyes that he was telling the truth.

"I'm not thrilled about you being my control, frankly," Whittaker said. "But it was the only way I could think of to get you out of that school."

"Why did you do that?" Cynthia snapped. "What gave you the right?"

"I already told you," he said. "I love you, and all's fair in love and war. This seems to be both, so anything goes."

"Damn you, Jimmy!" she said, furious that she felt like crying.

"That may pose certain problems between us, Captain," Hammersmith said.

"How is that?" Whittaker asked.

"I'm in love with her, too," Greg Hammersmith said.

"Oh, Greg!" Cynthia said.

"From this point, then, Lieutenant, you are advised not to turn your back on me," Whittaker said.

"Fair enough," Hammersmith said.

"You look vaguely familiar to me, Lieutenant," Whittaker said. "Do we know each other?"

"No, Sir," Hammersmith said.

"He's the actor, Captain," Chief Ellis said. "Greg Hammer?"

"Oh, yeah," Whittaker said. "I'll be damned. How'd a movie star get in the OSS?"

"I'm a friend of Stan Fine's," Hammersmith said. "When the Army announced that I would be stationed as an instructor at Fort Monmouth for the indefinite future, I asked him to get me out of it."

"I'm really sorry you told me that," Whittaker said. "I always find it difficult to cut the throats of friends of friends of mine."

"Catch me asleep," Hammersmith said. "I'm very vulnerable when I'm asleep."

"You just volunteered to run around in the Philippines, Lieutenant," Whittaker said. "How do you feel about that?"

"I thought I had to prove I was a radio wizard first," Hammersmith said.

"That was before you told me you have the hots for our girl . . ." Whittaker said.

"Damn you!" Cynthia said.

"Obviously," Whittaker went on, "I could not go off to run around in the jungle and eat monkeys and leave you here to pursue yon fair maiden by yourself."

"Obviously not," Hammersmith said, and chuckled.

Damn it, Cynthia thought, *they like each other!*

3

Fersfield Army Air Corps Station
Bedfordshire, England
7 February 1943

First Lieutenant Henry "Hank" Darmstadter, U.S. Army Air Corps, a stocky, round-faced young officer of twenty-three was not sure why he had volunteered for a "classified assignment involving great personal risk" or why he had been accepted.

As a simple statement of fact, rather than from modesty, he understood that he was not the world's greatest airplane driver. There was proof of this. He had twice—once in basic and again in advanced—been sent before the elimination board. The first time, the reason had been simple. He had suffered airsickness.

The only reason he had not been eliminated in basic and sent to navigator's or bombardier's school, or for that matter to aerial gunner's school, was that his class had an extraordinary number of cadets who also suffered from airsickness, plus half a dozen guys who had just quit. The elimination board had considered all those cadets who had an airsickness problem and decided that Darmstadter, H., was the least inept of the inept.

They really couldn't eliminate all of those who under other circumstances should have been eliminated. Pilots were in short supply, and the demand was growing. When he had been given another "probationary period" by the elimination board, it had two conditions. The first was official: that he "demonstrate his ability to perform aerobatic maneuvers without manifesting signs of illness or disorientation." Translated, that meant that he do a loop without getting airsick. The second, unofficial, unspoken, condition was that he understand he would not get to be a fighter pilot or a bomber pilot, and that there was a good likelihood, presuming he got his wings, that he would be assigned to a liaison squadron, flying single engine two-seaters. Or even be assigned to the Artillery to fly Piper Cubs directing artillery fire.

Hank Darmstadter had conquered his airsickness. He wasn't sure whether this was because he had grown accustomed to the world turning at crazy angles or to being upside down, or because he had simply stopped eating when he knew that he was going to be flying.

He had been given his wings and his second lieutenant's gold bar and sent to advanced training. Not in P-51s or P-38s or B-17s or B-24s, but in C-45s. The C-45 was a small, twin-engine aircraft built by Beech. It had several missions in the Army Air Corps, none of them connected directly with bringing aerial warfare to the enemy. It was used as a small passenger transport, and it was used as a flying classroom to train navigators and bombardiers.

Two weeks before Hank Darmstadter was to graduate from advanced training in the C-45 aircraft, he had, flying solo, dumped one. He had lost the right engine on takeoff, and if he had had one hundred feet less altitude, he would have gone into the ground. But the hundred feet made the difference, and he had been able to stand it on its wing and make a 360-degree turn and get it back onto the runway, downwind and with the wheels up, just as the second engine cut out.

Thirty seconds after he had scrambled out the small door in the fuselage, there had been a dull rumble, and then a larger explosion as the fuel tanks ignited and then exploded.

When he appeared before that elimination board, they had discussed the accident and Darmstadter, 2nd Lt. H., as if he were not there. In the opinion of one of his examiners, if he was that far along in the course, he should have known and demonstrated the proper procedure to follow in the case of engine failure on takeoff. And the proper procedure was not to make a dangerous 360 and land the wrong way on the runway as Darmstadter had done, but to make the proper adjustments for flight on one engine, and then to circle the field and gain sufficient altitude to make a proper approach (that is, from the other direction, into the wind).

Another of his examiners, to Darmstadter's considerable surprise, had taken the position that since no one was with him in the cockpit, they didn't know what had happened, and that it wasn't really fair to assume that he had done what he had done from panic; that he was entitled to the benefit of the doubt; and that Darmstadter's best judgment had been to do what he had done.

There had been seven officer pilots on the elimination board. The vote (it was supposed to be secret, but the President of the Board told him anyway) was four to three not to eliminate him. He would be permitted to graduate and to transition to Douglas C-47 aircraft. The C-47, Darmstadter knew, was supposed to be the most forgiving aircraft, save the Piper Cub, in the Army Air Corps. Douglas was building them by the thousands, and each of them needed two pilots. They were used as personnel transports (they were the Army Air Corps version of the DC-3 civilian airplane) and cargo aircraft. Most of the C-47s being built would be used in support of airborne operations, both to carry paratroopers and to tow gliders.

Hank Darmstadter had understood that his glamorous service as an Air Corps pilot would be in the right (co-pilot's) seat of a C-47 gooney bird. He would work the radios and the landing gear and the flaps while a more skillful pilot would do the flying.

And that's what he had done at first when he'd come to England. But then the system had caught up with him. He had received an automatic promotion to first lieutenant, based solely on the length of his service. It was the policy of the Troop Carrier Wing commander that the pilot-in-command, wherever possible, be senior to the co-pilot. And Darmstadter had picked up enough hours, and enough landings and takeoffs as a co-pilot to be qualified as an aircraft commander.

Ten days before, when his squadron had returned from a practice mission—in empty aircraft practicing low-level formation flight as required for the dropping of parachutists—the Troop Carrier Wing commander had gathered the pilots in a maintenance hangar and told them Eighth Air Force was looking for twin-engine qualified pilots for a "classified mission involving great personal risk" and that those inclined to volunteer should see the adjutant.

Only three gooney-bird pilots had volunteered. The other two were pilots who desperately wanted to be fighter pilots, and believed that unless they did something, anything, to get out of gooney birds, they would spend the war in a gooney-bird cockpit.

Hank Darmstadter, who himself would have loved to be a fighter pilot, didn't think there was any chance at all of getting to be one by volunteering for this "classified mission." He could think of no good, logical reason for his having volunteered. Without false heroics, he understood that there was hazard enough in either towing gliders or dropping parachutists when there were a hundred gooney birds all doing the same thing at the same time in a very small chunk of airspace.

The one reason he had volunteered was that he had wanted to, and he was perfectly willing to admit that it was probably a goddamned dumb thing to do.

When he saw the Adjutant, there was a short questionnaire to fill out. It asked the routine questions, and a couple of strange ones. One question was to rate his own ability as a pilot, with five choices from "completely competent" down through "marginally competent." Darmstadter had judged himself in the middle: "reasonably competent, considering experience and training." Another question wanted to know if he spoke a foreign language, and if so, which one and how well. And the last question was whether or not he had any relatives, however remote the connection, living on the European continent, and if so, their names and addresses.

He was tempted to answer "no" to both questions, but in the end, he put down that he understood German, and that he had a great-uncle, Karl-Heinz Darmstadter, and presumably some other relatives, in Germany but that he didn't know where.

He hadn't quite forgotten about having volunteered, but he had put it out of his mind. For one thing, he felt pretty sure if they were making a selection of volunteers, they would probably have a dozen better qualified people than a gooney-bird driver to pick, and for another, considering the Army Air Corps bureaucracy, it would take three weeks or a month before they told him "thanks, but no thanks."

At four o'clock this morning, the charge of quarters had

come to his Quonset hut, and told him the Adjutant wanted to see him. The Adjutant had handed him a teletype message:

PRIORITY
HQ EIGHTH US AIRFORCE
COMMANDING OFFICER 312TH TROOP CARRIER WING
1ST LT HENRY G. DARMSTADTER 03434090 2101 TROOP CARRIER SQUADRON TRANSFERRED AND WILL IMMEDIATELY PROCEED FERSFIELD ARMY AIR CORPS STATION REPORTING UPON ARRIVAL THEREAT TO COMMANDING OFFICER 402ND COMPOSITE SQUADRON FOR DUTY. OFFICER WILL CARRY ALL SERVICE RECORDS AND ALL PERSONAL PROPERTY. CO 312TH TCW DIRECTED TO PROVIDE MOST EXPEDITIOUS AIR OR GROUND TRANSPORTATION.
BY COMMAND OF LT GENERAL EAKER
A.J. MACNAMEE COLONEL USAAC ADJUTANT GENERAL

At 0400 there was soup thick enough to cut with a knife, and the weather forecast said "snow and/or freezing rain," so the most expeditious air or ground transportation had been a jeep. It had been a five-hour drive, and Darmstadter had been stiff with cold when they were passed inside the Fersfield gate by an MP wearing his scarf wrapped around his head against the cold.

"The 402nd's way the hell and gone the other end of the field, Lieutenant. When you see a B-17 graveyard, you found it," the MP said.

As they drove down a road paralleling the north-south runway, past lines of B-17s in revetments, Darmstadter was surprised to hear an aircraft approaching, engines throttled back for landing. He stuck his head out the side of the jeep and looked at the sky. It was neither raining nor snowing, but conditions were far below what he thought of as minimums of visibility.

And then he saw the airplane. It was a B-25, and for a moment he thought the pilot had overshot the runway and would have to go around. But the pilot set it down anyway.

Damned fool! Darmstadter thought, professionally.

They reached the end of the runway. There was, as the MP had said, a B-17 graveyard: fifteen, maybe twenty, battered and wrecked and skeletal B-17s, some missing engines, some with no landing gear, their fuselages sitting on the ground. Three battered B-17s, Darmstadter saw with confused interest, were still flyable, to judge by their positions near the taxi ramp, and by the fire extinguishers and other ground equipment near them. But the tops of their fuselages, except for portions of the pilots' windshields, were gone, as if someone had simply taken a cutting torch and cut them away. Someone, for reasons Darmstadter could not imagine, had turned three B-17s into open cockpit aircraft.

There were half a dozen Quonset huts and a homemade arrangement of tent canvas and wooden supports that obviously served as some sort of hangar, or at least a means to work on engines out of the snow and rain.

As the jeep approached the area, the B-25 he had seen land taxied down a dirt taxiway, turned around with a roar of its engines, and stopped. Three sailors . . . it took Darmstadter a moment to be sure that's what they really were, trotted up to the B-25 and started to tie it down and put chocks in place. The crew door dropped open and an Air Corps officer jumped to the ground. Darmstadter waited for the rest of the crew to come out, and then, when the pilot turned and pushed the door closed, he was forced to conclude that, in violation of regulations (and, so far as he was concerned, common sense) the B-25 had been flown without either a co-pilot or a flight engineer.

The jeep, all this time, had been moving.

"This must be it, Lieutenant," the jeep driver said, and pointed to a small sign reading simply "Orderly Room" nailed to the door of one of the Quonsets.

"I'll see," Darmstadter said, and got out of the jeep and walked to the Quonset.

He knocked and was told to come in. Inside were two Navy enlisted men, three Air Corps enlisted men, and three Naval officers, all three of them wearing gold Naval Aviator's wings. Two of them were wearing USN fur-collared leather, zipper jackets. The third wore a navy blouse, with pilot's wings, the gold sleeve stripes of a lieutenant commander, and an impressive row of ribbons. Some of them Darmstadter had never seen before, but he recognized both the Distinguished Flying Cross and the Purple Heart.

Darmstadter saluted.

"Sir, I'm looking for the 402nd Composite Wing."

"You've found it, Lieutenant," the Navy flyer with the DFC said. He offered his hand. "I'm Commander Bitter."

"How do you do, Sir?" Darmstadter said.

"You must be Darmstadter," the lieutenant commander said.

"Yes, Sir," Darmstadter said. He handed over a Certified True Copy of the teletype message from Eighth Air Force.

The door opened and a tall Air Corps officer, a major, the one Darmstadter had seen climb out of the B-25 entered the Quonset hut. For the first time, Darmstadter got a good look at his leather A-2 jacket. There was a Chinese flag and what was apparently some kind of a message in Chinese characters painted on the back.

"What the hell are you doing flying in that shit?" one of the other Navy flyers said. He was the oldest of the three, a ruddy-faced middle-aged man.

"Oh, ye of little faith!" the Air Corps major said, and then turned to Darmstadter. "You must be Darmstadter."

"Yes, Sir," Darmstadter said.

"I could tell because you looked confused," the major said. "And like the kind of guy who would dump a C-45." He paused a moment. "You're in good company, Lieutenant. Commander Bitter also dumped one, didn't you, Commander?"

The middle-aged Navy flyer laughed.

"Goddamn, I'd forgotten about that," he said. "He did, didn't he?"

"Presumably," Commander Bitter said, his voice revealing that he was a little annoyed at the reference to a dumped C-45, "you're going to explain what this is all about?"

"I'm going to borrow Dolan for a couple of days," the major said, and then, as if he had just remembered his manners, offered his hand to Darmstadter. "I'm Dick Canidy, Darmstadter. Welcome aboard."

"Sir," Darmstadter said, "I'm a little confused."

"So am I," Commander Bitter said. "Where are you and Dolan going?"

"An island called Vis in the Adriatic Sea," Canidy said, and then turned to Darmstadter. "You checked out in the B-25, Darmstadter?"

"No, Sir," Darmstadter said. "I've never even been in one."

"Fine," the major said. "I was afraid you might have picked up some bootleg time."

Darmstadter was now wholly confused.

"No, Sir," he said.

"Eric needs a ride home," Canidy said. "We're going to take Lieutenant Darmstadter along with us."

"He just said he's never even been in a B-25," Commander Bitter said.

"That's the whole idea," Canidy replied. He turned to face Darmstadter. "What I want to find out is whether a pilot with about your level of skill can be taught to land and take off from a dirt runway with a stream running through the middle of it."

"Sir?"

"It'll be two or three days before we go," Canidy said, "time enough for Commander Dolan to check you out in the B-25. That is, presuming you're still an eager volunteer?"

"Sir, I'm still confused," Darmstadter said.

"But maybe you've heard enough to rethink a little? Reconsider volunteering? If you want to walk, you can walk right now. No hard feelings, and no black marks on your record."

"You aren't pulling my leg, are you, Major?" Darmstadter said. "You're making a joke of it, but you really meant everything you said, didn't you?"

Canidy nodded.

"And that's all I'm going to be told, isn't it?"

The major nodded again.

"In or out, Darmstadter?" Canidy asked. "It's up to you."

"In, Sir," Darmstadter said.

"Commander Dolan," the major said, "may I suggest we follow that delightful naval custom of splicing the main brace to welcome a new officer to the wardroom?"

"Aye, aye, Sir," Commander Dolan said, and took a bottle of bourbon from a file cabinet.

"For Christ's sake," Commander Bitter said, "it's half past ten in the morning!"

"I'm Joe Kennedy," the third naval aviator said to Darmstadter, offering his hand. The gold letters below the aviator's wings on the leather patch sewn to his flight jacket identified him as LT. J.P. KENNEDY, JR., USNR. "It's a little crazy around here, but you get used to it."

Dolan passed around glasses that had once contained Kraft cheese spread. They now held a good two inches of the bourbon. Commander Bitter shook his head but took one.

Canidy took a small swallow of the whiskey.

"Rule One around here, Darmstadter," he said, "is that you don't write home to Mommy about what you're doing, or what you've seen. And you don't tell your pals, either. The Second Great Commandment is like unto the first. You don't ask questions. But before we put that into effect, you can have one question."

There were at least a dozen questions spinning around in Darmstadter's mind. He was surprised at the one he blurted:

"Why are the tops cut off those B-17s?"

"That's not the question I expected," Canidy said. "I thought you'd ask what's going on around here. Then I would have told you that you have just joined the OSS on a probationary status. If you turn out, you'll join the OSS's private air corps. If you don't . . . you won't like what will happen if you don't. Not a threat, a statement of fact."

Darmstadter had heard about the OSS. Very hush-hush, involved in all sorts of things involving espionage and sabotage and dropping agents behind enemy lines.

Canidy saw the shock on Darmstadter's face and smiled.

"As far as the B-17s are concerned," Canidy went on, "what we're trying to do with them is turn them into radio-controlled flying bombs. We fill them with an English explosive called Torpex. Then Joe gets in, fires it up, and takes off. We cut the roof off so he can bail out. The plane is then flown to the target by radio control. If we can get the sonofabitch to work twice in a row, we're going to fly one into the German submarine pens at Saint-Lazare. So far we haven't been able to get it to work twice in a row."

Darmstadter looked into Canidy's face and saw that he had been told the truth. "You've had your question," Canidy said. "I answered it. That's all you get."

"I understand, Sir," Darmstadter said, seriously.

The door of the Quonset creaked again as it opened. Darmstadter saw an enormous Packard limousine sitting outside. It had been adopted for military service by having a serial number stenciled onto the hood and the words "U.S. Army" on thc doors. But it still looked, Darmstadter thought, as if it should be rolling up to Buckingham Palace and not a Quonset hut in a B-17 graveyard.

A tall, attractive woman wearing the uniform of a sergeant of the Women's Royal Army Corps came in. The uniform was of rough woolen material and ill-fitting, but it did not hide the fact that beneath it was a very well set-up female, indeed.

She looked curiously, hesitantly, at Darmstadter.

In the prescribed British manner, the WRAC sergeant came to stiff attention and stamped her foot.

"Sir," she said to Canidy. "Sorry to be late, Sir. There was a dreadful smashup on the way."

"It's all right, Agnes, he's now one of us. Lieutenant Darmstadter, Sergeant Agnes Draper."

"Hello," Sgt. Draper said. Her smile was dazzling.

"To answer your unspoken question, Commander Bitter," Canidy said, drily. "Yes, Sergeant Draper and I can find time in our busy schedule to take lunch with you. And how lucky for you both that I have just given Darmstadter the 'no questions allowed' speech."

Commander Bitter's face tightened in anger. Commander Dolan and Lt. Kennedy laughed. Sgt. Draper blushed.

"Damn you, Dick," Sgt. Draper said.

"Military courtesy around here, you may have noticed, Lieutenant Darmstadter, is sometimes a bit lax. In the future, Sergeant Draper, you will make that 'damn you, Sir.'"

"Oh, go to hell," she said, but she smiled at him.

4

Petty Officers' Club
Navy Yard, Washington, D.C.
2130 Hours 7 February 1943

Radioman 2nd Class Joe Garvey, USN, moved his beer glass in little circles on the bar, spreading the little puddle of condensation in ever larger circles. Joe Garvey was more than a little drunk. He had been drinking in the Petty Officers' Club since half past five, when he'd come to the club from the Petty Officers' Mess. And he was not used to drinking. Sometimes, out at Mare Island, after he'd made Radioman Third, he had a beer. It was bad enough in boot camp being a skinny little guy with glasses who had never been afloat on anything bigger than a whaleboat, without getting the reputation for being a teetotal too. Real sailors drank. It was as simple as that.

Joe Garvey hadn't wanted to be a radioman when he joined the Navy. He had wanted to go to sea as maybe a gunner on a twin-Bofors 20-mm, something like that, maybe on a destroyer. Maybe even in a submarine. If he had known more about the Navy, he would have kept his mouth shut about having a ham license. But he'd been a boot, and when they'd asked him, he'd told about being a ham. So they gave him a code test, at 20 words per minute, and he'd flown through that; he'd been copying 40 words a minute since he was fifteen.

So he'd gone right from Great Lakes Naval Training Station to Mare Island as a Radioman striker,[1] instead of going to sea. And they'd made him Seaman First and given him the exam for Radioman Third, and he'd passed that with a 98.5. And then he'd been on the next promotion list. And six months after that, he'd made 97.4 on the exam for Radioman Second.

And when he'd asked his Chief about maybe getting sea duty, his Chief told him the Navy needed him right where he was; there weren't all that many guys around who could handle a key the way he could; and it made more sense to have the best operators in an important commo center, rather than afloat, where they might average maybe fifteen minutes a day on the air.

The first interesting thing that had happened to him since he'd been in the Navy was the Chief coming to him and telling him to pack his gear, that he'd been placed on TDY[2] to Washington, and that they were holding the courier plane for him.

A couple of times at Mare Island, when he couldn't think of

[1]A USN enlisted man working to qualify for a rating.
[2]Temporary duty.

a way to get out of it, he'd sometimes had two beers, or even three, but he was not used to just sitting at a bar and drinking one beer after another.

They had been treating him real well at the Navy Yard. Instead of what he expected—a bunk and a wall locker in one of the big bays reserved for in-transit whitehats—he had a private room, with a desk and even a telephone.

"These are chief's quarters," the master-at-arms had told him. "If anybody asks what you're doing in them, you tell them to see me."

"What am I doing in them?" Garvey had asked.

"Let's just say that's where Chief Ellis said to put you," the master-at-arms said.

"What about formations?"

"You don't have to stand no formations," the master-at-arms said. "All you got to do is be available, in case they need you. You can go anywhere you want to go, so long as there's a telephone where you're going and I know where you are and what the number is—and you can get back here in thirty minutes. You want to go get your ashes hauled, Garvey, just make sure she's got a telephone and that you'll be able to pull your pants on and get back here in thirty minutes."

Joe Garvey had not been summoned, and neither had he gotten his ashes hauled. The truth of the matter was that they had shown him a technicolor movie in boot camp that had scared the hell out of him. Guys with balls as big as basketballs, and guys with their dicks rotting off. And the Chief who had given that lecture had said that if you didn't want to get promoted and wanted to spend the rest of your time in the Navy cleaning grease traps or chipping paint, catching a dose of clap was a good way to do that.

The smart thing to do, the Chief had said, was to keep your pecker in your pocket and wait until you got home and could stick it in some nice, clean, respectable girl you knew wasn't going to give you nothing that would fuck up your life permanently.

There were a couple of nice girls Joe Garvey knew back in Louisville, but none who had given him any hint that they would go to the movies with him, much less let him do *that* to them, but he had decided to keep his pecker in his pocket anyway. He didn't want his dick rotting off before he had a chance to use it.

And he wanted to get promoted. He was already a petty officer second, and if you were a skinny little shit who wore glasses, he knew that was a good thing to be. What he had wanted most out of life, at least until they'd put him on a plane at Mare Island and flown him here, was to make Chief Radioman. That wasn't such an impossible dream. Not only was he one hell of a radio operator—he could knock out fifty words a minute and read sixty—but he *knew* about radios. There were a lot of radiomen who were good operators, and there were a lot of radiomen who were good technicians, but there weren't all that many who were both. Since the Navy wasn't going to send him to sea, the next best thing was to make Chief Radioman. Nobody would believe that a Chief Radioman had never been to sea. Or if that came out, people would understand that the Navy had its reasons for keeping him ashore. If he was a chief, it wouldn't matter that he was a skinny little shit who wore glasses. A chief was a chief, period.

And making Radioman First was going to be easier than he had thought it would be. He was going to go back to Mare Island when they were through with him with a letter of commendation from a goddamned Navy captain.

"Makes you sound like John Paul Jones, Garvey," Chief Ellis had told him. "I know, 'cause I wrote it."

The next time the promotion board sat, he was probably going to be the only Radioman Second going for First with a letter of commendation like that. He had already taken the Radioman First examination, and he'd made 91.5. If he just kept his mouth shut, he was going to make Radioman First, and a little later, he would make Chief Radioman.

But that was no longer good enough. He didn't want to sit out the war in the commo section at Mare Island. He wanted to get into the war. When somebody asked him, later, what he'd done in the war, he didn't want to have to tell them he'd been at Mare Island, period.

And he thought he had figured out what to do about it.

"Fuck it!" Radioman Second Joe Garvey said aloud, which made the bartender look at him strangely.

Then he got off the bar stool, shrugged his arms into his peacoat, put his hat at a jaunty angle on his head and walked, somewhat unsteadily, out of the bar of the Petty Officers' Club.

He didn't stop to pick up his Liberty Card. He was afraid the master-at-arms would smell the beer on him and not give it to him. He had been given an "any hour in and out" duty card which would get him past the Marine MP at the gate.

As he went through the gate, a taxicab rolled up and an officer got out. Joe Garvey saluted and got in.

"Q Street, Northwest," he ordered. "I'll show you where."

On the way, he fell asleep, and the cabdriver had to stop the cab and reach in the back and shake him awake when they were on Q Street.

"Further down," Joe told him, and the cab drove slowly down the street until Joe recognized the brick wall.

"Right there," he said, and handed the cabdriver a five-dollar bill. "Keep the change."

He had almost made it to the door in the gate when a large man in a heavy overcoat appeared out of nowhere.

"Hold it right there, Sailor!"

"It's all right," Garvey said. "I'm to report to Chief Ellis."

"You missed him then," the man said. "He left an hour ago."

Another, equally burly man appeared.

"What have you got, Harry?" he asked.

"I got me a drunken sailor," the first man said. "The sonofabitch can barely stand up."

"Fuck you," Joe Garvey said.

"I got me a belligerent drunken sailor," the man said, laughing. He put his hand on Garvey's arm.

"What the hell do we do with him?"

"I'll take him inside and ask the duty officer," the first man said. "He says he's supposed to report to Ellis."

"Kid," the second man said. "I think you just fucked up by the numbers."

The first man, firmly gripping Garvey's arm, propelled him a hundred yards further down the street, and then through the automobile gate to the property, then up the drive, and finally into the kitchen.

Joe Garvey recognized the two men in shirt sleeves sitting

at the kitchen table drinking coffee. As well as he could, he came to attention and saluted. "Sir," he said (it came out 'Shir'), "Radioman Second Class Garvey, J., requests permission to speak to the captain, Sir."

"What have we here?" 1st Lt. Horace G. Hammersmith, Signal Corps, U.S. Army, asked, smiling.

"He just got out . . . fell out . . . of a cab," the burly man said.

"Garvey, my boy," Capt. James M.B. Whittaker said, "if one didn't know better, one would suspect that you have been communing with John Barleycorn."

"You know him?" the burly man asked.

Whittaker nodded.

"Sir, I wish to volunteer," Garvey said, very thickly.

"Volunteer? For what?"

"You're going into the Philippines," Garvey said. "I want to go with you."

"So much for the big secret," Lt. Hammersmith said, chuckling.

"You're drunk, Garvey," Whittaker said.

"No, I'm not," Garvey said, righteously.

"I'll take care of Garvey," Whittaker said. "Thank you."

"I don't know, Captain," the burly man said. "I think I better see what the duty officer has to say."

"Hey," Whittaker said, smiling, but with a layer of steel just beneath the surface. "I said, I'll take care of Garvey."

"Not only am I a much faster operator than the lieutenant," Garvey said, "but you'll be working a Navy net . . ."

"Garvey!" Whittaker said, sharply.

"Shir?"

"Sssshhhh," Whittaker said.

"Yes, Shir," Garvey said, obediently. Hammersmith laughed. Garvey looked at him with hurt eyes.

"That will be all, thank you," Whittaker said to the burly man.

"You understand, Captain, that I'll have to make a report of this," the burly man said.

"You just report that you turned him over to me," Whittaker said, evenly. "OK?"

"Yes, Sir," the burly man said, after a moment's hesitation. Then he left the kitchen.

Garvey was making a valiant and unsuccessful effort to stand at attention. He swayed.

"If I may make a suggestion?" Lt. Hammersmith said.

"By all means," Capt. Whittaker said.

"Why don't we each take one arm and guide him to a place of rest? Before he falls down, I mean?"

"Splendid suggestion, Lieutenant," Whittaker said, as he made for Garvey.

They had just about made it to the kitchen door when it swung inward and Cynthia Chenowith came in.

"What in the world?" she demanded.

"You remember Garvey, of course, Cynthia?" Whittaker said.

"He's drunk!" Cynthia said.

"Didn't I tell you Cynthia was perceptive?" Whittaker said.

"What's he doing here?" Cynthia said. "Where are you taking him?"

"We're putting him to bed," Hammersmith said.

"Not here, you're not," Cynthia said. "I'm going to get Chief Ellis back here and let him handle this."

"Don't be a bitch, Cynthia," Whittaker said. "Make a real effort."

"Now just a minute, Jimmy!" Cynthia said.

"Cynthia?" Whittaker said.

"What?"

"Sssshhhh," Whittaker said, and by that time, Whittaker and Hammersmith were through the kitchen door, with Garvey more or less suspended between them.

Six

1

Fersfield Army Air Corps Station
Bedfordshire, England
0615 Hours 12 February 1943

CANIDY WAS LATE. He had been expected at 0600. And Lt. Hank Darmstadter had been waiting to go since he had awaked, after a restless night, at quarter to four. When he looked out the window, there was thick fog, so thick that flight in his Troop Carrier Squadron would not even have been considered. It was likely that the fog would keep them from flying, but there was no one at 0345 whom he could ask.

Dolan knocked on Darmstadter's door at 0500 and seemed surprised to find him wearing the high altitude flight gear over his uniform.

"Why don't you leave that sheepskin gear here?" Dolan suggested. "I thought we'd ride over and get breakfast in the Air Corps mess."

Dolan ate a hearty, air-crew-about-to-go-on-a-combat-mission breakfast, complete with real fresh eggs and a slice of ham. Darmstadter's Troop Carrier Squadron had not gone on combat missions and consequently had been issued no fresh eggs, so they should have been a real treat. But he was so nervous he had no appetite, and he ate them only because he told himself he needed the nutrition.

A jeep took them to the revetment where the B-25G had been readied for flight. Dolan made a careful, if leisurely, preflight examination of the aircraft, and then hoisted himself onto the hood of the jeep and waited for Canidy to show up.

"You think we're going to go, Commander?" Darmstadter asked. When Dolan's eyes rose in question, Darmstadter added, "the fog?"

"What I'm wondering about is 'where's Canidy?'" Dolan said.

For lack of some better way to kill time, Darmstadter walked around the airplane again. Knowing that he was not only to be checked out in the B-25G, but that they were about to make a long distance flight in it, Darmstadter had studied at length and with great interest TM 1-B-25-G, "Flight Operations Manual, B-25G (Series) Aircraft."

He had realized the moment Commander Dolan had taken him out to the airplane for his first ride that most of his dedicated study had been a waste of time.

"You'll notice," Dolan had told him, "that we've modified this one a little."

It was a massive understatement.

The B-25G had been delivered to the Eighth Air Force with a twin .50 caliber machine gun position in the tail; with another pair of .50s in a rotating turret on top of the fuselage at the leading edge of the wing; with two single .50 caliber machine gun positions ("waist guns") in the sides of the fuselage; and with two fixed .50s and a 75mm M4 cannon in the nose.

All of the guns had been removed and their positions faired over. The bomb-dropping racks and mechanism were gone, and the bomb-bay doors were riveted permanently closed. Auxiliary fuel tanks had been installed in what had been the bomb bay, where the bombs were supposed to be.

In the fuselage aft of the trailing edge of the wing, where the radio operator's and waist gunner's positions had been, there were now five (as many as would fit) light brown leather civilian airliner passenger seats.

The seats had been "salvaged," Dolan told Darmstadter, from a US Navy Boeing "Strato-Cruiser" transport, that Canidy had "dumped in Africa."

Darmstadter was very curious to learn more about that, but he had come to understand that while Major Canidy and the others seemed to make jokes about everything else, Canidy had been dead serious about the "Ask No Questions" rule.

Dolan had given Darmstadter seven hours of in-flight instruction in the B-25G, which was really more than it sounded like, because with the exception of the first takeoff and landing, Dolan had never touched the controls again.

Somewhat to Darmstadter's surprise, he had been an apt pupil. Dolan's only criticism had come right at the start, "Don't try so hard. It's not that hard to fly, and you're a better pilot than you think you are."

He had made mistakes, of course, but after Dolan had shown him what he was doing wrong, he had not made that particular mistake again. He had had the most trouble, not surprisingly, in landing. The B-25G came in a lot hotter than the C-47, and if the power settings were not right on the mark, it dropped like a stone. The gooney bird was a very forgiving aircraft; the B-25 was not.

But he'd shot hour after hour of touch-and-go landings until his technique satisfied Dolan. Then he'd spent another two hours trying to touch down right at the end of the runway and to bring it to a complete stop as quickly as possible. He was aware that he had not been able to accomplish that to Dolan's satisfaction. And he was embarrassed about that, even after he told himself that he should not be. What Dolan was asking would have been difficult for a good, experienced pilot, and he knew he was neither.

They heard the crunch of automobile tires a minute before they could see the glow of headlights in the fog. But then the distinctive grill of the Packard limousine appeared.

"I stopped to get the latest forecast," Canidy said by way of greeting. "I presume that the rubber bands are all wound up and we can go?"

"It'll take five minutes to light the runway," Dolan said.

"It'll take that long to warm it up," Canidy said. "Tell them to light it."

Darmstadter was confused by that. There were no landing field lights at Fersfield. If there were, he thought, he would have seen them.

Commander Bitter and Lt. Kennedy drove up in a jeep.

"I would suggest that you wait until you've got at least 1,000 feet," Bitter said. "But Weather says it's going to be this way until noon, maybe later."

"I think we can get off," Canidy said. He turned to Darmstadter. "Get aboard, Darmstadter," he said. "Strap yourself in the seat that faces backward."

Then he gestured for Dolan to precede him aboard. It was more than a gesture of courtesy, Darmstadter saw. He was telling Dolan that Dolan would function as aircraft commander.

As Darmstadter was strapping himself in, Canidy appeared momentarily in the cabin to wedge a canvas Valv-Pak between one of the seats and the fuselage ribs. Then he disappeared. The plane shook as the left engine started to turn, and then caught.

From where he was sitting, Darmstadter could look out the small window where the waist gunner position had been faired over with Perspex. Though he couldn't see much, he did see Sgt. Draper standing beside Commander Bitter, both of them with their hands raised in farewell. And then there was nothing to see but the edge of the taxiway as the B-25G trundled to the threshold of the runway. Then he saw a fire at the end of the runway. He unstrapped himself for a better look, and saw that it was a GI can (a No. 10 tin can) and that the fire burning in it was gasoline. Pressing his head against the Perspex, he looked as far as he could down the runway. It was lined at fifty-foot intervals with flaming GI cans.

He realized that the burning sand-and-gasoline-filled cans were the runway lights Canidy and Dolan had been talking about. They would not "light" the runway, in the sense of illuminating it, but they would provide an indication where the runway was. He quickly counted cans. He got to fourteen. That meant seven hundred feet. Not nearly enough to take off.

And at that moment, having completed the run-up of engines, the B-25 started to move.

As Darmstadter watched with something approaching terror, the dull glow of another burning can appeared through the fog, and then another. Despite the thick fog, he realized, it would be possible to take off by staying on the runway between two lines of burning GI cans.

And then the rumbling of the undercarriage suddenly stopped. A moment later the nose of the B-25 lifted, so steeply that he fell against the seat which he was supposed to be strapped into, and he heard the whine of the hydraulics as the gear was retracted.

The reddish glow of the burning cans disappeared; there was nothing whatever to be seen through the Perspex window now but gray.

Darmstadter found the heavy sheepskin flying gear, put it on, and plugged it in. Then he put earphones over his ears and adjusted the oxygen mask, with its built-in microphone, over his lower face.

"Do you read?" he asked.

"We have been calling you, Lieutenant," Canidy's dry voice came through the earphones, "with no response. We thought maybe you'd had a last-minute change of heart."

"Sorry, Sir," Darmstadter said. "I was putting on the sheepskins."

"We're passing through eight thousand," Canidy said. "I'll let you know when we pass through ten. Make sure the oxygen is working."

Darmstadter opened the valve and felt the cold oxygen in his nostrils and throat.

"Oxygen OK," he said.

"Couple of things," Canidy said. "Make sure you've got a walk-around bottle and a spare. We're going way up, so stay on oxygen."

"Yes, Sir."

"If you feel like it," Canidy went on, "and it might be a good idea, move around a little. Wave your arms, bend your legs. But don't work up a sweat. If you do that, the sweat will freeze and weld your skin to the oxygen mask. Then it will smart when you try to take it off."

"Yes, Sir," Darmstadter said, chuckling.

"And stop calling me 'Sir,'" Canidy said.

It grew colder very quickly as the B-25 maintained its climb.

And by the time the B-25 leveled off, and the sound of the engines changed as they throttled back and leaned off for cruising, it was bitter cold in the fuselage, and the bulky, sheepskin, electrically heated flying suits and boots did not provide comfort, only protection from frostbite and freezing.

Every fifteen minutes or so, Darmstadter got out of the leather upholstered, civilian airline seat, and within the limits of movement the flexible oxygen hose gave him, stamped his feet and flailed his arms around. Carefully, for he believed what Canidy had said about working up a sweat and freezing the mask to his face.

They had been airborne an hour when Canidy came over the intercom and asked him to bring up some coffee. Darmstadter hooked up a portable oxygen bottle and found the wooden crate that held two narrow-mouthed stainless steel thermos bottles of coffee and one much larger, wide-mouthed thermos holding sandwiches in waxed paper. He took one of the thermos bottles and two china mess-hall cups forward.

He poured coffee and handed a mug to Canidy, who indicated with a jerk of his thumb that it should go to Dolan. Dolan took it, moved his mask away for a moment, sipped the coffee, and then put the mask back on.

"Shit," his voice came over the earphones. "Burned my fucking lip!"

Darmstadter glanced at the altimeter, and then looked at it again, more closely, to be sure he had read it right. It indicated 27,500 feet, which was three thousand five hundred feet higher than the "maximum service altitude" for a fully loaded B-25G, according to TM 1-B-25-G.

Had Canidy rigged the engines so they would function at that altitude? he wondered. *Or was the greater altitude possible because the weight of the guns and the parasitic drag of their turrets and mounts was gone?*

Then he thought that the only thing he knew for sure to explain what he was doing at 27,500 feet over the Atlantic Ocean was that they were headed for an island called Vis. He had a hundred questions in his mind about that, including how come there was a landing field in an area shaded in red—indicating "enemy occupied"—on every map he had ever seen of the Adriatic area.

And, of course, there was the big question: "Why had they picked a C-47 pilot with a mediocre record like his to go along?" It was almost impossible to accept the reason Canidy had offered, that they wanted to see if a pilot of his skill level could manage a takeoff and a landing on a strip which had a stream running through the middle of it.

Canidy surprised him by getting out of the co-pilot's seat

and motioning him into it, then pointing to the altimeter, and then handing him the chart.

That was the first time he'd seen the chart. They had politely but carefully kept him from seeing it before they'd left. Dolan had even kept him from attending the final weather briefing at Fersfield by going there before he came to Darmstadter's room to wake him up.

The chart for the first leg of the flight showed a course leading out to sea in a general south-southwest direction so they would pass no closer than two hundred miles to the coast of France. Then it turned southeast, with Casablanca, Morocco, as their destination.

There were cone-shaped areas drawn on the chart, the small end in France, the wide end over the Atlantic. Canidy explained that they indicated the normal patrol areas for German Messerschmidt ME109F fighters based in France. There were larger cones, which Canidy identified as the patrol areas for German Heinkel bombers used as long-range reconnaissance aircraft. The larger cones covered much of the B-25's projected route.

"The theory," Canidy said drily, "is that the Heinkels fly at about 10,000 feet, which gives them their best look for convoys and the best fuel consumption. And we hope that if one of their pilots happens to look up here and see us, he will decide that prudence dictates he keep looking for ships."

"But what if one of them sees us?"

"We have two defenses," Canidy said. "We're a little faster. If that doesn't work, Brother Dolan will lead us in prayer."

"We're faster because you removed the guns? That weight is gone?" Darmstadter asked.

"The weight, sure, but primarily because of the parasitic drag," Canidy said. "By taking the two turrets out of the slipstream, we picked up twenty knots at 20,000 feet. We got another five or six knots when we faired over the waist-gun position. We can go either faster or farther at the same fuel consumption rate."

"Clever," Darmstadter said. "The engineers obviously knew their stuff."

"Thank you," Canidy said, smiling.

"You did it? You're an engineer?" Darmstadter blurted, remembering as he spoke that it was a question and questions were against the rule. But Canidy didn't jump on him.

"You will doubtless be awed to hear that you are dealing with R. Canidy, BS, Aeronautical Engineering, the Massachusetts Institute of Technology '39."

Darmstadter bit off just in time the question that popped to his lips: "How'd you get involved in something like this?"

He was beginning to understand that there were questions he could ask, but that asking personal questions was taboo.

The answer, anyway, seemed self-evident. Whatever the OSS really did (some of the stories he'd heard about the OSS simply couldn't be true), it obviously had a high priority for personnel and equipment. The big brass had apparently decided that an MIT-trained aeronautical engineer could do more good working and flying for the OSS than he could, say, as a maintenance officer in a Troop Carrier or Heavy Bombardment wing.

Canidy connected a portable oxygen bottle to his face mask, and then went into the cabin. Ten minutes later, he returned.

"I'll sit there a while, John," he said to Dolan, motioning him out of the pilot's seat. "Take a nap."

When Dolan had hooked up a portable oxygen mask and gone back into the fuselage, Canidy's voice came metallically over the intercom.

"Dolan's a hell of a fine pilot," he said. "He was a gold-stripe Chief Aviation Pilot before the war."

Darmstadter had heard that both the Navy and the Marines had enlisted pilots in peacetime, and the legend was that they were better pilots than most of the officers because all they did was fly.

"And then he got a commission?" Darmstadter asked.

"No," Canidy said. "First, they took him off flight status. Bad heart. Then he got out of the Navy and went to China with the American Volunteer Group as a maintenance officer. *Then* he got a commission."

"But he's flying!"

"How Commander Dolan passed a flight physical, Darmstadter, is one of those questions you're not supposed to ask,"

Canidy said. "When you were in preflight, and they were giving you those fascinating lectures on military tactics, did they touch on 'conservation of assets'?"

Darmstadter thought about it, and then shook his head.

"I don't remember," he said.

"What you're supposed to do, if you're a general or an admiral and about to enter battle, is decide what 'asset' you absolutely have to have if things get tough. Then you squirrel that asset away so it's ready when you need it. I just sent my asset back for a nap. If anybody can sit this thing down safely on a mountain strip with a stream running across the runway, Dolan can. You follow?"

"Yes, Sir," Darmstadter said. He was more than a little uncomfortable. Canidy was obviously a highly skilled B-25 pilot and comfortable doing things with it that most people would not try (his solo flight of the B-25 through the soup the day Darmstadter had first met him was proof of that). And he had just admitted that he didn't think he could make the landing on the island of Vis.

"There is an additional problem," Canidy said. "Commander Dolan thinks he is still twenty-two years old and that the doctors are dead wrong about the condition of his heart. He will take affront unless handled properly. Kid gloves are required."

"I understand, Sir," Darmstadter said.

"And I told you before, stop calling me 'Sir,'" Canidy said.

Six hours and fifteen minutes after taking off from Fersfield, the B-25G landed at Casablanca. Darmstadter made the landing. He had to tell himself there was no reason to be nervous. Landing on the wide, concrete runway of a commercial airport on a bright, sunny afternoon should be a snap, compared to landing on the rough, narrow gravel runways at Fersfield. But he was aware that it was sort of a test. Major Canidy was in effect giving him a check ride to see how well Dolan had done as an instructor pilot.

Darmstadter was enormously pleased and relieved that the landing was a greaser.

A Follow-Me jeep, painted in checkerboard black and white and flying an enormous checkerboard flag, met them at the end of the runway and led them away from the terminal to a remote corner of the field. There was an old hangar there, with the legend "Air France" barely legible through a layer of rust.

As they approached, the doors opened, and a ground crewman gave Darmstadter hand signals, directing him to taxi to the doorway and then shut it down. The moment the engines died, a dozen Air Corps ground crewmen manhandled the B-25 inside the hangar and closed the doors.

2

The Mark Hopkins Hotel
San Francisco, California
12 February 1943

It had been decided in Washington that Whittaker, Hammersmith, and Garvey would spend the night at Mare Island. Cynthia, to avoid the curiosity and comment that a civilian woman in the Mare Island Female Officers' quarters would cause, would stay in a San Francisco hotel.

"I know someone who can get you into the Mark Hopkins," Jimmy Whittaker had said, innocently, when the issue of where she would stay in San Francisco came up in Captain Douglass's office. "What the hell, you might as well go first class."

"Go ahead and do it, Jim," Captain Douglass had answered for her. "Hotel rooms are in damned short supply in San Francisco."

When they arrived in San Francisco, by commercial air, they went first to the hotel. Cynthia's reserved "room" turned out to be the Theodore Roosevelt suite, four elegantly furnished rooms on an upper floor.

"It was all they had available," Jimmy said innocently.

Cynthia knew that simply wasn't true. What had happened was that Jimmy had told the hotel something like "I'd like something very nice for a very good friend of mine," and the hotel had come up with the Theodore Roosevelt suite. The hotel had been very obliging to Jim Whittaker because Jimmy was a very rich man, and the hotel knew it.

Jimmy's father and his two uncles had inherited the Whittaker Construction Company from their father. There was more to it than the Construction Company, though God knew that was enough. The Whittaker fortune was based in railroads. They had built them before the Civil War, and grown very rich during the war building and operating railroads for the Union Army.

After the Civil War, there had been more railroads. And harbors, and heavy construction. Whenever they could, which was most often, they took part of their pay in stock of whatever they were building. The company had large real estate holdings in New York City and elsewhere. It was possible, Cynthia thought, looking around the Theodore Roosevelt suite, that Jimmy even had an interest in the hotel.

Jimmy's father had been killed in World War I. And his third of Whittaker Construction had gone to his only son. Both Jimmy's Uncle Jack and his Uncle Chesty had died childless. Jack Whittaker's third would pass to Jimmy on the death of his widow. Jimmy had already inherited the house on Q Street, Northwest, from Chesty, as well as some other property.

Chesty Whittaker, Jimmy's uncle and Cynthia's lover, had told her all about the financial position of James M.B. Whittaker. Not subtly. Chesty had thought she should marry Jimmy.

"You've got to think of the future, my darling," Chesty had said. "We can't go on."

"Why can't we?"

"Well, for one thing, I'm a little long in the tooth. You'll still be a young woman when I am long gone."

"Goddamn you!" she had screamed. "This is obscene. You're not going to die, and I'm not going to marry Jimmy. Jimmy's a kid."

"There is only three years' difference . . ."

"Four," she had snapped.

"Four years," he'd said. They had looked at each other for a moment, before he went on, "Presumably, you meant it when you said you didn't want my wife to ever find out about us."

"The way I put it was 'I'd rather die than have her find out,'" Cynthia had said. "Yes, of course I meant it."

"The reality of our situation is that you are as poor as a church mouse," Chesty had said. "And what do you think she would think if I made provision for you in my will? In addition to her many other virtues, she is intelligent and perceptive."

"Then don't 'make provision' for me," Cynthia had said.

"I love you," he'd said. "I could not not do that."

"And the convenient way to do it is to marry me off to Jimmy? Damn you, Chesty."

"Jimmy stopped off here on his way to Randolph Field," Chesty Whittaker had said. "He said that it was his intention, when he graduated, to ask you to marry him, and what did I think of that?"

"What did you say?" she'd asked.

"I told him I thought it was a splendid idea," Chesty'd said. "Actually, what I said, making my little joke, was 'name the first son after me.'"

"Oh, damn you!" she'd said, and she'd started to cry, and he'd held her.

Three months after that happened, Chesley Haywood Whittaker had dropped dead. And he had not made provision for her in his will, and she was as poor as a church mouse.

Cynthia decided not to make an issue of the Theodore Roosevelt suite. It would be pointless to protest, for one thing, and for another, it wasn't as if there was a suggestion he would share it with her. He had just made a generous gesture. In the family tradition, she thought. In many ways, Jimmy reminded her of Chesty.

The Navy sent a Plymouth staff car to carry them from the Mark Hopkins to Mare Island. Waiting for them in a hangar there, guarded by a platoon of Marines under a Gunnery Sergeant, was a five-foot-high stack of wooden crates that would at 0500 the next morning be loaded aboard the Naval Air Transport Service Douglass C-54 that would carry them to Pearl Harbor in the Hawaiian Islands.

Jimmy, very seriously, ordered Radioman Second Class Joe Garvey to take charge of the guard detail. Cynthia had to restrain a smile at the slight sailor's obvious feeling of importance at being given the responsibility.

Garvey's status was still undecided. Since he had correctly

deduced that Whittaker and Hammersmith were going into the Philippines, he could not be simply returned to duty. But on the other hand, it had not been decided that he would go with Whittaker and Hammersmith. For the meantime, taking him with them to San Francisco and Hawaii would serve two purposes. An extra hand was going to be helpful, and he already knew what was going on. And if he was with them, he was considered to be secure. He could, at any point, be put on ice if it was ultimately decided not to take him to Mindanao.

They then went to the Mare Island Officers' Club for dinner. Whittaker ordered a steak dinner with all the trimmings to go, and sent their Navy driver to the hangar to deliver it to Garvey.

There was an orchestra in the club. After dinner, after first, with great mock courtesy, asking Whittaker's permission, Greg asked Cynthia to dance. Whittaker graciously gave his permission, then rose and gave a little bow as Greg led her off to the dance floor.

Then it was Jimmy's turn to dance with her. Thirty seconds after he had put his arms around her, she had felt his erection stabbing at her stomach. He didn't grab her and press her close or try to move his hands so they would come against her breasts, but he had an erection, and it was obvious that he was not only not embarrassed by it, but seemed pleased that she had no choice but to be aware of it.

And since she had learned in a class euphemistically called "Human Hygiene" in college that the male erection was an "involuntary vascular reaction," she had not been able to tell him to "stop that."

He held her hand as they returned to the table.

Jimmy picked up his glass and, smiling, looked over the rim of it at Greg.

"I have been thinking, Ronald Reagan . . ." he began.

"I saw the furrowed brow," Hammersmith interrupted, "and it's 'Greg Hammer.' Ronny Reagan is the one they call the 'Errol Flynn of the B Movies.'"

"Right," Whittaker said. "Hammer, as in the baking soda."

"Now you've got it," Hammersmith said. "What have you been thinking, oh, worthy leader?"

"That despite my initial unflattering impression of you, you may be reasonably trustworthy after all."

"Oh, *thank* you, Sir."

"To the point where I would feel comfortable in leaving you in sole charge of Radioman Garvey while I escort the lady to her hotel."

"I can get to the hotel by myself," Cynthia protested.

They ignored her.

"So that you can protect our girl from the unwanted attentions of sailors in the Mark Hopkins?"

"Correct," Whittaker said. "I have heard all sorts of tales about sex-starved Naval Officers making indecent proposals to unaccompanied young ladies such as Miss Chenowith, right in the lobby of the Mark Hopkins."

"We couldn't have that, could we?" Greg replied. "You sneaky sonofabitch."

" 'You sneaky sonofabitch, *Sir,*' " Whittaker corrected him.

The two men, pleased with their own wit, smiled at each other, which infuriated Cynthia.

"I don't need an escort," Cynthia said.

"The way she says that," Whittaker replied, "you'd think she thinks I have designs on her body, wouldn't you?"

"I don't think you're funny, Jimmy," she said.

"Let's go," he said. "We have an early day tomorrow."

He took her arm when he put her into the Navy car, but as soon as Greg had gotten out at the hangar, he slid away from her on the seat, so that their hips were no longer pressing together. And he did not try to hold her hand, put his arm around her, or kiss her on the way to the hotel.

He did speak to the driver:

"How are we going to get Miss Chenowith back out to Mare Island in the morning?"

"My orders are to stick with you, Sir, until you get on the plane."

"All night?"

"Yes, Sir."

"Well, you go get yourself some sleep," Whittaker ordered. "Be at the hotel at 0400. I'll catch a cab back out there tonight."

"Why don't you go back out with him?" Cynthia asked.

Whittaker ignored her for a moment, and then somewhat

lamely said, "I want to check in with Ellis. I'd rather do that from your room than try to get a long distance authorization at Mare Island or feed quarters to a pay phone."

He might, indeed, actually call Ellis from the Theodore Roosevelt suite, once he gets there, Cynthia thought, but he obviously just thought up that excuse to get into the room.

There was also a good chance that the moment he got her behind the closed doors of the Theodore Roosevelt suite, he would make a play for her, she thought. She really didn't want that. But she didn't want to make an issue of it now. If it happened, she could handle him.

When they got to the suite, he went directly to the telephone on the table in front of the couch and put in a call to Chief Ellis in Washington.

He seemed genuinely disappointed that Ellis was not immediately available.

"I'm in Miss Chenowith's room in the Mark Hopkins," he said to the telephone. "I'll wait here for his call."

He put the telephone in its cradle.

"Not there? That's surprising," Cynthia said.

"He would have been there if I had called when I was supposed to," he said. "I didn't even think of calling him until I needed an excuse to be alone with you."

She smiled at him.

That should have been my cue, she thought, *to say something cutting—"don't get any ideas, Jimmy," something like that. I wonder why I didn't?*

It was, she decided, because his honesty disarmed her. And then she realized there was more than that. She had tried to force the thought from her mind whenever it had appeared. But that had been hard, and it kept reappearing, as it was doing now.

The thought was that the clock was running down, like the clock at a basketball game. Very soon, Jimmy and Greg (and maybe even Garvey, whom she thought of as "the boy in the sailor suit") would get on the submarine and try to establish contact with this man Fertig and his guerrillas in the Philippines. There was a very good chance that they would be caught, and if they were caught, they could count on being executed. Cynthia had seen photographs of Japanese executions of Americans. It was done ritually, according to the

Japanese warriors' code of Bushido, which prescribed execution by beheading.

And this was followed by another thought, alarming in its implications: There seemed to be little morally wrong with going to bed with a man who stood a very good chance of being executed by beheading in the very near future. It seemed little enough to do for him.

But that presumed he would be executed. Jimmy, God bless him, seemed to have an incredible ability to stay alive. And if he stayed alive, he would be back. And he would interpret her taking him into her bed as a reciprocation of love. And he would want to marry her.

There were a number of reasons she couldn't marry Jimmy. For openers, she was convinced that the love she felt for him was not the sort of love a woman should have for the man she would marry, whose children she would bear. He was younger than she was. And she had been his uncle's mistress. She sometimes thought that she owed the love she felt for Jimmy simply to his likeness, in so many subtle ways, to Chesty Whittaker. Sometimes, when he looked at her, it was as if Chesty was behind the eyes.

And she didn't reciprocate Greg's affection, either. Greg said it jokingly, but she believed that he thought he loved her. And she didn't want to sleep with him, either.

It would be better all around if she were a slut, she thought every so often. Not an absolute, four-star slut, but just a little bit of a slut, like Charity Hoche. The situation Cynthia found herself in would pose no great problems for Charity. If Charity believed that two men like these, both of them handsome and rich, and head and shoulders above most other men, thought they were in love with her, and if she was as fond of both of them as Cynthia was, Charity would sleep with both of them. One at a time, of course, but with both of them.

"I think we should talk about Joe Garvey," Cynthia said. "Ellis will want to know when he calls back."

Whittaker nodded.

"On the one hand, you need a backup for Greg," Cynthia said, all business.

"And on the other, Joe Garvey looks and acts as if he

should be working the lights for the senior play," Whittaker said.

He walked to the bar and made himself a drink, then returned to the couch and sat down, slumped against the rear cushion, his legs stretched out straight in front of him, holding his glass on his stomach.

"He's not trained for anything like this," Cynthia said.

"Neither am I, according to good old Eldon Baker," Whittaker said.

"You're going out of your way to be difficult, aren't you?"

"I'm about to start," he said.

"Excuse me?"

"While I was off in Merry Old England," Whittaker said, "I was fucking a Duchess."

"For God's sake, Jimmy!"

"Elizabeth Mary Alexandra, Her Grace The Duchess of Stanfield," he said. "Her family owns Whitbey House. He's in the RAF. Missing in action. I'm sure there is a word for what I was doing. And it was my fault, not hers."

He met her eyes until she averted them.

"And then when I was in Cairo, I was fucking another married woman. Her husband was off with Charles de Gaulle and the Free French."

"Why are you telling me this?" Cynthia asked. "You think it's funny?"

"There's a punch line," he said.

"I don't think I want to hear it," she said.

"I used to ask myself, Cynthia," Whittaker said, looking at her, "sometimes at *very* inappropriate moments, 'Why are you doing this? If you love Cynthia, why the hell are you screwing somebody else?' "

He looked at her as if he expected a response.

"No answer came, Cynthia," he said. "The conclusion to be drawn, therefore, is that I am an unprincipled sonofa-bitch."

"Another possibility is that you don't really love me," she said. "Not that way. For God's sake, Jimmy, we have known each other since we were kids. I used to take care of you when you were a little boy."

"I have loved you since you were about fourteen," he said,

matter-of-factly. "You were climbing out of Chesty's pool in Palm Beach, and I got a look down your bathing suit. My heart stopped, and then jumped. My heart still stops and then jumps sometimes when I look at you. What this equation means, I'm afraid, is that I do in fact love you. *That way.*"

"What about Garvey?" she said.

Whittaker nodded his head as if he expected not only her change of subject but even that particular question.

"She said," he said, "changing the subject."

He drained his drink, and then stretched across the couch to put the empty glass on a table.

"I'm not going to let you off the hook there, Cynthia," he said, and started to cross the room to the bar.

"What the hell is that supposed to mean?"

"There's more to playing Mata Hari, my dear Cynthia, than running around the woods in Virginia with a rifle, or flashing your OSS credentials to impress people."

"Now that's a cheap shot!"

"It involves things like making decisions," he said. "For example, 'do I send a nice little boy in a sailor suit off someplace where he is liable to drown, or have his head sliced off with a sword?' "

My God, he's seen those pictures! He knows what he's getting himself into. He's frightened!

He looked at her out of Chesty's eyes.

"Goddamn you!" she said.

He didn't reply. He walked back to the couch and sat down.

She felt a sudden infuriating urge to cry. She fought it down, then went to the bar and poured an inch of brandy into a snifter.

She wondered why Whittaker was being such a sonofabitch about Garvey. Why he didn't just say, "we'll take him," or "we better not take him." He damned well was equipped to decide whether the contribution Garvey could make to the mission overrode his youth, and inexperience, and lack of training, and for that matter, physical stamina.

That's what had to be judged. Whether Garvey was drowned or beheaded was important only insofar as it would affect the mission.

Clearly, Garvey should go. Why had Jimmy been unwilling to come out and say that?

Because, she suddenly understood, he was being a sonofabitch again—a *male* sonofabitch. He was simply unable to understand that she thought as he did. He still thought she was playing at being a spy; the bastard had even called her "Mata Hari" and accused her of flashing her OSS credentials to impress people.

Goddamn him!

"Garvey will go," she announced.

He nodded.

Their eyes met.

"If I asked you a straight question, could I have a straight answer?" Cynthia heard herself ask.

"That would depend on the question," he said.

The telephone rang. It was Ellis.

"Sorry I didn't call earlier, Ellis," he said. "I just forgot."

He reported that the material was on hand, that the weather was good, and unless Ellis heard to the contrary, they would depart Mare Island for Hawaii on schedule.

"And we're taking Garvey," he concluded. "Get him transferred officially as soon as you can. Get him overseas pay, and hazardous duty pay . . . whatever you can."

Ellis said something else, to which Whittaker replied:

"Thanks, Chief, I'll damned well try."

Cynthia knew that Ellis had told him to take care of himself.

Whittaker hung the phone up again.

"You were asking?" he said, meeting her eyes.

"Are you afraid?"

"I'll tell you what I'm afraid of," he said seriously, after a pause. "I'm afraid I'll answer that dumb question the wrong way, and that'll give you your excuse to throw me out of here."

"Are you afraid, Jimmy?" Cynthia asked.

"This is probably the wrong answer, but fuck it. Truth time. No, I'm not. I'm good at this sort of thing. There's a thrill, Cynthia. It's even better than flying."

She looked at him first in disbelief, and then in astonishment when she realized he was telling the truth.

"The wrong answer, I gather?" he asked, drily.

"It wasn't the answer I expected," she said.

"Do I get to stay?"

She felt her face flush. She felt faint. There was a contraction at the base of her stomach.

She forced herself to look at him.

"If you like," she said, very softly.

And then, more quickly than she would have thought possible, he erupted from the couch and came to her.

Embarrassed, she averted her face.

His hand came up, and the balls of his fingers touched her cheek and gently turned her face to his. She met his eyes.

His fingers moved down her cheek, and down her neck, and onto her shoulders. He buried his face in her hair. She felt his arms around her, pressing her to him, and then felt his body shudder.

And then he picked her up and carried her into the bedroom.

3

St. Gertrud's Municipal Prison
Pécs, Hungary
12 February 1943

There was just barely room enough for the Tatra diesel dump truck to pass through the tunnel to the courtyard of St. Gertrud's. Scrape marks on the granite walls of the tunnel and on the fenders of the truck testified that the drivers didn't always make it through on the first try.

The Tatra pulled into the courtyard, and with a great clashing of gears and bursts of sooty diesel exhaust backed up to within ten feet of an interior door.

The heavy wooden door opened inward, and three guards came out. They were middle-aged men in gray uniforms and black boots. Carrying billy clubs and small .32 caliber automatic pistols in closed top holsters, two of them took up positions facing each other between the truck and the door. The third, holding a clipboard in gray woolen gloved hands stood to one side by the door. As the prisoners came out of the door and started to climb onto the truck, he checked their names off on a roster.

The prisoners, of various ages and sizes, wore loose-fitting black duck jackets and trousers over whatever clothing they had been wearing when they were arrested. On their heads were black cotton caps with brims, universally too large. These covered their ears as well as the tops of their heads. There were more than thirty of them, more than the Tatra's dump body could comfortably accommodate sitting down. It was necessary for them to line the three walls of the truck bed (the rear wall of the dump truck was slanted) standing up and hanging onto the wall and each other.

It was just after six in the morning, and they had just been fed. Breakfast had been a hunk of dark bread and a veal, potato, and cabbage soup. It was hearty fare and tasty. The intention of the prison authorities was obviously to provide adequate nutrition for the prisoners. There would be a second meal, bread and lard, and a third at night, always a gulyás (stew). This sometimes had paprika, making the traditional Hungarian stew, and sometimes just chunks of meat floating in a rich broth with potatoes and cabbage.

When all the prisoners had climbed onto the Tatra truck, the guard with the clipboard went back inside the prison. The other two guards went to a small BMW motorcycle, kicked it into life, and waited for the truck to leave the courtyard. Then they followed it, ten or fifteen yards behind, making a series of slow turns on the cobblestones so they would not catch up with it and have to stop.

St. Gertrud's prison was on the edge of Pécs. Three minutes after leaving the prison, the truck was groaning in low gear as it climbed a narrow and winding cobblestone street. The motorcycle had to come to a stop three times to wait for the truck to get ahead.

The truck climbed to the top of a hill, and then started down the other side, equally steep and winding. The truck moved very slowly, in low gear, for it had snowed the night before, and there was a layer of slush over the cobblestones. When the road was clear, the truck went down the hill at a terrifying rate.

When it had almost reached the bottom of the hill, the

truck turned off onto a road that appeared to be paved with coal. There was a dirt road under the coal, but coal falling from trucks had then been crushed under other trucks, so that there was in fact a three-inch-deep layer of coal paving the road.

When the truck reached the minehead and stopped, the prisoners, without being told what to do, got off the truck and walked to the shaft head. There, suspended from an enormous wheel, like a monstrous water bucket over a well, was a steel-framed elevator. The prisoners filed onto it until they closely packed it.

Then the basket descended into the mine.

Fifty feet from the surface, it began to get dark. At one hundred feet, they could see nothing at all; it was like being blind. By three hundred feet, however, their pupils had reacted to the absence of light and dilated to the point where some sight returned.

At five hundred feet, when the basket stopped with a groan and then bounced up and down until the elasticity of the cables had expended itself, there were faintly glowing electric lights.

The prisoners were issued carbide headlamps by a foreman. They gathered around a table to clean them. Then they filled the brass fuel tanks with fingernail-sized pellets of carbide, adding water, and quickly screwed the covers in place. The headlamps began to hiss, as the water reacted chemically on the carbide and produced gas. The prisoners ignited the escaping gas from a lamp burning on the table, and then adjusted the lamps to their heads.

The foreman looked over the prisoners and gestured at two of them. They went to him as the others walked into a tunnel.

I have been selected to shovel donkey shit, First Lieutenant Eric Fulmar, Infantry, Army of the United States, thought. *I wonder why. That job usually goes to the old men; shoveling donkey shit and spreading straw doesn't require as much strength as wielding picks or sledgehammers or coal shovels.*

The basic motive power in the mines was donkeys. They were hitched to a coal car and dragged the full car to the elevator. They were then unhitched, the coal car manhandled onto the basket, and the basket hauled to the surface.

The donkeys were then hitched to an empty coal car, which they dragged back along the rails to be filled again with coal.

Eric at first had been horrified at what appeared to be cruel and inhumane treatment of the animals, even though he was aware that, in the circumstances, there was little room for him to pity anything, human or animal. He had then expected any minute that the Gestapo or the SS (or the Hungarian version thereof, the Black Guard) would show up and introduce themselves by knocking him down and kicking his teeth out to put him in the right frame of mind for the interrogation to follow.

But that had not happened. Except for one man, the last Black Guards he had seen were the ones who had carried him and Professor Dyer to St. Gertrud's prison. That man had been a corporal or a sergeant (Fulmar was not sure about their rank insignia) he had seen the next morning. That morning, the one Black Guard had been sitting backward on a chair watching, as prison guards went through the paper work.

A prison guard had dumped on the table the contents of a gray paper envelope containing all the personal property taken from him when they had arrested him on the barge. Except for his wristwatch and his money. The prison guard, in soft German, had told him to identify the property taken from him, and to sign a form he handed him. It had not seemed to be a propitious time to bring up the missing money or the wristwatch.

"Your property will be returned to you at the completion of your sentence," the guard had said.

Fulmar had said nothing, praying that his relief would not be evident on his face. He had quickly come up with a scenario that seemed to make sense, but was frightening because it seemed to be too good to be true: He and Dyer had been arrested not because the Gestapo and the SS-SD were looking for them all over German-occupied Europe, but because they seemed to be black marketeers who had come to Hungary with a good deal of money in search of foodstuffs.

Painfully aware it was wishful thinking, he began to realize that the Black Guards who had stopped and searched the barge and found them had been looking for black marketeers

—not to bring them before the bar of justice, but to find them with large amounts of cash that could "disappear" between the time they were arrested and the time they got to the police station.

If the Black Guards charged them with black-marketing, which was a serious crime, requiring a formal trial, the state would take the money Fulmar had with him. If, on the other hand, they were charged with "unauthorized travel," the euphemism for Austrians and Germans who came privately to Hungary to buy sausage and smoked ham and salami for their own use, there was no need for the subject of the money to come up at all.

"May I ask, Sir, what my sentence is?" Eric had asked very carefully.

"You have been sentenced by the Municipal Magistrate to three months' confinement at hard labor for unauthorized travel to Pécs," the prison guard had said.

"Yes, Sir," Fulmar said. "Thank you, Sir."

"Three months in the mines," the Black Guard had said, in barely understandable German, "will be good for you. And maybe it will even teach you that you can't slip things past the river patrol."

There was a suggestion there that if he had offered the Black Guard on the boat a little money, he would not have been arrested at all.

There was a terrible temptation to press his luck, to offer them more money to let them go. But he realized in time that he was so overexcited by fear that he couldn't trust his own judgment. He was deeply aware that a vein on his temple was pulsing in time with his heart. And his ears rang.

"I will remember that, Sir," Fulmar said, managing a weak smile.

Smiling, the prison guard waved him out of the little office.

As quick as the first scenario had come to him, others followed, and they were not nearly as pleasant. A hundred things could go wrong: Professor Dyer might panic. He might decide to try to save his own skin by turning on Fulmar. And Gisella had not been arrested. So he might decide that turning himself and/or Fulmar in would somehow help her.

But above all, there was the alarm sounded for all of them by the Gestapo and the SS-SD. It was wishful thinking gone mad to hope that no connection would be made between the two men the entire German security services were looking for and the two "persons traveling to Pécs without authorization."

But there had been nothing to do about that possibility but pray.

On his second day in the mines, Professor Dyer had crushed his fingers under the wheels of one of the coal cars. He had been taken from the mine howling in pain. It had been easy then to imagine that the accident would attract the authorities to him, but that hadn't happened, either.

Dyer's hand had been treated and bandaged. And he now spent his days one-handedly sweeping out the cells in St. Gertrud's and replacing the straw in the mattresses.

Every night, when he got back, Fulmar had to display a confidence that he did not feel at all. He had to reassure Dyer they had nothing to worry about, that all they had to do was avoid attracting attention to themselves, and they would be turned free.

And every morning, he gave the Professor what he hoped was an encouraging wink as he filed out of the cell block to get on the truck.

The donkeys in their stalls stood waiting stoically to be led out and hitched to the coal cars. They didn't seem to mind, obviously, doing what was expected of them. Being in the mines, for them, was the way things were.

The mine corridor where the donkeys had their stalls was several hundred feet long; the donkey stalls occupied the center portion. It smelled, not unpleasantly, of donkey manure. There was a sharp odor on top of that, ammonia-like, from donkey urine.

Three-quarters of the way down the line of stalls the donkey-shit car sat waiting for attention. As they approached it, Fulmar understood why he and another muscular young prisoner had been selected from the line of incoming miners. There was more than donkey shit to be loaded aboard the donkey-shit car today. There was a dead donkey.

"*Tot* (dead)," the foreman said, quite unnecessarily.

Then he showed them how one of the sides of the donkey-shit car could be removed, and how, with the aid of a block and tackle, they were to load the carcass onto the car. The donkey's eyes were open, a curious white. And he was already starting to decompose, and to smell. When they got the block and tackle in place and hauled him out of the stall onto the tracks, the movement caused the contents of his lower bowel, not ordinary donkey shit, but a foul-smelling, bluish semiliquid, to pass from his anus.

More of it came out after they had rearranged the block and tackle and dragged him onto the car. Fulmar felt nauseated, tried to fight it down and failed.

The foreman laughed at him and said he could tell that he was a city boy who had never lived on a farm.

After they got the donkey carcass into the car and closed the side, they went down the line of donkeys and shoveled the donkey shit into the car. By the time they were finished, you couldn't see the donkey carcass.

And then they hooked a donkey to the car to drag the car to the elevator.

Fulmar had another unpleasant thought. He didn't know how long he had been in jail and working in the mine, and therefore did not know how much longer he would be in the mines. He thought he was a damned fool for not having made a scratch on his cell wall once a day. Then he would have known.

Then he thought it really didn't matter. Long before his 90-day sentence was up, they would find out that he wasn't a black marketeer.

And soon after that, some other prisoner would roll his dead body off somewhere in a cart, just as he was doing with the donkey. The donkey, Fulmar thought, was actually better off than he was. The donkey had not had the ability to stand around imagining what was going to happen to him.

Seven

1

Headquarters, Commander-in-Chief, Pacific
Pearl Harbor Naval Base
Oahu Island, Territory of Hawaii
0915 Hours 13 February 1943

LIEUTENANT COMMANDER STUART J. Collins, United States Navy, Cryptographic Officer, Headquarters, CINCPAC, was aware that the Lieutenant Commander in the crisp white uniform in the outer office of CINCPAC was looking askance at his uniform. Commander Collins's khaki uniform was mussed and wilted, and there were sweat stains under the armpits.

The cryptographic section, in the basement of the neatly white-painted, red-tile-roofed headquarters office building, was of course air-conditioned. But it had been air-conditioned in 1937, when no one could have guessed how many people and how much equipment it would be necessary to stuff into the three small rooms. It was hot down there, and people sweated.

If the Commander in the crisp white uniform in the Admiral's cool and spacious office didn't like his sweaty, shapeless uniform, fuck her. Goddamn women in the Navy, anyway.

"The Admiral will see you, Commander," the WAVE Lieutenant Commander said, quite unnecessarily. Commander Collins was not deaf; he had heard the Admiral tell her, over the intercom, to send him in.

Commander Collins walked into the CINCPAC's office.

"Good afternoon, Sir," he said, and extended a clipboard to the Admiral, who scrawled his name on the form, acknowledging receipt of TOP SECRET Incoming Message 43-2-1009. Commander Collins then handed him the message, hidden beneath a TOP SECRET cover sheet.

CINCPAC read it:

URGENT
TOP SECRET
FROM CHIEF OF NAVAL OPERATIONS WASHINGTON DC
TO [EYES ONLY] COMMANDER IN CHIEF PACIFIC, PEARL HARBOR TERR HAWAII

DP YOU WILL MAKE AVAILABLE GATO CLASS SUBMARINE FOR SUCH TIME AND FOR SUCH MISSION AS SPECIFIED BY C.J. CHENOWITH OF THE OFFICE OF STRATEGIC SERVICES. CHENOWITH AND PARTY OF THREE [3] EN ROUTE BARBERS POINT NAS ABOARD NATS FLIGHT 232 ETA 1530 HOURS 14 FEBRUARY. CARGO ACCOMPANYING CHENOWITH PARTY OF APPROXIMATELY TWO [2] TONS GROSS WEIGHT IN THIRTY TWO [32] WOODEN CRATES WILL REQUIRE TREATMENT AS TOP SECRET MATERIEL. OCNO DOES NOT DESIRE TO DISCUSS THIS ORDER. OCNO WILL BE ADVISED IN DETAIL BY MOST EXPEDITIOUS MEANS OF REASONS FOR INABILITY TO COMPLY WITH THIS ORDER. BY DIRECTION: SOLOMON VICE ADMIRAL.

CINCPAC looked up at Lt. Commander Collins.

"No reply, Commander," he said.

"Yes, Sir," Collins said and started to do an about-face.

"Collins?" CINCPAC said.

Collins faced CINCPAC again.

"Hot in the basement?"

"Yes, Sir."

"You talk to the Engineer about it?"

"Yes, Sir."

"And what did he say?"

"He said that the ambient temperature is within the operating range of the equipment, Admiral, and there's no way he can authorize more air conditioning."

"Collins," CINCPAC said. "There's a Chief Kellerman over in Civil Engineering. We were aboard the old *Des*

Moines together. You go see him, tell him I sent you, and ask him to cool your shop down."

"Yes, Sir," Commander Collins said. "Thank you, Admiral."

"And on your way out, ask Commander Oster to get COMSUBFORPAC in here just as soon as possible."

"Aye, aye, Sir."

COMSUBFORPAC[1], Rear Admiral (Upper Half) Geoffrey H. Keene, USN, a ruddy-faced, freckled man of forty-three, who looked much younger, was a professional officer, and thus accustomed to carrying out any order given with cheerful, willing obedience.

"Gerry, what boat, or boats, Gato class, have you got here ready for sea?"

"None this minute, Sir," Admiral Keene said. "But the *Drum*'s just about through with her sea trials. She's off Kahoolawe Island right now, and she's scheduled to go on patrol in three or four days, as soon as they correct what needs fixing."

"There will be a mission for her," CINCPAC said. "Apparently, a people-carrying mission."

"Yes, Sir?" Admiral Keene said. His tone made it clear he wanted more information.

"If the *Drum* is all that's available, it'll have to be the *Drum,*" CINCPAC said.

"Admiral, may I suggest that the *Narwhal*[2] will shortly be available? She's about to leave Diego."

"It'll have to be the *Drum,* Admiral," CINCPAC said. "And if you had anything special planned for her, it will have to be put on the back burner."

COMSUBFORPAC could not help but question the wisdom of using a multimillion dollar naval vessel and its highly trained crew as a kind of seagoing taxicab. Transporting people somewhere was something that submariners did from

---

[1]Commander, Submarine Force, Pacific.

[2]The USS *Narwhal* and her sister ship, USS *Nautilus,* laid down 1929–1930, were the largest submarines in the U.S. Navy. They were sixty feet longer than Gato class submarines, with nearly twice (2730 vs. 1526 tons) the displacement. Although they carried two 6-inch cannon (as opposed to one 5-inch on Gato class) they were not routinely sent on combat patrols, but reserved for transport and other special assignments.

time to time—but at the pleasure of the submariners, if and when that could be reasonably fitted into the normal duty of submariners: That, first, last, and always, was the destruction of enemy men-of-war and the interdiction and destruction of enemy shipping.

But CINCPAC had addressed Keene as "Admiral," rather than by his Christian name, a subtle reminder that he was giving an order.

"Aye, aye, Sir," COMSUBFORPAC said.

CINCPAC handed him the TOP SECRET folder.

"If you can find the time, Gerry," CINCPAC said, "it might be a good idea if you met this Mr. Chenowith at the airfield. Present my compliments, and as tactfully as possible, let him know that I would be grateful to learn what the hell this is all about."

"Aye, aye, Sir," Admiral Keene said.

2

Waikahalulu Bay, Kahoolawe Island
Territory of the Hawaiian Islands
0945 Hours 13 February 1943

The Alenuihaha Channel (depths of at least 1,000 fathoms)[3] runs between the Hawaiian Islands of Hawaii, Maui, and Kahoolawe.[4]

There is a shelf approximately forty miles off the southern coast of Kahoolawe Island, where the depth changes abruptly from about 1,400 fathoms to 650. Then, five miles off the Kahoolawe shore, the depth changes again abruptly to approximately 40 fathoms.

The final sea trial after refitting of the USS *Drum* (*SS-228*, a 311-foot-long submarine of the Gato class) required her to approach the Alenuihaha Channel from the open Pacific, on

[3] 1 fathom = 6 feet.

[4] Pearl Harbor and Honolulu are on the island of Oahu, 600 miles to the northeast.

the surface, in the hours of darkness, navigating by celestial navigation.

She would remain on the surface, crossing the channel until she reached the shelf, whereupon she would submerge to maximum operating depth on a course which would bring her off Waikahalulu Bay. She would then rise to near periscope depth and maintain that depth and course in the 40-odd fathom water until visual contact with their assigned target was established, by periscope, in daylight.

She missed Waikahalulu Bay by five miles. Her skipper, Lieutenant Commander Edwin R. Lennox, USN, a stocky, round-faced, sandy-haired officer who had three days before celebrated his thirtieth birthday, was disappointed, but not surprised. There was really no good way to read the currents of the Alenuihaha Channel or the offshore waters of the island.

When his periscope picked up the targets, without taking his eyes from the rubber eyepieces of the periscope, Commander Lennox softly ordered, "Battle stations, Mr. Rutherford. Gun crews to stand by."

"Aye, aye, Sir," Lieutenant William G. Rutherford, USNR, the *Drum*'s twenty-seven-year-old executive officer, a tall, black-haired, skinny man, said. He pushed the heel of his hand against a round brass knob. A bell clanged throughout the submarine, and there was frenzied activity everywhere but around the periscope itself.

"Steer zero eight five," Commander Lennox ordered.

"Coming to zero eight five, it is, Sir," the helmsman said. And a moment later, "Sir, the course is zero eight five."

"Periscope down," Commander Lennox said. "Take her to one hundred feet."

Commander Lennox slapped the handles of the periscope in the up position.

"Down periscope," he ordered, and the periscope moved downward.

"One hundred feet, Sir," the chief of the boat reported.

"Hold her so," Commander Lennox ordered. He crossed the crowded area and pushed down on the lever which activated the public address system.

"This is the captain speaking," he said. "If I have to say it again, and I think I do, the way to achieve speed is to be sure of what you're doing, and then to do it carefully. We will lose time if somebody falls down a ladder, or over the side."

There was a murmur of chuckles throughout the boat.

"Gun crews standing by, Sir," the chief of the boat said.

"Very well," Commander Lennox said. "Bring her around to two sixty-five."

"Coming to two six five it is, Sir," the helmsman replied. The *Drum* banked like an airplane as she changed course. And then she straightened up.

"Up periscope," the Captain ordered, and the periscope rose.

"Sir, the course is two six five," the helmsman reported.

"Keep her so," Commander Lennox said, and turned to the executive officer. "Got your watch, Bill?"

"Yes, Sir."

"Punch it," Commander Lennox said, then: "Surface, surface!"

Twenty seconds later, in boiling water, the bow of the *Drum* emerged from the sea.

There was a burst of black smoke as she went from battery to diesel power.

Commander Lennox, Lt. Rutherford, and a talker came onto the conning tower.

"Make turns for ten knots," Commander Lennox ordered. "Gun crews man your guns, report when ready."

The talker repeated his orders into his microphone.

Bluejackets in steel helmets and life vests poured from hatches in the conning tower. Some made their way to the 5-inch cannon mounted forward of the conning tower, and began to prepare it for firing. Others went to a rapid-firing 40-mm cannon mounted on a platform just below where the skipper, the exec, and the talker stood. A third group went to the 20-mm rapid-firing cannon mounted on the rear of the conning tower.

Other sailors formed a human chain, passing ammunition from the submarine to the guns.

One by one, the guns signaled (the gun chiefs raising a hand overhead) their readiness to open fire.

"The guns are ready to fire, Sir," the exec reported, and then added, "One hundred eighteen seconds."

"Commence firing," Commander Lennox ordered.

"Commence firing," the talker repeated.

Commander Lennox and the exec put binoculars to their eyes and trained them on the shore of Waikahalulu Bay. There were targets in place, wooden frameworks covered with canvas, fairly credible replicas of oil storage tanks.

The five-inch fired five rounds; one fell nowhere near the targets, but the other four went where they were supposed to go. Meanwhile, the 40-mm and 20-mm rapid-firing cannon fired continuously, the 20-mm in a rapid staccato, the 40-mm in a slower, more measured cadence. The targets were obscured by dust and smoke.

Commander Lennox counted the 5-inch rounds. The moment he saw the muzzle flash of the fifth round, without taking his eyes from his binoculars, he ordered, "Cease fire, secure the guns, clear the decks."

The talker repeated the orders. The sailors at the guns now prepared them for submersion. The crews of the rapid-firing cannon began to pass unfired ammunition back into the hull, and then they all went below.

"Sir," the talker said, "chief of the boat reports gun crews secure from firing."

"Dive!" the Captain ordered.

"Dive!" the talker said. "Dive!"

A Klaxon sounded. The Exec, the talker, and finally the Captain went through the hatch and secured it after them. By then, the decks were already awash.

"Take her to a hundred and fifty feet," Commander Lennox ordered.

"One fifty feet, aye," Lt. Rutherford repeated.

"What have we got, Helmsman?" Commander Lennox asked a minute later.

"Sir, we are steering two six five degrees . . ." The helmsman paused and waited until the needle on the depth gauge was where it was supposed to be, and then went on, "at one five zero feet, Sir."

"Keep her so," Commander Lennox ordered, and then he stepped to the public address system again.

"This is the captain speaking," he said formally. "For a bunch of Kansas hayseeds and Brooklyn thugs, that wasn't half bad. And the chief of the boat would have told me by now if somebody had gone over the side."

Chuckles and laughter ran through the boat.

Leaving the microphone open, Commander Lennox said, "Take her up, make turns for sixteen knots, and set us on a course for Pearl Harbor."

He let the spring-loaded microphone switch go, and motioned for the chief of the boat to come to him.

"Chief," Commander Lennox said, "I would not be too upset, when you check the guns, if you were to find something that would take, say, thirty-six hours to fix."

"Aye, aye, Sir," the chief of the boat said.

"And, of course, if the men aren't needed to help with the repair, there's no reason I can see why they shouldn't be given liberty."

"Aye, aye, Sir," the chief of the boat said.

"Surface, surface!" Lt. Rutherford ordered.

3

Headquarters, U.S. Forces in the Philippines
Misamis Occidental Province, Mindanao
14 February 1943

They had worked out a cipher:

On the fifth of February KSF had sent a message, as opposed to responding to one of Fertig's messages. So far, all that establishing a radio link with the United States had done was to enable Fertig to get word to his wife that he was alive and not in a Japanese POW camp.

KSF FOR MFS NAMES OF TOWN AND STATE WHERE PATRICIA LIVES WILL BE USED AS CODE PHRASES FOR DOUBLE TRANSPOSITION STOP SEND TEST MESSAGE IMMEDIATELY KSF BY

Patricia, Fertig's daughter, was living with her mother in Golden, Colorado.

Using that as the basis for a rudimentary double transposition code, Fertig's homemade transmitter sent a meaningless phrase to KSF. Receipt of the message was acknowledged, but the reply, in the new code was only:

KSF FOR MFS NO TRAFFIC FOR YOU AT THIS TIME KSF OUT

Two days later, on February 11, 1943, there had been another message for MFS:

YOUR STATION DESIGNATED WYZB REPEAT WYZB STOP ALL REPEAT ALL FUTURE TRAFFIC WILL BE WITH KAZ REPEAT KAZ STOP KAZ HAS FILE OF ALL PAST TRAFFIC KSF OUT

KAZ was the call sign of General Douglas MacArthur's General Headquarters, Southwest Pacific Command, in Australia. They heard KAZ on the air all the time, but had been unable to get KAZ to respond to their calls.

Now, things might be different. But several hours of calls to KAZ had produced no response whatever. There were several possible explanations for that, the most likely that radiations from Gerardo Almendres's homemade transmitter were for some reason unable to reach Australia. Fertig did not permit himself to dwell on the possibility that MacArthur did not want to talk to him.

While Fertig did not personally know MacArthur, he had a number of friends who did. To a man, they reported that Douglas MacArthur, one-time Army Chief of Staff, later Marshal of the Philippine Army, and now once again in U.S. Army uniform, had an ego on a par, say, with Charlemagne's.

While Fertig did not believe that the fall of the Philippines was MacArthur's fault . . . indeed, he had acquired a deep respect for MacArthur's military ability; MacArthur's delaying actions with his limited resources had been undeniably brilliant . . . he suspected that MacArthur was personally shamed by his defeat.

If that were the case, that shame might be deepened by proof that not all American officers and Philippine Forces had hoisted the white flag and marched docilely into Japanese captivity.

During his brief service as an officer, Fertig had quickly learned an old soldiers' requisitioning trick. If you need something for one hundred men, and you want to be sure you get it, you requisition a quantity sufficient for two hundred. Or four hundred. Then, when the supply authorities cut your requisition by fifty percent, or seventy-five percent, you still wind up with what you really need.

Fertig had been "generous" in his communications with KSF with regard to his estimated strength report for the troop strength of the U.S. Force in the Philippines. Not dishonest, just generous. He had elected to take the word of Philippine Army officers who had not elected to surrender (putting his own serious doubts aside), when they told him how many men they had at their disposal, and how anxious—providing he could supply and pay them—they were to put themselves and their men under the command of Brigadier General Wendell W. Fertig and the U.S. Forces in the Philippines.

If they told him, for example, that they had five hundred troops just waiting for the arms and food that would permit them to engage the Japanese, he took them at their word, even if it looked to him as if the five-hundred-man force consisted of a couple of officers and maybe sixty Philippine Scouts.

He had added up all the Philippine forces he was told were anxious to place themselves under his command and come up with a figure just in excess of six thousand officers and men. His "requisitions" for arms and food and gold coins had been based on this strength figure.

MacArthur, according to the radio message from San Francisco, had been made aware of this troop strength.

Fertig wondered how Douglas MacArthur was going to react to learning that, after he had reported his forces had fought to the last man and the last bullet, there were six thousand troops under a brigadier general still fighting on Mindanao.

When Second Lieutenant (formerly Private) Robert Ball of USFIP came to report that MacArthur (or at least KAZ, his radio station) was finally being heard from, Brigadier General Fertig, a Thompson submachine gun beside him, was drinking a cup of tea on the shaded veranda of his combined headquarters and quarters. The tea was Lipton's. It had been grown in the Far East, sent to the United States, blended, put in tea bags, and then sent back to the Far East. How it had passed into the hands of the Moro tribal chief who had given it to Fertig, Fertig didn't know.

All he knew was that Lipton was putting out a better product than he had previously suspected. The tea bag which had produced the tea he was now drinking was on its fourth brewing cycle. (Brew, dry, brew again, dry, et cetera.) He knew this because he was a methodical man, and each time he drenched the tea bag in boiling water, he tore one of the corners of the tea-bag-tab off. The tea-bag-tag drying on the bamboo railing beside him was cornerless.

He felt that it behooved him to conceal from his subordinate staff the excitement he felt now that MacArthur was finally being heard from.

"Thank you, Ball," he said, with as much savoir-faire as he could muster. "How long do you think it will take Captain Buchanan to decrypt the message?"

"About thirty minutes, Sir," Ball said.

"Fine," Fertig said. "I expect to be here in half an hour, when Captain Buchanan is finished."

Forty-five minutes later, Captain Horace Buchanan handed Brigadier General Fertig the two sheets of paper on which he had neatly lettered (Hq, USFIP did not possess a typewriter) the decrypted message. From the look on Buchanan's face—disappointment and embarrassment—Fertig knew that there was little good news in the radio message.

"Thank you," Fertig said, and read the message:

KAZ FOR MFS

ONE LT COL WENDELL W. FERTIG CORPS OF ENGINEERS US ARMY RESERVE DETAILED INFANTRY

TWO COLONEL MARCARIO PERALTA PHILIPPINE SCOUTS DESIGNATED MILITARY GUERRILLA CHIEF OF TEMPORARILY OCCUPIED ENEMY TERRITORY

THREE THE ISSUANCE OF MILITARY SCRIP IS EXPRESSLY FORBIDDEN REPEAT EXPRESSLY FORBIDDEN

FOUR COMMAND OF GUERRILLA FORCES WILL BE EXECUTED ONLY BY OFFICERS PRESENTLY IN DIRECT COMMAND OF SAME

FIVE THIS HEADQUARTERS WILL ENTERTAIN REQUISITIONS FOR SMALL IN SIZE URGENTLY NEEDED EQUIPMENT ONLY

BY COMMAND OF GENERAL DOUGLAS MACARTHUR COMMANDER IN CHIEF SOUTHWEST PACIFIC COMMAND
WILLOUGHBY BRIGADIER GENERAL USA

Fertig looked up and met Buchanan's eyes.

"I took out the 'stops' and stuff, General," Buchanan said.

There had been a faint hesitation, Fertig noticed, before Buchanan had called him "General."

It wasn't only a little bad news, it was all bad news.

So far as MacArthur was concerned, he was a reserve lieutenant colonel in the Corps of Engineers, not a Brigadier General in command of U.S. Forces in the Philippines.

Colonel Marcario Peralta was "military guerrilla chief of temporarily occupied enemy territory." Fertig did know Peralta. Peralta had been a successful lawyer in Manila before the war. The last Fertig had heard, just before the surrender, Peralta had been a major. Now he was a colonel, which meant that Fertig was supposed to be subordinate to him.

That could explain why MacArthur had pointedly reminded him that he was a lowly lieutenant colonel.

There was another possibility: If he had not promoted himself, and thus offended MacArthur's sense of the military proprieties, it was possible (now that he thought of it, even likely) that he would have been promoted to colonel and named "military guerrilla chief of temporarily occupied enemy territory."

The really worrisome paragraph was the one about forbidding him to issue scrip. He'd been issuing the scrip, signing each one-, five-, and ten-dollar bill himself; and the crude money had been accepted by the Filipinos; they had taken him at his word that, when the war was over and the Japanese had been driven from the Philippines, it would be redeemed at face value.

And since MacArthur obviously was not about to send him gold, the scrip he was "expressly forbidden repeat expressly forbidden" to issue was the only way he had to pay the troops and to buy whatever the natives were willing to sell.

That was even more important than his rank, or Colonel Peralta's appointment as "military guerrilla chief." Peralta was on the island of Panay. There was little or no chance that he would try to exercise command over Fertig. Peralta was no fool; he knew that Fertig would simply ignore him.

"Captain Buchanan," Fertig said, "I presume that no one but you has seen the contents of this message?"

"No, Sir."

"It is herewith classified top secret," Fertig said, and put a match to it. "No one else is to be made privy to its contents."

"Yes, Sir."

"You may tell Lieutenant Ball and whomever else you wish," Fertig said, "that the message dealt with our reinforcement in the future."

"Yes, Sir," Buchanan said. "Sir, what do I call you?"

"That would seem, Captain Buchanan," Fertig said, looking at him, "to be entirely up to you."

There was a just perceptible hesitation before Buchanan spoke. Then he said, "Will there be a reply, General Fertig?"

"No, no reply," Fertig said. "That will be all, Captain, thank you."

"Permission to withdraw, General?"

"Granted," Fertig said. Then, suddenly, "Yes, there will be a reply, Captain." Fifteen minutes later, MFS went on the air:

MFS FOR KAZ

PERSONAL FOR GENERAL MACARTHUR

REFERENCE PARA FIVE YOUR VALENTINES DAY MESSAGE STOP URGENTLY REQUEST VIA FIRST AVAILABLE TRANSPORTATION NECESSARY DRUGS TREAT VENEREAL DISEASE CONTRACTED BY KEY PERSONNEL STOP FERTIG

4

Croydon Airfield
London, England
14 February 1943 St. Valentine's Day

"I think the thing to do with Charity Hoche, Helene," Lt. Colonel Stevens had said to Helene Dancy earlier that morning, "is for you to meet her at the airport, run her past the clothing store, get her into uniform, and take her out to Whitbey House. She is a young lady who attracts a great deal of attention, and to the extent we can, I think we ought to keep her out of sight."

Colonel Stevens had then decided that it would be best to put Charity Hoche into the uniform of a WAC First Lieutenant.

"We'll think about actually getting her a commission," Stevens had said. "In the long run, that might be the thing to do. But for the short run, anyway, I think it makes more sense than putting her into a civilian specialist's uniform. That attracts attention."

The first impression Capt. Helene B. Dancy had of Miss Charity Hoche was not particularly favorable.

Miss Hoche descended the stairway from the door of the ATC C-54, "the Washington Courier," wearing the uniform of a War Department Civilian,[5] with the uniform cap perched perkily atop a mass of long golden hair. Neither Capt. Dancy nor Colonel Stevens had expected that Miss Charity Hoche would arrive in England in a civilian specialist's uniform.

She also managed to display a good deal of shapely thigh and lace-hemmed black petticoat as she came daintily down the stairs. She wore the gabardine uniform topcoat over her shoulders.

Two officers (one of them, in Capt. Dancy's opinion, old enough to know better) hovered solicitously around her. They were rewarded for their efforts with a radiant display of perfect white teeth between lips that Capt. Dancy thought had entirely too much lipstick of a too dazzling shade.

A double-decker London bus had been driven onto the field to transport the arriving passengers to SHAEF Billeting. There they would be given a two-hour orientation lecture, known as the "Be Kind to Our English Cousins speech." The trouble with Americans, in the opinion of many Englishmen, was that they were "overpaid, oversexed, and over here."

The purpose of the orientation lecture was to remind the

[5]The uniform prescribed for WAC officers, but with an embroidered blue insignia with the letters U.S. inside a triangle sewn to the blouse lapels where a WAC officer would have gold U.S. and WAC insignia.

newly arrived Americans that England had been at war for more than three years; that there was a "ration scheme" for practically everything the English needed to live; and that the British quite naturally resented the relative luxury in which the American taxpayer was supporting its citizens in the United Kingdom.

The lecture, Capt. Dancy decided, seemed to have been prepared with Miss Charity Hoche in mind. But she would not hear it.

Capt. Dancy showed her identification card to the guard and walked out of the terminal building and intercepted Charity Hoche as she was being escorted to the bus.

"Miss Hoche?" she said. "I'm Capt. Dancy. Will you come with me, please?"

The pudgy lieutenant colonel who was carrying Charity's makeup kit looked crushed.

Capt. Dancy happened to meet Charity Hoche's eyes and found herself being examined very carefully by very intelligent eyes.

"My luggage?" Charity asked.

"It'll be taken care of," Capt. Dancy said.

Charity said good-bye to the two officers and followed Capt. Dancy into the terminal, and then to the Ford staff car.

"Where are we going?" Charity asked, when she was in the car, and then without waiting for a reply, "Is it hard to drive one of our cars on the wrong side of the road?"

"The 'other' side of the road is the way I think of it," Capt. Dancy said. "And the answer is 'no, you have to be careful, but you get used to it.'"

"How did I get off on the wrong foot with you so soon, Captain?" Charity challenged.

Because you're young and spectacularly beautiful and look and act as if a serious thought and a cold drink of water would kill you.

"If I gave that impression, Miss Hoche, I'm sorry," Capt. Dancy said. "Where we're going is to my billet. There, we're going to put your hair up, take some of that makeup off, and do whatever else is necessary to make you credible as a WAC officer."

Charity Hoche seemed oblivious to the reproof.

"Captain Douglass thought you might want to put me in a

WAC uniform, but he wasn't sure. I've got the insignia and AGO card of a first lieutenant in my purse."

Dancy looked at her in surprise.

"So, all we'll have to do then," Charity said, sweetly, "is pin on the insignia, put my hair up, and take some of the makeup off, right?"

She gave Capt. Dancy a dazzling smile.

"But before we do that," Charity went on, just as sweetly, "I think we should go by Berkeley Square. Not only do I have three 'Eyes Only' for Mr. Bruce, but I have crossed the Atlantic with a Colt 'Banker's Special' hanging from my bra strap. It hurts like hell, and I want to get rid of it."

"I'll be damned," Capt. Helene Dancy said.

"Won't we all be, sooner or later?" Charity asked.

"Apparently, I was wrong about you," Capt. Dancy said.

"I don't know about that," Charity said, "but you were wrong about Colonel Stevens. You should have known he wouldn't have let me come over here if I was a complete fool."

5

OSS London Station Berkeley Square, London, England
1610 Hours 14 February 1943

David Bruce, Chief of London Station, was surprised to sense his office door being quietly opened, and when he looked up, to see the face of Capt. Helene Dancy waiting to catch his attention.

"Sorry to disturb you, Sir," Capt. Dancy said.

Bruce's eyebrows rose in question.

"Miss Hoche is here," Capt. Dancy said.

Bruce frowned. He didn't want to see Charity Hoche. He wanted in fact to nip in the bud any idea of hers that she would enjoy with him the same close personal relationship she was supposed to have with Bill Donovan.

He had directed that Helene Dancy pick the girl up at Croydon and take her directly to Whitbey House in one of the station's 1941 olive-drab Ford staff cars. En route, Helene was supposed to relay his orders to her to make herself useful wherever Lieutenant Robert Jamison felt she would fit in.

Jamison was Adjutant of Whitbey House Station. His job had been to relieve Canidy of as much of the administrative burden as he could. He had done a good job, but not only was he admittedly unhappy with what he called his chief clerk's role, but he was also qualified, in Bruce's opinion, to assume greater operational responsibility.

Jamison wanted to go operational, which was different from assuming greater operational responsibility.

Bruce had already decided that was out of the question, not because Jamison couldn't do it, but because he knew too much for the OSS to risk having him captured. With Canidy the exception that proved the rule, OSS personnel privy to OSS plans and intentions in more than one (their own) case were not permitted to go operational.

No attempt had been made to brief Jamison on any particular operation, but he did the paper work, and he was as bright as a new dime. There was no question in David Bruce's mind that Jamison knew far too much about too many things to send him off somewhere where he was likely to find himself being interrogated by the Sicherheitsdienst.

But Bruce had always thought there were areas where Jamison's intelligence and other talents could be put to better use than requisitioning sheets and towels and keeping abreast of the paper work. Canidy had been giving him jobs of greater importance than these. And he had accomplished them admirably.

Jamison had handled, for example, and handled well, a project in connection with "Operation Aphrodite":

There was only one way to test the practicality of the drone bomber project, and that was by setting up a target and trying to blow it up with an explosives-laden, radio-controlled B-17. This of course had to be done with as much secrecy as possible, so when they finally flew the flying bombs against the German submarine pens, they would have the necessary element of surprise.

Jamison had scoured the maps of the United Kingdom until he found a lonely bay in Scotland which could be used as a target range. It had required coordination with the English, the local Scottish government, the U.S. Army (from whom he had borrowed a detachment of Engineers to build a target, a mock-up of the entrance to the Saint-Lazare submarine pens) and the U.S. Navy (who had provided ships to clear the area, and a yard boat to be available to pluck "Operation Aphrodite" aviators from the water, if that should prove necessary).

And Jamison had carried this responsibility (which was, of course, in addition to his "chief clerk" duties) with a skill, imagination, and discretion that had pleased Bruce. Jamison had come up with a different cover story for each set of outsiders involved, with just enough truth in each to make it credible, and far enough from the real truth to keep the secret of what was really going on away from German agents.

When the first EYES ONLY PERSONAL message from Colonel William B. Donovan regarding Miss Charity Hoche had come to Berkeley Square asking Ed Stevens if he could find useful work for her, Bruce had seen in it a solution to the problem of more efficient utilization of the talents of First Lieutenant Robert Jamison. She would be assigned first as Jamison's assistant. There, she would do such things as learn how to requisition flour to bake bread—or a similar looking white powder which had extraordinary explosive power when detonated, say, against the supports of a bridge in France or Yugoslavia.

The sooner she could take the paper-work burden from Bob Jamison's shoulders, the sooner Jamison could be put to work doing other, more important, things.

"Why is she here?" Bruce asked. There was more than a hint of displeasure, even reproof in his voice.

"She has three EYES ONLY for you," Captain Dancy said.

"Oh?" Bruce was surprised that Charity Hoche had been put to work as a courier. Couriers were most often officers traveling to Europe for assignment, or sometimes warrant officers whose duty it was to travel around the world, providing armed, personal guard to documents which could not be trusted to the mail pouches.

"Send her in, please," Bruce said.

"She's in the ladies' room," Capt. Dancy said, and then added, "taking off her pistol."

Charity Hoche appeared a minute later. She had three

letter-sized envelopes in her right hand and a Colt "Banker's Special" .38 Special revolver in her left.

She was stunning. She exuded, David Bruce thought personally, a subtle sexuality, even a sort of refined lewdness that would make a saint tend to forget his vows. Professionally, David Bruce had wondered if all of his happy plans to have this young woman relieve Jamison of his administrative chores might be shot out of the water by her blatant sex appeal.

Bruce had been amused to learn that the Army had *officially* approved the policy of inserting slides of attractive and scantily attired or nude young women into slide trays containing other slides demonstrating the proper technique of waterproofing a truck or assembling a pontoon bridge. It caught the men's attention, woke them up, got the blood flowing.

Bruce was genuinely concerned about the degree to which Charity Hoche's simple presence among the men in training and awaiting assignment at Whitbey House would catch the men's attention. There were some women at Whitbey House, and some local women, but not nearly enough of the opposite sex to go around.

Miss Charity Hoche, Bruce suspected, would wake them up and get their blood flowing to an undesirable degree.

"Mr. Bruce," Charity said, in a low and sexy voice, "I'm Charity Hoche. Daddy said when I saw you to give you his best regards."

She thrust the envelopes at him. They were of lightweight, airmail paper, double enveloped, the outer envelopes stamped TOP SECRET.

They were warm to the touch. After a moment, he figured that out. She had been carrying them on her person. In her girdle, specifically; there was no other place where they could have been carried unfolded. It made sense, of course, but there was still something unsettling about it.

Bruce forced his thoughts from Charity's girdle to the pistol. The way she was holding it—upside down, her finger nowhere near the trigger, not waving it around, the muzzle pointed safely toward the floor—showed that she was quite at home with firearms. But one did not expect to see a snub-nosed revolver in the soft white hands of a long-haired blonde with a face that brought to mind candlelight dinners.

Charity Hoche saw the surprise in his eyes. She flashed Bruce a dazzling smile.

"I didn't mean to startle you, Mr. Bruce," she said. "But I . . . I can't tell you where I've had the damned thing for the last thirty-six hours . . . just had to get it out of there. I'm scarred for life."

David Bruce had been a little chagrined at how eagerly his mind considered in glorious technicolor the various places Miss Hoche might have had the pistol concealed on her person for the past thirty-six hours.

"Not at all," David Bruce said, somewhat lamely.

Charity handed him next three *Receipt for Classified TOP SECRET Documents* forms, and watched as he compared the numbers of the forms with the numbers on the outer envelopes, and then signed them. When he gave them back to her, she folded them into a small wad and stuffed them inside her uniform blouse. He averted his eyes in a gentlemanly fashion as she did this.

"Let me take a quick look at these," David Bruce said, furious with himself for acting like a high-school boy before this stunning young woman. "And then we'll have a little chat."

"Yes, Sir," said Charity Hoche.

"Helene," Bruce heard himself say, "why don't you get us some coffee?"

She went to get the coffee, but he saw the look on her face, and reminded himself again that although she was functioning as his secretary, she was a commissioned officer of the United States Army, and aware that captains are not sent to fetch coffee.

The first of the three PERSONAL—EYES ONLY messages from the Director of the Office of Strategic Services dealt with logistic matters. He glanced at it, and then opened the second. That dealt with the suspicions held by the FBI that a Technical Sergeant recruited for the OSS (and, he recalled from a remote portion of his memory, about to finish training at Whitbey House) had uncomfortably close connections with the Communist Party, USA. As he replaced that one in its envelope, he thought he would have to read that one very carefully indeed. Then he opened the third EYES ONLY. It dealt with Miss Charity Hoche:

Dear David:

While I would suggest that we leave intact the in-house gossip that Charity Hoche has been sent to you because she batted her eyes at Uncle Bill, and the old softie gave in, the truth of the matter is something else.

Beneath the very attractive facade is an unusually bright (genius level IQ) young woman with a master's degree in political science earned in four years, summa cum laude. As this came out, first as Charity proved far more useful working at the house on Q Street than frankly I thought she would be, and then officially, from a belatedly administered CBI,[6] *Pete Douglass and I began to involve her in more and more higher level operations.*

The last time I was in England, I brought Ed Stevens into one such operation, together with a direct order that he was not to tell you I had done so. I should not have to tell you the decision to keep you out of this was not in any way a reflection on you. I will tell you that it is the only operation currently under way in Europe to which you are not fully privy, and that those, including Charity, who are privy to it are a very small number of people personally approved by the President.

And neither Ed nor Charity are privy to all the details. I brought Ed into it, with the President's permission, because the operation is of such importance that nothing else being done can be permitted to interfere with it. He was told what he has been told solely so that he can make sure nothing that happens over there will get in the way. His orders are to reason with you, first, to see if he can talk you out of whatever it is you plan to do that might get in the way, and, failing that, to communicate directly with either myself or Pete Douglass. We would then, without explanation, cancel the planned operation. We have done that twice.

---

[6]Complete Background Investigation, normally conducted by the FBI as a prerequisite for a TOP SECRET security clearance.

Charity was brought into it, again with Franklin Roosevelt's specific permission, for the simple reason that this operation's in-house administration cannot be conducted through our normal channels, as secure as we believe them to be. Pete and I needed, in other words, a clerk-typist and file clerk with not only a TOP SECRET–PRESIDENTIAL clearance, but one with the intellectual ability to comprehend the implications of the project, and to deal with the people involved.

It was only, frankly, after I pointed out to the President that none of the other people he proposed, in particular one Navy captain of our mutual acquaintance, to assume responsibility for in-house administration and liaison for this project could type or file, and that adding the Navy captain to the cleared list would leave us no better off than we then were, that he approved adding Charity to the list of those cleared for the project.

That situation has now changed, as a result of growth in the project. We now have the Navy captain, and he has an administrative staff of two. And as both the project, and your operations, have grown, so has the possibility that you will undertake something that could get in the way, and that it would somehow slip past Ed Stevens's attention.

We cannot take that risk. My recommended solution to the problem was what I thought to be the obvious one, to add your name to the list. Unfortunately, I made it hours after the President had become aware that, on his own, one individual on the list had made his deputy privy to some details of the project.

Roosevelt was enraged . . . at the time I didn't know why . . . at my suggestion that we add "every Tom, Dick, and Harry" to the list, and, at my persuasive best, when I told him what I considered to be the risk of something slipping past Ed Stevens in London, all I could get from him was permission to send someone already on the list over there to keep that from happening.

That boiled down to one of the Navy captain's men, a commissioned warrant officer, absolutely trustworthy, but a sailor to the core, or Charity.

My decision is to send you Charity. On my authority,

she has the presumed Need-to-Know anything concerned with any of your projects, to the same degree as Ed Stevens. I have instructed her, should something come to her attention that she feels has missed Ed's, to first bring it to his attention, and then to yours, and finally, if it comes to this, to communicate directly with Pete Douglass or me.

How you arrange for this is of course up to you, and I don't think I have to tell you this project review function of hers is to go no further than you or Ed.

I am, of course, David, uncomfortable with keeping you in the dark, and can only hope that you will forgo judgment until the time when I can tell you what's been going on; when, I really believe, you will understand why all this has been necessary.

You may have noticed the strikeovers and other symptoms of amateur typing. This is because neither Miss Broyle, nor even the ever-faithful Chief Ellis, are in on this either, and this has been writ by hand by

Your old friend,
Wild Bill

David Bruce recognized that, despite Wild Bill Donovan's liberally dispensed soft soap, his reaction to learning that the President of the United States, an old friend, had decided there were some secrets with which he could not be trusted was mixed hurt and anger.

And he realized he was hurt and angered by learning that Ed Stevens, of whom he was very fond and whom he considered a true friend, had been involved in a months' long deception.

And he realized that he was humiliated to learn that while he couldn't be trusted with this great goddamned secret, whatever it was, the long-haired blonde who had crossed the Atlantic with TOP SECRET–PERSONAL–EYES ONLY documents in her girdle enjoyed the confidence of the President. And Donovan.

Bruce was a man of great will. He forced the anger and humiliation down, succeeding after a long moment in convincing himself that the President must have his reasons, and that it was his duty not to question his judgment.

Capt. Helene Dancy entered the office with three cups of coffee and coffee accoutrements on a tray.

"Miss Hoche," David Bruce said, "I presume you are familiar with the EYES ONLY that deals with you?"

"In general terms, Sir," Charity Hoche said. "I haven't read it. I've read the other two."

"I think you should read it," Bruce said, and handed it to her. He heard the sound of his voice, and told himself to be careful. He was still acting emotionally.

He looked at Helene Dancy and saw in her eyes that she sensed that something extraordinary was going on. He looked again at Charity Hoche as she read Donovan's letter. Twice, her eyebrows went up, apparently in surprise.

Then she looked at him, and met his eyes.

"Captain Dancy," Bruce said, "would you ask Colonel Stevens to come in, please?"

"Yes, Sir," Helene Dancy said. "Would you like me to log those EYES ONLYS in?"

Meaning, of course, Bruce thought, *that your curiosity is aroused and that you'll get a quick look at them between here and the safe.*

"You can take these two, Helene," Bruce said, looking at Charity Hoche. "I'm not sure about the third."

"I don't mean to be forward, Sir," Charity Hoche said, "but I think it would be better if Captain Dancy saw that letter."

Bruce handed it over. He saw that Charity Hoche was watching Helene Dancy's face as carefully as he was for her reaction. And they were both disappointed. Her face showed no reaction. She did look at Charity, however, as she folded the letter and stuffed it back in the envelope.

"May I make a suggestion?" Capt. Dancy asked.

"Certainly," Bruce said.

"If you were to tell Lieutenant Jamison that Miss . . . or Lieutenant, which would probably be better . . . that *Lieutenant Hoche* will be devoting half of her time to dealing with female personnel at Whitbey House for me, there would be no reason not to go ahead and send her out there as originally planned."

"Good idea," Bruce said, after a moment. "We'll just have to get Jamison some other help."

"I would say that it would take her two or three days to read the files here," Dancy said. "In the meantime, she can stay with me."

"That's very kind," Charity said.

"Not at all," Captain Dancy said. "I'm going to run you by the bar in the Dorchester. Maybe I can latch onto one of your rejects."

Charity laughed with delight. They smiled at each other.

Womanly smiles, Bruce thought. *Even girlish.*

But there was more to both of them than that. He reminded himself that another of his weaknesses was underestimating the female animal.

"I'll go fetch Colonel Stevens, Sir," Capt. Dancy said.

6

Pearl Harbor U.S. Naval Base
Oahu Island, Territory of Hawaii
1615 Hours 15 February 1943

Commander Edwin R. Lennox, wearing the trousers and shirt of a tropical worsted uniform—the blouse hung from a protruding bolt on the *Drum*'s conning tower—watched as the last of the fresh food was carried aboard. An hour before, an officer courier had delivered his sailing orders. They were in two sealed envelopes, numbered "1" and "2."

The first order, by authority of COMSUBFORPAC, directed Lennox to take the *Drum* to sea at 0600 16 February 1943. He was to sail to coordinates which would put him two hundred miles south-south west of Pearl. Upon arrival there, he was directed to open envelope "2." The second envelope would define the area the *Drum* was to patrol, engaging enemy naval forces and shipping "until such time as the expenditure of torpedoes, fuel and victuals, in your sole judgment, dictates your return to Pearl Harbor."

As soon as the last of the fresh food was stowed aboard, it was Lennox's intention to go ashore, mail his last letter to his wife, and then go to the Officers' Club for a steak and as many drinks of Kentucky sour mash bourbon as he could handle and still make it back to the *Drum* under his own power by midnight.

A Navy gray Plymouth sedan came onto the wharf and stopped beside the ton-and-a-half rations truck. A whitehat jumped out from behind the wheel, opening the rear door and then standing to attention as a full commander in a crisp white uniform got out and walked to the center of three gangplanks laid from the wharf to the deck of the *Drum*. The thick golden rope of an aide to a flag officer hung from the shoulder of the crisp white uniform.

The admiral's aide walked down the gangplank, stopped, and crisply saluted the officer of the deck, who was wearing shorts, a T-shirt, an incredibly dirty brimmed cap he thought was a lucky piece, and a .45 in a holster slung low on his hip like a gunfighter's.

"Request permission to come aboard, Sir," the admiral's aide said in the prescribed nautical manner.

"Permission granted," the officer of the deck said, returning the salute far more casually than it had been rendered. There was in it faint overtones of the scorn felt by submarine officers about to go back on patrol for officers who walked around Pearl Harbor in crisp white uniforms dog-robbing for an admiral.

The admiral's aide saluted the colors and stepped onto the deck.

"I wish to see the captain, Sir," the aide said.

"Ask the commander to come up," Lennox called down. He didn't want to go into the hull. It was hot down there, and he was freshly showered and in a fresh uniform.

Very carefully, so as not to soil his uniform, the admiral's aide climbed the ladder welded to the side of the conning tower.

"What can I do for you, Commander?" Lennox asked.

"I have two documents for you, Captain," the admiral's aide said. "Your operational order has been revised. May I suggest we go to your cabin?"

"Yes, Sir," Lennox said. "You want the original back?"

"Please," the admiral's aide said.

"Watch yourself," Commander Lennox said, as he entered the conning tower. "It's pretty greasy in here."

They made their way to the captain's cabin, which was the

size of a small closet. Lennox worked the combination of the safe, and exchanged the #2 envelope in it for an identical envelope handed him by the admiral's aide.

"Can I lock it?" Lennox asked. "You said 'two documents'?"

"You can lock it," the admiral's aide said, and when Lennox had closed the safe and twirled the dial, handed him a second envelope.

Lennox opened it and looked at it incredulously.

Mr. and Mrs. H. Frederick Dennison
Request the Honor of the Presence of
Lt. Commander Edwin R. Lennox, USN
At Cocktails and Dinner
5:30 pm February 15, 1943
411 Ocean Drive, Waikiki

"What the hell is this?" Lennox blurted.

"Beautiful place," the admiral's aide said. "Mr. Dennison owns most of the movie theaters in Hawaii. And some other things, like maybe half of downtown Honolulu."

"Well, would you please express my regrets to Mr. Dennison?" Lennox said. "I have other plans."

"The admiral thought you might," the admiral's aide said. "That's why he sent me to deliver the invitation. It is the admiral's desire, Commander, that you accept Mr. Dennison's invitation."

"I'm sailing at 0600," Lennox said.

"The admiral is aware of that, Commander," the aide said.

"He's going to be there?" Lennox asked.

"Oh, yes," the admiral's aide said. "The Dennisons really know how to throw a party. Ever been to a luau, Commander? I mean a real one?"

"Oh, what the hell!" Lennox said. "But why me?"

"The Dennisons like to do what they can for the fleet," the admiral's aide said. "I don't suppose you've got whites, do you?"

"No, I don't," Lennox said.

"Pity," the admiral's aide said. "You about ready to go?"

Eight

1

"Rolling Waves"
Waikiki Beach, Oahu, Territory of Hawaii
15 February 1943

It was a forty-five minute drive from Pearl Harbor to the Dennison estate on the beach at Waikiki. The party was well under way by the time Lennox got there. The red-brick curved driveway before the long, low house was packed with cars, more than half of them military and naval staff cars. Lennox saw that many of the service cars had what looked like a second license plate covered with a canvas sleeve. He knew what they concealed: the starred plates identifying the passengers as admirals and generals.

Lennox realized that not only was he going to be out of place in his tropical worsted uniform but outranked by a platoon of brass hats and their entourages. This was no place for a submarine sailor to be.

And when they were inside, and a houseboy had led them to a two-bartender bar set up by a large swimming pool, he saw two movie stars. Floating around in the pool with sort of inner tubes under their arms and drinks in their hands were Lana Turner and one of those too handsome, too perfect, actors. It took him a minute to place the guy as Greg Hammer.

How does a large, splendid physical specimen like that avoid his draft board?

He realized there must be two hundred people in the Dennison mansion. One in five was female. For woman-scarce Hawaii, that was an unusual percentage of females. Some of them were wives, but many were unattached.

Why am I surprised? Where did I expect the pretty girls to be, in downtown Honolulu trying to pick up sailors?

He saw COMSUBFORPAC, which wasn't surprising, and CINCPAC, which was. He wondered why the hell COMSUBFORPAC had wanted him at the party. Probably, he thought somewhat bitterly, to give the condemned man a last hearty meal.

COMSUBFORPAC saw him, nodded, and gave him a quick smile, but made it clear by quickly looking away that Lennox was not expected to pay his respects to him in person at that time.

And then the admiral's aide disappeared, and Lennox was left alone. He finished his first drink, had the bartender make him another, and then wandered around until he came to the buffet.

What he would do, he decided, was eat. They weren't serving the steak he had been looking forward to, but it was beyond reasonable argument a hearty, luxurious meal. There were roast pigs, restaurant rounds of roast beef, fish, and chicken. He tried to remember where he had seen a more luxuriant display of food, but nothing came to him.

He carried his tray outside the building and sat on a low brick wall beyond which was the white sand beach and the ocean. The food turned out to taste as good as it appeared, and he ate everything he had heaped on his plate.

Lennox had just lit a cigar when the admiral's aide came for him.

"I wondered what had happened to you," the aide said.

"I was about to come looking for you, Commander," Lennox said. "I've got to think about getting back to Pearl."

"We'll get you back to the *Drum,*" the aide said. "But right now, will you come with me, please?"

"Where are we going?"

The aide did not reply. Lennox followed him around the pool, then through a long, high-ceilinged living room, and then down a corridor. The aide stopped before a door and knocked.

"Come!" a male voice said.

It was a den, a private office.

Inside were CINCPAC, COMSUBFORPAC, CINCPAC's aide, a very good-looking young woman, an Air Corps Captain, and movie star Greg Hammer in the uniform of a first lieutenant in the Army's Signal Corps.

Lennox was a little embarrassed about what he had imagined when he saw Hammer floating around in the pool. He was clearly not a draft dodger. But not too embarrassed. He'd heard about Hollywood movie stars going into the services. There was a Marine aviation squadron with Macdonald Carey and Tyrone Power in it, conveniently stationed in Diego, where they had rented a hotel so they wouldn't be forced to put up with the discomfits of a BOQ. Clark Gable had been commissioned a lieutenant in the Air Corps. Ronald Reagan was making training films in Hollywood as a first lieutenant. It was therefore not surprising to find Greg Hammer in an officer's uniform.

"Miss Chenowith," CINCPAC said, "may I present Commander Lennox, captain of the *Drum*?"

Cynthia Chenowith gave him her hand and said she was glad to meet him. Her hand was the first female hand Lennox had touched in a year, and it was warm and soft, and he unkindly wondered who was privileged to jump Miss Chenowith.

"Miss Chenowith is connected with Continental Studios," CINCPAC said. "And I'm sure you recognize Lieutenant Greg Hammer?"

"Yes, of course," Lennox said, shaking the movie star's hand.

"And this is Captain Whittaker, of the Air Corps," CINCPAC said.

"How are you, Commander?" Whittaker said, and gave Lennox his hand.

Lennox couldn't remember having seen Whittaker in a movie, but then he had never paid all that much attention to Hollywood pretty boys. At least Whittaker had gone to flight school; there were aviator's wings, if no ribbons, on his blouse.

"You may have wondered, Commander," CINCPAC said, making his little joke, "why I have called this meeting."

Lennox laughed, dutifully.

"Yes, Sir," he said, "I have."

"Continental Studios," CINCPAC said, "has decided to make a motion picture documentary of a submarine patrol. The Navy has promised its full cooperation, and, after consulting with Admiral Keene, I have selected the *Drum* to participate."

"I don't quite understand, Sir," Lennox said. He didn't quite believe what he was hearing.

"Captain Whittaker and Lieutenant Hammer will be sailing with you, Lennox. Plus a Navy enlisted photographer's assistant."

"On patrol, Sir?" Lennox asked, incredulously.

"As I understand the way it will work," CINCPAC said, "Greg Hammer will serve as narrator, Captain Whittaker will function as director/producer, and the whitehat will operate the camera."

If you open your mouth and say one word, Lennox, it will run away with you, and you will tell CINCPAC, COMSUBFORPAC, and the pretty lady with the gorgeous teats precisely what you think of the dumbest fucking idea you have ever heard of.

"Yes, Sir," Commander Lennox said.

And then, in desperation, he thought of something which just might keep them from putting this idiotic idea into practice.

"I presume that you gentlemen and the sailor have gone through the school at New London?" Lennox asked.

"No," Captain Whittaker said. "We thought about it, but we couldn't find time in the schedule."

"Sir, may I respectfully suggest that poses a pretty severe problem?" Lennox said. "We have no way of knowing if these gentlemen can take the atmospheric pressures of the boat?"

"We checked with the fleet surgeon about that, Lennox," COMSUBFORPAC said. "He feels that, after examining their last physical examinations, there is no reason they will have trouble."

"Sir, may I suggest there are psychological considerations as well? There is the question of confinement, claustrophobia . . ."

"Perhaps Admiral Keene didn't make himself clear,"

CINCPAC said, a little sharply. "The potential medical problems have been considered, and judged to be manageable."

"Yes, Sir," Lennox said.

"Captain Whittaker and Lieutenant Hammer, and the whitehat, will come aboard the *Drum* at 0530," COMSUBFORPAC said. "Their gear will be loaded aboard between now and then."

"Their gear, Sir?" Lennox asked.

"Their cameras and recording equipment and film," COMSUBFORPAC said.

"And the rubber boats," Captain Whittaker said. "And their outboard motors."

"We plan to inflate them when we're at sea," Greg Hammer offered, "for what we call long shots, location shots."

"I don't know where we're going to find the room to store any rubber boats," Lennox said.

"Perhaps," CINCPAC said, "it might be a good idea for you, Lennox, to go aboard now and supervise the loading yourself."

"Aye, aye, Sir," Lennox said. "Your permission to withdraw, Sir?"

"Granted," CINCPAC said. He offered Lennox his hand. "Good hunting, Commander."

"Thank you, Sir," Lennox said. He nodded at the others and walked out of the room.

"Good hunting?" Jesus H. Christ! How the hell can I hunt for anything with a couple of second-rate movie stars and a photographer on board? What the fuck did I do to deserve this?

The admiral's aide followed him back down the corridor and through the living room and to the bar by the swimming pool, where Lennox ordered a double bourbon and drank it neat.

He looked the admiral's aide in the eye.

"Have they lost their fucking minds, or what? If it's so important to make a fucking movie, why not send a couple of photographer's mates, submarine-qualified photographer's mates? Two fucking movie stars? It's absolutely insane!"

"Yours not to reason why, Commander," the aide said. "Yours but to do and die—meanwhile being very courteous to your passengers. They have friends in high places."

He was never to know how close he came to being decked by the captain of the USS *Drum.*

When the Plymouth dropped him off at the wharf where the *Drum* was tied up, there were half a dozen sailors staggering under the weight of small wooden boxes.

Lennox went aboard.

"What the hell is going on, Skipper?" the officer of the deck asked.

"We are taking two movie stars, plus a movie cameraman with us," Lennox said.

"What?"

"There are supposed to be rubber boats and outboard motors," Lennox said, ignoring the question.

"I put two rubber boats with motors in the aft torpedo room," the officer of the deck said. "I don't know how the hell anybody will be able to move in there. For sure, we won't be able to load the tubes with the boats in there."

"And the rest of their equipment?"

"That wasn't so hard to store," the officer of the deck said. "There were a couple of boxes maybe five feet long. Everything else is in those little boxes. They're heavy as hell. What's in them?"

"What does it say on the boxes?"

"'Photographic film, Do Not X-Ray.'"

"Then, presumably, they contain motion picture film," Lennox said. "See the chief of the boat, and tell him we'll have one more whitehat with us. The movie stars will share bunks with the officers."

"Aye, aye, Sir," the officer of the deck said. "May I ask which movie stars?"

"Greg Hammer is one of them," Lennox said. "The other is a guy named Whittaker. Never heard of him. An anonymous celebrity, so to speak."

"I know Hammer," the officer of the deck said.

"By the time this patrol is over, you will know him intimately," Lennox said. "Good night, Mr. Downey."

"Good night, Skipper."

2

Ford Island, Pearl Harbor Navy Yard
Oahu, Territory of Hawaii
16 February 1943

At five minutes to six, twenty-five minutes late, CINCPAC's Cadillac limousine came onto the wharf. CINCPAC's aide, the two movie stars, and the woman from Continental Studios were in the back, CINCPAC's aide sitting on a jump seat. There was a very slight, bespectacled, very boyish-looking sailor in front with the driver.

The driver opened the door for them, and then, as they waved cheerfully at Lennox, the boyish-looking sailor took two small canvas bags from the trunk and carried them aboard.

The crew looked at the wharf in unabashed curiosity.

Capt. Whittaker suddenly grabbed Miss Chenowith and kissed her on the mouth. The crew of the *Drum* whistled and cheered.

Miss Chenowith freed herself, turned to Lt. Hammer, and kissed him on the mouth.

The crew whistled and cheered again.

Whittaker and Hammer walked down the gangplank and stepped onto the deck of the *Drum.* They did not salute the officer of the deck, nor ask permission to come aboard. They just walked on board and went into the conning tower as if they were boarding the Staten Island ferry.

"Make all preparations to get under way," Commander Lennox ordered.

The Navy band on the wharf, following tradition, began to play "Anchors Aweigh."

"Remove the gangplanks, loosen up all lines fore and aft," Lt. Rutherford ordered.

Commander Lennox sensed movement behind him. He turned and saw Capt. Whittaker's head and shoulders coming through the hatch.

"Morning," Whittaker said, cheerfully.

A moment later, Lt. Hammer came through the hatch.

With a massive effort, Commander Lennox smiled.

"If you gentlemen will be good enough to stand back there," he said, pointing.

"Sure," Whittaker said. "We don't want to be in the way."

Both of them waved at the girl on the wharf. Both of them, Lennox saw, wore evidence of her lipstick. She waved back.

"Cast off all lines," Lennox said. "Secure all deck hatches. Half left rudder. Ahead dead slow."

The *Drum* shuddered just perceptibly as the engines engaged. Very slowly, she moved away from the dock.

When they were in the channel, moving past Battleship Row, Lennox turned to Rutherford.

"You have the conn, Mr. Rutherford," he said. "Take us to sea."

"Aye, aye, Sir."

"And if you gentlemen don't mind, I would like a word with you in my cabin."

Commander Lennox delivered a brief, precise, and pungent lecture on the customs of the Naval Service as they applied to submarine service, starting with the information that one was supposed to ask permission before boarding a Naval vessel and touching on such items as the prohibition from entering the bridge without the specific permission of the captain.

And then he warmed to his subject.

So far as he was concerned, he told them, this movie documentary was the dumbest goddamned thing he had heard of in his eight years in the Navy.

In addition to that, he didn't like the attitude of either of them. He was the captain of a vessel at sea, and when they spoke with him, they would call him either "Captain" or "Sir." But for the time being, he said, he would be pleased if they didn't speak to him unless spoken to, and he would consider it a personal favor if they would take their meals in the wardroom when he was not there. Movie actors in officers' uniforms ruined his appetite.

So far as he was concerned, his business was sinking Japanese ships, not making some kind of bullshit movie. They should conduct themselves accordingly.

Capt. Whittaker and Lt. Hammer took the speech without

comment, which Lennox found disturbing. He had hoped they would argue with him, which would have given him the chance to really eat ass, and possibly even an excuse to throw their goddamned rubber boats and movie cameras over the side.

"Sir," Whittaker said respectfully, "we will do our best to keep out of your way."

"See that you do," Lennox said. "You are dismissed."

Once he had finished blowing his top, Lennox was a little ashamed of himself. He told himself they had their orders too, even if those orders were to make a fucking movie. And now that he had calmed down a little, he understood that he had been something of a prick to them.

They were still several hundred miles from the position in the Pacific where he was authorized to open envelope "2," but he went to the safe and got it, anyway. Maybe, once he knew where they were going, he would be able to suggest to the movie stars something they could take pictures of. Maybe that would make up for his having acted like a horse's ass.

He tore the envelope open.

TOP SECRET

COMMANDER SUBMARINE FORCE PACIFIC

Pearl Harbor, Territory of Hawaii

To: Commanding Officer USS Drum [SS *228*]

1. By Direction of the President, you will proceed to the Island of Mindanao, Territory of the Philippines, and there put ashore, at such place and at such time as he may designate, Captain James M.B. Whittaker, USAAC, and such personnel and equipment as he may desire.

2. While the nature of Captain Whittaker's duties while ashore in the Philippines are classified and are not to be inquired into, you are hereby informed that his duties have the highest priority, and that the entire efforts of the *Drum* and its crew are to be devoted to its accomplishment, to the exclusion of all else.

3. After putting Captain Whittaker and his party ashore, you will put out to sea to a position determined by Captain Whittaker where you will maintain a radio

communications schedule with Captain Whittaker, or his designate, at such times as he may require.

4. On receipt of the appropriate orders from Captain Whittaker, you will take him, and whomsoever else he designates, together with whatever materiel and/or equipment he may designate, from the shore of Mindanao at such time and place as he may designate. You will then transport him and boarded personnel and/or equipment and materiel to such destination as he designates.

5. You are specifically forbidden to engage in any action against the enemy unless specifically authorized to engage by Captain Whittaker.

6. You are directed to insure by whatever means necessary that your officers and crew understand both the priorities of this mission, its classification and the absolute necessity that it remain TOP SECRET.

BY DIRECTION:
Geoffrey H. Keene, Rear Admiral, USN

Commander Lennox said, "Oh, *shit!*" so loudly and with such fervor that his voice penetrated the baize curtain that served as the door to his cabin and could be heard above the rumble of the diesel.

The chief of the boat put his head past the curtain. "You called, Captain?"

"Moaned was more like it," Lennox said. "Would you tell the Exec to come here right away, Chief? And then ask the Army officers to join me at their convenience?"

"Aye, aye, Sir," the chief of the boat said.

"And I'll want you in on this, too, Chief," Lennox said.

Everyone was there in a matter of minutes.

"Chief, I don't want anybody using the passage while this is going on," Lennox said. "Put some guards out, and then come back in here."

When they were all crowded into the tiny cabin, waiting to hear what he had to say, Lennox said:

"Except to announce that I really showed my ass a while back, for which I apologize, I don't really know what to say. May I have your permission to show my orders to my Exec and the chief of the boat, Captain Whittaker?"

"I think that would be a good idea," Whittaker said.

The chief of the boat read the orders over the Exec's shoulder. Both of them registered surprise on their faces, but said nothing.

"No questions?" Whittaker asked.

"What's in the boxes?" the chief of the boat asked.

"The long ones are packed with carbines," Hammersmith answered.

"And half the others are filled with ammo," Whittaker added.

"And the other half?"

"A million dollars' worth of gold coins," Whittaker said.

The chief of the boat accepted that stoically.

"Gonna be a bitch getting that stuff ashore in rubber boats," he said. "I don't suppose the people who'll be meeting you would have boats, real boats, something big enough to handle that weight?"

"That's one of our problems, Chief," Whittaker said. "Nobody knows we're coming."

"Holy shit!" the chief of the boat said, and then immediately got control of himself. "Well, we'll figure something out, Captain."

3

16 Degrees 20 Minutes North Longitude
43 Degrees 5 Minutes North Latitude
(Over the Adriatic Sea)
1520 Hours 16 February 1943

The B-25G "Mitchell" had been alone for hours high in the bright blue sky, its passage around the heel of the Italian boot and up the center of the Adriatic marked by twin trails of condensation (contrails) behind it. Far beneath it was an unbroken bed of clouds, stretching as far as the eye could see, looking like a vast layer of cotton wool.

Dolan was at the controls, Canidy in the co-pilot's seat, and Darmstadter was sitting on a fold-down jump seat immediately behind the pilots' seats. It was uncomfortable on the jump seat, but the foam-rubber and leather seats in the fuselage had little appeal for Darmstadter. When he was alone in the fuselage, he had too great an opportunity to think of what could go wrong. He was finding what reassurance he could from being close to Canidy and Dolan.

Darmstadter had been in the left seat when they left Malta, and had made the takeoff. But Canidy had taken over the controls after they had left the ground, and he was the one who had set the course and rate of climb and fine-tuned the engines and the mixture.

And then, matter-of-factly, he had told Darmstadter where they were going (but not why) and pointed out their course on a chart.

And then he had told him, patiently, even kindly, as a flight instructor teaches a student pilot, how it was planned for them to find Vis and what would happen if things went wrong.

Canidy explained that the OSS agent with the British SOE force on Vis had a radio transmitter-receiver capable of operating on the frequencies used for aviation. Using the radio direction-finding equipment[1] on the B-25G, they would home in on Vis very much as they would home in on Newark Airport after a flight from Washington.

With several significant exceptions:

"The trouble with RDF transmitters," Canidy said, "is that they can be picked up by anybody tuned to that frequency. For example, German or Italian aircraft. A curious Luftwaffe pilot looking for the way home from a patrol over the Adriatic might come across the signal from Vis and wonder what the hell it was.

"The worst possible scenario is that two pilots, or for that matter, two ground stations, might hear the Vis transmission at the same time, and mark their position and the relative position of the Vis transmitter on a chart. If they did that, all that would have to be done would be to put the chart marks together. Triangulation. You with me?"

Darmstadter nodded. He knew that without actually following a signal to its source, the location of the transmitter

[1]A rotating loop antenna mounted atop the fuselage, and a signal strength meter mounted on the instrument panel.

could be easily determined. "Triangulation" simply meant the drawing of straight lines on a chart from two different points of reception toward the source of the signal. The intersection of the straight lines indicated the location of the transmitter.

"So what they're going to do to reduce the odds of getting caught," Canidy said, "is to go on the air as little as possible. The first signal we'll listen for when we get close enough will be on the air for only five minutes. Then it will go off and come back on fifteen minutes later for sixty seconds on a different frequency and using different call letters."

He handed Darmstadter a typewritten list.

There were three columns. The first gave times, starting at 1500 and ending at 1745. Sometimes there was nineteen minutes between transmissions, and sometimes as little as eleven minutes. But there were no two intermissions alike. The second column listed the frequency of the transmissions. No two of these were alike. The third column listed the three-letter identification code which the transmitter would send, endlessly repeating them for the period of time it would be on the air.

"Clever," Darmstadter said.

"It presumes our guy on Vis has the transceiver, and that it's working, and that we'll be able to pick it up when we have to," Canidy said.

"And if we don't?" Darmstadter asked.

"That could pose some problems," Canidy said. "You'll notice that the Point of No Return[2] on the chart is here, and the point where we hope we can pick up the Vis RDF transmitter is here."

Darmstadter saw that the first place they could hope to pick up the direction-finding signal was at least two hundred miles from the Point of No Return.

"And if we don't get the RDF signal?"

"Then we go down on the deck and try to find it by dead reckoning," Canidy said.

"That would be kind of hard, wouldn't it?" Darmstadter asked.

---

[2]On an aviation course, the point beyond which return to the departure airport (or an alternate field) is impossible.

"Think positively, Darmstadter," Canidy said, drily. "But since you posed the question, I think it would be impossible."

"And then what?" Darmstadter asked.

"Then you have a choice," Canidy said. "You can take the airplane over the Yugoslav mainland, bail out, and take your chances that the Partisans might get you before the Germans do. If the Partisans get you, you're home free. If they don't, you'll have to take your chances with the Germans."

"What do you mean by that?"

"You tell them you were on a bombing raid, got lost, and bailed out when you ran out of gas. If they believe you, you sit out the war in a Stalagluft[3]. If they don't, you're in trouble."

"And where are you and Dolan going to be while I'm taking my chances with the Partisans?"

"Dolan and I will have drawn the 'Go Directly to Jail, Do Not Pass "Go" and Do Not Collect $200' card," Canidy said, matter-of-factly. "We can't get captured."

"Why not?" Darmstadter blurted.

"Because the Germans can find out anything they want to know from anybody, if they put their mind to it," Canidy said. "And there are certain things that Dolan and I know that you don't, and that the Germans shouldn't."

"What are you going to do?" Darmstadter asked, horrified, "to keep from getting captured?"

Canidy ignored the question. Instead, he handed Darmstadter another typewritten sheet of paper.

"There will be a bombing raid by B-25 aircraft on the boot of Italy," he said. "Here're the details, what you would be expected to know if you had gone on the mission. Memorize as much as you can, especially your unit, your aircraft number, your departure field. Use your imagination for the names of the crew. I think you can probably get away with it."

"And what, exactly, are you and Dolan going to do?" Darmstadter asked.

"To coin a phrase," Canidy said, "we'll cross that bridge when we get to it."

"I'd really like to know," Darmstadter persisted.

---

[3]Prisoner of War camp for aviation personnel.

Canidy thought it over a moment before replying.

"They gave us a pill," he said. "Actually, it's a small glass vial, filled with what looks like watery milk. When you bite it, it's supposed to work before you feel the little pieces of glass in your mouth. The idea is that we're supposed to bite it when it becomes clear we're not going to make it to Vis. But what I think we'll do is bail out over the mainland and take a chance the Partisans will find us before the Germans do. If we land in the lap of the Wehrmacht, *then* we'll bite the pill."

"What the hell do you know that makes suicide necessary?" Darmstadter blurted.

Canidy had not responded.

Just over an hour before, Canidy had turned on the radio direction finder. By then, the three of them had relieved for each other at the controls at roughly hourly intervals, and Dolan was then sitting in the pilot's seat. At first, the signal strength indicator needle on the instrument panel had made no response as Canidy turned the crank which rotated the loop antenna mounted atop the fuselage.

Then the needle jumped, just perceptibly, and he reversed his cranking motion, aiming the antenna at the source of the radiation. The needle crept very slowly, barely perceptibly, upward as the signal strength increased.

And then, very faintly, over the static in his earphones, Darmstadter began to be able to recognize one Morse code letter, Dah-Dah-Dah, D, and then another, and finally a third, until there was in his earphones, endlessly repeated Dah-Dah-Dah Dit-Dit-Dit-Dit Dah-Dah-Dah. He wondered if DHD meant something, or whether it had been selected because it was a long, readily recognizable string of letters.

"I don't think," Canidy's voice came drily and metallically over the earphones, "that's what they call 'right on the money.'"

Dolan looked up at the roof of the cabin, at the needle on the antenna rotating mechanism. Then he put the B-25G into a very gentle turn, in a very slightly nose-down attitude, and made small adjustments to the throttle and richness controls.

Finally, his voice came metallically over the earphones.

"Fuck you, Canidy."

A moment later, he straightened the B-25 on a course corresponding with that indicated on the radio direction finder, made a minute adjustment of the trim wheel, and then touched his intercom mike button again.

"And if you can refrain from walking up and down, Darmstadter, like a passenger on a ferry boat, I would be obliged."

Then he folded his arms on his chest.

The B-25 dropped very slowly toward the layer of cotton wool far below them.

The indicator needle on the signal-strength meter suddenly dropped back to the peg.

"You've lost the signal," Darmstadter said.

"That's probably because they've stopped transmitting," Dolan said drily. The B-25 flew on, in a very shallow descent.

Eleven minutes later, when they were still above the cloud cover, there was a one-minute transmission from Vis, and Dolan made a tiny course correction to line the plane up again on course before the signal-strength meter fell back to its peg again.

They were in the cloud bank when Vis came on the air again. Darmstadter could see about one inch past the windshield. There were a dozen or so drops of condensation on the window frame just past the plexiglass, for some mysterious aerodynamic reason undisturbed by the air through which they were passing at an indicated 290 knots. But beyond the drops of condensation there was nothing but a gray mass.

"You don't want to go down to the deck and see if we can get out of this shit?" Canidy asked. It was a question, Darmstadter understood, not a suggestion, certainly not an order.

Dolan shook his head, "no," in reply. And then a full minute later, spoke.

"If it looks like it's working, don't fuck with it," he said.

It sounded more as if Dolan was thinking aloud than replying to Canidy, or, Darmstadter thought a moment later, as if Dolan had called that old pilot's cliché from the recesses of his memory to reassure himself.

The point of the needle on the vertical speed indicator was indicating a descent only on close examination; on casual glance, it seemed to indicate level flight. The needle on the altimeter moved counterclockwise very slowly. But it was moving, and they were going down.

Twenty-odd minutes later, during another Vis transmission, Canidy said, "I wish that transmitter wasn't working quite that well."

It took Darmstadter a moment to understand what he meant. Then he did. The needle on the signal-strength meter was now resting against the upper limit peg; there was no way to judge if they were moving ever closer to the transmitter. The signal-strength meter was accepting all the signal strength it was capable of.

When the altimeter indicated 12,000 feet, Canidy pulled his oxygen mask free from his face and rubbed his cheeks and under his chin with his fingers. When Darmstadter removed his own mask, the fresh air passing through his nostrils and mouth seemed warm and moist. Dolan did not take his mask off. Darmstadter wondered if this was a manifestation of the declaration he'd made earlier, "if it looks like it's working, don't fuck with it," or if Dolan's concentration was on other things and he simply hadn't noticed they were at an altitude where it was safe to fly without bottled oxygen.

And then, suddenly, startlingly, they dropped out of the cloud cover. There was an ocean down there, and land to the front and the sides.

Canidy frantically searched through his aviator's briefcase and came up with a handful of 8″ x 10″ glossy photographs.

Dolan ripped his oxygen mask off.

"What was that you were saying, Dick, about 'right on the money'?" he asked.

"Jesus," Canidy said. "And I was right on the edge of agreeing with David Bruce that they shouldn't let old men like you fly."

The two looked at each other and beamed.

"Take her down to the deck, and make your approach around that hill on the left," Canidy said.

"Hey," Dolan said, annoyed, "I'm driving."

But he lowered the nose of the B-25, until they were no more than a thousand feet off the choppy seas of the Adriatic, and made a wide sweeping turn around the hill Canidy had indicated.

When they crossed the rocky beach, they immediately encountered the steep hills of Vis; so an indicated altitude of one thousand feet, which was based on sea level, put them no more than two or three hundred feet over the side of the hill, and then the level valley on shore.

"Go strap yourself in," Dolan ordered. "Quickly."

Reluctantly, Darmstadter made his way back to the leather upholstered passenger chairs in the fuselage. He had just sat down and was fumbling for the seat belt, when the nose of the B-25 lifted abruptly. Ignoring the seat belt, he pressed his nose against the plexiglass.

There were fifteen or twenty people on a crude runway, their arms waving in a greeting.

Then Dolan stood the B-25 on its wing and began a one hundred eighty degree turn. As the plane leveled off, there came the sound of hydraulics as the flaps and gear came down, and the engines changed pitch.

Darmstadter got his seat belt in place just as the plane touched down. There was a far louder than he expected rumble from the landing carriage, followed immediately by the change of pitch as the engine throttles were retarded. And then the plane lurched as if something had grabbed it.

Instantly, Darmstadter's view through the plexiglass disappeared in a gross distortion, and then almost as quickly the distortion seemed to be wiped away. He realized that what had happened was that water, a great deal of water, had splashed against the window.

The plane was now braking hard. Darmstadter felt himself being pressed against the upholstery of the rear-facing chair.

And then it stopped for a moment, and then turned around. As Darmstadter unfastened his lap belt, the engines died. The silence, broken only by the faint pings and moans of cooling metal, was surprising.

"Vis International Aerodrome," Canidy called cheerfully from the cockpit. "Connections to Budapest, Voodapest, Zoodapest, and all points east. *Thank you* for flying Balkan Airlines."

Chuckling, Darmstadter got to the access hatch in the floor behind the cockpit just after Canidy had dropped through it to the ground. Darmstadter jumped after him.

4

Headquarters, 344th Fighter Group
Atcham Army Air Corps Station, England
1650 Hours 16 February 1943

When Lt. Colonel Peter Douglass, Jr., returned to his quarters from the post-mission debriefing, the Underwood typewriter and the service record were waiting for him on the old and battered desk in his room.

It was SOP (Standard Operating Procedure). There was a system. There had to be a system. The SOP Lt. Colonel Douglass had set up was that in the case of pilots within a section, their section leaders wrote the letters, subject to review by squadron commanders. In the case of section leaders, squadron commanders wrote the letters, subject to review by the Group Exec. In the case of squadron commanders, or squadron executive officers, the Group Commander wrote the letters himself.

Douglass kicked off his sheepskin flying boots, sending them sailing across the small room in the curved-ceilinged Quonset hut. He took off his battered, leather-brimmed hat and skimmed it three feet toward a hook on the wall. It touched the hook, but bounced off and fell to the floor. He made no move to pick it up.

He reached into the pocket of the sheepskin flying jacket and came out with two miniature bottles of Old Overholt rye whiskey. Eighth Air Force SOP provided for the "post-mission issue of no more than two bottles, 1.6 ounces, bourbon or rye whiskey 86 proof or 100 proof to flight crew personnel, when, in the opinion of the attending flight surgeon, such issue is medically indicated." The Eighth Air Force SOP went on to stipulate that "in no case is the issue of more than two bottles permitted" and that "wherever possible, the issue of medicinal whiskey will be made only after flight crews have undergone post-mission debriefing."

And finally, the Eighth Air Force SOP stated that "medicinal whiskey so issued will be ingested in the presence of the prescribing flight surgeon."

Translated, that meant that unless you watched those crazy pilots, or, in the case of bombers, navigators, bombardiers, flight engineers, and aerial gunners, they were liable to hoard their "bottles, 1.6 ounces" of medicinal whiskey until they had enough to tie a load on, or worse, share it with people not entitled to medicinal whiskey.

Lt. Colonel Douglass walked to the battered desk, pulled the drawer open, and carefully laid his miniature bottles in it. There were already a dozen other bottles there. It was the 344th Fighter Group Commander's unofficial SOP to pass out his ration of medicinal booze to his pilots when he thought such issue was indicated for morale purposes. Sometimes, he passed it out to the enlisted men, too, in contravention of the spirit and letter of the Eighth Air Force SOP.

It bothered the hell out of the ground crews when their plane and pilot didn't come home. And some took it worse than others.

Saving the miniatures to pass out as he saw fit did not represent any sacrifice, booze-wise, on the part of Lt. Colonel Douglass. He had his own out-of-supply-channels source of booze, and when he had a couple of medicinal post-mission nips, he took them from a bottle of Scotch.

He shrugged out of the sheepskin, high-altitude flying jacket and threw it toward his bed. It too fell short of the target and slid to the floor. He left it there, and then pushed the suspenders holding up the sheepskin trousers off his shoulders. He stood on one leg to pull the trousers off, and then on the other leg to get them completely off. He then threw them toward his bed. This time he made it.

He then picked up a telephone.

"Meteorology," he said, when the operator came on the line. And then a moment later, "What have we got, Dick?"

His weather officer predicted perfect (that is absolutely unflyable) weather in England and over the European Land Mass for not less than 48 hours, and probably for as much as 72 or 96 hours.

"There's a stationary front, Colonel, a massive chunk of arctic air, which, meeting with an equally massive chunk of warm air from the Mediterranean . . ."

"What your colonel had in mind, Captain," Lt. Colonel Douglass interrupted him, "is whether or not it would be safe for him to get drunk for a day or two."

"In my professional meteorological opinion, Sir," the weather officer said, "you have that option."

"Thank you," Douglass said.

"Colonel, I'm sorry about Major Till," the weather officer said.

"Yeah," Lt. Colonel Douglass said, after a moment. "Thank you."

Then he hung up.

He went to a large, sagging-to-one-side wardrobe and worked the combination of the long-shafted bicycle padlock that, looped through two eye-rings, locked it. He opened the left door and looked inside, and then, frowning, the right door.

One lousy, half-empty imperial quart of Scotch! What the hell had happened to the rest of it?

He didn't like his own answer. *I have drunk the rest of it, that's what had happened to it. A couple of little nips here, and a couple more there, and the four imperial quarts of straight malt Scotch have evaporated.*

Well, what the hell, there was more where that came from. There was a sturdily locked room at Whitbey House stacked to its high ceiling with booze. Canidy ran the OSS Station at Whitbey House on the philosophy that unless his people were now given by a grateful nation the best available in the way of booze and food, there was a good chance that his people would not be around to get it later.

He would just have to run over to Whitbey House and replenish the larder, that was all there was to it. Canidy had declared him to be an Honorary Spook, with all the rights and privileges there unto pertaining, such as access to the booze larder.

And then he remembered that Canidy was gone. He was off on one of his nobody-knows-anything-about-it missions in his souped-up B-25G. Canidy had given Douglass no details, of course, other than that he "would be away for a couple of days." But then Douglass had learned that Dolan was off somewhere, too. And he'd flown over Whitbey House, and the B-25G normally parked there was gone.

Ergo: Canidy and Dolan were off somewhere doing something secret and important in the souped-up B-25G.

There was a steady, sometimes nearly overwhelming, temptation for Douglass to ask Canidy (or, probably smarter, to ask OSS London Station Chief David Bruce) to have him transferred to the OSS. And there was little question in his mind that it could be easily arranged: For one thing, if the OSS wanted somebody, they got him. No matter what assignment an officer (or for that matter an enlisted man) had, that was not considered as essential to the war effort as an assignment to the OSS would be.

And he was sure that David Bruce had at least considered that Lt. Colonel Peter Douglass, Jr., knew more about the OSS than he was supposed to.

Douglass had flown with Canidy and Bitter with the Flying Tigers in China and Burma, where their airplanes had been maintained by "Mr." John Dolan. It made no sense to indulge the notion that any of them would regard Doug Douglass as someone who couldn't be trusted with classified information, even if all of them, in fact, tried to keep him in the dark.

He had learned, for example, that Eric Fulmar was in Germany. He hadn't asked. Canidy had told him. He hadn't asked what Fulmar was doing in Germany. And he had tried, unsuccessfully, not to put two and two together. So he had come up with the answer that if Canidy and Dolan had gone off somewhere in the B-25G, it was very likely that they had gone to bring Fulmar home.

Finally, the Deputy Director of the Office of Strategic Services was Captain Peter Douglass, Sr., USN, Doug's father. Considerations of nepotism aside, it made sense to have Peter Douglass, Jr., in the OSS, since he knew so much about it.

There were reasons Douglass had not asked to be taken in. He would have been embarrassed to speak them out loud, for they would, he thought, seem both egotistical and overly noble. But in his own mind, he was one hell of a fighter pilot, and one hell of a commander. By staying where he was, he believed that he was probably saving lives.

He did not allow himself to dwell on the counter-argument, that Canidy and Bitter and Jimmy Whittaker and the others were also saving lives. Not directly, by shooting down a Messerschmidt on the tail of one of his pilots, nor even less directly, by doing the things that a good commander does to keep his men alive, but in an almost abstract sense. If what the OSS was doing could shorten the war by a week, or a day, or even by six hours, that would mean that the guns would fall silent around the world, and more lives would be saved in six hours than he could hope to save by being a good fighter group commander for the rest of the war.

That argument seemed to be buttressed by the fact that Canidy and Bitter and Whittaker had proven themselves as fighter pilots.

Douglass understood that he would not be asked to join the OSS. If they wanted him in the OSS, he would have been transferred into it long ago. He was going to have to join, submit an application, no matter how informal, and he didn't want to do that.

Lt. Colonel Doug Douglass carried what was left of the imperial quart of Scotch whiskey to the battered desk. He unscrewed the top, took a healthy swig from the neck, and then set the bottle on the desk.

He sat down, and rolled a sheet of printed stationery into the typewriter. Then he typed the date.

He would, he thought wryly, have been one hell of a squadron clerk.

He opened the service record and found what he was looking for. His fingers began to fly over the keys.

Mr. and Mrs. J. Howard Till
711 Country Club Road
Springfield, N.J.

Dear Mr. and Mrs. Till:

By now, you will have been notified by the Adjutant General that David has been killed in action.

He was my executive officer and my friend, and I share your grief.

The 344th Fighter Group was assigned the mission of protecting B-17 and B-24 bombers of the Eighth Air Force on a heavy bombardment mission to Frankfurt,

Germany. The Group was divided into two echelons. David commanded one, and I the other.

Some distance from the target, we were engaged by a large group of German Messerschmidt fighter aircraft. In the engagement that followed, David shot down two German fighters. He was going to the aid of another pilot when his aircraft came under fire from several Messerschmidts. David's aircraft was hit in the fuel tanks, which then exploded.

David was instantly killed, probably without warning.

He died, I think, as he would have wanted to, in aerial combat, leading his men as they protected other men.

"Greater Love Hath No Man Than He Lay Down His Life for Another."

The two German fighter aircraft he shot down brought his total kills to six. The posthumous award of the Air Medal (6th Award) has been approved. I have, in addition, just been informed by Eighth Air Force that David will also be awarded the Distinguished Flying Cross, and the citation will reflect his flying skill, devotion to duty and courage, not only on his last flight but during the entire period of his assignment to the 344th Fighter Group.

I am aware that military decorations are small consolation to you at this time, and can only hope that you will accept them as a token of the respect and affection in which David was held, not only by the officers and men of the 344th Fighter Group, but by the highest echelons of the Eighth Air Force.

David was a splendid officer and a fine human being. He will be missed.

If there is anything that I can do for you, please do not hesitate to let me know.

Sincerely,

Peter Douglass, Jr.
Lt. Col., USAAC
Commanding

When he had finished typing, he rolled the sheet of paper out of the typewriter and read it.

Then he ran an envelope into the machine and typed the envelope. He folded the letter, put it into the envelope, and then wrote "Free" on the envelope where a stamp would normally go.

He picked up the telephone, and when the operator came on the line said, "Find Captain Delaney and get him over here, will you?"

He walked to a small door beside the wash basin. Beyond was a small cubicle holding a shower and an ancient English water closet with a warped and cracked wooden seat. The shower consisted of a rusting shower head pointing straight down from the slanted ceiling to the brick floor of the shower. A three-tier layer of bricks kept the shower water in place, and a shower curtain, cut from a condemned parachute, hung from a wooden rod.

An oil temperature gauge, somehow modified by Douglass's crew chief, who had also laid the bricks and found the crapper somewhere, was mounted on the wall. The needle, pointing to a green "OK" strip, indicated 280 degrees Fahrenheit, but it had been explained to Douglas that he should ignore the indicated temperature; when the needle pointed to the "OK" strip, the water was at the proper temperature for a shower.

Douglass went to the wardrobe and took out fresh underwear and a clean uniform. Then he stripped. As he pulled his T-shirt over his head, he winced at the sharp, acrid odor. He knew what it was. It was the enduring odor of sweat-while-terrified. Literally, the smell of fear.

He relived for a moment the absolute terror he had felt for about twenty seconds when it had looked like the pilot of the Messerschmidt on his tail was going to succeed in turning inside Douglass's turn. It had been as if time had somehow slowed down, like a movie newsreel in slow motion; and while things had been in slow motion, he had been able to see the stream of German tracers moving ever closer to him.

And then the stream of tracers had stopped when the German pilot, who was good and knew his trade, realized that he wasn't going to make it. He had turned and dived sharply to the left.

As Douglass had turned to try to get on the German's tail, he had become aware that he was sweat-soaked.

"Jesus H. Christ!" Douglass said, disgustedly, throwing the T-shirt to the floor.

He went to his shower and turned it on full. It was hot, hotter than he liked, even too hot for comfort, but he stood under it, furiously rubbing red Lifebuoy soap over his skin, and then rinsing himself until the entire fifty-five gallons of the water supply in a former oil drum on the roof was exhausted.

He shut the head off and quickly opened a valve which would replenish the water in the drum. He heard a momentary hiss as the cold water struck whatever it was his crew chief had installed in the drum to heat the water, and he remembered that the crew chief had sternly warned him never to use all the water in the drum, otherwise the heating element would burn out.

"I've probably fucked that up, too," Douglass said aloud.

"Sir?"

"Nothing."

Douglass wondered how long he had kept Delaney waiting.

He wrapped a gray-white towel around his middle and went into his bedroom.

Delaney was a serious-faced Irishman from someplace in Iowa, a devout Roman Catholic with a wife and several kids, although he was only twenty-two or twenty-three years old. He had been sitting in the chair by the desk and had gotten up when Douglass entered the room.

"Sit!" Douglass said, and walked to his bed and pulled a clean T-shirt over his head.

"Who do you recommend to assume command of your squadron, Major Delaney?" Douglass asked.

"Sir?"

"By the authority vested in me by Eighth Air Force, you have been appointed Executive Officer of the 344th Fighter Group," Douglass said. "The job carries with it a gold leaf."

"I'm sorry about Major Till, Sir," Delaney said.

"Yeah," Douglass said. "I asked you a question, Major."

"I'm not sure I can handle it, Colonel," Delaney said.

"I made that decision," Douglass said. He had his undershorts on by then and was in the process of working his feet into Half Wellington boots. When he had them on, he walked to the desk and unscrewed the cap on the imperial quart of Scotch.

"Till, you unlucky bastard," he said, holding the bottle up. "I hope you went quick."

He handed the bottle to Delaney.

Delaney wiped the neck on his blouse jacket and took a swig.

"Maybe he was dead before he went in," Delaney said. "Needham followed him down, and he said he never got the canopy open."

"I just wrote his family that his ship blew up," Douglass said. "One of the things a field grade officer must know, Major Delaney, is when to lie."

Delaney looked at him and nodded, but said nothing.

"I will be gone for the next twenty-four to thirty-six hours," Douglass said. "You will tell whatever lie you think you can get away with if there are inquiries as to my whereabouts. I'm going to leave a number where I can be reached. You will use it only if necessary, and you are to give it to no one."

"May I ask, Sir, where you will be?"

"Repeating the caveat that you are to tell no one, I will be at Whitbey House in Kent. It's where the OSS hangs out."

"Yes, Sir."

There was relief in the way he said that, and on his face. The moral sonofabitch was afraid that I was going to tell him that I was going to be shacked up somewhere.

"It takes me about an hour and a half to get back here from there," Douglass said. "In case I am needed. I will not be needed to fly. I have checked the weather, and nobody will be flying."

"Yes, Sir."

"If you keep up that 'Yes, Sir' crap," Douglass said, "you will almost, but not quite, succeed in making me feel guilty for leaving my new executive officer in charge."

Delaney gave him a hesitant smile.

"Am I allowed to ask what you'll be doing with the OSS?"

"I am going to get drunk, Major Delaney," Douglass said. "I do that sometimes when something like Dave Till happens. It ill behooves a commanding officer to get shit-faced somewhere where his subordinates can see him in that condition."

"Yes, Sir," Delaney said.

"You will personally see to Till's personal effects," Douglass said. "Collect them, go through them to make sure there are no dirty pictures, love letters, or anything else that might suggest he was a healthy young male. Make an inventory of what's left, and leave it on my desk."

"Yes, Sir," Delaney said.

"How are you fixed for money?"

"Sir?"

"You have been promoted, Major," Douglass said. "It is a hoary tradition of the service that you have a promotion party."

"I have money, Sir," Delaney said. "But thank you."

"In this case," Douglass explained, "your party will also serve to keep our young warriors on the base tonight. You will lie again. You will tell them that just before the colonel left for High Wycombe[3] he left word that 24-hour passes for pilots are authorized as of—and not before—0400 tomorrow. It has been my experience that if I turn them loose after a mission like the one we flew today, they tend to behave in a manner unbefitting officers and gentlemen. And as you are about to find out, there is a good deal of paper work involved when one of our young heroes punches out an English cop, or steals a taxicab."

"I understand, Sir," Delaney said.

"You do, Jack, you really do. That's why I gave you the job."

"I hope I can measure up to your expectations, Sir," Delaney said.

"You may leave, Major," Douglass said. "And you may take the Scotch with you." Delaney looked surprised.

"If I took it with me," Douglass said, "I would never make it to Whitbey House."

"Thank you," Delaney said.

"By the time I get back, Jack," Douglass said, "I expect you to have made up your mind about who'll take over your squadron."

---

[3]Headquarters, Eighth Air Force was in a former private school for girls at High Wycombe.

Nine

1

The Island of Vis
1615 Hours 16 February 1943

FOUR MEN WERE on hand to greet Canidy, Dolan, and Darmstadter in the B-25.

One was a British officer wearing the red beret of a parachutist. The pips of a captain were on the shoulders of a sweater. Around his neck he wore a white silk scarf. There were two other Englishmen in British uniform. They were hatless and without insignia of rank. All three of the English had Sten submachine guns. The fourth man was in civilian clothing, a tie-less white shirt, a double-breasted, heavy suit jacket and baggy, unmatching trousers.

The British officer came to attention and saluted, an almost parade-ground salute, his hand, palm outward, quivering as he touched his temple with his finger tips.

"Afternoon, gentlemen," he said, casually. "My name is Hughson. Welcome to Vis."

Canidy returned the salute.

"You're the aircraft commander, Major?" Captain Hughson asked.

Canidy jerked his thumb upward to the cockpit of the B-25G.

"Commander Dolan's the aircraft commander," he said.

"With his permission, of course," Captain Hughson said, "I would suggest the thing to do is get the aircraft under cover."

"How do we do that?" Canidy asked.

Hughson gestured toward the hillside. Darmstadter saw there was a short, steep-sided indentation in the rocky hillside, a natural revetment, and that above it were rolls of camouflage netting.

As if reading his mind, the British officer said, "Except as netting, the camouflage isn't worth a damn. Unless, of course, we wish to give the impression that a North Africa wadi has been miraculously transplanted to the island."

"What do you do?" Canidy asked, chuckling.

"We artistically arrange local evergreens atop the netting," Hughson said. "And devoutly pray that it works."

"Let's get at it, then," Canidy said.

Capt. Hughson raised his hand above his head and snapped his fingers.

Eight Englishmen, in various combinations of uniform trotted up. One of them, with sergeant's chevrons sewn to his rough woolen jacket, stamped his foot and gave the captain a quivering-hand salute.

"Sir!" he barked.

Darmstadter saw Canidy's eyebrows go up at the noncom's parade-ground behavior.

"Would you have the chaps roll the aircraft into the revetment?" the British officer asked, conversationally.

"Sir!" the sergeant barked, and stamped his boot again.

The English soldiers, without further orders, went to the B-25G and started to push it. When they had trouble getting it moving, Canidy went to the left wheel, put his back against it, and tried to help. Darmstadter went to the other wheel and did the same thing. As he heaved, he saw that neither the British officer nor the civilian were helping. They even seemed surprised that Canidy and Darmstadter were lending a hand.

Once the initial inertia was overcome, their help was no longer needed, and they walked back to where the captain and the civilian stood.

Darmstadter saw Dolan finally drop through the access hatch, and then, taking a quick look around to see what was going on, begin to give directions to the pushers.

"Commander *Dolan,* you say?" the British captain asked.

"Right," Canidy said, "and this is Lieutenant Darmstadter."

The two shook Darmstadter's hand.

"I didn't catch your name," Canidy said to the civilian.

"Ferniany," the civilian said.

"Yachtsman," Canidy said, confirming his suspicion that the civilian was the OSS agent.

"We try not to use that identification unless we have to," Ferniany said.

"We're among friends, I think," Canidy said.

They all watched as the B-25G was turned, and then rolled backward into the natural revetment. And they continued watching as the British soldiers, with a skill that could have come only from practice, unrolled the camouflage net and propped it up over the airplane with trunks of young pine trees, and then covered the camouflage netting with branches.

Then Dolan walked over to them, and there was an exchange of salutes between Dolan and the British officer. Darmstadter saw that Dolan was as surprised by the display of parade-ground military courtesy as Canidy had been.

"This is Yachtsman," Canidy said.

Dolan smiled and shook Ferniany's hand.

"Where's Fulmar?" Dolan asked. He chuckled. "Or what is it we're calling him, 'Ex-Lax'?"

"I was about to ask," Canidy said.

"There is a minor problem with Fulmar," Ferniany said. "Actually, it's almost funny."

"What's almost funny?" Canidy snapped.

"He's doing ninety days in the coal mine at Pécs," Ferniany said. "For black marketing. Him and the professor. The girl is here."

"Go over that again," Canidy snapped. "Spare me the humor."

"The barge we were to travel on was boarded, just before we were supposed to leave Pécs," Ferniany said. "That happens sometimes. They found a lot of money on Fulmar. They naturally concluded that he was a black marketeer and hauled him and the professor off."

Darmstadter saw that B-25G was now well hidden from where they stood; from the air, it would be invisible. And the soldiers who had erected the netting over it were now walking down the "runway" where they had landed, sweeping the tire tracks with pine branches. Then he saw something that for a moment baffled him.

Two of the soldiers were rolling a boulder onto the center of the "runway." The boulder was taller than they were. There was no way that a bulldozer, much less two men, could move a boulder that size with such ease. Unless, of course, it was phony, like the boulders that careen down a mountain in the movies. That's obviously what it had to be, Darmstadter realized, and then saw three more boulders farther down the field on the far side of the stream that cut the runway in half.

"May I suggest, gentlemen," Captain Hughson said, "that we go to our digs? Every once in a while, Jerry flies a Storch[1] over for a look. It would probably arouse his curiosity to see us all standing about in this deserted meadow."

They followed him toward the hillside, where, hidden behind a bush, was the start of a narrow, steep path which wound its way up through the boulders and stunted trees. After they had climbed for five minutes, they came to the first of what turned out to be a series of caves in the side of the hill.

Captain Hughson led them into one of them.

A hissing Coleman lantern inside illuminated a small stone altar and crude paintings of people with halos on the cave walls.

They don't look like Jesus, Canidy thought, *they must be saints.*

He thought that his father would know whom the paintings depicted, what sort of Christian had painted them on the wall here, and when. The Reverend Dr. George Crater Canidy was an expert on early Christianity. It was the first time he had thought of his father recently. Whenever he did, he thought that his father would disapprove, if he knew what his son was doing.

The British SOE captain saw his interest.

"Orthodox," Hughson said. "I don't know *what* orthodox, but orthodox. They tell me that they came here after training

---

[1]The Feisler Storch was a small, two-place, high-winged monoplane, the German equivalent of the U.S. Army's L-4—or Piper Cub as it was better known.

in a monastery, and they carved out these caves, and then spent the rest of their lives in silence and prayer. Communal farm, that sort of thing, but all they did otherwise was think and pray. Rather unsettling, what, to think about it?"

"Well, at least they left us their bomb shelters," Canidy said, and then looked for Ferniany. When he had his attention, he went on, "Who carried Fulmar off where?"

"The Black Guard and some local cops," Ferniany said. "To the municipal jail in Pécs. That happens all the time, with legitimate black marketeers, I mean . . . how about that? a 'legitimate' black marketeer . . ."

"Hey!" Canidy said, sharply. "I've had about all of your scintillating wit I can handle."

"Just who the hell do you think you are?" Ferniany said.

"My name is Canidy. I'm both the action officer and your control, OK?"

"I thought you said Commander Dolan was the aircraft commander," Ferniany said, half accusingly.

"I did," Canidy said. "He *is* the aircraft commander."

"Major," Ferniany said, "I'm really sorry. It never entered my mind that you would show up here."

"A lot of things apparently 'never entered your mind,'" Canidy said. "Now, what the hell happened, one step at a time?"

"The cops in Hungary are like the cops in Hamtramck, Michigan, Major," Ferniany said. "They have their hands out. They want a slice of the pie, and then they look the other way. So far as they're concerned, if a Hungarian farmer sells a ham, or a couple of salamis to a 'tourist,' instead of selling it to the state, that's his business, providing they get their cut. They make sure that everybody understands the rules by picking people up every once in a while and putting them in jail. Like the cops raid the whorehouses in Cicero, on a roster basis. You understand?"

"And Fulmar got picked up . . . on a roster?"

"The Black Guard had a good day with him," Ferniany said. "I saw them counting the money they took away from him. How much did he have, anyway?"

Canidy ignored the question.

"How come they didn't pick you up?" he asked. "And you said the Dyer girl's here?"

"I'm not making my point," Ferniany said. "And it's important that I do."

"So make it," Canidy said.

"They didn't pick me up, or anybody else on the barge, because that would be killing the goose that lays the golden egg. They picked up Fulmar because he hadn't paid the toll."

"You mean beforehand?" Canidy asked. Ferniany nodded. "Well, if you knew about this system, why didn't you pay whatever had to be paid?"

"I had a decision to make," Ferniany said. "I decided it would be worth the risk . . . the word I got, presumably from you, Major . . . was to keep this operation as quiet as possible. I decided the best way to do that was to try to slip them through without paying off the cops . . ."

"You should have paid the cops," Canidy said.

"When you pay the cops, it's for a round trip," Ferniany said. "They would have been curious when these people didn't head back to Vienna with suitcases full of salami and ham."

"Your orders, Captain," Canidy said, icily, "were to see that under no circumstances were Fulmar and Professor Dyer to fall into German hands."

"You mean, I was supposed to 'eliminate' them?" Ferniany asked. "The thing is, Major, I'm new at this. I'm not used to the euphemisms: 'eliminate' for 'kill,' specifically. So far, it hasn't been necessary for me to kill people on our side. I don't know, frankly, what I would have done if I had thought they were going to be turned over to the Sicherheitsdienst or the Gestapo."

Canidy, his face rigid, looked at Ferniany a long time before he spoke.

"I don't know if I could have done it, either," he said finally, softly. "It's easier to order people to do something like that than it is to do it yourself."

"Major, it's five-to-one that long before their 90 days is up, they'll be turned loose. They're not making any money for the cops in the coal mines. The coal mines are a lesson, you understand?"

"I know what you're trying to tell me," Canidy said. "But there's more to this than you understand."

"Like what?"

"Like there was a very good reason for the elimination order," Canidy said.

"Are we back to that?"

Canidy didn't reply. He walked away from the others for a few moments, thinking. Then he came back to the group and turned to Captain Hughson.

"There is avgas here? Nothing 'almost funny' has happened to that?"

"There are twenty-five 55-gallon drums of aviation gasoline, Major," the British officer said. "Twelve, thirteen hundred American gallons."

"And some kind of a pump?" Canidy pursued.

"Hand pumps," Ferniany said. "Three of them."

"Are we sure it's clean gas?" Dolan said.

"The tanks are sealed," Ferniany said. "And there're both metallic filters and chamois."

"You better get on the refueling right away, John," Canidy said. "At first light tomorrow, after you put Darmstadter through a couple of touch-and-gos, I want you to make for Cairo."

Dolan accepted the order without question, with a nod of his head. But he was curious:

"Why Cairo? And aren't you coming with us?"

"Cairo because we have a pretty good radio link with our station chief there, and no, I can't go back with you."

"We have radio contact with London, Major," the SOE captain said.

Canidy ignored him.

"While you're fueling the plane," he went on, "I'll start encrypting a message for London. You give it, personally, to the station chief. His name is Wilkins, Ernest J. Wilkins, and he's a lot more competent than he looks. Tell him to get it right out, and then you wait there for further orders."

Dolan nodded.

"You'll take the Dyer girl with you," Canidy said. "If the decision is for you to go on to London, take her with you. If it isn't, turn her over to Wilkins, and have her put on ice. *His* ice. Make damned sure he understands that. She is not a prisoner, but I don't want her talking to anybody but you and the station chief."

Dolan nodded again. "Daylight will be at 0513," he said.

"Say twenty minutes to shoot two or three touch-and-gos, another half an hour to land, top off the tanks, and put the girl aboard. That'll get us out of here at no more than quarter past six."

"Fifteen minutes to shoot two touch-and-gos, and you'll be on your way at half past five. It's 1,500 miles, give or take a hundred, from here to Cairo. Presuming no bad head wind, that'd put you into Cairo in six hours, say noon Cairo time."

"Two other presumptions," Dolan said, drily. "That you have your reasons for taking a passenger while Darmstadter's shooting touch-and-gos, and that you have your reasons for us not to make a refueling stop at Malta."

"There are reasons, John," Canidy said, "but none you can't figure out yourself."

"Right," Dolan said.

Canidy turned to Captain Hughson.

"How do you cook your meat here, Captain?" he asked.

The British officer's eyebrows went up.

"Actually, there are two methods," he said, drily. "We usually heat the tins in boiling water. But sometimes, if the meat is your Spam, we take it from the tins and fry it for a treat."

"Could you rig up some sort of a spit over a fire?" Canidy asked.

"I'm sure you have a reason for asking," Captain Hughson said.

"There's four hundred pounds of Four-in-One beef[2] on the plane," Canidy said. "I thought perhaps SOE might like to entertain its visitors with the roast beef of Merry Old England."

For the first time, Captain Hughson smiled.

"Well, we'll give it a bloody good try, Major," he said.

"There's also some vegetables, but God only knows if they survived the cold," Canidy said. "You stick around, Ferniany," he ordered, "while I do the paper work."

"Yes, Sir," Ferniany said.

It took Canidy longer than he thought it would to get what details he needed from Ferniany, then to write his report,

[2]Boned beef packed for the U.S. Army Quartermaster Corps, prepared so that it could be roasted whole; cut into steaks; chunked for stew; or ground.

then to edit it down to as short a version as possible for encryption, and then for the encryption itself.

He carried with him simple transposition codes on water soluble tissue paper, one for each day, each five letter code block representing a word or a phrase he and the OSS Cryptographic officer had thought might be useful. But they had not considered the possibility that Fulmar and Professor Dyer would be locked up in a Hungarian municipal prison as petty criminals, so coming up with paraphrases for that situation from the available words and phrases was difficult. He had to laboriously build a second code from the code he had available, and by the time he had finally transferred the message Dolan would carry to Cairo for transmission, and had burned his notes and that day's code, a lot of time had passed. It was dark when they walked out of the cave.

They stood in the dark for a minute, until their eyes adjusted to the darkness, and then they followed their noses farther up the hill to the cave from which came the smell of roasting beef.

2

OSS Station Whitbey House
Kent, England
1905 Hours 16 February 1943

Captain the Duchess Elizabeth Alexandra Mary Stanfield, WRAC, Liaison Officer of His Majesty's Imperial General Staff to OSS Station Whitbey House liked First Lieutenant Charity Hoche, WAC, newly appointed Assistant Adjutant, from the moment she had first seen her getting out of the Ford staff car in front of Whitbey House.

Why she liked her, she could not explain. There were some women the Duchess liked at first sight, and some she didn't. But by and large her snap judgment first impressions were proven correct. Maybe in this case it was because Charity Hoche, although she looked up and somewhat shyly smiled at the Duchess and Lieutenant Bob Jamison as they started down the wide shallow stairs toward her, she did not ask for help, hauled her luggage from the back seat and, staggering under the weight, started to carry it up the stairs herself. And then with a look of chagrin on her face—and an "Ooops!"—Charity Hoche put down the right suitcase and saluted.

The Duchess returned the salute.

"Welcome to Whitbey House," the Duchess said. "And thank you for the salute, but we do rather little of that around here."

"I'm Bob Jamison," Jamison said. "Let me give you a hand with your bags."

"What a marvelous house," Charity said, reaching to take the Duchess's extended hand.

"Small and unpretentious," Jamison said drily, "but comfy. Sometime, when you have a free week or ten days, I'll show you around."

The Duchess liked Charity's smile and peal of laughter.

"My name is Elizabeth Stanfield," the Duchess said.

"Charity Hoche," Charity said. "How do you do?"

"Have you eaten?" the Duchess asked.

"Colonel Stevens took me by the Savoy Grill," Charity said, "for a final lecture on the conduct expected of me as an officer and a gentlewoman."

"Well, I think, under the circumstances, you're doing quite well," the Duchess said as they entered the foyer.

Jamison had been informed, and he had so informed the Duchess, of the decision to put Charity into an officer's uniform.

The Duchess found Charity's eyes on hers and saw in them both gratitude and appraisal. This was a highly intelligent woman, the Duchess decided. She wondered what her real role at Whitbey House was to be. There was a reason for the decision to put her into an officer's uniform, and it had nothing to do with the one offered: "that it would make things a little easier when she's dealing with the female personnel."

Charity laughed again, a pleasant peal of laughter, when she saw the signpost erected at the foot of the main staircase. It was ten feet tall and festooned with lettered arrows, and it gave the direction and miles to Washington, Berlin, Tokyo, Moscow, as well as to the mess, the club, and the officers' and billeting areas within the huge mansion.

"Don't laugh," Jamison said. "You'll need it. We have

three bloodhounds who do nothing but search for people who get lost on the premises."

Jamison set Charity's suitcases down in the corridor outside his office and motioned Charity inside.

"Before we go through the paper work," Jamison said, "let me make it official. On behalf of our beloved commanding officer, Major Richard Canidy, who is regrettably not available at the moment, let me welcome you to Whitbey House."

"Thank you very much," Charity smiled.

The Duchess saw on Charity's face that Charity had known that Canidy would not be here. And then she had the sure feeling that Charity knew why Canidy wasn't here, and very probably where he was and what he was doing.

There were documents for Charity to sign, and Jamison handed her an identity card overprinted with diagonal red stripes and sealed in plastic.

"The red stripes are what we call 'anyplace, anytime' stripes," Jamison explained, "meaning you go anywhere on the station whenever you wish. You'll probably be asked for the card a lot, until the security people get to know you, and you *will* be asked for it whenever you leave the inner and outer perimeters."

Charity nodded her understanding, glanced at the card, and tucked it in the breast pocket of her uniform tunic.

"That, except for the question of your billet, is it," Jamison said. "You have two choices. You can have a private room in the female officers' wing on the second floor, or you can move in with Captain Stanfield in the servants' quarters on the third floor."

"I'm in what used to be the apartment provided for . . ." she hesitated, just perceptibly, and then went on, "the Duchess's personal maid. There are two bedrooms and a sitter, and a private bath with a bathtub. There are only showers in the female officers' quarters."

"That's very kind of you," Charity said, "and I think I'd prefer that. But it raises a question."

"What's that?" the Duchess asked.

"You're my very first duchess," Charity said. "I knew a baroness one time, at school. But I don't know what to call you."

"Elizabeth, or Liz, will do just fine," the Duchess said.

Stevens had told her, the Duchess decided. Or David Bruce. Or possibly she had known even before she had arrived in England that the Imperial General Staff Liaison Officer to OSS Whitbey House Station had before the war occupied the house as The Duchess Stanfield.

"I'm perfectly prepared," Charity said, with a smile, "to curtsey . . . for that matter to prostrate myself . . . if it means access to a hot bath. What I had in London was a trickle of rusty tepid water. More like a bad leak than a shower."

The Duchess laughed.

"Well, come on then, we'll get you a hot bath. And you won't have to prostrate yourself, either."

The Duchess was surprised, almost astounded, to see what Charity Hoche's heavy suitcases contained. There was one spare uniform and several spare shirts, but the rest of the space was filled with cosmetics, soap, perfume, underwear and silk stockings.

Charity saw the surprise on the Duchess's face.

"We have a marvelous old sailor in Washington," she said. "Chief Ellis. He told me what to bring. He said that I could get anything GI over here without any trouble, but that if I wanted 'lady-type-things,' I should take them with me."

"You were given good advice," the Duchess said. "That's the first time I've seen more than three pairs of silk stockings at once in years."

"Help yourself," Charity said.

"Oh, I couldn't," the Duchess said.

"Oh, I wish you would," Charity said. "Sooner or later, there will be a chance for you to scratch my back. And there's three dozen pair, more than I can possibly use before Mommy sends me some more."

"Would you like me to prostrate myself now, or later?" the Duchess asked.

They smiled at each other, and the Duchess understood that her snap judgment of Charity Hoche had been on the money. A good woman, and a nice one. Charity handed her a dozen pair of silk stockings.

"Wear them in good health," Charity said.

Charity went to the tub, put in the stopper, and started to fill it. She then somewhat discomfited the Duchess by taking off all her clothes and walking around the bedroom starkers as she loaded her treasure of "lady-type-things" into a chest of drawers.

Then she got into the tub. The Duchess went to her room, threw away with great pleasure her remaining two pairs of silk stockings (which had runs in them) and put on a pair that Charity had given her. They made her feel good.

Then she saw her own hoard of "lady-type-things." It primarily consisted of twenty-two jars of Elizabeth Arden bubble bath. Her eyes teared. Just before he'd gone off wherever the hell he was, Jimmy Whittaker had helped himself to her last half-tin of bubble bath, and she had been furious.

Not too furious, she recalled, to accept his invitation to join in the bubbles. In fact, she'd probably really been more sad than angry. She had resigned herself to doing without bubble bath as she had resigned herself to doing without Jimmy Whittaker.

And then Bob Jamison had called her into his office, handed her a U.S. Army package from The National Institute of Health, Washington, D.C. (which was how the OSS identified its packages) stamped URGENT AIR PRIORITY SHIPMENT and a shipping label reading "Crystals, Soluble, Non-Explosive," and addressed to the "Officer-in-Charge, Agricultural Research Facility, Whitbey House, Kent."

"I think this is for you," Jamison had said.

It was a case of 24 bottles of Elizabeth Arden bubble bath crystals.

God, how I miss Jimmy!

And to hell with thinking about the illegal use of scarce air freight facilities and interfering with the war effort.

The Duchess took one of the bottles and carried it into the bathroom. Charity was slumped down in the tub, so that only her chin and her nipples broke the surface of the water.

"How about a little bubble bath?" the Duchess asked.

"Oh, I see it got here," Charity said. "I was afraid to ask."

"You know where it came from?"

"Yes," Charity said, "I know."

"I won't ask where Jimmy is," the Duchess said.

"I'm glad, because I can't tell you," Charity said.

The Duchess filed that away, professionally. Charity Hoche

was privy to upper echelon secrets. And knew how to keep them. And then she was a little ashamed for being professional.

"Actually, I had something specific in mind before," Charity said, "when I said there would come a time when you could scratch my back."

"Tell me," the Duchess said.

"How would I get Lieutenant Colonel Peter Douglass, Jr., on the telephone?"

"Doug's a friend of yours?"

"Understatement," Charity said. "At least on my part."

"The way we do that," the Duchess said, "is I get on the telephone, and when I have Colonel Douglass on the line, I bring the phone in here to you."

"Oh, nice!"

Two minutes later, the Duchess went back into the bathroom.

"Colonel Douglass is not available," she said. "He will not be available for the next thirty-six hours. I'm sorry."

"Damn," Charity said. She sat up abruptly, splashing water. "That means he's out spreading pollen."

"I don't think so," the Duchess said.

"Oh, come on," Charity said. "He doesn't know I'm here. And if you know him, you know he's just like the others. I'm not complaining. If I was in his shoes, I'd probably be doing the same thing. 'Live today . . .' "

"I would guess that he's off somewhere getting drunk," the Duchess said.

"Oddly enough, that would make me happy. Compared to what I really think he's up to. Why do you say that?"

The Duchess hesitated.

"Oddly enough, it's classified," she said.

"Oddly enough," Charity said, "I'm cleared for anything going on around here. Didn't Jamison tell you?"

"No," the Duchess said. "Are you really?"

"Yes, I am," Charity said. "Does that mean you're not?"

"I am accused," the Duchess said, "of being the resident spy for the Imperial General Staff. There is a grain of truth in the accusation. But I know about this."

"I really am cleared," Charity said. "Am I going to have to get Jamison up here to confirm that?"

"He'd love that, dressed as you are," the Duchess chuckled. "We'd better not."

Charity Hoche was obviously telling the truth.

"Probably because of his father," the Duchess said. "Or maybe just because he's Dick's good buddy, and Dick just uses that for an excuse, whenever Doug goes off on a mission, Eighth Air Force tells us. And they tell us when he comes back. TWX to Berkeley Square with info copy here. He flew a mission today. He made it back, but his executive officer was killed. I saw the TWX just before you got here. Under the circumstances, I don't think he's out . . . how did you put it? . . . 'spreading pollen.'"

"Thank you," Charity said, almost solemnly.

"You want the bubble bath?" the Duchess asked.

"What I would really like is a drink," Charity said, suddenly standing up and reaching for the flexible pipe shower head to rinse herself off. "I'll save the bubble bath for sometime when it'll be useful."

"That I can offer," the Duchess said. "We have a nice bar here, and sometimes even a piano player."

3

Lieutenant Ferenc "Freddy" János, the piano player, was a very large man. Which was, he thought, the reason he had broken his ankle. If one was six feet four inches tall and weighed two hundred and thirty pounds, one could not expect to be lowered to the ground by parachute as gently as could someone who weighed, say, one hundred sixty pounds.

And it wasn't really that bad. The doctor had, perhaps predictably, told him that it "could have been a lot worse." It had hurt like hell on the drop zone, and while the medics, heaving with the exertion, had carried him to the ambulance. But once they'd gotten a cast on it, there had been virtually no pain. A maddening itch under the cast, but no pain.

And the X-rays had shown a simple fracture of one of the major bones; he'd been told that "knitting, for someone of your age and physical condition" would be rapid. It was an inconvenience, nothing more. It had, of course, kept him from going operational. The bad landing and the resulting broken ankle had taken him off the team. He had been replaced by a lieutenant flown hastily from the United States.

Going operational would have to wait until they took the cast off (in three days; today was Tuesday, and the cast would come off on Friday) and probably for a couple of weeks after that; a week to become intimate with a new team, and however long it took after that to schedule and arrange for a mission.

The major problem that faced Lt. Ferenc "Freddy" János, as he saw it, was arranging to get laid between the time the cast came off and the time he went operational. That would require getting to London, and that was going to pose a problem, for the OSS did not like its people going into London once they had been made privy to a certain level of classified operational information.

He had been made privy to that level of classified information two days before the bad landing. It had then been intended that the men on his team parachute into Yugoslavia three days later. They had been taught—and had committed to memory in case the drop had not gone as planned—several alternate means to establish contact with the guerrilla forces of Colonel Draža Mihajlović.

This information was quite sensitive, and those in possession of it could not be trusted to go off and tie one on in London, or for that matter, anywhere off the Whitbey House estate. Freddy János understood the reasoning, for lives were literally at stake, and he was perfectly willing to grant that liquor loosened tongues, especially his. But he thought it would be a truly unfortunate circumstance if he had to jump in Yugoslavia following a long period of enforced celibacy. God alone knew how he could get his ashes hauled in Yugoslavia.

It wasn't that there were not a number of females here at Whitbey House (including two leaning on the piano at that moment as he played) who could with relatively little effort be enticed into his room. But he had what he thought of as his standards. For one thing, he did not think officers should make the beast with two backs with enlisted women.

This belief had not come from The Officer's Guide, which had euphemistically dealt with the subject, but from Lt.

János's own experience as an enlisted man. He had been enraged when he had suspected that his officers were dazzling enlisted women into their beds with their exalted position, and he was unwilling to enrage the enlisted men here by doing the same thing himself. He had even gone further than that. He had had a word with several officers about the matter; he had let them know their behavior displeased him, and that when he was displeased, he sometimes had trouble keeping his displeasure nonviolent.

There were female officers at Whitbey House (three American and one British), but the American WACs did not measure up to Freddy János's standard for a bed partner, and the British officer, Captain The Duchess Elizabeth Alexandra Mary Stanfield, WRAC, whom Freddy János would have loved to know much better, had proven to be the exception to the rule that upper-class women, when he looked at them with his large, sad, dark eyes, usually wished to comfort him with all the means at their disposal.

Freddy János had learned about the effect of his large, sad, dark eyes on women when he was fifteen. At fifteen, he was already nearly six feet tall and pushing one hundred eighty pounds. He had been accepted as a "protégé" piano student at the Juilliard School of Music in New York City. He had still spoken with something of an accent then, his father having brought them from Budapest to accept an appointment as concertmaster of The Cleveland Symphony only four years before.

Arrangements had been made for him to stay with friends of the family in a large and comfortable apartment on Riverside Drive overlooking the Hudson River. The friends had also been Hungarians and musicians, and it was their custom to hold Sunday afternoon musicales, in the European manner, sometimes trios, sometimes quartets, sometimes quintets; and he was naturally asked to play when a piano was required.

After one musicale, Mrs. Lizbeth Vernon, the lady in 6-B, one floor up, a tall, lithe woman of thirty-four, whom he had noticed smiling softly at him when he played, came to him and told him how much she had enjoyed his playing. And she went on to say that sometime when he had a few minutes, she hoped he would drop by her apartment and see if her piano was in tune. She had just had it tuned, but it didn't sound right, and she wanted a second opinion before she called Steinway & Sons and complained.

When he went to her apartment the next day after school, Lizbeth Vernon answered the door in a thin silk robe and told him that she had been under the sunlamp and hoped he wasn't embarrassed. Lizbeth also told him that she thought he was lonely, that she had seen it in his eyes, and that she understood his loneliness, because her husband, a regional manager for Merrill Lynch, the stockbrokers, was on the road from Monday to Thursday, so she was lonely herself.

There were a couple of awkward moments that afternoon, after Lizbeth learned that not only was he only fifteen, but that he had never been with a woman before.

"Jesus Christ!" Lizbeth said, horrified, as they lay sated in the biggest bed he had ever seen.

But she quickly recovered.

"Well, I'll say this," Lizbeth said, laughing deep in her throat as she grabbed him, "you *are* big for your age. And you *are* a protégé, aren't you?"

And Lizbeth told him that what had "driven me crazy" from the first moment she'd seen him was his eyes.

That had been, from beginning to end, a fine relationship. And it had lasted long after his "protégé" status had ended. Two years at Juilliard had convinced everybody, his father included, that despite his "early promise," he just didn't have what it would take to become a concert pianist.

He had often come down to Manhattan to visit Lizbeth (when her husband was out of town over a weekend) when he had been at Yale, working toward a degree in European history (with a minor in Slavic languages); and there'd been harsh words between them only twice: once when she had come to New Haven to surprise him and had found him in bed with a red-haired, white-skinned, Irish Sarah Lawrence student who had amazingly freckled breasts; and the other, in January 1942, when he had told her that he was going to enlist rather than wait until he graduated the following June.

Lizbeth had told him (actually screamed at him) that he was going to regret it when he woke up and found out what the Army was all about. If he had any sense at all, he would at least stay in school until he graduated and could get an officer's commission.

The Army had sent him to Fort Dix, New Jersey, for basic training, and then to Fort Knox, Kentucky, for tank training. He had loved all of it, even basic training. There was something about it that had made him feel for the first time in his life (out of bed) like a man. Piano protégés play pianos, not baseball or football, and as lousy as the Yale football team was, there had been no place on it for someone even of his size who had never handled a football.

He had made expert with the Garand rifle in basic training, the first firearm he had ever touched, and to his great delight and satisfaction had proven to be just as skilled firing the 75-mm tube on the M4A3 tank on the ranges at Knox. His record, education, and physical condition quickly got him into Officer Candidate School, and he was the Honor Graduate of his class of "ninety-day wonders."

But instead of being ordered to a tank company, Second Lieutenant Ferenc János was ordered to the 576th Military Government Detachment at Fort Benjamin Harrison, at Indianapolis, Indiana. There, a very military lieutenant colonel who four months before had never worn a uniform crisply informed him he was an officer now, and the Army made the decision about officer assignments. He spoke Hungarian and Croatian and German, and his services would be required to govern a defeated Germany and/or a defeated Hungary.

He had been compiling a list (because of his musical background) of German, Austrian, Hungarian, Bohemian, Moravian, and Yugoslavian church organs of historical and/or cultural importance when he had seen a notice on the bulletin board at Fort Benjamin Harrison that applications from officers speaking any of a list of foreign languages would be accepted for an unspecified assignment involving "great personal risk."

The lieutenant colonel who had told him that the Army made the decisions about officer assignment now told him that his application "bordered on the disloyal" and that he felt he should tell him that he would do everything in his power to have the application disapproved.

Two weeks later, Freddy János had found himself reporting

to a requisitioned estate in Virginia, known as OSS Virginia Station. So far as Freddy János was concerned, it was even better than Forts Dix and Knox. Here he was taught really fascinating things, such as how to blow up bridges, and parachute from airplanes, and kill people with your bare hands.

And then, just before he was to go back to Hungary, he broke his goddamned ankle.

"Hey, Freddy!" an officer called in disgust from across the room, "Jesus Christ!"

It took Freddy János just a moment to understand the nature of the complaint. Lost in thought, wallowing in self-pity over his enforced celibacy, he had without thinking gone from Gershwin to Prokofiev. He listened to what his subconscious had selected for him to play. He smiled. It was the Sonatina in G Minor, Opus 54, Number Two, from "Visions Fugitives." Very appropriate.

"You just ain't got no couth, Sanderson," Freddy called back, and then segued into "I'm Gonna Buy a Paper Doll."

He smiled at the two women leaning on the piano.

And then he looked beyond them to the bar. Captain The Duchess Stanfield was walking up to it, and she was not alone.

Absolutely gorgeous! God was obviously feeling good when he made that one!

And an officer! No restrictions!

What he would do, Freddy decided, was wait until they got their drinks and sat down someplace. Then he would just wander over and say "Hi!"

It was too much to hope that they would come by the piano, where he would have a chance to dazzle the absolutely ravishing blonde with some piano pyrotechnics and then smile sadly at her.

But they did just that.

God is on my side! Virtue is its own reward!

"Hello, Freddy," the Duchess said, as she hopped onto the piano itself.

"Hello," he said.

"Charity, this is Freddy János," the Duchess said.

"Hello," Charity said, smiling at him, giving him her hand, meeting his eyes.

"I'm overcome," Freddy said, taking her hand, marveling at the softness of it, the warmth, the *utter femininity* of it.

"Freddy has a broken ankle," the Duchess said. "I'd get my hand back if I were you, but after that you're fairly safe; he can't run at all well."

"How did you break your ankle?" Charity asked, compassion and sympathy in her eyes and voice.

And where there is compassion and sympathy, can passion be far behind?

"Small accident, landing by parachute," Freddy said, with a smile and what he thought was just the right touch of becoming modesty.

"Oh, Jesus!" Charity breathed.

Freddy hadn't expected quite that reaction and looked at her in surprise. She wasn't looking at him, but over his shoulder at the door.

A flyboy had come into the bar. Freddy had seen him before. He was a buddy of Canidy, the headman. It was rumored that he was the son of some big shot in the higher echelons of the OSS. He was also supposed to be an ex-Flying Tiger. He was also pretty goddamned young to be a lieutenant colonel.

He headed straight for the bar, without looking toward the piano.

"Doug!" the absolutely stunning blonde called. Or tried to call. She seemed to be having trouble with her voice.

He didn't hear her.

"Colonel Douglass!" the Duchess called, in her clear, crisp voice.

The flyboy looked for her, found her, and waved casually, dismissing her.

And then did a double take.

Then he walked to the piano, right to the blonde. He didn't look at anyone else, and he didn't speak.

He put his hand up, very slowly, very carefully, as if afraid when he made contact that the apparition would disappear, as does a soap bubble when touched, and touched the blonde's cheek.

"Doug," the blonde said again, as if she was about to cry.

The flyboy took his fingers from the blonde's cheek and

reached down and caught her hand, and led her wordlessly out of the room.

"Sorry about that," the Duchess said. "I saw your eyes light up."

"One gathers they have met before." Freddy said.

The Duchess chuckled.

"Did my eyes really light up?" he asked.

"Yes, they did," she said.

"Why are you so sure they didn't light up for you?"

She met his eyes.

"Sorry, Freddy," the Duchess said.

She had sad eyes, he saw. There was something in them that made him want to comfort her. Really comfort her, not screw her. Well, maybe both, but first comfort her. And then he saw in her eyes that she was neither going to let him comfort her or screw her.

"Me, too," Freddy said.

4

The Island of Vis
0525 Hours 17 February 1943

Canidy was sitting on a ten-foot-tall boulder, half buried in the side of the valley, his legs dangling over the side, sipping coffee from a gray pottery mug. Ferniany was sitting beside him, and Capt. Hughson was standing behind them.

Canidy winced when the B-25 on its landing roll came to the shallow stream in the middle of the runway and set up an enormous cascade of water.

But the B-25 did not deviate from its path.

It rolled another three yards, braking hard, so that inertia depressed the piston on the nose gear almost completely. Then it stopped and turned, and began taxiing back down the runway.

When it passed the boulder, Dolan, in the co-pilot's seat, made a "what now?" gesture with his hands, holding them out palms up, and shrugging.

Canidy made a "take it up" gesture, followed by a "bye-bye" wave. Dolan nodded and smiled, and then put his hands over his face in a "Oh my God! we're going to crash!" gesture.

The B-25 reached the inland end of the runway sixty seconds later, turned, ran up its engines, and then started to move. As it passed the boulder, Canidy could see the expressionless face of Gisella Dyer through the plexiglass window in the fuselage. He waved at her. There was no response.

There was another eruption of water when the B-25 passed through the stream again, and it visibly slowed. But then it picked up speed again quickly, the nose wheel left the ground, and a moment later it was airborne.

The wheels went up, and the flaps, and then it climbed steeply.

Canidy watched for a minute until the plane was barely visible, and then he stood up, draining the coffee mug.

"OK, Ferniany," he said, "let's get our show on the road."

They walked off the top of the boulder where it joined the wall of the valley, and then slid rather than walked to the valley floor. A three-wheel German Hanomag truck, sort of an oversized three-wheel motorcycle, was parked there. The Hanomag had a canvas-covered truck bed; Canidy and Ferniany got in the back and closed the canvas tail-curtain over them, then Hughson kicked the engine into life and got behind the steering wheel.

They made their way about four miles down a path that turned first into a narrow cobblestone road and then into a rough macadam street. In a little while, they turned off onto a steep, narrow dirt path that led them to the water's edge.

When Canidy climbed out of the Hanomag, he saw a 38-foot-high prowed fishing boat two hundred yards offshore dragging a net to the regular explosive snorting of a two-cylinder diesel engine. Just as he thought he saw the glint of binoculars in the small wheelhouse, the sound of the diesel engine changed pitch, the fishing boat slowed and then went dead in the water, and men started to retrieve the net.

When it was aboard, the boat headed for the beach in a wide curve.

"I don't know how he's going to like this," Ferniany said.

"I hadn't planned to ask him," Canidy snapped. "Maybe he'll be smart enough not to volunteer an opinion."

The moment he said it, he was a little sorry. There was something in the chemistry between him and Ferniany that produced dislike without real reason. But that wasn't why he had snapped at him. The reason for that was that Ferniany was close to the truth. "Saint Peter," the OSS agent on the fishing boat, was probably not going to like what he was about to learn. Nor would Stevens and Bruce, and if it got that far, Capt. Douglass or Colonel Donovan.

The OSS agents on the scene would be annoyed both by having their thunder stolen by a visiting brass hat and by the extra risk his grandstanding would mean. And Stevens and Bruce would bitterly question his decision to go into Hungary himself. First and foremost was the question of his running the risk of falling into German hands. And right on the heels of that was the equally valid question of whether he could do what had to be done any better than Yachtsman and Saint Peter could do it.

Captain Hughson touched Canidy's arm.

"There's a rock over the water," he said. "You can jump from it to the boat."

He nodded toward it.

"Would you like to take this with you?" Hughson asked, unslinging his Sten submachine gun from his shoulder and offering it to Canidy.

"Have you got another one?"

"Actually," Hughson said, "there's a Schmeisser[3] in my cell I've been looking for an excuse to carry."

"Then thank you, Hughson," Canidy said, and took the submachine gun from him.

"You will be a good chap, won't you, Major, and make an effort to return the Sten to me, in person?" Hughson said.

"Despite what everybody apparently thinks," Canidy said, "I am *not* charging foolhardy into the valley of death."

---

[3]The German Erma (Erfurter Maschinenwerk) 9mm submachine gun, standard for the Waffen-SS, was a reliable, accurate weapon held in high regard by the British, Russians and Americans, who for reasons never satisfactorily explained, insisted on calling it "The Schmeisser." The genuine Schmeisser was a far inferior weapon.

"No, of course, you aren't," Hughson said. He put out his hand, and Canidy took it.

The boat nosed in to the rock. First Ferniany and then Canidy jumped onto the deck. Immediately, the boat headed offshore.

There were two men in the wheelhouse, both dark-haired and dark-skinned, both needing a shave, and both dressed in dark blue fisherman's trousers and rough brown sweaters. It was only when one of them spoke in English to Ferniany that Canidy had any idea which was the genuine fisherman and which the SOE agent with the code name "Saint Peter."

"And what, might one dare inquire, is one supposed to do with this downed, if intrepid aviator?" Saint Peter asked in an upper-class British accent.

Ferniany chuckled. "Major Canidy, may I introduce Lieutenant J.V.M Beane-Williams, late of the Household Cavalry?"

"How'd'ja do?" Lt. Beane-Williams said with a smile, offering his hand. "I hate to put it to you so bluntly, Major, but you have, so to speak, just entered the 'Out' door. England . . . I presume you came from England . . . is in quite the opposite direction."

Canidy chuckled. He liked this Englishman.

"Hughson tells me that you can put us ashore on the mainland," Canidy said.

"I presume there is a reason?" Saint Peter said.

"Some place where we can make contact with Mihajlović's guerrillas," Canidy said. "Our ultimate destination is Budapest, and the sooner we can get there, the better."

"Budapest is rather nasty this time of year," Saint Peter said. "Snow and slush, and ever-increasing numbers of the Boches. But I daresay you've already considered that, haven't you?"

Without waiting for a reply, he entered into a conversation with the Yugoslavian captain.

Finally, he turned to Canidy.

"Tódor suggests we put you ashore at Ploče," he said. "He has a first cousin twice removed there. Or did he say a 'second cousin, once removed'? He also asked that I express his practically boundless admiration for your wristwatch."

Canidy looked at the Yugoslavian captain, who was smiling warmly at him, exposing two gold and two missing teeth.

Then he unstrapped his chronometer and handed it to him.

The Yugoslavian said something, and Saint Peter translated.

"He says, 'Oh, I couldn't.' "

"Tell him I insist," Canidy said.

The Yugoslav unstrapped his cheap watch and handed it to Canidy.

"He says," Saint Peter said, "that if you insist . . ."

Canidy chuckled.

"It's sixty miles, or thereabouts, to Ploče," Saint Peter said. "If we're not stopped, it should take us four, perhaps four and a half hours."

"And if we're stopped?"

"Then none of us will get to visit Ploče's many historical and cultural attractions," Saint Peter said.

Ten

1

Cairo, Egypt
1220 Hours 17 February 1943

First Lieutenant Hank Darmstadter was riding in the co-pilot's seat working the radios when Commander John Dolan suddenly reached over and grasped his upper arm in a very tight grip.

Startled, Darmstadter looked at him. Dolan's face was white and beaded with sweat. He seemed to be in pain.

"Indigestion," Dolan said, with a terrible effort. "There's a bottle of medicine in my briefcase. Get it, will you?"

The first thing Darmstadter remembered, as he hastily unfastened his seat and shoulder harness, was that Dolan had been medically retired from the Navy before the war because of a heart condition.

Jesus, he's having a heart attack!

Dolan's black leather Navy-issue briefcase was on a shelf in the passageway between the cockpit and the auxiliary fuel tanks that had been installed in the bomb bay. Its contents expanded the accordian folds, and Darmstadter grunted with the effort it took to open the catch and the straps that held it closed.

As he started rummaging through the briefcase, he glanced past the auxiliary fuel tanks into the fuselage. The German girl was looking at him. She had her hair done up in braids, which she had then coiled on the sides of her head. Darmstadter wondered who she was and why getting her and her father out of Germany had been worth all the effort it had cost.

They had been introduced, and she had politely shaken hands, but had remained silent. From the way her eyes had followed the conversation, however, Darmstadter had known that she at least understood English. And yet, she had asked no questions, not even about where they were taking her. He wondered if she was in some kind of emotional shock, or simply acknowledging that for the moment she had no voice whatever in what happened to her.

Then he had a strange thought. He wondered what she had done during the flight about taking a leak. There was a relief tube in the cockpit, but that wouldn't have done her any good, even if she had known about it and asked for it.

He returned his attention to Dolan's briefcase. There was everything in it, from a copy of *TM B-25-1 Flight Operation B-25 Series Aircraft* to a change of socks and underwear and a toilet kit. And a pint bottle of a bright red liquid with a label reading "Medical Corps, U.S. Army" and the typewritten message: "Lt. Commander J.R. Dolan, USNR, Take As Required for Indigestion."

Darmstadter hurried back to the cockpit.

Dolan reached for the bottle. Darmstadter unscrewed the cap and handed it to him.

"Sit down and take it," Dolan ordered. Then he waited until Darmstadter had gotten back into the co-pilot's seat, fastened his seat and shoulder belts again, and nodded to show his readiness to fly the airplane before he put the bottle of bright red liquid to his lips.

He took a large swallow, hesitated, and then took a second. In a moment, the look of pain on his face went away, and he managed a weak smile.

Darmstadter looked at the instrument panel. They had been homing in on the Cairo RDF for the past thirty minutes. The needle on the signal-strength gauge was almost at the upper peg. They were flying ten degrees to the left of the direction indicated by the needle on the RDF antenna indicator.

Darmstadter made the course correction and then looked at Dolan again. The startling paleness was gone from his face.

"You better start letting down," Dolan ordered. "Thousand feet a minute."

Darmstadter nodded, then reached over his head for the trim wheel and lowered the nose. After that, he retarded the throttle just a hair.

There was time to reconsider his first alarmed conclusion that Dolan was having a heart attack. That had been, he decided, a fear reaction. What was wrong with Dolan was what Dolan had told him: an attack of indigestion. He probably had them often, for he was carrying the bright red indigestion medicine with him.

Dolan said something, and Darmstadter missed it.

"Excuse me?"

"I said it must have been Canidy's goddamned steaks," Dolan said, leaning over to make himself heard over the roar of the engines. "Every time I eat charred meat, it does it to me."

Darmstadter nodded.

He was right back to *Dolan was having, had had, a heart attack.* He'd smelled Dolan's breath when the older man had leaned over. Whatever was in that bottle, bright red or not, usually came in a narrow-necked bottle with a label reading "Sour Mash Bourbon."

"You better sit it down," Dolan said, leaning over again and sending Darmstadter another cloud of bourbon fumes. Then he slumped back against the cushions of the pilot's seat and took another healthy swallow of "indigestion medicine."

Darmstadter reached for the microphone and put it before his lips.

"Cairo, Army Four Three Three."

A voice with the unmistakable tones of Brooklyn came over the earphones.

"This is Cairo, go ahead, Army Four Three Three."

"Army Four Three Three, a B-25 aircraft, is passing through niner thousand about thirty miles north of your station. Request approach and landing."

"Four Three Three, Cairo. The winds are from the north at ten, gusting to twenty. Visibility is unlimited. The altimeter is Two Niner Niner Niner. Descend to three thousand feet and report when you have the airfield in sight."

"Cairo, Four Three Three. Understand three thousand," Darmstadter said and hung his microphone up.

Then Dolan's voice came over his earphones, and he turned and saw that he had his microphone in front of his lips.

"Cairo," Dolan said. "Four Three Three. Four Three Three is Ninth Air Force flight Four Zero Five. Acknowledge."

Darmstadter wondered what the hell that meant. It didn't surprise the Cairo tower.

"Four Three Three," the operator with the Brooklyn accent said, "Cairo. Roger your Flight Four Zero Five."

Darmstadter could see three large pyramidal structures to his left.

My God, those are the *pyramids!! The real ones!*

And then he looked to his left and picked up his microphone again.

"Cairo, Four Three Three, I am at four thousand five hundred. I have the field in sight."

"Four Three Three, Cairo. Maintain present course and rate of descent. You are cleared as number one to land on Runway Three Four. The altimeter is Two Niner Niner Niner. The winds are from the north at ten, gusting to fifteen. Report on final."

"Four Three Three, Roger."

Darmstadter looked at Dolan as he reached for the throttle quadrant. Now, there was a sort of dazed look on his face. And he had not reached for the plastic sealed landing checkoff list hanging from the instrument panel.

Darmstadter realized that he was going to have to land the airplane himself, without help. But he was more concerned about Dolan's condition than he was about getting the flaps and gear down without help.

He turned to the right, and then the left.

"Cairo, Four Three Three on final."

"Roger, Four Three Three. You are number one to land. Look out for the C-47 on the threshold."

Darmstadter put on twenty degrees of flaps, and then lowered the gear. He came in low and slow and put it on the ground within a hundred yards of the threshold.

"Four Three Three on the ground."

"Four Three Three, take Taxiway Five, a Follow Me will meet you."

"Roger," Darmstadter said.

Taxiway Five was the last turnoff. As he taxied down the runway to it, Darmstadter saw a jeep racing down a taxiway parallel to the runway. The jeep was painted in a black-and-white checkerboard pattern, with a huge checkerboard flag above it flapping in the wind.

When he turned the B-25 off the runway, the jeep was there waiting for him. It led him to a remote corner of the field. There was a large hangar there whose doors were being opened as they arrived. The Follow-Me jeep stopped, and a ground handler hopped out and signaled for Darmstadter to move to the hangar doors. When the nose of the B-25 was ten feet from them, he gave the throat-cutting sign to stop engines.

Immediately, a dozen GIs came out the hangar and manhandled the B-25 inside the hangar. Darmstadter sensed, from the decreasing light inside the hangar, that the doors were being closed.

He looked at Dolan.

"You all right, Commander?" he asked.

"The word you have to keep in mind, Darmstadter," Dolan said, "is 'indigestion.' Am I going to have trouble with you about that?"

"No, Sir," Darmstadter said, after a moment.

"Thank you," Dolan said, simply and sincerely.

"What happens now?" Darmstadter asked.

"I don't know," Dolan said. "Canidy gave me that 'Flight Four Zero Five' message just before we took off. I expect somebody will show up shortly. In the meantime, you might have them start to refuel it."

When Darmstadter dropped from the belly of the B-25, he saw that there were two Military Policemen, armed with Thompson submachine guns, guarding the airplane. And there was a captain, wearing an AOD (Aerodrome Officer of the Day) brassard.

Darmstadter walked over to him and saluted.

"I'd like to get this fueled," he said.

"Someone will be along for you shortly, Lieutenant," the

AOD said. "In the meantime, nothing comes into, or goes out, of this hangar."

"We have a female passenger aboard," Darmstadter said. "She has to use the can."

"I don't know if there's one available," the AOD said.

"There has to be something," Darmstadter said.

"Jesus Christ!" the AOD said in annoyance.

"Sorry as hell to inconvenience you," Darmstadter flared.

The AOD glared at him.

"Who the hell do you think you are, Lieutenant?"

"I'm only a lieutenant," Darmstadter said, "but I can ask Commander Dolan to come down here if you have to have that as an order."

"Sergeant!" the AOD said, and one of the submachine gun armed MPs came over.

"There is a female aboard this aircraft who needs the facilities," he said. "Take her there and bring her back."

Darmstadter climbed back into the aircraft.

"Would you like to . . ."

"I must have the ladies' room," Gisella Dyer said, in precise if uneasy English.

"Come with me," Darmstadter said.

Five minutes later, before Gisella had come out of the men's room at the rear of the hangar, a side door opened and two men in U.S. Army Civilian Technician uniforms came in.

The AOD indicated Darmstadter with a nod of his head.

One civilian walked up to him and held a leather folder in front of Darmstadter's eyes. They were OSS credentials, but Darmstadter had never seen any before, and it took him a moment to realize what they were.

The man's name was Ernest J. Wilkins.

"You're the flight Four Zero Five?" Wilkins asked.

"That's right," Darmstadter said.

"You want to tell me what this is all about? Before that, you want to show me your identification?"

"I think maybe you better go aboard and talk to Commander Dolan," Darmstadter said. "I'm just an airplane driver."

"Why don't *you* go aboard and ask Commander Dolan to join us?" Wilkins said, sarcastically.

"He's a little under the weather," Darmstadter said.

"What's wrong with him?"

"Indigestion," Darmstadter said.

"Jesus H. Christ!" Wilkins said, but he went to the access hatch and climbed aboard the B-25.

There was a marked change in Wilkins's attitude when he climbed back down from the airplane.

"Captain," he said to the AOD. "Get on the horn and get an ambulance over here. There is no medical emergency, we will not need a physician. I will require one of the MPs to come with us. This airplane is to be refueled and kept under guard in this hangar. I presume you have cautioned your men to keep their mouths shut?"

"Yes, Sir," the AOD said.

Gisella Dyer, trailed by the MP sergeant, walked up.

"Good afternoon, Miss Dyer," Wilkins said to her in fluent German. "Welcome to Egypt. We're going to go from here to a place where you'll be staying for a while. I'm afraid, for reasons of security, that you'll have to travel by ambulance. It'll be a little warm in the back, but we don't have far to go."

Thirty minutes later, Dolan, Darmstadter, and Wilkins were in what had once been the pool house by the swimming pool of a wealthy Egyptian banker. The blue, tile-walled room now held an impressive array of communications equipment under the supervision of a gray-haired, distinguished-looking man who wore a ring, an amethyst surrounded by the legend "20 Years Service-AT&T."

Dolan seemed to be completely recovered from his "indigestion." The color was back in his face, and he was no longer tensed with pain.

Darmstadter was uncomfortable. There was no doubt in his mind that there was a hell of a lot more wrong with the old sailor than indigestion. What was his duty, to tell Wilkins (who had identified himself as Station Chief, Cairo) so that Wilkins could, by force if necessary, get him medical attention? Or to obey Dolan's admonition to "keep in mind that the word was indigestion"?

Dolan himself answered the question.

When London acknowledged receipt of the encrypted message from Canidy and ordered Cairo to stand by while the message was decrypted, Dolan handed the man with the AT&T ring a sheet of paper.

"Encrypt that, and send it, urgent, before they get off the air," he ordered.

When the communications officer had run the message through the encryption device and begun to transmit the encoded message, Dolan reclaimed the sheet of paper and handed it to Darmstadter.

"To OSS London Station. Eyes Only Bruce and Stevens. Suffering severe intestinal distress and fever. Probably recurrence of malaria. Have made Darmstadter aware of all repeat all operational details in case his assumption command necessary. Dolan, Lieutenant Commander, USNR."

When Darmstadter looked at him, Dolan shrugged.

"What the hell, kid," the old sailor said. "You didn't really want to go back to flying gooney birds, did you?"

2

OSS London Station Berkeley Square
London, England
1105 Hours 17 February 1943

There is a three-hour time difference between Cairo and London. The message transmitted from the pool house of the villa in Cairo at 1405 Cairo time was acknowledged by London at 1110 London time. The second acknowledgment (confirming satisfactory decryption in London) was sent to Cairo at 1124, London time, and the second acknowledgment of Dolan's message at 1141, London time.

Both encrypted messages had come out of the encryption/decryption device in Berkeley Square in the form of punched tape. It was necessary to feed the punched tape into another machine (a converted teletype machine), which then typed out a copy on paper. The messages were next entered in the Classified Documents Log, and finally they were put, separately, inside two cover sheets. The outer was the standard TOP SECRET cover sheet, and the inner one was stamped with both TOP SECRET and EYES ONLY BRUCE AND STEVENS.

It was by then 1158.

Rank hath its privileges, and the privilege the senior Cryptographic Officer of OSS London Station, twenty-six-year-old Captain Paul J. Harrison, Signal Corps, had claimed for himself was the day shift, 0800 to 1600. And just as soon as he could get the personnel section at SHAEF (Supreme Headquarters, Allied Expeditionary Force) off their ass to pin second lieutenants' bars on two of his sergeants, he intended to take no shift at all. But now, with his perfectly qualified sergeants barred from acting as Cryptographic Duty Officer by a bullshit directive from David Bruce, he had the duty.

As was his custom with EYES ONLYs (the 40-page SOP for Classified Documents made no specific reference to who should physically carry messages), Capt. Harrison personally took both messages up from the cryptographic room in the subbasement to the Station Chief's office.

Capt. Helene Dancy told him that David Bruce had moments before left the building. He was to have lunch with Lieutenant General Walter Bedell Smith, General Dwight D. Eisenhower's deputy at SHAEF. "Beetle" Smith and David Bruce were friends as well as professional associates. Knowing this, Eisenhower had for all practical purposes given General Smith carte blanche in dealing with the OSS.

"Where's the colonel?" the cryptographic officer asked.

"Whitbey House," Helene Dancy replied. "What have you got?"

"An EYES ONLY Operational Immediate . . . two of them . . . for Bruce and the colonel. From Canidy and Dolan."

The SOP was very clear on the handling of Operational Immediate messages:

"16. [B]. OPERATIONAL IMMEDIATE MESSAGES WILL BE IMMEDIATELY DELIVERED TO THE ADDRESSEE, OR IN HIS ABSENCE, TO THE SENIOR OFFICER PRESENT POSSESSING THE APPROPRIATE SECURITY CLEARANCE. IN NO CIRCUMSTANCES WILL A DELAY OF MORE THAN TEN [10] MINUTES BETWEEN DECRYPTION AND DELIVERY BE TOLERATED."

"Can I see it?" Helene Dancy asked.

"You're not next on the list," Captain Harrison said reluctantly, obviously uncomfortable.

"That's right," she said, just a little tartly. She picked up her telephone.

"Sergeant, do you know where Captain Fine is?" she asked a moment later, and then, when there had been a reply: "Send someone for him, please. Get him back here as soon as you can."

"Well, who's next on the list after Fine?" Harrison asked.

"Oddly enough, I am," Capt. Dancy said, a little ice in her voice. She put out her hand for the documents.

"Hey, Dancy," Capt. Harrison said, as he handed them to her. "I don't make the rules. I just try to obey them."

"I know," Helene Dancy said. "Damn, why does everybody have to be gone at once?" And then she quickly glanced at the first message: Canidy's.

"Oh, Christ!" she said.

"My thought exactly," Capt. Harrison said.

She flipped back the cover sheet on the second EYES ONLY: Dolan's.

"I think you'd better get both of these off, Operational Immediate, to Washington, EYES ONLY, Donovan and Douglass," Capt. Dancy said.

She saw the look on his face.

"OK, I'll make it official. As the senior officer present, I order you to transmit these messages to Washington, EYES ONLY, Donovan and Douglass."

"I'm not trying to be chickenshit about this," Harrison said. "You heard Bruce eat my ass out the last time I 'acted without thought and authority . . .'"

"Well, I just took you off the hook for this time," she said.

"Yeah," Harrison said. "Helene, I'm not asking you to make it official, but should I try to run down Bruce at SHAEF?"

"That would make a second copy necessary," she said. "The sergeant major will get Fine in here in a couple of minutes."

The SOP was specific about that, too:

"16. [F]. IN NO CASE, EXCEPT WITH THE SPECIFIC PERMISSION OF THE CHIEF OF STATION, OR THE DEPUTY CHIEF OF STATION, WILL MORE THAN ONE [1] COPY OF AN EYES ONLY DOCUMENT BE PREPARED. IT IS EMPHASIZED THAT ADDRESSEES OF EYES ONLY DOCUMENTS, WITH THE EXCEPTION OF THE CHIEF OF STATION AND DEPUTY CHIEF OF STATION, ARE SPECIFICALLY FORBIDDEN TO MAKE COPIES OF EYES ONLY DOCUMENTS FOR THEIR OWN FILES, OR FOR ANY OTHER PURPOSE."

"What the hell," Capt. Harrison said. "How mad can Bruce get?"

"Pretty mad," she said. "I don't know, Paul."

"Is Bruce eating at the SHAEF general's mess?" Capt. Harrison asked, having made up his mind.

"He wasn't sure," Capt. Dancy said. "When he can get Beetle Smith out of the building for an hour or so, he likes to butter him up at the Savoy Grill."

"And if I call either place to find out, no one will tell me," Harrison said. "I think I'll take a chance on the Savoy."

Five minutes later, after having made copies of the EYES ONLY messages and ordered their transmission to Washington, Capt. Harrison went onto Berkeley Square to get in a Ford staff car. There he saw Capt. Stanley S. Fine getting out of a jeep driven by the sergeant major.

He waved at Fine, but said nothing to him about the EYES ONLYs, or about where he was going. If he told Fine, Fine might forbid him (he had the authority) to take copies of the EYES ONLYs to Bruce. More likely, once he'd explained the situation, Fine would also decide it was the thing to do, and to hell with Bruce's SOP. That would put him in the line of fire if Bruce didn't like the decision, and that wasn't necessary. Fine was a good guy.

The maître d'hôtel of the Savoy Grill blandly denied the presence of either Lt. General Walter Bedell Smith or Mr. David Bruce. He smilingly announced he hadn't seen either of them in days.

Capt. Harrison looked around the large, elegantly appointed room, and found what he was looking for. A major having a solitary lunch at the far end of the room. Behind the major was an ornately carved moveable screen, so placed that it could conceal a table for two. And hanging from the epaulets of the major's green tunic was the golden rope of an aide-de-camp.

"Thank you very much," Harrison said to the maître d'hôtel. And then he ducked past the maître d' and headed for the screen. The maitre d' scurried after him, but unless he broke into a run, Harrison knew he wouldn't catch up with him.

But Beetle Smith's aide-de-camp saw him and rose quickly to his feet, obviously intending to block his path. Harrison reached in his pocket and was enormously relieved to find his OSS credentials there. He was terrified of the consequences of losing them, and since he rarely had need of them, he usually kept them in the TOP SECRET safe.

He got them out of his pocket and held them up for General Smith's aide-de-camp to see.

"Just a moment," the aide-de-camp said. "I'll tell Mr. Bruce you're here."

Harrison smiled and kept going.

David Bruce looked at him with surprise and annoyance.

The Chief of London Station and the Deputy Commander of SHAEF were lunching on small steaks, oven-browned potatoes, and asparagus. Harrison knew that the steaks and asparagus had come from OSS stocks. The usual fare at the Savoy Grill was broiled fish and Brussels sprouts. The Savoy was, however, happy to prepare whatever ingredients a guest might wish to send to its kitchen ahead of time. The price charged was the same as if they had furnished the ingredients.

What that meant was that Bruce, as Helene Dancy had suggested, was buttering up Beetle Smith by providing an unusually nice luncheon at the Savoy. And that meant he was likely to be greatly annoyed to have the nice luncheon interrupted.

"I'm sorry to disturb you, Sir," Paul Harrison said. "But I could see no other choice."

He thrust a large manila envelope at him.

"Captain Fine is not available?" Bruce asked, courteously enough.

"He was sent for, Sir," Harrison said. "He was out of the office."

"Oh, excuse me," Bruce said. "Beetle, this is Captain Harrison. And this is General Smith. Or do you know each other?"

Hell, yes, we're old pals. How the hell are you, Beetle?

"No, Sir," Capt. Harrison said. "How do you do, Sir?"

General Smith smiled, and offered a firm handshake.

"Captain," Smith said. " 'Harrison,' is it?"

"Yes, Sir."

Bruce tore the envelope open carefully, glanced inside, then took the EYES ONLY documents from it.

"I'm happy to meet you, Captain," General Smith said.

Harrison could not think of a reply.

Dear Harriet, You'll never guess who I met at lunch at the Savoy Hotel.

Smith, naturally curious, turned his attention to David Bruce.

"Important, David?" General Smith asked.

"Not particularly," Bruce said. And then he corrected himself. "I don't mean to suggest that you should not have brought this to my attention here, Harrison. That was the correct thing to do."

"Yes, Sir," Harrison said.

"You said that Captain Fine has been sent for?"

"Yes, Sir."

"I don't think there's any point in involving Captain Fine in this, Captain," Bruce said. "What I think you should do is see that Washington gets a copy of this as quickly as you can. And then get in touch with Colonel Stevens and ask him to be in my office at four. A little earlier, if he can make it. And I think it might be a good idea if you were to ask him to bring Lieutenant Hoche with him."

"Yes, Sir," Harrison said.

Lt. Hoche, Capt. Harrison recalled, was the newly arrived, absolutely splendiferous blonde who was supposed to be Helene Dancy's man . . . woman . . . at Whitbey House.

What the hell has she got to do with this?

Bruce returned the documents to the envelope and handed it back to Harrison.

"Thank you, Captain," he said.

Harrison was wondering whether or not the Customs of the

Service required him to salute a three-star general in a hotel dining room, when General Smith solved the problem.

He gave Harrison his hand.

"Pleasure to have met you, Captain," he said. "I look forward to seeing you again."

"Yes, Sir," Harrison said. "Thank you, Sir."

3

Office of Strategic Services
National Institute of Health Building
Washington, D.C.
0655 Hours 17 February 1943

Chief Boatswain's Mate J.R. Ellis, USN, pushed open the plate glass door, marched into the lobby of the building, and crossed to the elevator, his metal-tapped heels making a ringing noise on the marble floor.

He was almost at the elevator when a guard, whose nose had been in the sports section of the *Washington Star,* spotted him. The guard, in a blue, police-type uniform erupted from his chair.

"Hey!"

Ellis looked over his shoulder and saw the guard headed for him.

"Where do you think you're going?" the guard demanded as he caught up with Ellis and put his hand on Ellis's arm.

Ellis fished in his trouser's pocket with his free hand and came up with an identity badge sealed in plastic and fitted with an alligator clip. He held it out for the guard to see. The card bore his photograph, diagonal red "anytime, anyplace" stripes, his name, and in the Duty Assignment box, the words "Office of the Director."

The guard was satisfied with Ellis's bona fides, but not mollified.

"You're supposed to wear that badge, you know," he said.

"Sorry," Ellis said. "I forgot."

Ellis got on the elevator and rode up.

When the second lobby guard returned from the men's room, the guard who had stopped Ellis was curious enough to ask him, "Who the hell is the sailor with the anytime, anyplace badge?"

"Navy Chief? Big guy? Ruddy face?"

"That's him. He walked in here like he owned the place."

"He almost does," the second guard told him. "That's Chief Ellis. Donovan's shadow. Nice guy. Just don't fuck with him. The best way to handle him is to remember the only people around here who tell him what to do are Colonel Donovan and Captain Douglass."

Upstairs, Ellis got off the elevator and walked down the marble-floored corridor to the Director's Office.

"Good morning, Sir," he said to the slight, balding man in his late thirties sitting at Colonel Donovan's secretary's desk.

William R. Vole was in civilian clothes, but he was a Chief Warrant Officer of the Army Security Agency,[1] a cryptographer, on what had turned out to be permanent loan to the OSS.

There were eight such cryptographic experts assigned to the OSS in Washington, and one of them was always available to the Office of the Director. They had become *de facto* duty officers in the Director's Office, in addition to their cryptographic duties. It had been made official by Colonel Donovan, at Ellis's suggestion. Ellis had pointed out that their cryptographic duties had already made them privy to the contents of incoming and outgoing encrypted messages, so they would learn little they already didn't know by keeping the Director's Office manned around the clock. And there were other ways they could make themselves useful in the Director's office.

"Chief," CWO Vole responded with a smile.

Vole liked Ellis, and felt a certain kinship with him as well. They both had long enlisted service before the war. And

[1]The Army Security Agency, originally formed to provide security for Army communications (hence the name), monitored Army radio and wire communications nets to insure that no classified information was being transmitted in such a manner that it would become available to the enemy. It had developed a capability, however, to intercept enemy radio transmissions and to break enemy codes, and thus in addition to its counterintelligence and security functions, it became an intelligence source.

unlike many of his peers, he did not resent Ellis's authority to speak for Colonel Donovan, or Donovan's deputy, Captain Peter Douglass. He had been around the OSS long enough to see how Ellis used that authority, and he had never seen him abuse it.

And there was enough vestigial enlisted man in Chief Warrant Officer Vole to take some pleasure in the annoyance and discomfiture of a long line of brass hats who had tried and failed to pull rank on the salty old chief. Vole could not remember an incident where Ellis had not been backed up by Captain Douglass when some brass hat had complained to him about a decision of Ellis's, and he had several fond memories of incidents where some brass hat, having gotten no satisfaction from Captain Douglass, had gone over Douglass's head to Colonel Donovan.

The response then had been a furious, if brief, ass-chewing of the brass hat, done with the skill and finesse only a former Infantry Regimental Commander (as Donovan had been in the First War) could hand out.

Ellis took off his brimmed cap and hung it atop a bentwood clothing rack. Then he removed a white silk scarf and folded it very neatly and hung it on a wooden coat hanger. Finally, he took off his blue overcoat and hung that carefully on the hanger. Then he turned and looked at the ASA warrant officer.

"The Colonel's home," Chief Warrant Officer Vole reported. "Staley's with him. The Captain's home. I sent Marmon with a car for him. He's going to the Pentagon and will be in about ten, maybe a little later."

Marmon was a former District Policeman who served as combination chauffeur and bodyguard to Captain Peter Douglass.

"That's it?" Ellis asked.

"Mrs. Foster's going to be in late," Vole continued. "She has a dental appointment, but says she can reschedule if you need her. Miss Haley, she says, can handle everything she knows about."

"Fine," Ellis said.

"And I just made a pot of coffee," the ASA warrant officer said.

"And can I use one!" Ellis said. "It's as cold as a witch's teat outside."

He went to the small closet where the coffeepot sat on an electric hot plate and poured a cup.

When he came out, the ASA Warrant Officer had taken the overnight messages from the safe and laid them out, together with the forms for the receipt of classified documents, on an oak table. Ellis sat down at the table.

"Anything interesting in here?" he asked, as he began to sign the forms.

"Mostly routine," Vole said. "The Philippines have been heard from again, but that's about all."

Ellis looked at him with a question on his face.

"Seventeen," the ASA warrant officer said.

When Ellis had finished signing the receipts and pushed the receipt forms away from him, he picked up file number seventeen, and opened it. The first thing he saw was that it was an intercept, rather than a message intended for the OSS.

On his own authority, as "Special Assistant to the Director," he had sent a "Request for Intercept" to the ASA, asking that the OSS be furnished with whatever ASA intercept operators around the world heard on either American or enemy frequencies that had anything to do with American guerrilla activity in the Philippine Islands. Inasmuch as the ASA and every other military and naval organization knew that the alternative to not giving the OSS whatever it asked for was explaining to the Chairman of the Joint Chiefs of Staff why this could not be done, the "request" had been in fact an order.

Ellis had decided that if Douglass or Donovan asked him why he had done so, and he didn't think they would, he would tell them it was because of the Whittaker mission. That was logical, of course. But the truth was that Ellis had put in the Request for Intercept long before it had been decided to send Whittaker into the Philippines. He had suspected that the reason there had been no reply to Fertig's original transmissions to MacArthur's headquarters in Australia was that some brass hats of MacArthur's palace guard, or perhaps even MacArthur himself, considered the very existence of guerrillas embarrassing. MacArthur's liaison officer to Washington had flatly announced that "effective guerrilla operations were impossible."

The ASA intercept operators were good. They had furnished Ellis with the radio message from MacArthur appointing Philippine Scout Major Marcario Peralta "military guerrilla chief of temporarily occupied enemy territory," and with Fertig's response to that, a request for drugs to cure venereal disease—as much as telling MacArthur he considered himself fucked.

Today's message showed that Fertig had his temper under control and was thinking:

URGENT FROM WYZB FOR KSF PASS TO SECRETARY OF WAR WASHINGTON DC

AS SENIOR AMERICAN OFFICER IN THE PHILIPPINE ISLANDS I HAVE ASSUMED COMMAND OF MINDANAO AND VISAYAS WITH RANK OF BRIGADIER GENERAL.

I HAVE REACTIVATED UNITED STATES FORCES IN THE PHILIPPINES.

USFIP HAS REESTABLISHED PHILIPPINE CIVIL GOVERNMENT IN THE HANDS OF ELECTED COMMONWEALTH OF PHILIPPINES OFFICIALS.

LAWFUL GOVERNMENT OF PHILIPPINES IN AREA OF RESPONSIBILITY OF USFIP IS PRINTING AND PLACING INTO CIRCULATION MONEY.

USFIP IS BORROWING NECESSARY OPERATIONAL FUNDS FROM COMMONWEALTH OF PHILIPPINES GOVERNMENT.

USFIP URGENTLY REQUIRES MINIMUM ONE MILLION DOLLARS IN GOLD.

USFIP URGENTLY REQUIRES FOR MORALE OF PHILIPPINE POPULATION ANY SORT OF AID. MEDICINE FIREARMS AND AMMUNITION PREFERABLE.

FERTIG BRIG GENERAL USA COMMANDING USFIP

Ellis frowned.

"What the hell is that all about?" Vole asked.

"Fertig is being fucked by the system," Ellis said. "But he's too mean to lie down and take it."

The telephone rang. Vole answered it, and then held his hand over the microphone.

"There's an EYES ONLY Operational Immediate for either Donovan or Douglass," he said. "They want to know if anybody's here that can take it."

"Decrypted?" Ellis asked.

"Yeah. Dispatched at 1207 London time."

"Would you run down there and get it?" Ellis asked.

Vole nodded, and took his hand away from the telephone microphone.

"Put it in a cover," he said. "I'll be right down."

Vole was gone no more than five minutes. By the time he returned, Ellis had gone through the overnight messages and arranged those he felt Colonel Donovan should personally see in the order of their importance.

He took the two EYES ONLYs from Vole.

"I thought you said one EYES ONLY," he said.

"They're related," Vole said.

He opened Dolan's message first, read it, and grunted. Then he opened the message Canidy had laboriously encrypted in the monks' cave on the Island of Vis.

TOP SECRET

OPERATIONAL IMMEDIATE

OSS LONDON STATION OSS WASHINGTON

EYES ONLY COLONEL DONOVAN; CAPTAIN DOUGLASS

FOLLOWING FROM CANIDY RECEIVED 1110 LONDON TIME FORWARDED AUTHORITY DANCY CAPT WAC.

BRUCE AND/OR STEVENS WILL HAVE MESSAGE IN HANDS NO LATER THAN 1230 LONDON TIME.

QUOTE TOP SECRET OPERATIONAL IMMEDIATE EYES ONLY BRUCE AND STEVENS

1. ON SAFE ARRIVAL STATION VII INFORMED BY YACHTSMAN EXLAX AND TINCAN ONE IN HANDS OF CIVIL AUTHORITIES STATION V. TINCAN TWO SAFE WELL STATION VII.

2. SURPRISE BOARDING BY BLACKGUARD AND RIVER POLICE YACHT STATION V RESULTED DISCOVERY EXLAX OPERATIONAL FUNDS. HUNGARIANS PRESUMABLY BELIEVE FUNDS INTENDED FOR PURCHASE BLACK MARKET FOOD. EXLAX AND TINCAN ONE ARRESTED AS BLACK MARKETEERS. SENTENCED NINE ZERO DAYS HARD LABOR COAL MINES STATION V.

3. YACHTSMAN REPORTS DOCUMENTS NOT REPEAT NOT QUESTIONED.

4. YACHTSMAN STATES SITUATION FAIRLY COMMON. ABSENCE PREPAYMENT GRAFT BLACKGUARD AND RIVER POLICE REGULARLY ARREST BLACK MARKETEERS CONFISCATE GOODS OR MONEY CONFINE LOCAL JAIL AT MINE HARD LABOR AS LESSON. YACHTSMAN BELIEVES THEY WILL BE RELEASED WITHOUT FURTHER DIFFICULTY PRIOR COMPLETION SENTENCE.

5. HAVE TAKEN FOLLOWING ACTION.

A. WILL REMAIN HERE PENDING DECISIONS ACTIONS ENUMERATED LATER HEREIN.

B. TINCAN TWO FLOWN CAIRO FOR ICING THERE. RECEIPT THIS MESSAGE WILL CONFIRM SAFE ARRIVAL.

C. YACHTSMAN ORDERED TO STATION V TO PERSONALLY CONFIRM LOCATION OF EXLAX AND TINCAN ONE AND TO EXPLORE POSSIBILITY ESCAPE OR RELEASE BY FORCE. EXPECTED TRAVEL TIME FOUR REPEAT FOUR DAYS. STATION V TO STATION VII COMMUNICATIONS SLOW AND UNRELIABLE REPEAT UNRELIABLE.

6. REQUEST PERMISSION EFFECT RELEASE EXLAX AND TINCAN ONE BEST MEANS AT MY DISCRETION. IF SO REQUIRE IMMEDIATE DISPATCH VIA STATION VIII NEXT AVAILABLE HUNGARIAN SPEAKING TEAM. STANDARD TEAM EQUIPMENT SHOULD BE AUGMENTED WITH THIRTY POUNDS COMPOSITION C2 AND EQUIVALENT TWENTY THOUSAND US DOLLARS IN HUNGARIAN, GERMAN AND YUGOSLAVIAN CURRENCY. TEAM SHOULD HAVE HUNGARIAN AND OR YUGOSLAVIAN IDENTIFICATION.

7. IN VIEW NECESSARY ABSENCE EXLAX CONTROLLER SUGGEST FINE AS TEMPORARY REPLACEMENT.

CANIDY END QUOTE

TOP SECRET

"Oh, *shit!*" Chief Ellis said.

He picked up the telephone and dialed a number from memory.

Staley's familiar voice came on the line: "Capitol 3-1991."

"Is he up yet?" Ellis asked.

"I heard the crapper flush," Staley reported.

"Well, don't say nothing unless he tells you to go anywhere but here," Ellis said. "If he does, say I called and said I think he should come here straight from there."

"What's up, Ellis?" Colonel Wild Bill Donovan's voice asked.

"There's something I think you ought to see as soon as you can, Sir."

"Will it wait until after breakfast, would you say?"

"Yes, Sir, it'll keep that long."

"We'll be there inside of forty-five minutes," Donovan said, and the line went dead.

Ellis tapped the cutoff button on the telephone with his finger and dialed another number from memory.

"Capitol 3-2772," a male voice answered.

"Captain Douglass?" Ellis asked.

"Who's calling, please?" the man asked.

"Marmon, goddamn you, is that you?"

"You don't have to bite my ass off, Chief," Marmon said righteously. "I thought I recognized your voice."

"Is the Captain there?"

"You want me to get him?"

"No. Shit! I'm taking a census."

In a moment, Captain Douglass came on the line.

"Good morning, Chief," he said. "What's up?"

"I don't know what's going on where you're going, but if you can put it off, I think it would be a good idea if you came in."

"He ask for me?"

"No, Sir, but I think he probably will."

"I'll be there in half an hour," Captain Douglass said. "Thank you, Chief."

Ellis hung the telephone up.

"That important, huh?" Warrant Officer Vose asked.

Ellis looked at him.

"If you're fishing for an explanation," Ellis said, "don't."

"I read the decrypt," Vose protested.

"That's only because we haven't figured out a way for you to decrypt stuff without reading it," Ellis said, matter-of-factly.

He got up and walked to the safe and worked the combination. From a two-foot-high stack of folders piled precariously in the bottom, he pulled a thick one with a TOP SECRET cover sheet and the words EXLAX written on it with a thick pointed pen.

He carried it to the desk and started going through it. There was no more of a question in his mind that the Colonel would want the paper work in front of him than there was that he would want to talk Canidy's EYES ONLY OPERATIONAL IMMEDIATE over with Captain Douglass. By the time either of them walked into the office, the paper work would be ready for them.

Ellis's eye fell on the overnight traffic. He should get that out of the way before he laid this stuff out.

Then he had another thought. He opened a drawer and took out a lined pad and a pencil and wrote quickly on it.

"You want to make yourself useful," he said to Vose. "Get this encoded and out right away. And then stick around. I think there will be a reply to the EYES ONLYs."

Vose took the sheet of lined paper from Ellis and read it.

URGENT VIA KSF FOR WYZB HQ US FORCE IN PHILIPPINES ATTENTION BRIGADIER GENERAL FERTIG KEEP YOUR SHIRT ON STOP J.R. ELLIS CHIEF USN STOP END

"You really want me to send this?" Vose asked.

"Just that way," Chief Ellis said.

4

Office of the Station Chief
OSS London Station
Berkeley Square, London
1600 Hours 17 February 1943

"Is something wrong, David?" Lt. Colonel Edmund T. Stevens asked.

Bruce looked at him with his eyebrows raised.

"I would say so, wouldn't you?" he replied drily.

"I mean, right now, here," Stevens said. "You were frowning."

"Oh," Bruce said, and then managed a faint smile. He gestured vaguely around his office. "Actually, I was thinking, paraphrasing Churchill, that 'never have so few been commanded by so many.' "

The three visitors' chairs in the office were occupied by

Colonel Stevens, Capt. Helene Dancy, and Lt. Charity Hoche. Capt. Stanley S. Fine was leaning against the wall.

"I don't see that it could be avoided," Stevens said.

"No," Bruce agreed, then: "I presume this is one of those things in which Miss Hoche has a special interest?"

Stevens nodded.

"Well, let's get on with it, then," Bruce said. "You, first, Charity, please."

She didn't seem surprised, but neither did she say anything.

"The way we do this, Charity," Bruce explained, "is 'in the military manner.' That is to say, the junior member of this panel is asked for his . . . her . . . opinion first, so that it will not be influenced by that of more senior members."

Charity nodded.

"I don't see that we have any choice but to give Dick Canidy what he's asked for," she said, and then quickly added, "at least until we hear to the contrary from Washington."

"That doesn't address the question of authorizing him to try to get Fulmar and Professor Dyer out of the jail in Pécs," Bruce said.

"I think we'll be told what to do about that," Charity said.

Bruce looked at Stevens, who just perceptibly nodded his head in agreement.

"What he's asked for, specifically, is the next available Hungarian-speaking team, thirty pounds of C-2, and twenty thousand dollars in mixed currency," Bruce said. "That's what you mean?"

Charity nodded. "That, and Captain Fine to step in as control."

"We'll start with that, then," Bruce said. "Unless I hear an objection, I will ask Fine if there is some reason he cannot, or thinks he should not, take over as control."

He looked at Stevens, then at Helene Dancy, and finally at Fine.

"No, Sir," Fine said.

"So ordered," Bruce said.

"One thing, Stanley," Stevens said. "Charity is cleared for this. All the way."

"Yes, Sir," Fine said.

"I want to clarify that, Stan," Bruce said. "Charity is to be brought into anything connected with this that Colonel Stevens and myself are."

"Yes, Sir," Fine repeated.

"Well, why don't you sit here," Bruce said, "and take over this meeting?"

"I don't mind standing, Sir," Fine said.

"I'd rather walk around," Bruce said, and gestured for Fine to sit down.

Fine sat down at Bruce's desk, put a lined pad on the green blotter in front of him, and took a pencil from a dozen sitting, point up, in a gray pottery orange-marmalade jar.

"Helene," he said. "You'll take care of the money? Is that going to pose any problem?"

"We don't have that much," Capt. Dancy said. "But I can have it by, say, nine in the morning."

"And the C-2?"

"I'm sure there's at least that much at Whitbey House," Colonel Stevens said.

"There should be," Helene Dancy agreed. "But I'll check."

"That, then, brings us to the team," Fine said.

"First," Charity Hoche said. "To the question of their documents. Canidy said Hungarian and/or Yugoslavian. If we can, I think we should give them both."

Fine's face was expressionless, but Colonel Stevens thought he saw in his eyes a hint of surprise, even annoyance.

"Helene?" Fine asked.

"Documents Section can handle that," Capt. Dancy said. "They'll need four hours."

"Why so long?" Charity asked.

"They don't have very much of the proper paper for the photographs," Dancy explained. "We have to use their paper; it produces a characteristic grain, and image flatness. The Hungarian is different from the Yugoslavian. And the only place we can get it is on the local black markets. It is also lousy paper, and it takes that much time to be sure. In case they have to print the photographs twice, or even three times."

"But they will be able to come up with what we need?" David Bruce asked.

"Probably in forty-five minutes," Helene Dancy said. "I'm using the worst possible scenario."

"Have we got a team to photograph?" Fine asked.

"They have all been photographed, Stanley," Helene Dancy said. "Several times, in work clothes, suits, even in Black Guard uniforms. *Printing* is the problem."

"That's not what I really meant," Fine said. "I'll rephrase. Is a team available? If there is more than one available, which is the better of them?"

"I was out there when this came up, Stanley," Colonel Stevens said. "There are two teams finished with training, one in the last week."

"Did Jamison give you any indication which was better?" Fine asked.

"There is a problem," Stevens said. "The teams which have finished their training have been trained to go in to Tito, not Mihajlović."[2]

"God!" Bruce said.

"It was necessary, David," Stevens said. "We had to appear level-handed, and that meant sending teams to Tito."

"What about the team in training?" Bruce asked.

"Mihajlović," Stevens said. "But it's a communications team. No specific training for something like this."

"What about János?" Helene Dancy asked. "When does he get out of his cast?"

"Friday," Charity said.

"Who the hell is János?" Bruce asked.

"The first lieutenant who broke his ankle," Dancy furnished.

"Well, we can hardly take his cast off one day and jump him in the next," Bruce said.

"János was trained to go in to Mihajlović," Dancy said.

"And we're not going to jump them in anyway," Charity said. Bruce snapped his head around to look at her. Charity smiled, and added, "Are we?"

"We may have to," Stevens said. "With Dolan under the weather, I think we have to leave him out of the equation.

---

[2]There were two major guerrilla forces in Yugoslavia. Colonel Draža Mihajlović led a force of Royalists, and Josip Broz, who called himself "Tito" led a larger force of Communists.

And that means there's no one but that young pilot . . . whatsisname?"
"Darmstadter," Helene Dancy furnished.
"Darmstadter," Stevens said, ". . . to fly the B-25. Which means either parachuting them onto Vis, or for that matter into Hungary, or sending them by submarine."
"I can fly the B-25," Fine said.
"No," Bruce said. "You're the control."
"Doug Douglass can fly the B-25," Charity said.
Bruce looked at her.
"He's not . . . assigned to us," he said.
"Can't that be arranged?" Charity asked. "TDY or something?"
"We're getting ahead of ourselves," Fine said. "The first decision that has to be made is about the team. Do we send in a Tito team?"
Charity looked at Colonel Stevens.
"No," Stevens said flatly.
"What's the difference?" Helene Dancy asked.
"For the men, none," Stevens said. "But we will not send an officer on this who has been selected to go in to Tito."
"May I ask why, Sir?" Fine asked.
"No, I'm afraid I can't tell you, Stan," Stevens said.
Fine looked curious, but shrugged.
"It looks as though we're back to János," he said. "And to flying him in rather than jumping him in, because of his ankle. And since I can't fly the B-25, we're also back to Douglass. May I ask that you reconsider, Sir, my flying the B-25?"
"Out of the question," Bruce said.
"And we're not even sure of János," Stevens said. "Helene, get the medical officer at Whitbey House on the horn and get a report on János's ankle. Specifically, what shape he will be in when they take the cast off, and for how long."
"While she's doing that," Fine said, "what about transport of the team from here to Cairo? If they're going to Cairo?"
"What do you mean by that?" Stevens asked.
"I thought perhaps Malta," Fine said.
"Oh," Stevens said.
"We'll send them to Cairo," Bruce said. "They'll attract less attention there. And we'll send them on the ATC courier.

There's a daily flight. If we send one man a day, starting right now, they should attract no attention at all. Wilkins is good at distracting attention."

"Mr. Bruce," Fine said, almost hesitantly. "I'm afraid that you will think I'm rephrasing a request that has already been denied . . ."

"What, Fine?" Bruce asked, impatiently.

"Project Aphrodite has two new B-17s," Fine said.

"One of which you would like to fly to Cairo?" Bruce asked, icily sarcastic.

"May I explain my thinking, Sir?"

"No," Bruce said.

"I would like to hear it," Charity said.

Bruce glared at her and opened his mouth to speak. Before he could, there was a knock at the door, and instead of saying what he'd intended, Bruce said, his voice angry and impatient:

"We are not to be disturbed!"

"Operational Immediate EYES ONLY for you, Sir," Capt. Harrison's voice came through the door.

"Oh, hell," Bruce said, "now what?" He raised his voice. "Bring it in, Harrison!"

Harrison came into the room, extended a clipboard with a Receipt for Classified Document on it, and when Bruce had signed it, handed him a document with a TOP SECRET cover sheet on it.

"Thank you," Bruce said. "I didn't mean to snap at you, Paul."

"No problem, Sir," Harrison said. He made no move to leave.

"That'll be all, thank you," Bruce said.

"An action is required, Sir," Harrison said.

Bruce snorted, and lifted the cover sheet.

TOP SECRET

OPERATIONAL IMMEDIATE OFFICE OF THE DIRECTOR OSS WASHINGTON FOR OSS LONDON FOR OSS CAIRO EYES ONLY BRUCE STEVENS WILKINS

RELAY FOLLOWING CANIDY MOST EXPEDITIOUS MEANS:

QUOTE 1. OSS LONDON AND CAIRO DIRECTED AS HIGHEST

PRIORITY TO SUPPORT WITH ALL MEANS AVAILABLE ATTEMPT FREE EXLAX AND TINCAN ONE.

2. RESCUE WILL BE ATTEMPTED AT EARLIEST POSSIBLE TIME AND IN ANY CASE NOT LATER THAN TEN REPEAT TEN DAYS FROM RECEIPT OF THIS MESSAGE.

3. IN EVENT ATTEMPT IMPOSSIBLE OR ATTEMPT FAILS EXLAX AND TINCAN ONE WILL BE TERMINATED REPEAT WILL BE TERMINATED.

4. NO DISCUSSION OF THIS ORDER WILL BE ENTERTAINED. UNQUOTE

STATION CHIEFS LONDON AND CAIRO WILL ACKNOWLEDGE RECEIPT AND COMPREHENSION OF CANIDY MESSAGE.

STATION CHIEF CAIRO ADDITIONALLY WILL REPORT TIME AND PLACE OF DELIVERY OF MESSAGE TO CANIDY WITH INFO COPY TO LONDON.

DONOVAN

Bruce handed the message to Colonel Stevens, and then looked at Capt. Harrison.

"Would you please message Colonel Donovan that Colonel Stevens and myself acknowledge receipt and comprehension of this message?" he said, almost formally.

"Yes, Sir," Harrison said.

"My God!" Stevens said, when he had read the message. He extended it to Bruce. "May I see that, please?" Charity Hoche asked.

"Oh," Stevens said, as if he had just remembered she was present. "Sure."

When she had read it, she handed it to Fine. He frowned when he read it, but said nothing.

"You were saying, Stan," Charity said, "something about new B-17s?"

Eleven

1

OSS Whitbey House Station
Kent, England
1815 Hours 17 February 1943

First Lieutenant Robert Jamison found First Lieutenant Ferenc János where he thought he would be at this time of day, in the bar, at the piano, with a drink adding yet another scar to the varnished finish of the piano, and with two of the WRAC drivers listening to him play.

"Freddy, could I see you for a moment?" Jamison asked.

"Ladies," Freddy János said, "duty calls."

"Not here, János," Jamison said.

János's eyebrows rose in curiosity, but he didn't say anything. He hoisted himself from the piano stool with a grunt, reached for his drink, finished it, and then squatted on his one good leg to pick up his crutches from the floor.

He followed Jamison down the center corridor of the first floor of the left wing of the mansion to the dispensary, which had been set up in what had been the ballroom. There were sixteen beds, eight on each side of the high-ceilinged room. Eleven of them were occupied.

At the far end of the ballroom was a small, flat-roofed "building," roughly framed in with exposed two-by-fours and plywood. It held a simple, if surprisingly complete operating room, an X-ray room, a pharmacy, two examining cubicles, a dentist's chair and equipment, and an office for the two physicians attached to Whitbey House station.

Both of them, and a nurse, were waiting for Jamison and János.

"What's going on?" János asked, when he saw where Jamison had led him.

"First things first," Jamison said. "We want an X-ray of your ankle."

"I will repeat, Lieutenant Jamison," one of the doctors, a captain, said, "that I don't like this."

"Whether or not you approved didn't come up, Doctor," Jamison said, "when the colonel said to do it."

The doctor gave him a cold look.

The nurse took János into the X-ray room, motioned for him to hop on the table, and then took his crutches and leaned them on the wall. She wordlessly arranged his leg on the table under the X-ray apparatus, then stepped behind a crudely built, raw lumber six-foot wall.

"Don't move," she ordered, and there was a whirring sound from the X-ray apparatus. She made six X-rays before she was finished, and then issued another order: "You'd better stay there until I get these out of the soup."

The two doctors and Jamison came into the room.

"What's going on?" János asked from the X-ray table.

"We want to see if we can take your cast off safely," Jamison said.

"Why?"

"If we can, I'll tell you," Jamison said.

János, who had been lying down, sat up on the table and let his legs hang over the side.

The nurse returned with still damp 11 by 14 inch X-ray photographs, put three (all it would handle) on a viewer, and turned it on.

The two doctors examined the X-rays and then replaced them on the viewer with the other three.

The captain turned to Jamison.

"It appears to have healed and knitted satisfactorily," he said.

"The question, Doctor," Jamison said, "is, in your professional medical opinion, can the cast be safely removed?"

"There's a difference, Jamison, between taking it off and declaring this officer fit for duty."

"Can it be safely removed?" Jamison replied. "If so, please remove it."

"Jesus Christ," the other doctor, a lieutenant, said disgustedly.

"Would you get me the cutter, Nurse?" the captain asked.

János didn't like what he saw when the cast was removed. The skin beneath, where it was not marked with angry red marks, was unhealthily white, and although he couldn't be sure without actually comparing it side-by-side with his good ankle, it looked to him to be much thinner.

Both doctors manipulated the ankle and the foot. There was no pain, but it was uncomfortable.

"Well?" Jamison asked.

"The fractures," the captain said, "seem to have knitted satisfactorily. There is no pain or impediment of movement that I can detect."

"He can walk, in other words?" Jamison asked.

"Before he can be determined to be physically fit for duty," the captain said, "he will require therapy. Do you concur, Doctor?"

"Jamison," the younger doctor said, "there is muscle atrophy . . ."

"What kind of therapy?" Jamison asked.

"Walking, actually," the captain said. "Short walks, gradually extended. Manipulation of the foot and ankle to restore movement."

"That'll be all, János," Jamison said. "Thank you."

"You said you would tell me," János protested.

"You're being considered for an operation," Jamison said. "When and if it is decided you're going, you'll be told about it."

"When will that decision be made?"

"Tomorrow morning, probably," Jamison said. "Do you think you can manage without your crutches?"

"I don't know," János said.

"Give it a try," Jamison said. "If you can, leave the crutches here. If you go back to the bar, go easy on the booze. I don't want you falling down and breaking it again."

The lieutenant, shaking his head, chuckled.

The captain said, "Jamison, I might as well tell you, the moment Major Canidy returns, I'm going to protest this."

"Captain," Jamison said, "all I'm doing is obeying my orders. That's what you do when you put a uniform on, obey orders."

He turned and walked out of the room.

The captain called after him. "Jamison, in my capacity as the senior medical officer present, I absolutely forbid this officer to participate in a parachute jump."

"Your position has been noted, Doctor," Jamison called, over his shoulder.

János got off the X-ray table and gingerly lowered his bare, sick, white foot to the floor.

"Any pain?" the captain asked.

"No," János said.

"Fuck him," the captain said. "You use the crutches, János. You start using that leg carefully. I'll deal with Jamison."

János hoisted himself back onto the X-ray table and removed his other shoe and sock.

"With the shoe off," János said. "I think I can manage."

He lowered himself to the floor again, and then, awkwardly and carefully, walked very slowly out of the X-ray room.

2

OSS Whitbey House Station
Kent, England
0600 Hours 18 February 1943

First Lieutenant Ferenc János marched into the office of the Commanding Officer, came to attention, and saluted. He was wearing a wool OD (olive drab) Ike jacket and trousers. Parachutist's wings were on the jacket, and his trousers were bloused over glistening Corcoran jump boots. His woolen "overseas" cap was tucked in an epaulet of his jacket.

"Sir, Lieutenant János reporting as directed, Sir."

Lt. Colonel Edmund T. Stevens returned the salute.

"Stand at ease, Lieutenant," he said.

János was surprised to see the good-looking blond WAC lieutenant in the room. He wondered why. The story about her (which had quickly circulated through Whitbey House) was that she would work for Jamison, taking care of the women.

"How's your ankle, János? Straight answer, please," Stevens said.

"With the boot on, Sir," János said, "no problem."

"How far do you think you could walk on it?" Stevens asked.

"As far as I have to," János said.

"An overestimate of capability is dangerous, János," Colonel Stevens said.

"Yes, Sir," János said.

"A mission of the very highest priority has come up," Stevens said. "You have already expressed your willingness to participate in a mission involving great personal risk in enemy-occupied territory. You were also made aware that if you were captured, you would not be treated as a prisoner of war, but as a spy, and treated accordingly. I ask you here and now if you still wish to volunteer for such a mission?"

"Yes, Sir," János said.

"From this point, Lieutenant," Stevens said, "this conversation is classified TOP SECRET. Divulging what I am about to tell you to anyone, or discussing it with anyone not now present in this room, will constitute a court-martial offense. Do you fully understand that?"

"Yes, Sir."

"The mission is to free certain people from confinement in the hands of civil authorities in Hungary. I am now going to pose a question to you that I want you to think over very carefully before replying," Stevens went on. "If the mission goes sour, or if the mission cannot be accomplished within a set time frame, you will be required to eliminate, by which I mean kill, or cause to have killed, the people presently imprisoned. Now, are you willing to accept the mission, knowing that may be necessary?"

János hesitated, but not for long.

"Yes, Sir," he said. He became aware that the good-looking blond WAC was looking at him. More than looking at him, he realized—evaluating him and doing that very coldly.

"You believe you would be able to . . . and this is the only phrase that fits the situation . . . kill in cold blood the people presently imprisoned. And possibly a substantial number of others who can only be accurately described as 'innocent bystanders'?"

"You're not going to tell me what this is all about?"

"Just please answer my question," Stevens said.

"With your assurance that it's a military necessity, Sir," János said.

Stevens nodded.

"Charity?" he asked.

"Even, Freddy," Charity Hoche asked, "if the people who had to be eliminated were known to you? Even if you had met them here?"

"Holy Mother of God," János blurted, and then found control again. "With the same caveat as before, that Colonel Stevens assures me this is militarily necessary."

There was a knock at the door.

"Yes?" Stevens called, impatiently.

"Colonel Douglass is on the phone for Lieutenant Hoche, Sir," a male voice said.

"I guess I better take it," Charity said after a moment's thought. "He probably just got his orders and wonders what they're all about."

She walked out of the office.

"That was *the* important question," Colonel Stevens said. "But there is another important question. For reasons I cannot go into, it is impossible for us to send Lieutenant Shawup on this mission. But the team which he commands will make it. There will be a certain resentment on their part toward you. Can you handle it?"

"Yes, Sir," János said without hesitation.

"They will resent—after having received promises to the contrary—not being under Shawup's leadership. And they will resent being told . . . they will not be asked, they will be told . . . that elimination of the people being held may be necessary. They will resent that, too."

"They'll do what I tell them to do," János said, confidently.

"You sound very sure of yourself," Stevens said.

"Look at me, Colonel," János said. "As big as I am, wouldn't you hate to make me mad?"

Stevens's face went blank for a moment, and then he chuckled.

"Yes, I guess I would," he said.

He leaned over the desk and offered János his hand.

"I have every confidence that you can handle this, Lieutenant János," he said. "Good luck!"

3

Fersfield Army Air Corps Station
Bedfordshire, England
1200 Hours 18 February 1943

When the P-38 flashed over them, Lieutenant Commander Edwin W. Bitter, USN, Captain Stanley S. Fine, USAAC, and Lieutenant j.g. Joseph P. Kennedy, Jr., USNR, were sitting on folding wooden chairs outside the Quonset hut that served officially as the orderly room of the 402nd Composite Squadron and secretly as the headquarters for Operation Aphrodite.

They were taking the sun. There was precious little sun in England in February, and when it did pop out, everyone who could take the time tried to get out in it.

"I have been told by everybody from Bill Donovan to that ferocious WAC Captain in David Bruce's office that asking questions is like farting in the Sistine Chapel," Kennedy said, "but I would still dearly like to know where the hell you are taking my brand-new airplane."

"Come on, Joe," Commander Bitter said, a mild reproof.

"Yours not to reason why, Lieutenant," Fine said, smiling at him, "yours but to take yon fighter jockey aloft and see how much you can teach him in an hour or two about driving the B-17."

He gestured in the direction of the P-38, which the pilot had stood on its wing to line it up with the main Fersfield runway.

"I am also just a little curious why that is necessary," Kennedy said, "since here sit Commander Bitter and myself, both fully qualified B-17 pilots, and in my case at least, an extraordinary 'Look Ma, No Co-pilot' 17 chauffeur."

Bitter and Fine laughed.

"Your country, Lieutenant," Fine said, "is saving you for more important things."

"You aren't going to tell me, are you, you sonofabitch?" Kennedy said.

"I can't, Joe," Fine said seriously.

They stood up to watch the P-38 land. It came in hot, in a crab, lining up with the runway at the last moment before touching down.

"If yon fighter jockey tries that in a 17," Kennedy said drily, "we will have one more to park over there."

He pointed to the "graveyard" where remnants of more than two dozen crashed and shot-up B-17s were scattered around.

"Without any whistling-in-the-dark self-confidence," Kennedy went on, "what are our chances of getting that 17 back?"

"That will depend on how much you can teach Doug," Fine said.

A Follow-Me jeep had driven out to the taxiway to meet the P-38. Fine started to walk toward the revetment in which it would be parked, and Bitter and Kennedy followed him.

"I think I'll go along in the 17," Bitter said. "Maybe I could help Joe."

"No," Fine said, politely enough, but there was no mistaking it was an order. "We want to keep you around to fly the other new one."

They reached the revetment as the P-38 taxied up to it.

A ground crewman made a throat-cutting signal with his hand, and the engines died. A ground crewman laid a ladder against the cockpit, and Lt. Colonel Peter Douglass, Jr., climbed down it.

He was wearing a pink Ike jacket, matching trousers, a battered, oil-spotted, fur-felt brimmed cap with the crown stiffener removed on the back of his head, Half Wellington boots, and a parachute-silk scarf in the open collar of a gabardine shirt.

He is absolutely, totally, out of uniform, Fine mused. And then he corrected himself. *No, that is the uniform prescribed by fighter pilots for themselves. And there is no question that Doug is one hell of a fighter pilot. There were Japanese meatballs and German swastikas painted in three neat rows on the cockpit nose, plus a submarine. And something brand-new. Douglass had named his airplane "Charity."*

"Where the hell is my brass band?" Douglass asked, wrapping his arm around Commander Bitter's shoulders and (because he knew it annoyed Bitter immensely) kissing him wetly on the temple.

Fine and Kennedy smiled.

"Who's Charity?" Kennedy asked.

"As in 'Faith, Hope and,'" Douglass said. "If I don't get a band, how about lunch? I'm starved."

"You're going flying with Lieutenant Kennedy," Fine said. "You can have lunch when you come back."

"Where am I going flying with you, Kennedy?" Douglass asked.

"Up and down, up and down," Kennedy smiled. "Fine wants me to teach you to line an airplane up with the runway while you're still in the air."

"Only bomber pilots have to do that," Douglass said. "It's because their reflexes are so slow. You're serious about this, aren't you? *Before* I have lunch?"

"If you're a good boy, I'll have a surprise for you when you get back," Fine said.

"I already talked to her," Douglass said, "which raises the question of RHIP (Rank Hath Its Privileges)."

"How?" Fine asked.

"A senior officer such as myself," Douglass said, "cannot be expected to share a room with low-grade underlings such as you guys. Do I make my point?"

"Oh, I think Commander Bitter will be happy to accommodate you, Colonel, Sir," Kennedy said, chuckling. "He already has had the troops spiffing up the transient female quarters. You'll notice the smile of anticipation on his face."

"Doug," Bitter said very seriously, changing the subject, "if you really want something to eat, I'll have some sandwiches prepared and get them to the aircraft."

"Shame on you, Lieutenant Kennedy," Douglass said, "you are embarrassing the commander."

For a moment, looking at Bitter, Fine was afraid the situation was going to get out of hand, but with a visible effort, Bitter finally managed a smile.

Douglass looked at his watch.

"The girls are due here at two fifteen," he said. "That gives you just about two hours to teach me all you know, Kennedy. That shouldn't be a problem."

Douglass and Kennedy flew for nearly two hours before landing a final time and taxiing the B-17F back to the 402nd Composite Squadron area. As they stood by the aircraft with the crew chief, giving him a list of things to check to prepare the plane for flight, a small convoy rolled past the B-17 graveyard and stopped before the Quonset hut.

The convoy consisted of an Austin Princess limousine, a Packard limousine, and a three-quarter-ton Dodge Weapons-Carrier. The Packard and the Austin Princess were driven by sergeants of the WRAC, and the canvas-bodied Dodge by a U.S. Army sergeant.

Lt. Colonel Ed Stevens and Lt. Charity Hoche got out of the Princess, and five men in olive-drab U.S. Army uniforms got out of the Packard.

"Let that be a lesson to you, Lieutenant Kennedy," Douglass said, " 'Virtue is its own reward.' If you had allowed me to land this aerial barge when I wanted to, I wouldn't have had to stand around panting until just now."

"One gathers that the colonel would be panting over the blond lieutenant?" Kennedy asked. "Who the hell is she, anyway?"

"A senior officer such as myself," Douglass said, "does not of course discuss either ladies or his personal affairs with a junior officer. But I will say this, Kennedy. If it were to come to my attention that anyone, say a lowly reserve swabby officer, paid any but official attention to a certain WAC officer while I am off saving the world for democracy, I would feed him his balls."

"That's Charity," Kennedy said.

"That's Charity," Douglass confirmed, possessively.

"I hate to tell you this, Colonel," Kennedy said. "But the lady doesn't seem prone to throw herself in your arms."

"That's because she doesn't want to make you feel jealous," Douglass said.

They smiled at each other.

"Thanks for the lessons," Douglass said. "How did a fair-to-middling airplane driver like you wind up flying aerial barges?"

"Just lucky, I guess," Kennedy said. "And just for the hell of it, Colonel, if that were a check ride, you would have passed it."

They smiled at each other again.

"Let's go see if we can make Bitter blush again," Douglass said.

4

Budapest, Hungary
0350 Hours 19 February 1943

Canidy didn't see the policeman with his hand held up until he was almost on him.

He had been too busy watching the road in front of him. It had been a long time since he had ridden a bicycle, and while it was true, he had found out, that once you learned how, you never forgot, it was also true that pedaling a bicycle required muscles he hadn't used in a long time. Even moving as slowly as they had been riding, his calves and upper thighs were heavy with exhaustion.

And the road was covered with frozen slush, which caught the wheel of the bicycle when it rode in one of the ruts. He had taken four spills; and one of them was a bad one, throwing him heavily on his right shoulder and bruising his right knee.

There was no chance to stop before he got to the policeman, although he made a valiant effort. And, he saw, there was no place to run either, no corner to duck around. The policeman had appeared from nowhere because he had been inside a small, wooden guard shack almost hidden by the buttresses of the Árpád Bridge. There was nothing ahead but the bridge itself, and if the policeman couldn't run him down on foot, which seemed likely, then he would have no trouble shooting at him.

The policeman got out of his way, as Canidy locked the

hand brakes and skidded to a stop on the icy slush, the bike slipping out from under him.

He heard Ferniany laugh behind him as Canidy fell to his knees.

And then the policeman said something. Canidy had no idea what he said, but he thought there was a tone of laughter in it.

Canidy got to his feet, picked up the bicycle, and walked to where the policeman was now examining Ferniany's identity documents. Canidy rested the bicycle against his leg, reached inside his ragged shepherd's coat for his papers, and held them ready in his hand until the policeman was ready to take them.

He looked toward the far end of the bridge. He could not tell if there was another policeman in another hidden shack at the far end. Probably not. The Árpád Bridge crossed a branch of the Danube between Pest and Margit Island. The Margit Bridge crossed the other branch of the Danube to Buda. If there was another guard shack, it would be on the Margit Bridge, not at the end of this one.

If it became necessary to kill this policeman—by breaking his neck or cutting his throat—it would still be possible to continue across the Danube here.

The policeman handed Ferniany's papers back and turned to Canidy. He was shaking his head. He said something. Canidy had no idea what it was, but he shrugged.

The policeman took his papers. Canidy saw Ferniany take his garrote[1] from his pocket.

The policeman returned Canidy's papers with what could have been a courteous bow. Then he turned Canidy around and unfastened the straps of the rucksack Canidy had on his back. He came out with a small cheese and a small sausage.

Canidy gestured that he was welcome to it. The policeman smiled and then politely fastened the straps on the rucksack. Then he went to Ferniany's bicycle and began to unfasten the straps holding a limp rucksack over the fender. Canidy put his hands up his sleeves, hoping it looked as if he was trying to

[1]A length of piano wire with a wooden handle at each end. Properly placed, a garrote was not only an effective killer, but kept the victim from crying out while being strangled.

warm his hands. He jerked the strap around the hilt of his Baby Fairbairn[2] free and tested to see if he could quickly get it out of its sheath.

Fulmar and Whittaker had given him a quick course in assassination. Neither of them liked the garrote. *("What if the wire gets hung on a button or something?"* Fulmar had calmly argued, *"Or if he gets his fingers under the wire before you can bury it in his neck? Put your hand over his mouth and stick him behind the ear. As soon as you scramble his brains, you can let him go. It takes a hell of a long time to strangle somebody.")* Whittaker's preferred technique of assassination was throat-cutting. *("Once you cut into the throat, all they can do is gargle."* Whittaker had said. *"I don't trust the itty-bitty point on the Fairbairn, especially the little one. You hit a bone or something, and it breaks, and there you are with your hand over the mouth of some highly pissed-off character you can't put down.")*

Canidy had decided the Fairbairn was best, because it was far more concealable than a throat-cutting knife, and because Jimmy Whittaker had somewhat reluctantly conceded that there was a lot of blood when you cut someone's throat and very little when you scrambled his brains.

Canidy felt bile in his throat at the prospect that he might now have to put theory into practice, but it did not become necessary. The policeman helped himself to a tub of butter from Ferniany's rucksack and waved them on.

They rode to the end of the bridge and then crossed Margit Island. He could see what looked to him like an amusement park closed for the winter, small wooden shacks in a line; an oblong building that could have concealed a dodgem ride; a larger round building that almost certainly contained a merry-go-round.

There was no policeman at the Buda end of the Margit Bridge.

Two blocks into Buda, the cobblestone street became too steep and too slippery to pedal the bicycles, and they got off and pushed. And for some reason, here the slush had begun

---

[2]A dagger developed by Captain Bruce Fairbairn of the Shanghai Municipal Police. The "Baby" was the smaller of two versions and was used when concealment was desirable.

to melt (Canidy wondered about this and decided they were over a tunnel of some kind, maybe a sewer, that gave off enough heat to melt the frozen slush). So his feet, in rough leather work shoes and thick cotton socks, quickly became wet and then even colder than they had been.

Between the Margit Bridge and Batthyany Palace, they passed two more policemen, but neither of them showed any interest in the bicyclists.

When Ferniany finally pushed his bicycle off the street and onto the sidewalk before the facade of what looked like a museum, Canidy was sweat-soaked from exertion and annoyed that Ferniany seemed immune to both fatigue and cold.

The doorbell was just that, a handle which when pulled caused a bell somewhere inside the building to just audibly tinkle.

By the time a small door built into the larger door opened a crack, Canidy had his breath back, but his sweat-soaked clothing had chilled, and he was shivering and his feet hurt.

A small old man with white hair and very bright eyes exchanged a few words with Ferniany, and then opened the door to let them pass.

There were more cobblestones inside the door, and at the end of a passageway a courtyard. The little old man led them into a huge kitchen and said something to Ferniany, apparently an order to wait. The kitchen, Canidy saw, was not in use. There was a huge icebox, and each of its half dozen doors was wedged open. More important, none of the three wood-burning stoves held a fire.

A door opened, and a rather startling redhead came into the kitchen. Her hair, a magnificent mop of dark red, hung below her shoulders. She was wrapped in an ankle-length, somewhat bedraggled, Persian lamb coat. The hem of a woolen nightgown was exposed at the bottom, and her feet were in what Canidy at first thought were Half Wellington boots, but which he saw after a moment were really sheepskin-lined jodhpurs.

She shook Ferniany's hand, and they had a brief exchange. Then she turned to Canidy. She spoke British-accented English.

"I am the Countess Batthyany," she said. "How may I be of service, Major?"

"I'm Pharmacist," Canidy said.

Her eyebrows rose in genuine surprise.

"You would be far more welcome," she said, "if I didn't suspect that you wouldn't be here unless there is trouble."

"Have you got any brandy?" Canidy said. "I'm chilled to the bone."

"Yes, of course," she said. "Forgive me."

She turned and motioned for them to follow her. There was a narrow, rather steep flight of stairs, and then a door. They stepped into a dimly lit room. The room was well furnished, and when Canidy glanced around, he saw that the door they had come through was cut through the paneling of the room so that it would fit in with the decor. A servant's passageway, he decided.

When he turned around again, there was a man in the room. Tall, aristocratic, wearing a silk dressing gown. He held a Walther Ppk .32 ACP pistol in his hand. It was pointed at the floor.

"Was ist los?" he asked.

"Liebchen, this is Major Canidy," the Countess said, adding, "'*Pharmacist.*' Major, may I introduce His Excellency Brigadeführer-SS von Heurten-Mitnitz?"

Von Heurten-Mitnitz's expression did not change, but he spent a long moment examining Canidy before he spoke.

"The major and his friend look frozen," he said. "Could you ring for some brandy? Something for them to eat?"

"Yes, of course," the Countess said.

Then von Heurten-Mitnitz looked at Canidy again.

"You don't happen to know Putzi's son's name, do you?"

"I was wondering if you were going to ask," Canidy said, and then gave his part of the prearranged countersign. "Ergon."

Von Heurten-Mitnitz nodded coolly and managed a brief smile.

"My next question," he said, "obviously, would be to ask what brings you here. But I'm a little afraid to ask."

"Eric Fulmar and Professor Dyer are in the municipal jail in Pécs," Canidy said. "You didn't know?"

"Jesus, Maria und Josef!" the Countess breathed.

"No," von Heurten-Mitnitz said, "I didn't."

"We're done for," the Countess said, matter-of-factly.

"Can you at least get Helmut and me out? Is that what you've come for?"

"I came in to arrange for a site into which we can paradrop a team," Canidy said.

"'Paradrop?'" von Heurten-Mitnitz asked. "You mean parachute?"

Canidy nodded.

"You've got to get us out!" the Countess said, furiously.

"That may not be necessary," Canidy said. "Fulmar and the professor have been arrested as black marketeers."

"How do you know that?" von Heurten-Mitnitz asked, calmly.

"I was there when they were arrested," Ferniany said.

"Then there is a *chance,*" von Heurten-Mitnitz said, searched for the words, and smiled wryly, "'that the jig is not up?'"

"There's a chance," Canidy said. "Ferniany is more confident about that than I am."

"The function of your team will be to get them out of prison?" von Heurten-Mitnitz asked.

"The team leader will have my orders, I'm sure," Canidy said. "I don't know what they will be."

Canidy saw in von Heurten-Mitnitz's eyes that he would not have to explain that his orders might be to make absolutely sure that neither Fulmar nor Professor Dyer would be available for interrogation by the SS or the Gestapo. And when he looked at the Countess Batthyany, he saw in her face that she understood, too.

"I want to try to get them out," Canidy said.

"A question of priorities, then?" von Heurten-Mitnitz said.

"Yes," Canidy said.

"And where on that list would be the priority to get out the Countess, or for that matter me?"

"If it comes to that," Canidy said, "we'll get you out."

"We will go out," the Countess said, "or stay, together."

Von Heurten-Mitnitz looked at her for a moment, and then at his wristwatch.

"It's too early," he said. "But later, I will call Müller and ask him to pick me up here." He saw the look on Canidy's face. "It is necessary."

After a moment, Canidy nodded.

"Just so long as he understands that I will make the decision about trying to get Fulmar and the professor out."

"I thought you implied that decision will be made by your superiors?" von Heurten-Mitnitz asked.

"I'll decide," Canidy said, flatly.

5

Fersfield Army Air Corps Station
Bedfordshire, England
0410 Hours 19 February 1943

"There's no reason for you to get up," Douglass said, as he sat up in the narrow bed and swung his feet out onto the floor.

Charity sat up in bed.

"I've been pretending that we're in Bala-Cynwyd . . ." she said.

"Where?" he asked, chuckling.

"It's a suburb of Philadelphia," she said, ". . . and that the alarm clock has just gone off, and that you're going to get up and put on a suit, and that when you have had breakfast you'll kiss the children. And then I'll drive you to the station, and you'll get on the commuter train and go in to your office in Philadelphia . . ."

"What kind of an office?"

"You're a lawyer, like my father," she said.

"Why a lawyer?"

"Because when lawyers leave their loving wives and adoring children to go to their offices, they know they'll be coming home that same night, not going off to some impossible island nobody ever heard about . . ."

"Stanley's a lawyer," Douglass said.

"Damn you, come back to me," Charity said.

"I'll have to, to make you an honest woman," he said.

"And to give the baby a name," Charity said.

"What baby?"

"The one I think we made last night," Charity said.

"Last night, or ten minutes ago?" he replied.

"I hope we did. Whenever," Charity said. "How do you like them apples, Colonel?"

"Hey, is this the right time to discuss something like that?" Douglass asked.

"The best time," Charity said. "If a man doesn't believe that a woman loves him after she says she wants his baby, he'll never believe it. I want you to *know* it, Doug."

He stopped in the act of pulling his shorts on and went to the bed and sat on it.

"Me, too," he said.

"That's close," Charity said.

"I love you," he said.

"Correct," she said. "That wins you your choice of a trip to the sunny and romantic Adriatic isle of Vis, a cement bicycle, or whatever else your little heart desires. Me, for example."

"Jesus, Honey, they're waiting for me."

"I thought RHIP."

"It does," he said. "Fuck 'em, let 'em wait."

" "em? 'em?' " Charity asked.

6

Headquarters, U.S. Forces in the Philippines
Misamis Occidental Province, Mindanao
19 February 1943

There was now some official stationery available to Headquarters, U.S. Forces in the Philippines. It was a good quality 24-pound watermarked bond paper, with an engraved letterhead. The letterhead read,

THE DOLE CORPORATION
Pineapple Plantation Three
"There Are None Finer"
Mindanao, Territory of the Philippine Islands

Headquarters, United States Forces in the Philippines used the blank side of the paper, but only for important official documents. After some thought, General Fertig decided that it was necessary to maintain certain files, and to use his available stock of stationery (one and one half boxes, totaling precisely 741 sheets of paper) to do so.

USFIP had acquired some other desperately needed supplies from the mountainside cottage of the manager of the Dole Corporation's Pineapple Plantation Number Three. The cottage, some miles from the plantation itself, had been the manager's private retreat. It had somehow escaped Japanese attention, and so it had held a dozen sets of bed linen (which USFIP converted into bandages); a Winchester single-shot, bolt-action .22 caliber rifle and three and a half boxes of .22 shells; a motley collection of inexpensive tableware and pots and pans; a mixed assortment of condiments and canned delicacies (such as Planter's Peanuts, martini olives and miniature onions); a Zenith portable radio; and a Smith-Corona "Student's" portable typewriter with a nearly new ribbon.

General Fertig had his staff prepare copies for the record of the several pronouncements he had made as Commanding General, USFIP; the commissions he had bestowed upon certain members of his staff; and memorandums of record of the money issued by the Provisional Government of Misamis Occidental Province and which he had borrowed for USFIP.

And he instructed his Cryptographic Officer, Capt. Horace B. Buchanan, to assume personal responsibility for the Smith-Corona and the stock of stationery, and, aside from making copies of outgoing and incoming messages, to make sure that no one used either paper or typewriter in a manner that could by any stretch of the imagination be considered profligate.

When Capt. Buchanan went to General Fertig's quarters with the two messages that had come in within five minutes of each other, the general was having his evening cocktail. Second Lieutenant (ex-Chief Petty Officer, USN) Elwood Orfett, whom Fertig had placed in charge of a deserted cocoanut oil mill, had revealed another talent. He could convert mashed pineapple meat into alcohol, producing a lethal-smelling transparent intoxicant with the kick of a mule, but which, when mixed with pineapple juice, didn't taste half bad.

"Would you like a little taste, Buchanan?" Fertig asked as Buchanan came up the bamboo stairs of the general's quarters, shaking the whole building.

"Don't mind if I do, Sir," Buchanan said and helped himself to a glass of the mixture. He poured it from a pottery mug in the shape of a cow's head. This was originally intended for milk, and was also salvaged from the pineapple plantation manager's cottage.

Fertig read the two messages:

PRIORITY FROM KAZ FOR WYZB ATTENTION LT COL FERTIG

YOUR RADIO MESSAGE OF 15 FEBRUARY 1943 FOR SECWAR WASHINGTON HAS COME TO THE ATTENTION OF THIS HEADQUARTERS.

ALL REPEAT ALL COMMUNICATIONS FROM YOUR DETACHMENT OF WHATEVER NATURE WILL BE DIRECTED TO THIS HEADQUARTERS. NO DEVIATION FROM THIS POLICY WILL BE TOLERATED.

BY COMMAND OF GENERAL MACARTHUR. WILLOUGHBY BRIG GEN

"I rather expected this one," Fertig said. Then he read the second message.

URGENT FROM JOINT CHIEFS OF STAFF WASH DC VIA KSF FOR WYZB HQ US FORCES IN PHILIPPINES ATTENTION BRIGADIER GENERAL FERTIG KEEP YOUR SHIRT ON STOP J.R. ELLIS CHIEF USN STOP END

"I rather like the sound of this one," Fertig said, "even if I haven't the faintest idea what it means."

"I'd say it's the reason General Willoughby sounds just a little pissed," Capt. Buchanan said. "It's addressed to 'General Fertig,' you'll notice."

"You think Willoughby knows about it?" Fertig asked.

"He knew about our message to the Secretary of War," Buchanan said. "Sure, I think he heard about it. He's probably got the whole message."

"What do you mean by that?" Fertig asked, curiously.

"The signature on the message is incomplete," Buchanan said. "There had to be more to it than 'Chief USN.' Chief of something. What?"

"I thought it meant 'Chief Petty Officer,'" Fertig said.

"Chief Petty Officers don't sign messages from the Joint Chiefs of Staff," Buchanan said. "Admirals and generals do that."

He remembered—and then was a little ashamed of the memory—that General Fertig, who had been a civilian eighteen months ago, knew damned little about the military services.

"Then what the hell does it mean?" Fertig asked. "'Keep Your Shirt On' doesn't sound at all military, does it?"

Buchanan filled his glass again before replying.

"I thought about that, General," he said. "It may be . . . maybe even probably is . . . a reply to your message to the Secretary of War. And it just might mean exactly what it says."

"That we should be patient, that they *are* sending help?"

"I wonder at what point you want something so desperately that you lose sight of reality and imagine you see what you're looking for behind every bush," Buchanan said.

"But?"

"The message is from the Joint Chiefs," Buchanan said. "And we have a 'we are pissed' message from MacArthur. Which just might mean MacArthur has been asked to explain why no help has been sent to us. Or even that he has been ordered to get off his ass and send some."

"Yes," Fertig said, softly, thoughtfully. "Could be."

"And if I wanted to get a message to somebody who doesn't have any cryptographic equipment worth a damn," Buchanan went on, "it would run through my mind to send a message in slang, in the clear, and hope that the Japs wouldn't understand the slang, and would try to decode the slang."

"We have heard from MacArthur about the Secretary of War message," Fertig said, "and there was no reply to our message about VD medicine."

"That might be because it would be beneath the generalissimo's dignity to acknowledge. Nobody talks to MacArthur that way."

"You really think there was more to that message than what we got—specifically, a rank, and a job title?" Fertig asked.

"I think there just had to be."

"If there was a message, it seems common decency would

have required MacArthur, or Willoughby, to relay it to us. To make sure we got it."

Buchanan shrugged.

"'Common decency,'" he parroted, bitterly.

"The last time I saw the Generalissimo," Fertig said, "was in the Manila Club. There was a buffet. MacArthur, of course, and his queen and the crown prince didn't stand in the line. But I went through it with my wife. And as we walked to our table, we had to squeeze around their table. He was in a planter's white suit. I had a large bowl of shrimp bisque. I will regret for the rest of my life not having had an accident with it."

Buchanan laughed.

"It may be, Buchanan," Fertig said, "that help is on the way. But I think it more likely that you and I are sitting here with five ounces of Orfett's pineapple white lightning in us, seeing things we want to see behind bushes that just aren't there. I don't want any of this to go any further than you or me."

"No, Sir," Buchanan said. And then he blurted, "But sooner or later, Christ, they're going to have to do something, aren't they?"

"Sooner or later," Fertig said.

7

Batthyany Palace
Budapest, Hungary
0820 20 February 1943

Standartenführer SS-SD Johann Müller came into the sitting room of the Countess's apartment in Batthyany Palace and quickly glanced around the room, taking in Canidy and Ferniany, who were sitting on a couch before a gilt coffee table.

There was no expression on his face.

"'Tag," he said, and then started to unbutton his black leather overcoat. He hung it carefully on the back of a Louis XIV chair and then moved the chair to a position near one of the two white porcelain stoves. Then he moved the chair a foot further away.

"If you get it too close, it cracks and dries the leather," he explained.

And then he looked at Helmut von Heurten-Mitnitz, his eyebrows raised in question.

"Johann," von Heurten-Mitnitz said in German, "this is Major Canidy of the United States Army. *'Pharmacist.'*"

Müller examined Canidy carefully, then did the same thing to Ferniany. He was subjected to the same kind of an examination by the Americans.

"And him?" Müller asked.

"Ferniany's my name," Ferniany said.

"Canidy's man on the scene, I gather," von Heurten-Mitnitz explained.

"Everybody speak slowly," Canidy said. "My German is pretty weak."

"He was telling him who we are," Ferniany said.

"I got that," Canidy said. "But go slow. I don't want to miss anything."

"Gott im Himmel!" Müller said, exasperated. "They send someone in who doesn't even speak the language!"

"It was necessary," Canidy said.

"Why?"

"Eric Fulmar and Professor Dyer are in the Pécs city jail," Canidy said.

This produced the first hint of excitement in Müller.

"And Gisella?" he demanded, "Fräulein Dyer?"

"She's safe," Canidy said.

"Safe where?"

"Cairo," Canidy said.

"So what happened?" Müller demanded. He was back in control of his emotions, but there had been enough for Canidy to decide that there was more than a casual relationship between the SS-SD officer and Dyer's daughter.

"The barge was boarded by the River Police and the Black Guard," Ferniany said. "They found a lot of money on Fulmar and decided he was a black marketeer. They helped themselves to the money and arranged for them to get ninety days in the coal mines."

"It's only a matter of time until somebody finds out who

they are," Müller said. "I had a teletype yesterday—addressed to me personally, not to the senior SS-SD officer—from Von Hymme, Himmler's[3] adjutant, telling me to personally make sure that 'the investigation was being pursued with all diligence.'"

"They think they're here?"

"From the time they found the Gestapo agent's body, they really closed down the borders of Germany to the occupied countries and to the neutrals. Himmler's mouth ran away with him again, and he said he could personally state that nobody got out that way. That leaves only here."

"Another question," Canidy said. "Why all the interest?"

"It would be enough," Müller replied drily, "that the Reichsführer-SS has showed his ass by not catching them long before this. And on top of that, our friend Eric used his knife on a Gestapo agent, which has the Gestapo in a rage. And then he used it on Peis, the SS-SD commander in Marburg an der Lahn, which has the SS-SD upset."

"Tell me about 'pursuing the investigation with all diligence,'" Canidy said.

"After you round up 'all the usual suspects,' which was done and which came up with nothing," Müller said, "you start to recheck things like travel permits, hospital admittances, and jails. When I got the teletype, I ordered that done. I don't know how long it will take them to check the Pécs jail, but it won't be long. If I was doing it . . . instead, I mean, of having to ask the Black Guard for their cooperation . . . I would have them by now."

Müller waited for that to sink in, and then went on, "If you've got some idea of getting them out of that jail, you had better do it now."

"Major Canidy has asked for a team of specialists," von Heurten-Mitnitz said. "The reason he's here is to arrange for a landing site."

"A landing site? You mean for parachutists?" Müller asked.

Canidy nodded.

"How long will that take? What's wrong with using the underground?" Müller asked.

[3]Heinrich Himmler was Reichsführer-SS.

"The underground can't be involved in this," Canidy said.

"How long will it take to get your 'specialists' in here?"

"Forty-eight hours, maybe twenty-four, after we find a place to drop them," Canidy said.

"The story I get," Müller said, "is that there are parachutists dropping all over Yugoslavia and Hungary."

"This has to be kept separate from that," Canidy said.

"We may not have forty-eight hours," Müller said. "We may not even have twenty-four." He looked at Canidy. "If they catch Fulmar, he knows von Heurten-Mitnitz and me. And, sooner or later, he would tell them everything he knows."

"And me," the Countess said. "He knows me."

"We'll arrange to get you out," Canidy said.

"Von Heurten-Mitnitz's family would probably be all right if he disappeared," Müller went on, "and the Countess doesn't have anything to lose. But they would go after my mother and my brothers and sisters."

"Then the thing to do is get Eric and the professor out of the jail, isn't it?" Canidy replied.

"Under the circumstances," Müller said, "I would say the thing to do is arrange for them to be shot while being arrested," Müller said.

"If they are to be shot, I'll make that decision," Canidy said.

"I really don't need your permission, Herr Major," Müller said.

"How large an area do you need for your parachutists, Major?" the Countess asked.

Müller glared at her.

"For the time being, Johann," von Heurten-Mitnitz said, "we will go along with Major Canidy."

"A minimum of eight hundred meters by three," Canidy said.

"So large?" she asked, disappointed, and then went on: "There is a field, a meadow, in the mountains above Pécs. We have a hunting lodge there. But it's not that big."

"What's around it?" Canidy asked.

"A forest," she said.

"Would a low-flying aircraft attract attention?"

"Of course," she said.

Canidy exhaled.

"If that's all there is, we'll have to use it," Canidy said. "Could you find it on a map?"

"I don't know," she said. "And I don't have a map."

Canidy gestured impatiently at Ferniany, who went to his sheepskin coat, dug into a pocket, and came out with a map.

With some difficulty, the Countess found the meadow she was looking for on the map.

"It's damned small, and it's thirteen miles from Pécs," she said.

"But it hasn't been used, has it?" Canidy said.

"No," Ferniany said. "There's that."

"Take the coordinates," Canidy ordered, "and then burn the map. And then you better get going."

"Where's he going?" Müller asked.

"To radio the location of the drop zone," Canidy said. "And to make arrangements to move the professor and Eric once we get them out."

"And what do you plan to do?" von Heurten-Mitnitz asked.

"The next problem is to get me from here to the Countess's hunting lodge," Canidy said.

"How do you plan to do that?" Müller asked.

"Gisella told me you have an Opel Admiral," Canidy said. "How about that?"

"I can't afford to be seen anywhere near Pécs," Müller said.

"No," Canidy said. "You are going to be at the Austro-Hungarian border, noisily 'pursuing the investigation with all diligence.'"

Müller snorted.

"And the Countess and I will go to the hunting lodge?" von Heurten-Mitnitz said, thoughtfully, "in Müller's car? With you in the luggage boot?"

"Unless you've got a better idea," Canidy said.

"The plane will attract attention," von Heurten-Mitnitz said. "And it will come out that we were there."

"The day before, maybe two days before," Canidy said.

"But it will come out," von Heurten-Mitnitz repeated.

"Unless you've got a better idea," Canidy repeated.

Müller snorted again.

Canidy looked at him coldly.

"And in case you think you have a better idea, Standartenführer Müller," he said, "I think I had better tell you that if this operation goes sour, Reichsführer-SS Himmler will receive, mailed from Sweden, an hour-by-hour report of how you spent your last forty-eight hours in Morocco. With photographs, showing you with Eric in his U.S. Army uniform."

Müller's eyes, very cold, met Canidy's, but he didn't say anything.

"At the risk of repeating myself," Canidy said, "it may be necessary to do whatever is necessary to keep Fulmar and the professor from falling into the hands of the SS. But I will make that decision."

Müller snorted again, and pursed his lips.

"When I first saw you, Major," Müller said, finally, "what I thought was they had sent an amateur. Obviously, I was wrong."

8

Cairo, Egypt
1225 Hours 20 February 1943

Captain Stanley S. Fine resisted the temptation to let Lt. Colonel Peter Douglass, Jr., who was riding as co-pilot, land the B-17F. Doug Douglass, despite the expected fighter pilot's denigration of the "flying barge" was obviously fascinated with the bomber. He would have liked to make the landing, and he probably would have handled it onto the wide and long runway without any trouble at all. He was an experienced pilot, and he had been an apt pupil.

But the moment they had taken off from Fersfield, Fine had been very much aware that they had crossed a line. From now on, everything was dead serious. There was no excuse whatever for taking any kind of a chance, no matter how slight.

Nothing had been said between them, but Douglass had seemed to understand and had conducted himself as a co-pilot should, making no control movements at all without first getting Fine's permission.

Fine set the B-17F down smoothly within two hundred feet of the threshold, and then he lowered it gently down onto the tail wheel.

"Call the tower?" Douglass's voice came over the intercom.

"Please," Fine said.

"Cairo, Army Triple Zero Four on the ground at twenty-five past the hour," Douglass said. "Request taxi instructions."

"Triple Zero Four, take Taxiway Two Right and find yourself a place to park with the other B-17s on the line."

Douglass looked over at Fine. He was surprised. Ten minutes before, Cairo had acknowledged the "This is Eighth Air Force Flight Five Six Six" message which was supposed to alert OSS Cairo that they had arrived. Douglass did not expect the B-17 to be ordered to find itself a place to park with the other 17s on the line.

Fine looked surprised, too.

Douglass pressed the mike button.

"Cairo, Triple Zero Four, say again your last transmission. You were garbled."

Cairo repeated the order.

There were a dozen B-17s and B-24s, and twice that many other transient aircraft on the parking line, but there was no sign of Canidy's B-25.

Fine taxied the B-17 to the end of the line, parked it in a line with another B-17, shut it down, and prepared the flight documents.

A gas truck, a brand-new General Motors semitrailer, stopped just off the taxiway in front of them, and a crew got off and began to unroll fueling hoses.

"I'll go see what's going on," Fine said, unstrapping his harness. "I think we had better keep our passengers aboard."

Fine opened the access hatch and lowered himself through it. Douglass went through the bomb bay into the rear of the fuselage. The team was peering out the gun ports.

"Colonel?" János asked. "Can we get off?"

"Not yet," Douglass said. "Somebody fucked up. There's nobody here to meet us."

"That figures," János said.

It was already getting hot in the fuselage; Douglass felt sweat under his arms and on his forehead as he saw it pop out on János's face.

"Fuck it," he said. "I don't see any point in melting. Get out, get in the shade of the wing, but don't stray off. And don't take anything with you."

He went to the side door in the fuselage and opened it, and then waited until the last of the team had gotten out before getting out himself.

The team was gone when he got outside, and he saw that a Dodge ambulance had been backed up to the nose of the B-17. Normally, Dodge ambulance bodies had huge red crosses painted on their sides and roof; this one did not.

"You get to ride in front, Colonel," a voice called, and he saw a hand gesture toward the front of the vehicle.

Douglass walked to the ambulance and got in.

The driver was a sergeant, and Douglass had his mouth open to ask him where they were being taken when a familiar voice spoke.

"The shit's hitting the fan."

Douglass looked into the back of the ambulance. The narrow benches on each side were jammed with people, and one of them was Lt. Commander John Dolan.

"Canidy went into Hungary," Dolan went on.

"Jesus!" Douglass said, then: "How are you? There was word you had a terminal case of the GIs."

"I'm better," Dolan said.

"Where are we going?"

"They got a villa," Dolan said. "Very nice, swimming pool and everything."

"Does anybody know why Dick went into Hungary?" Douglass asked.

"Does anybody know why he does anything?" Dolan replied. "They're trying to get a message to him to get his ass out of there. Everything's on hold until we see if that works."

"Who's 'they're'?" Douglass asked.

"Donovan himself," Dolan said. "They're apparently really pissed."

Wilkins, the Cairo Station Chief, was waiting for them at the villa. A lunch had been laid out for everyone at the side of the pool. There was no sense of urgency, and both Fine and Douglass were annoyed. But as they were eating, a distinguished-looking man in a stiffly starched but tieless shirt came to the table and handed Wilkins a sheet of paper.

Wilkins glanced at it, and then handed it to Douglass.

"Sorry, Colonel," he said. "But I didn't know where exactly you fitted into this."

Douglass read it.

TOP SECRET

OPERATIONAL IMMEDIATE FROM OSS WASHINGTON TO OSS CAIRO

LT COL PETER DOUGLASS JR USAAC IS AUTHORIZED ACCESS TO SUCH CLASSIFIED MATERIAL IN CONNECTION WITH CURRENT MISSION AS IS DEEMED ABSOLUTELY NECESSARY REPEAT ABSOLUTELY NECESSARY BY STATION CHIEF CAIRO AND PHARMACIST TWO END DONOVAN

"Well," Douglass said, "It's nice to know I'm to be trusted, if absolutely necessary."

Wilkins did not seem amused.

"I understand Donovan is pissed at Canidy," Douglass said.

"I don't think 'pissed' is the word," Wilkins said.

"If Canidy went into Hungary, he had his reasons," Douglass said, loyally.

"I hope he finds his reasons worth it," Wilkins said.

"I don't think I follow you," Douglass said.

"Come with me," Wilkins said, "and you, too, Fine."

He led them to the pool house, where two radio operators sat with earphones on their heads. He motioned Fine and Douglass into chairs, and then dropped to his knees, worked the combination of a safe, and handed Fine a cover sheet stamped TOP SECRET.

TOP SECRET

OPERATIONAL IMMEDIATE FROM OSS WASHINGTON FOR OSS CAIRO EYES ONLY WILKINS

PASS FOLLOWING TO PHARMACIST TWO ON ARRIVAL CAIRO STOP

QUOTE YOU ARE HEREBY APPOINTED EXLAX CONTROL CANIDY RELIEVED STOP APPOINTMENT IS PERMANENT STOP CANIDY WILL NOT REPEAT NOT RESUME AUTHORITY OVER EXLAX UNDER ANY CONDITIONS STOP EVERYTHING POSSIBLE INCLUDING TERMINATION REPEAT INCLUDING TERMINATION WILL BE DONE TO PREVENT CANIDY FALLING INTO ENEMY HANDS STOP YOU WILL ACKNOWLEDGE TIME AND DATE OF RECEIPT DONOVAN UNQUOTE

Fine read it and handed it to Douglass.

"Jesus, he is mad," Douglass said.

"You have a code word for a situation like this?" Wilkins asked Fine. "To acknowledge receipt?"

"Yes, I do," Fine said.

"You want to give it to me?" Wilkins asked, on the edge of sarcasm.

"I don't think I will," Fine said. "I don't want to acknowledge that message."

"What?" Wilkins asked, incredulously.

"I'm not sure that was sent by Donovan," Fine said. "Before I acknowledge it, I want confirmation."

"That will take hours," Wilkins said.

"It doesn't sound like Donovan to me, either," Douglass said, loyally.

"What the hell are you trying to pull, Captain?" Wilkins demanded.

"Canidy was there," Fine said. "And he's not a fool. I certainly won't double guess him, and I don't think Colonel Donovan would, either."

Wilkins opened his mouth to argue, but didn't get a chance to speak. One of the operators called out.

"Hey, I got something from Vis . . ."

"What does it say?"

"It's not in the clear, for Christ's sake," the operator said, furiously pounding his typewriter.

Eight minutes later, the decryption process was completed:

FROM POSTMAN FOR CAIRO VIA STATION VIII

PHARMACIST REQUESTS EARLIEST POSSIBLE DROP RESCUE TEAM AT COORDINATES SEVEN FOUR NINE NINE THREE EIGHT

ONE EIGHT STOP DROP MUST REPEAT MUST TAKE PLACE AT FIRST LIGHT STOP ADVISE

It took another five minutes to find the map of Hungary, and then to mark the location indicated by the coordinates.

"We're how far from Vis?" Fine wondered aloud.

"Four hours thirty," Douglass said, immediately. "In the B-25."

Using his thumb and little finger as a compass, Fine measured the distance between Vis and Pécs.

"That's about an hour and a quarter," he said. "Maybe a little less."

"What about that 'must take place at first light' business?" Douglass asked.

"Jesus," Fine said. "You're asking, how do we take off from Pécs in the dark?"

"Yeah," Douglass said. "But we don't have to take off from Pécs. We can take off from here."

"We don't have the range," Fine said.

"More than enough, if we sit down at Pécs on the way back," Douglass said.

Fine was silent for a moment.

Then he said, "Message Pharmacist as follows. Team will be available for drop first light tomorrow."

Twelve

1

Pécs, Hungary
1330 Hours 20 February 1943

WHAT CANIDY HAD imagined was going to be adequate accommodation in the large trunk of Standartenführer-SS Müller's Opel Admiral quickly proved to be mildly, and then excruciatingly, uncomfortable.

Despite the generous proportions of the Admiral's trunk, he could not stretch his legs without arcing his torso painfully, nor raise himself on his elbows without simultaneously lowering his head so that his chin rested on his upper chest.

And the thick goose-down comforters and pillows which the Countess Batthyany had put into the trunk to keep him warm and serve as cushions had not been as helpful as everyone had cheerfully, almost gaily, believed. The comforter had quickly crushed down under him, so that he could feel every ridge and indentation in the trunk floor. And the comforter he had wrapped around himself for warmth, and the pillows on which he had planned to cushion his head, made things worse than nothing at all, for they retained enough bulk to get in the way when he shifted his body again and again to relieve the strain on his muscles.

He became uneasy, nervous, worried; and he began to wonder if he had some previously unsuspected problem with claustrophobia. He reasoned that through and decided his nervousness was perfectly reasonable: He was in the dark, and nobody liked that.

More important, it was fifty-fifty that von Heurten-Mitnitz was wrong when he said he "rather doubted they would be stopped at all, or subjected to more than the most perfunctory examination if they were." There was a fifty-fifty chance that the trunk lid would suddenly open and he would find himself looking up at a Black Guard, a Hungarian cop, or even a Gestapo agent. If that happened, he was not going to be in a position to do much about it. The Sten submachine gun Captain Hughson had given him in Vis was now in the hands of an admiring Yugoslav partisan. Canidy was armed now only with the Fairbairn and a snub-nosed Smith & Wesson "Chief's Special," neither of which would be of any real use if the car was stopped and checked. If that happened, in addition to being nearly paralyzed by the goddamned trunk, he would be blinded by the sudden light and helpless.

There had been time to remember where he had gotten the snub-nosed .38, and that hadn't helped his morale, either. Jimmy Whittaker had given it to him just before they'd taken off on the mission to the Belgian Congo. Moments before that, Jimmy had taken it away from the flight engineer. The flight engineer had been given the pistol by the Chief, OSS London Station, together with an order that he use it on Canidy the moment it looked as if Canidy was going to fall into enemy hands.

It was not difficult to proceed from that to the logical conclusion that if an elimination order (to keep him from falling into enemy hands) had been issued then, a similar order had doubtless also been issued to cover this circumstance. He knew now more information that the Germans shouldn't know than he had known when he and Jimmy had flown off to the Belgian Congo.

He wondered where Whittaker was at that moment. In Australia, more than likely, dazzling the Australian women with his good looks and all-pink uniform. Whittaker, he thought, should have been a sailor; he already had a girl in every airport.

Ann came to mind then, and he wallowed for a moment in the memory of the smell of her, and the feel, and the touch of her hand on him, and then he forced Ann from his mind.

And then he got a headache. He was suddenly aware of it,

a real bitch of a headache behind his eyes and across the base of his skull. He realized that he had been aware of *getting* a headache for some time.

"Oh, shit!" he said aloud.

He tried to look at his wristwatch to see how long he had been in the trunk. The Hamilton chronometer with the glowing hands was now adorning the wrist of the fishing boat captain. He couldn't even see the watch he had been given in return, much less tell what time it was.

In that ten seconds, the headache seemed to have grown even worse.

And then he knew why he had a headache.

"Pull over!" Canidy shouted. "Let me out of here!"

There was no reply. They apparently hadn't heard him. He could hear them talking. He couldn't make out what they were saying, but he could hear them.

He tried shouting again, and again there was no response. His voice was being muffled, he realized, by the thickly padded leather upholstery in the back seat of the Admiral; and what got through was not audible over the whistling of the wind on the convertible roof and the sound of the engine.

Then there was a momentary wave of terror. He was going to die in this fucking trunk, be quietly asphyxiated by carbon monoxide from the exhaust. When they got to the Countess's hunting lodge and opened the trunk, they would find him dead.

He thought first of his pistol. If he fired that, they would hear it.

But where was he to fire it? Out the top of the trunk, so there would be a bullet hole for the cops to become fascinated with? Into the trunk floor, where it would pierce the fuel tank?

And what would firing a pistol in the confined area of the trunk do to his ears?

He put both hands to his head and pressed inward as hard as he could against the pain of the carbon-monoxide-induced headache.

And then he twisted around, shoving to the side the goose-down comforter under him. He felt the floor of the trunk. It was covered with some kind of padding. He found the edge, and with a great deal of effort managed to pry the edge loose. Finally, there was enough loose so that he could grip it. He gave a mighty heave and it came loose. Now, there was nothing there but sheet metal.

He balled his fist and struck the floor of the trunk with all of his strength. And then did so again, and again, and again.

And finally, he sensed that the Admiral was slowing, and then there was the sound of gravel under the tires. The car stopped, and Canidy heard a door open. And then the trunk opened, just a crack. But the light coming through the two-inch opening was so painful Canidy closed his eyes against it.

"Are you all right in there?" von Heurten-Mitnitz asked.

"I'm being asphyxiated," Canidy said. "Is it clear? Can I get out?"

"Asphyxiated?" von Heurten-Mitnitz asked, doubtfully.

"The goddamned muffler leaks," Canidy said.

"Just a moment," von Heurten-Mitnitz said. From his tone of voice, Canidy knew that he now believed him.

And the trunk opened wide. Canidy heard the sound of the hinges and was aware of more light through his closed eyelids.

"Your lips are blue," von Heurten-Mitnitz said. "Here, take my hand."

Canidy opened his eyes just enough to see the hand, grabbed it, and closed his eyes again. Von Heurten-Mitnitz pulled him out of the trunk and led him to the curbside door.

"Lie on the seat," he ordered. "Beatrice, there's a flask in the map box. Give it to him."

"He's sick?" she asked.

"Exhaust poisoning," von Heurten-Mitnitz said. He closed the trunk, and then got behind the wheel and started off.

Canidy felt something cold and metallic at his lips. He took the flask from the Countess and took a deep pull.

He felt the warmth spread through his body, and then something else.

"I think I'm going to be sick," he said.

"Oh, please don't," the Countess Batthyany said, practically. "You never can get that smell out of a car!"

Canidy fought down the urge to vomit and took slow deep breaths. The desire to vomit passed, and he was able after a while to keep his eyes open. He found himself looking into the Countess's face.

"You're getting color back," she said. "You'll be all right, now."

There was genuine relief on her face, Canidy saw, and then decided it almost certainly wasn't for him.

There was another queasy feeling in his stomach. He fought it by sitting up, and it passed, but there was a wave of sharp pain behind his eyes.

He took another pull at the silver brandy flask and looked out the windshield. They were all alone on a narrow, curving road cut through a dense forest of mature pines.

"Where are we?" he asked. "How long was I in the trunk?"

"It's another couple of hours to Pécs," the Countess said. "We left Budapest at half past nine. You were back there about two hours."

"What's next on the road?" Canidy asked. "Am I going to have to get back in the trunk?"

"We just went through Dunaföldvár," the Countess said. "There's a couple of small towns between here and Pécs, Sioagárd and Pécsvárad, hardly more than villages. You'll be all right in the back, I think."

"Do we go through Pécs itself?"

"There's a way around," she said. "But it's dirt roads, and there's no telling how muddy they would be this time of year. And we would attract attention."

"I was wondering whether we could run by the jail," Canidy said, "and then trace the route the truck takes moving the prisoners to the mine."

"We'll take that road anyway," she said. "But it would be a detour to go past Saint Gertrud's."

"A conspicuous detour?" Canidy asked.

She thought that over before replying, "No. It's on the edge of town. But we wouldn't be more conspicuous there than we're going to be anyway."

"Then please tell Herr von Heurten-Mitnitz how to get there," Canidy said. "I want a look."

At quarter to two, the tires leaving a path across previously unbroken snow, the Opel Admiral pulled up before the hunting lodge. It was a long, low wooden building with elaborate scrollwork, now covered with dripping icicles, along the roof line. There was a chimney at each end and a much larger one in the middle. Smoke rose from one of the end chimneys, and as Canidy got out of the car, he could smell wood smoke.

"I think it would be better if you spoke German," the Countess said.

"Who's in the house?" Canidy asked.

"The caretaker and his wife," she said. "And there are foresters in small houses behind the lodge."

"And they can't be trusted?" Canidy asked.

"Of course, they can be trusted," she said. "They have been with my family for hundreds of years. But if the Black Guard comes here, I don't want to ask them to lie any more than necessary. They don't speak German, but they recognize it. I want them to be able to report they saw me with two German-speaking men."

"They're going to know what's going on," Canidy said.

"They will do what I ask them to do," the Countess said, "and then, because I ask them to, they will forget having done it."

Canidy's disbelief showed on his face.

"My father was active in the Independent Hungary movement," the Countess said. "Crown Prince Rudolf used to come here secretly. If my people could forget that he was here, they can forget you."

The look on his face confused her.

"Crown Prince Rudolf was the . . ." she started to explain.

"Heir apparent to the Austro-Hungarian throne," Canidy filled in. "The one who shot his girlfriend, and then himself. At Mayerling."

"Like Standartenführer Müller," von Heurten-Mitnitz said, "the Countess seems to have underestimated you, Canidy."

"And not you?"

"A good diplomat never underestimates anyone," von Heurten-Mitnitz said.

As they approached the hunting lodge, the door was opened by a hefty, large-bosomed woman with jet black hair. The hair was parted in the middle and done up in elaborate braids.

She curtsied to the Countess, and then to the men.

"She says," the Countess said, "that if she had known we

were coming, her husband would have of course been here, and there would be a meal prepared. As it is, all there is is simple boar gulyás. Paprika gulyás."

After they had eaten, Canidy was outfitted, from a wide selection, with a green loden cloth coat and lace-up boots, which were, he suspected, older than he was. Laughing, the Countess added a black cap of heavy wool.

"A real Magyar!" she said.

The caretaker showed up as the Countess was lacing up her boots. With him was a man Canidy's age, with a double-barreled shotgun hanging upside down on a woven leather strap from his shoulder.

"This is Alois, the chief hunter," the Countess explained. "His great-grandfather was my great-grandfather's chief hunter. We will take him with us to the meadow. If there is anything that has to be done, he will see that it is done, and then he will forget that he ever saw you."

"How big a place do you have, Countess?" Canidy asked. "In other words, how about the neighbors?"

"This estate is roughly an oblong," she replied, matter-of-factly. "It is twenty-three kilometers long and about fourteen wide. There are no neighbors, and the local authorities are my tenants. If I do not wish them to see me, or anything else, they will not see me, or anything else."

"You sound very confident of that," Canidy said.

"I am," she said.

A ten-minute walk over light snow brought them to the meadow. It did not meet any of the criteria for a drop zone. It was far too small, and it was surrounded on three sides by a mature pine forest, into which anybody who missed the drop zone would land.

But trees had been harvested at one end of the meadow, where the land dropped precipitously off toward a stream.

When Ferniany arrived with the radios and the panels, tomorrow or the next day, Canidy would arrange the panels either at the edge of the meadow by the forest or at the stream, depending on the wind. With a little bit of luck, they would be able to put three or four of the five parachutists down in the meadow. The others would have to take their chances on landing on his just-cut-over steep land at the end of the meadow.

There would be time to talk to the plane. Darmstadter had dropped parachutists before. He would know how to drop them here, once he had been told of the conditions by radio.

Canidy thought of the emergency backup procedures. There was always that in the planning. Here, in the case of radio failure or if there were no opportunity to put the signal panels in place, it was a smoky fire at the point in the drop zone that would indicate where the first parachutist in the string was supposed to land.

However, it didn't seem to make a hell of a lot of sense to bother about that particular backup. For one thing, there would be a chance to put the panels out and talk with the plane by radio. For another, unless the drop could be discussed with the plane, there would be no point in making the jump; it would be too risky.

But in the end, Canidy asked the Countess to have her chief hunter arrange for a five-foot-high stack of pine boughs at both ends of the drop zone. He showed, with his hands, how large the piles should be.

"And two cans of kerosene, preferably, or else gasoline, by each stack," he said.

She translated that for him.

And then, as if they were two old friends out for a walk in the woods, she took his arm and they walked back to the hunting lodge.

2

Cairo, Egypt
1715 Hours 20 February 1943

The first thing Freddy János realized when he saw that the bomb bay doors of the B-25 in the hangar were not functional was that he was going to have a hell of a hard time dropping out of the crew-access door when the time came.

Then he measured the access door with his hands and realized that there was no way *any* of the team could exit the aircraft wearing all their equipment.

"Something wrong, János?" Lt. Colonel Douglass asked him.

"That hatch isn't big enough," János said. "There's no way we can drop through that little hole."

"We've dropped people through that hole before," Douglass said.

"Only Fulmar," Capt. Stanley S. Fine said, entering the conversation. "The others went out the bomb bay. Before Canidy removed the racks and the door-opening mechanism. And Fulmar jumped in with a British chute. No spare. And it took him a long time to get through the door. *If* we could get them through the door, it would take so long they would land all over Hungary."

"Jesus Christ!" Douglass said furiously. "What the hell do we do now? How come this is the first time anybody thought about this?"

"The B-17 can't land on Vis," Fine said, answering that question before it was asked.

"What's Vis?" Freddy János asked.

Fine and Douglass looked at each other before Fine answered, "An island in the Adriatic. Where we will pick you up when this operation is over."

"Pick us up? We're not going to stay?"

"No," Fine said. "It has been decided to bring you out right away."

"Can I ask why?"

"You can ask, but I can't tell you," Fine said.

"I must be out of my mind," János said. "But that sort of pisses me off."

"Jesus, that's all we need, a hero," Douglass said.

János felt his face turn warm with anger. With an effort, he fought it down by telling himself that Douglass, by any criterion was a hero, and thus had the right to mock the word.

"I guess that sounded pretty dumb," he said.

"Yes, it did," Douglass said, not backing off. "I just hope you can restrain your heroic impulses when you do get in there, and that you do just what you're told, and nothing more."

They locked eyes for a moment. János, for the first time, saw that Douglass could have very cold and calculating eyes. And he sensed suddenly that Douglass was judging him, and that if Douglass found him wanting—if Douglass concluded that there was a risk he would foolishly take once he was in Hungary—there was a good chance he would be left behind.

"Can a gooney bird land on this island?" János asked.

There was no response from Douglass. He continued to look at János with cold calculating eyes.

"What the hell," Douglass said, finally. There was even the flicker of a smile. "When all the clever ideas fail, be desperate. Go by the book. Use a parachutist-dropping airplane to drop parachutists."

"Can we get our hands on a C-47?" János asked.

"Yes," Fine said, almost impatiently. He had seen a dozen of the twin-engine transports sitting on the field. There would probably be one they could have simply by asking for it. And if there was a problem, one would have to be "diverted from other missions." The OSS had the ultimate priority. "But does a 47 have the range?"

"I don't think it does," Douglass said. "I'm not even sure it will make it to Hungary. There's no way one of them could make it to Pécs, and then to Vis."

"Where's Darmstadter?" Fine asked. "He ought to know."

"He and Dolan are checking the weather," Douglass said.

"What's the priority?" Fine asked, rhetorically.

"To get János's team on the ground in one piece," Douglass said.

"We could . . ." Fine began. "I don't know what I'm talking about, and I won't until I know just what the gooney bird can do."

"Well," Douglass said, nodding toward a small door in one of the wide hangar doors where an MP, armed with a Thompson submachine gun, was checking the identification of Lt. Commander John Dolan, USNR, Lt. Henry Darmstadter, and Ernest J. Wilkins, "here comes the expert."

"Well," Wilkins said, cheerfully confident, as he walked up to them. "God loves us, apparently. The immediate and 24-hour weather over the drop zone is going to be perfect."

Douglass laughed nastily.

"Darmstadter," Fine asked. "What's the range of a gooney bird? Would a gooney bird make it one way to Pécs?"

"No," Darmstadter said immediately.

"What's wrong with the B-25?" Dolan asked.

"Canidy has cleverly modified the B-25 so that you can't drop parachutists from it," Douglass said, "or at least not a team of them, without scattering them all over Hungary."

"Good God!" Wilkins said.

"And we can't put the 17 into Vis," Dolan said.

"Right," Fine said.

"Jesus, now what?" Douglass asked. "Canidy expects us at daybreak."

"So we use the 17 for the drop," Dolan said. "And it comes back here. And we send the 25 to Vis. No problem."

"No," Wilkins said.

"What do you mean, 'no'?" Fine asked.

"Maintenance found landing-gear problems," he said. "They called me and told me it would take twenty-four hours, maybe a little more, to replace what was broken."

"Then you'll have to get us another 17," Fine said.

"There will be a lot of questions asked why someone wants to borrow a bomber," Wilkins said.

Darmstadter's mind had been racing. He thought he saw a solution. But he was reluctant to offer it. *These people,* he told himself, *know what they're doing. I'm just a mediocre gooney-bird pilot.*

And then he thought, *Fuck it!*

"If there would be only the team, five men, on the gooney bird," he said, "it would be very light. It would take another ton and a half, maybe two, before it got close to Max Over Gross."[1]

"If you're talking about fuel," Dolan said, not unkindly, "we just don't have time to rig auxiliary fuel tanks."

"I'm talking about 55-gallon drums," Darmstadter plunged on, "and hand pumps to replenish the fuel in the main tanks as it's burned off."

"Hey!" Dolan said, after a moment's thought.

"Would that work, John?" Fine asked.

"Eight 55-gallon drums would weigh 3,200 pounds," Dolan said. "A little over a ton and a half. And that would be another 400 gallons. More than enough to get a gooney bird from here to Pécs, and then to Vis."

---

[1]An over Maximum Over Gross Weight condition permitted under certain conditions.

"And you can get a gooney bird into Vis?" Douglass said.

Dolan thought that over a moment before replying.

"Yeah," he said after a moment, "I think Brother Darmstadter and I could sit a gooney bird down on Vis in one piece." He caught Darmstadter's eye and went on. "We'll have to get the tail wheel down before we hit the stream, going in. If we were still up on the main gear, we'd go over on our nose. Getting out will be easier; we'll just keep the tail wheel on the ground till we're through the water."[2]

Darmstadter nodded his understanding.

"Could Brother Darmstadter and me sit one down in one piece?" Douglass asked.

Dolan looked at him.

"You don't have hardly any gooney-bird time, Colonel," Dolan said, after a moment.

"But I don't have dysentery, either," Douglass said. "Canidy told me about your 'dysentery,' John."

"Canidy has a big mouth," Dolan said. "And I'm all right."

"I don't think we can take a chance on that, John," Douglass said.

"I'm missing something here," Wilkins said.

"I'm afraid Commander Dolan will not be able to go," Douglass said. "Whatever plans we make will have to exclude him."

"First of all, that'd be Fine's decision," Dolan said. "And you haven't heard me out."

"Go ahead, Commander," Fine said, and immediately wondered why he had called Dolan by his rank.

"Darmstadter knows more about dropping . . . what is it they say? 'sticks' . . . sticks of paratroopers than anybody else. And he's also the only one of us with any experience to speak of flying a gooney bird on the deck. And the only way we're going to be able to find Pécs and not get ourselves shot down is to go in on the deck."

"OK, that takes care of Darmstadter," Douglass said. "He flies the gooney bird. We're talking about who goes with him. We're talking about your 'dysentery,' Dolan."

"I was flying cross-country using a road map before any-

---

[2]The B-25 had a tricycle landing gear; the C-47, two main landing wheels and a smaller wheel at the tail.

body else here was out of diapers," Dolan said. "I'm the only one here who can, for sure, find this meadow Canidy has picked out for us."

"That presumes you don't have another . . . attack of dysentery," Douglass said.

"If, for example, you were to go in the gooney bird," Dolan went on, ignoring him, "that would leave me and Fine to fly the 25 to Vis. Captain Fine is not what you could call an experienced 25 pilot. I hate to think what would happen if he had to try to land the 25 on Vis."

"Dolan, do you think Colonel Douglass could land the 25 on Vis?"

"He stands a much better chance than you do," Dolan said. "And the kid doesn't need him in the 47."

"And what if you're not 'available' in the 47?" Fine challenged.

"That's the chance we have to take, that by me just sitting there in the right seat and letting the kid fly, my dysentery won't come back."

Douglass looked at Fine.

"I think we have to go with Dolan," Fine said. "His main advantage, I think, is that he's the one with the best chance . . . maybe even the only one with a chance . . . of finding the drop zone."

3

Pécs, Hungary
0515 Hours 21 February 1943

Lt. Hank Darmstadter thought that the most difficult part of the flight so far had been taxiing to the end of the runway in Cairo. They had taken off at 2100, which would put them over the meadow outside Pécs at just after daylight. The airfield at Cairo was blacked out, and while Wilkins had been able to arrange for the runway lights to be turned on long enough for them to take off, they had had to be led to the runway from the hangar by a man holding a flashlight in the back of a jeep.

The flashlight-in-the-jeep had been very hard to follow. It

was almost impossible to see directly ahead out over the nose of a C-47 with its tail wheel on the ground. C-47 pilots learned to taxi by looking out the side and by swinging the nose from side to side to provide a look ahead through the side windows.

It was difficult following the jeep, but they'd made it to the end of the runway all right, sometimes flicking the landing lights on to make sure of their position. Darmstadter had been a little surprised and flattered that Dolan had not taken over the controls and done the taxiing, but Dolan had left that to Darmstadter.

And from the moment they had lined up with the center line of the runway, things had gone without a hitch.

Dolan had waited until he'd run the final mag check for the engines, and then he'd called the tower for the lights, and they had come on immediately.

Despite what had turned out because of the air temperature to be four hundred pounds over Max Over Gross, the takeoff had been no problem at all. The only way Darmstadter could tell how heavy they were was a reluctance to pick up altitude. But they had never come close to a stall, and the climb was steady, if slow.

The first leg, the longest, was on a west-northwest course across the desert to the Mediterranean, and then across the Mediterranean far enough south of Crete to avoid a chance encounter with German aircraft based on the island. And then they turned north across the Ionian Sea.

There was almost a half moon, providing what Dolan described as the most they could ask for, enough light for them to make out land masses and shorelines, but not enough to make it easy for anyone to spot them.

The Strait of Otranto, which separates the heel of the Italian boot from Albania and the Adriatic from the Ionian Sea, came into view just when they expected it to, and they could see both shorelines for a while.

Dolan had planned that that leg of the flight would take six hours and twenty-five minutes. It actually took six hours and two, meaning that they were making better time than anticipated, even with the engines thinned back as much as possible for fuel economy.

Once they had crossed the Strait, Darmstadter had raised

the nose slightly, starting a slow climb to 9,000 feet, and Dolan had begun to peer intently out the window looking for the narrow strip of land that ran between the Adriatic and Lake Scutari on the Yugoslav-Albanian border.

Dolan had told him, jokingly, but meaning it, that the secret of "road map" navigation was to look for something on the ground that was large enough to be easily seen and that couldn't be confused with anything else.

Lake Scutari fit the bill. It was twenty-five miles long and was separated from the Adriatic by a strip of land as narrow as seven miles. It could be easily found, and it could not be mistaken for anything else.

"Steer straight north from the end of the lake," Dolan said when they had found Lake Scutari, and then he got out of his seat. "I think it's time to get rid of another drum."

Lt. János had been shown how to pump fuel from the 55-gallon drums into the main tanks. One of the drums had been "semi-permanently" installed, with a line running from its bottom to the main aircraft tank. Fuel from it had been pumped into the main tank, and then that fuel was replenished from other 55-gallon barrels.

The empty tanks didn't weigh much, but they could not be completely drained, and Dolan was worried that the avgas sloshing around in them would create fumes that would be dangerous. He had gone back into the cabin several times to make sure that as soon as each drum had been emptied, János had thrown it out.

The ground seemed to glow white about that time, and after a moment Darmstadter figured out what it was—the moonlight reflecting back from snow on the ground. That meant they were approaching the mountains in Montenegro, the highest of which was about 7,500 feet. There would be at least 1,500 feet between them and the highest peak, but it was important that they know when they passed over it, so they could safely descend.

Darmstadter had been worried that Dolan would want the controls after they started down and were flying on the deck. There was no question that Dolan was a better and more experienced pilot. But there was also no doubt that he had had a heart attack and might have another.

But Dolan lived up to what he had promised Douglass: that

he would "work the road map in the right seat and let the kid fly."

The only specific instructions Dolan gave him were course changes, and several times the "suggestion" that it would be "OK to go down another couple hundred feet."

According to the Corps of Engineers' map (which the Corps had apparently borrowed from *Le Guide Michelin)*, this part of Hungary was sparsely populated. There were here and there a few lights to be seen, but there was no way of telling whether they were a few lights in violation of a village blackout, or lights in single farmhouses.

At 0500, as the sky to the east was starting to glow dull red, Dolan unstrapped himself again and got off the co-pilot's seat.

"In eight minutes, maybe ten," he said, "we should see a few lights. That'll be Pécs. Or maybe Athens. If you see something round, that'll be Rome."

Darmstadter knew he was expected to laugh, and did.

"This has gone so well, I'm afraid to believe it," Dolan said. "I'll go back and tell our passengers. János said he wanted fifteen minutes to suit up."

Dolan was back in his seat before they came onto Pécs, and he was the first to see it.

"Go down on the deck," Dolan now ordered. "Put that line of hills between us and Pécs. It's damned near impossible to tell the direction of an airplane if you can't see it. And the more confused we can leave these people, the better."

Darmstadter concentrated on flying as close to the ground as he dared between lines of hills. It was light enough now to make out individual trees, and here and there a road and fields.

And then, surprising him, he flashed over a stream, then a cut-over section of hillside, then above that a meadow on a plateau.

"Christ, is that it?"

"It should be," Dolan said, "but I don't see any panels."

Darmstadter glanced quickly at him. Dolan had a headset on and was working the controls of the radio.

"Not a goddamned thing," he said.

"What do I do?"

"Stay on the deck under the hill lines," Dolan ordered.

"And make another pass over it. I'll go see what I can see from the door."

Five minutes later, from the other direction, the C-47 approached the meadow.

There was no doubt now that they had found their destination. A pile of tree limbs was burning furiously at the near end of the meadow by the cut-over area, the wind blowing the smoke across the meadow and into the forest.

Dolan came into the cockpit.

"It's up to you now, kid," he said. "The next pass is all we're going to get, or everybody will think we're having an air show up here."

Darmstadter smiled uneasily.

Dolan went back into the fuselage. There he would strap himself into a harness, and take up a position by the open door. When Darmstadter turned the red light on (there were supposed to be red and green lights, but the green wasn't working) and then off, he would push the first of the parachutists through the door. When they were all gone, he would throw the three equipment bags after them.

Darmstadter made his approach very carefully, slowing the C-47 down as much as he dared, coming in very low and shallow over the tips of the trees in the forest, one hand on the gooney bird's wheel, the other on the toggle switch for the light for the door.

And then he flicked the toggle switch.

He thought he could sense a slight change in the controls, which would mean that he had lost 1,000 pounds of weight—five parachutists—from his gross weight, and that the loss had changed the center of balance.

He had a strange, wild, arrogant thought.

"I could have landed this sonofabitch in that meadow! The way the wind is blowing up from the stream, I was making maybe forty knots over the ground. I was going so slow I could see Canidy's face! And I could have stopped it in plenty of time.

He looked over his shoulder into the aisle for Dolan.

He couldn't see him at first, and then he did.

Dolan was on the cabin floor on his side, curled up. Darmstadter looked out the windshield, and then back. Dolan straightened, grew almost stiff, and then went limp.

4

150 Degrees 20 Minutes West Longitude
08 Degrees 35 Minutes North Latitude
1725 20 February 1943

There were four people on the bridge of the conning tower of the USS *Drum* as she made 15 knots on a course of 275 degrees through oil-smooth, gently rolling seas. They were almost exactly halfway around the world from the Adriatic Sea and Budapest, Hungary, where at that moment it was 5:25 A.M., February 21, "the next day."

The *Drum*'s captain, Lt. Commander Edwin R. Lennox, USN, and Capt. James M.B. Whittaker, USAAC, were in clean and pressed but unstarched khakis. Commander Lennox wore a battered brimmed cap whose cover was once white, but was now nearly brown with oil stains. Captain Whittaker was hatless.

The talker, with a headset and microphone device over his head, was also hatless. He wore a light blue denim shirt and a darker shade pair of denim trousers, as did the lookout, who also wore a blue sailor's cap, the brim of which he had turned down all around.

The lookout, Commander Lennox, and Capt. Whittaker all had identical Navy issue Bausch & Lomb ten-power binoculars on leather straps around their necks.

Commander Lennox looked at his wristwatch, and then with a sailor's eye, at the darkening sky.

"Any time you're ready, Jim," Commander Lennox said, "you can go below."

Whittaker smiled.

"Aye aye, Sir," he said. "Permission to leave the bridge?"

"Granted," the *Drum*'s captain replied, smiling back.

They had grown to like each other on the voyage from Pearl Harbor. Lennox had thought about the growing friendship a good deal during that time—remembering what he had been told by a full lieutenant when he'd been an ensign aboard the *Kingfisher:* He'd been told that her skipper wasn't really such a hardnosed sonofabitch as he seemed, but that a skipper couldn't afford to have friends, that command was indeed a lonely thing.

He had accepted that then because he was an ensign, and ensigns believe what they are told by full lieutenants. But it was only after they had given him the *Drum,* his first command, that he'd really understood it. The master of a man-of-war could *not* have friends. He could be civil and courteous, but there had to be a wall between the skipper and everybody else aboard. It had a little to do with "familiarity breeds contempt," but there was more to it than that. The captain had to appear omniscient to his crew, and one of the best ways to do that, especially if you were convinced that at least two of your officers were far smarter than you were and better leaders of men, was to be aloof, to be somewhat mysterious, to share no opinion or confidences with anybody.

Lennox had seen in Whittaker somebody much like himself in character, and with similar command responsibilities, and with an *understanding* of command. Very early on, Lennox had decided that having Whittaker aboard was very much what it must be like to be captain of a cruiser flying an admiral's flag. Where the cruiser and the accompanying task force went, and what it would do, was the admiral's responsibility. But the operation of the cruiser was the cruiser captain's responsibility.

And Whittaker had acted as Lennox believed a good admiral would behave. Despite the authority the orders from COMSUBFORPAC had given Whittaker—which had in effect made the *Drum* his personal taxicab, he had leaned over backward to avoid even the suggestion of giving Lennox orders.

He had asked questions, and "wondered if it would be possible to" do what he had the clear authority to order done. He had always scrupulously referred to Lennox as "Captain" or "Skipper," even long after Lennox had started calling him "Jim."

And the night before, when they were alone with the talker on the bridge, Whittaker had asked "if it would be possible to" have a dry run of what would take place when they were off Mindanao.

"They assure me, Skipper," Whittaker said, "that the

outboards have been tuned by an expert. But cynical sonofabitch that I am, and with no reflection intended, Sir, on the U.S. Navy, I'd like to check that out."

"What you would really like, Jim, right, is a dry run?"

"Yes, Sir," Whittaker asked. "Is that going to be possible?"

"Does the Army use the phrase 'SOP'?" Lennox asked.

"Yes, Sir," Whittaker said.

"I violate mine," Lennox said. "The SUBFORPAC SOP clearly states that when we are within the operating range of Japanese aircraft and proceeding on the surface, we will always be in a 'prepared to dive' condition. That means all hatches except the one here will be secured, and that we will be making sufficient headway so that the sub's diving planes will have effect in case we have to make an emergency dive."

They had, during the voyage, exchanged technical lore. Whittaker had been surprised to learn that the diving planes on the *Drum* functioned like the ailerons of an airplane, controlling up and down movement of the submerged submarine. He knew that because of the dynamic forces acting upon the diving planes, the faster a submarine was moving across the surface of the ocean, the quicker it could be submerged.

"In other words, Skipper," Whittaker said, "a dry run is a lousy idea?"

"In these waters, if I follow the SOP," Lennox said, "what I get is a boat ready to make a dive, and a crew of sweat-soaked, temperature-exhausted sailors not only getting on each other's nerves, but not able to function fast when they have to. So what I do is leave the hatches open when I can in waters like these, stationing men by the hatches to close them if they have to, and I make damned sure my lookout has the eyes of a hawk."

"And to conduct a dry run would mean stopping the boat," Whittaker said, "increasing the time it would take you to submerge if a Jap plane spotted you."

Lennox nodded. "Spotted *us.*"

Whittaker shrugged.

"OK, if that's . . ."

Lennox interrupted him.

"Another unpleasant situation that comes to mind," he said, "is us sitting on the surface a half mile or so offshore of

Mindanao, and unable to submerge because there's a trio of Army guys in rubber boats with outboard motors they can't start."

Whittaker looked at him, but didn't say anything.

"And while I am being the high priest of doom and gloom," Lennox said, "I have another scenario. There we are off Mindanao, and we get the boats out of the torpedo room, blow them up, and they leak. Since I can think of no other way to get those heavy little boxes ashore, that would mean we would have come all this way only to have to go all the way back for more rubber boats."

"I'd like to add to that gloom and doom scenario, if I might, Sir," Whittaker said.

"Go ahead, Jim," Lennox said.

"We are on the surface off Mindanao, the boats have inflated properly, and the outboards have even started. Then the Army guys—whose total experience with rubber boats is limited to Lieutenant Hammersmith's time with an inner tube in a swimming pool—start loading those heavy boxes into the rubber boats and drop the boxes over the side, fall overboard themselves, and I'll let you figure out the rest yourself."

"You've had no training?" Lennox asked, surprised and concerned.

"No, Sir," Whittaker said. "There wasn't time."

"Well, then," Lennox said, "the question is not *if* we do a dry run, but when."

"I think, if it's possible," Whittaker said, "we should."

Lennox looked at Whittaker.

If I hadn't been so obliging, he wondered, *would you have pulled the rank the COMSUBFORPAC orders give you?*

"You told me, Jim," he said, "that to a pilot, darkness rises from the ground."

"Yes, Sir, it does."

"Then I think we should do the dry run tomorrow, at dusk," Lennox said.

"Thank you, Skipper."

The day had been spent preparing for the dry run. This was mostly a good thing for the boat, Lennox realized, though it was risky. The morale of the crew was helped by the chance not only to do something constructive, but to get out on deck. The risk of being spotted by a Japanese patrol plane was no greater with them there, but submerging would take longer because of the people and the equipment on deck.

Lennox posted extra lookouts and ordered the manning of the machine gun and Bofors cannon. He didn't plan to use them, but it gave their crews a chance to get on deck and to feel useful, and he decided the price, the extra forty-five or sixty seconds it would take the gun crews to drop through the hatches and close them, was worth it.

The rubber boats themselves, as Lennox had supposed they would, posed the greatest problems. If the chief of the boat, who by default became the rubber boat expert, had any thoughts about the idiocy of sending people with no training or experience with rubber boats to make a landing through the surf on an enemy-held shore, he kept them to himself.

The first problem was to get the boats from the forward torpedo room through the hatch and onto the deck. The chief of the boat considered his options and decided that because of the weight and ungainly bulk it would make more sense to uncrate them below and pass them through the hatch, despite the risk that they would be impaled and torn on something sharp on the way.

The boats, which carried their own air bottles, were designed to be inflated with the bottles. Even if the boats were thrown over the side uninflated and sank, if the pull-cord for the air bottles was pulled, the boats would inflate and pop to the surface.

Although spare air bottles had been provided, the chief of the boat decided that the smart thing to do was not to use the bottles until it was necessary. He called for the air hose normally used to charge the air bottles in torpedos, and when he had the first boat unrolled and lying limp on the deck, filled it with compressed air.

When that boat was expanded, he ran soapy water over it to check for leaks. When he found none, he opened the exhaust valves, and as they hissed and the boat collapsed, he looked at it thoughtfully.

Then he went aft and stood with his hands on his hips and spoke with Lennox and Whittaker, who were on the bridge.

"Two things, Skipper," he said.

"Go ahead, Chief," Lennox said.

"I think we could stow the boats aft of the conning tower,"

the chief of the boat said. "Properly stowed, we could even submerge with them."

"Good idea," Lennox immediately agreed.

"Second, there's no way the boats will carry all that weight."

"Then we'll have to use the spares, too," Whittaker said.

"I meant using the spares," the chief of the boat said. "The first time you flexed the boat in the surf, that weight'd rip the deck . . . or the bilge, whatever they call that sheet of rubberized canvas . . . free of the inflation chambers. If it didn't rip through before you got to the surf."

"What do you suggest, Chief?" Lennox asked.

"We got a hundred and sixty percent of life jackets aboard," the Chief said.

"I don't know what that means," Whittaker said.

"It means we got sixty percent more life jackets aboard than there is people," the Chief said.

"And?" Lennox asked.

"They're rated at 200 pounds," the Chief said. "Which is just about what them 'film' boxes weigh."

"You mean put a life jacket around a film box," Whittaker asked, "in case the bottom lets go?"

"I mean wrap jackets around the boxes, tie lines to them, and tow them ashore," the Chief said. "And around them boxes with the weapons and the ammo, too."

"Could they be towed?"

"There's only one way to find out, Skipper," the chief of the boat said.

"Put people on it, Chief," Lennox ordered.

"Carefully, Chief," Whittaker said. Both the Chief and Lennox looked at him in surprise and annoyance, but then smiled when Whittaker went on. "If we were to lose just one of those 'film' boxes out here, your beloved captain and myself would spend the rest of our days in Alcatraz."

"I take your meaning, Sir," the chief said with a smile.

By midafternoon, each of the boats had been brought on deck, inflated, checked for leaks, deflated, and then stowed, firmly tied to the mount of the twin Bofors aft of the conning tower.

The top was cut from an empty 55-gallon oil drum, and then the drum three quarters filled with sea water. Each outboard motor was test run for five minutes, the noise incredible inside the hull.

The chief torpedoman was placed in charge of floating the "film" boxes. He cut the flotation packets from life preservers and tied them around the wooden boxes. The available light line was soon exhausted, and two sailors made what was needed by first sawing through a length of four-inch Manila hawser and then untwisting the strands.

After that, there was nothing to do but wait until dusk fell.

Commander Lennox waited until he was sure that Whittaker was in the control room, and then he started the dry run.

"Close all hatches and watertight doors," he said, and the talker repeated the order.

Lennox could see the hatches on the deck closing, and he could hear a dull metallic clanging from all over the boat. With the exception of the hatch from the bridge, which would be his responsibility to close, the boat should now be watertight.

"All hatches and watertight doors secured, Sir," the talker confirmed.

"Prepare to dive," Lennox ordered. "Clear the bridge!"

"Prepare to dive," the talker repeated. "Bridge being cleared."

"Dive!" Lennox ordered.

"Dive! Dive! Dive!" the talker said, and dropped through the hatch. Lennox followed him, and then closed the hatch after him.

The sound of the Klaxon hurt his ears.

"Take her to 100 feet," the captain ordered, and put his hand out to steady himself as the bow of the *Drum* nosed downward.

Ten minutes later, the bow of the *Drum* broke the surface again.

The moment it did, Lennox started his stopwatch.

As soon as he was on the bridge, with water still spilling over the deck, he started issuing orders.

"Battle stations," he ordered.

The talker repeated the command, and the Klaxon went off.

"Man all cannon," Lennox ordered.

Submariners erupted from the hatches and went to the guns.

"All astern one third," he ordered. "Make her dead in the water."

The pitch of the just-started diesels changed.

It was time for another command, but there was nothing standard that Lennox could recall that fit the situation.

"Make all preparations to launch the rubber boats," he finally ordered.

Now, there was activity from every hatch on the deck.

As crewmen freed the rubber boats from the Bofors mount and handed them to crewmen on the deck, other crewmen emerged from other hatches. The weapons and ammunition boxes were first placed on the deck in a line, then tied together with ten-foot lengths of line.

By the time the crewmen carrying the limp boats had reached the forward deck, others had air hoses waiting. It took what seemed like a long time for the boats to be inflated, and by the time they were, Whittaker, Hammersmith, and Radioman Second Joe Garvey had come onto the deck, wearing their gear, and were waiting.

The chief of the boat and the chief torpedoman put the rubber boat over the side themselves, lowering it with ropes until it touched the nearly horizontal section of the hull, and then they jumped down onto it with ropes around their waists.

Then they pushed the boat off the hull into the water and raised their hands to help Whittaker from the deck to the sloping part of the hull and into the boat itself.

Whittaker jerked the starting rope of the outboard motor. When he had it running, he checked to see that the line tied to a grommet in the heavy black rubber was in place. Then he put the motor in gear, and the boat started off. When the line tied to the grommet drew taut, crewmen slid the first of the two larger ammunition and weapons boxes (now wrapped with life preserver flotation packs) into the water, then skidded the line of small "film" boxes after it.

Then the process was repeated for the second boat, except that both Hammersmith and Joe Garvey got into that one.

The atmosphere had been tense: to see if the boats could be

launched and whether or not the flotation packets would keep the weapons and film boxes afloat.

Then Lennox heard a guffaw, then a belly laugh, and then a high-pitched giggle. The first thing he thought, angrily, was that someone had fallen over the side. That, despite the genuine threat to life, was always good for a laugh from his men.

And then he saw the object of the amusement.

Jim Whittaker was fifty yards off the bow, making a wide turn to return to the *Drum*. The strain on the line towing the boxes behind the rubber boat, plus the weight of the outboard motor and of Whittaker himself, had caused the bow to rise almost straight up out of the water. The outboard was open full bore, but it was just barely moving, and Whittaker himself looked as if he was about to sink into the water.

Sound carries well over water, and Whittaker heard the laughter of the crew.

He rose to the occasion. Balancing himself precariously, he saluted crisply.

"Man overboard!" a shout went up, followed by a bellow of laughter.

Lennox looked quickly to see what had happened. The chief torpedoman had lost his footing and gone into the water. The chief of the boat was trying, with absolutely no success, to haul him back aboard by the rope around his waist.

The Captain of the USS *Drum* picked up his electric hailer and started to put it to his lips. Then he took it down and slammed it painfully against his leg until the pain was such that he was no longer overcome with hysterics.

"Attention on the deck," he finally announced. "Prepare to recover rubber boats!" And then the temptation was too much. "And while you're at it, see if you can recover the chief torpedoman."

Thirteen

1

Pécs, Hungary
0500 Hours 21 February 1943

CANIDY WOKE IN the dark in a large bedroom in the Countess Batthyany's hunting lodge. He was buried deep in goose down, his nostrils full of perfume.

But then he realized it wasn't perfume, it was something he had found in a bottle in his surprisingly ornate bathroom. The bottle bore a "Lanvin Paris-London-New York" label underneath the words "Pour les Hommes." His French was good enough to understand what that meant, and the stuff hadn't smelled half bad when he sniffed at the bottle neck, and so he had liberally splashed it over himself after he'd wiped himself dry with a thick towel about the size of a pup tent.

The cologne would be a nice change from the way he had smelled after the fishing boat from Vis to the mainland, and after the farm truck—redolent of horse manure—which had carried him across Yugoslavia to the neighborhood of the Hungarian border.

It was only when he had put on a pair of silk pajamas and the odor of the "Pour les Hommes" had not diminished—had in fact seemed to intensify—that he began to suspect the legend on the bottle was directed to the gentle sex. If they doused themselves in "Pour les Hommes," men would be drawn to the smell like moths to a candle.

It had confirmed the somewhat cynical impression he had formed not long after they'd first shown him his room that the

Batthyany family had apparently not only done their hunting in considerable comfort, but also that when they returned from the vigors of the field, the comfort they'd received then had been furnished by females. In his bathroom, he had found a bidet, and in a heavy bookcase by the bedside was a collection of leather-bound photo albums, the photographs portraying handsome men and women in their birthday suits performing what could only be described as sexual gymnastics.

He had at first wondered whether the albums had been purchased . . . they looked professionally done . . . or whether the Counts Batthyany had been unusually skilled amateur photographers. But when he got into the second volume, he recognized the huge fireplace in the main room of the lodge behind three dark-haired beauties and a hairy, skinny, mustachioed gentleman.

The thought passed through his mind that it might be fun to peel several of the neatly matted photographs free of the albums and take them home for Ann. It might brighten her day, he thought. But then he decided against that. Ann took sex very seriously. But then he was sure that as far as Ann was concerned, dirty pictures would be as high on her taboo list for him as carrying on with Her Gracefulness, the Duchess of Stanfield.

The next thought he had was that he would bring some of the dirty pictures back with him, to include them with his official report.

"The photographs attached as Inclosures 16 through 26 are included in the belief that they might suggest exploitable character flaws in the Hungarian aristocracy possibly useful in future operations."

That would shake up the system. Dave Bruce's near glacial dignity would crack; he might even blush. He would certainly hem, haw, and stammer.

And then he realized that he was already in enough trouble for having come to Hungary, without adding fuel to the fire. Did he need another demonstration that he didn't have the right attitude? Hardly.

Obviously, he thought, suddenly chagrined, he *did not* have the right attitude. Instead of sitting here drooling over dirty pictures like some high school junior, he should be wondering how to get Eric Fulmar and Professor Dyer out of St. Gertrud's prison without having to "terminate" them.

He put the leather-bound albums back in their case and went to sleep thinking over what he had just about decided to do—the final decision to be made after talking it over with Ferniany and whoever London sent in to command the team.

Ferniany would be here tomorrow, probably around noon. He would have with him two of his people, Hungarians he had recruited, and the signal panels, and the radio, and the Sten gun Captain Hughson had loaned him just before he left Vis. Canidy would be glad to have that back. There was plenty of room in the Lodge to put Ferniany and his men up for however long it took London to get off its ass and send him the team, and the worst possible scenario for that was five days.

Von Heurten-Mitnitz and the Countess would return to Budapest tomorrow. Canidy saw no problem with that. He didn't need the Countess now: She had told her servants they were to do what he asked. And he didn't think there would be any suspicion directed toward the Countess and von Heurten-Mitnitz for having been in Pécs several days before the prisoners had escaped from St. Gertrud's. Or several days before an unexplained explosion had destroyed a mine shaft in the Batthyany coal mine.

It would be a coincidence, nothing more, that His Excellency had been enjoying the overnight hospitality of the Countess at the Countess's rustic love nest ten or so miles away.

The most serious potential problem, Canidy had gone to sleep thinking, was not how to get Eric and the professor out of the hands of Hungarians, but how to do it without calling a hell of a lot of attention to the operation. He had been disturbed by Standartenführer Müller's report that the SS not only had not grown bored with looking for Fulmar and the professor, but quite the reverse, had intensified the examination.

St. Gertrud's prison would be swarming with SS and Gestapo just as soon as word got out that two prisoners had not only escaped but had been rescued by what it would take them about five minutes to figure out was a highly skilled team under the hands of either the SOE or the OSS.

When he woke up smelling like a Hungarian courtesan, Canidy rested on his back in the dark for several minutes in the hope that, as sometimes happened, his subconscious had been working on the problem while he slept and that there would be new solutions, or new questions, or both.

But none came.

He fumbled for the bedside lamp, turned it on, and then got out of bed and got dressed in the hunting clothes he had worn the day before. If nothing else, he decided, he would walk back through the woods to the drop zone and see for himself what it looked like at dawn.

Then he would come back to the house and see about something to eat.

He sensed, when he entered the main room of the lodge, that there was someone there, someone watching him.

The room was lit now only by embers in the huge fireplace before which in happier times the aristocracy had staged their little *tableaux vivants*. He looked around, but he saw nothing.

Then, Alois, the chief hunter, rose out of a huge upholstered chair near the fireplace. Its bulk and high sides had hidden him. He was fully dressed and had apparently slept overnight in the chair as a sort of guard. He was wearing a heavy poncholike garment of gray wool, and he had his shotgun.

"Good morning," Canidy said, smiling.

Alois grunted.

"I need a flashlight," Canidy said.

There was confusion on Alois's face.

Canidy mimed a flashlight, and lighting a path with one.

Alois grunted again and left the room. He returned with two flashlights, a square light with a handle, and a tiny two-cell that looked like a child's toy. He extended both to Canidy, offering him his choice.

Canidy took the larger light and walked to the door. Alois didn't move, but by the time Canidy had unlatched the chains and dead bolts, he became aware that Alois had moved soundlessly across the room and was standing behind him.

Somewhere, far off, there was the sound of aircraft engines.

The beam of his light picked out their footsteps in the snow from the day before, and Canidy, with Alois following him, walked away from the lodge toward the forest and the meadow beyond it.

Concentrating on not losing the path or his footing in the dark, Canidy didn't pay much attention to the sound of the aircraft engines far away—until they suddenly seemed much closer.

He looked up into the sky.

Jesus! Those sound like Twin Wasps![1]

He broke into a trot, slipping and sliding on the frozen snow.

When he reached the meadow, it was light enough to see the meadow and the area beyond. But there was no aircraft in sight, and it was only when he strained his ears that he could convince himself that he could just barely hear the sound of faraway engines.

Whatever it was, it was not for me. I should have known better. There's no way that could have been a gooney bird; no way they could have gotten a team here this quick. Now, I look like a horse's ass in front of Alois.

He met the large Hungarian's eyes and shrugged.

And then he was sure the sound of the engines receding had changed, that it was growing louder. And it kept going in and out, growing louder then fainter, then louder again.

And all of a sudden, it was very loud. A gooney bird appeared at the end of the meadow where the trees had been cut, its engine roar now deafening, and flashed overhead no more than two hundred feet off the ground. And there was no mistaking the star-in-a-bar U.S. identification painted on the wing.

"Jesus, Maria und Josef!" Alois said.

The gooney bird banked, and then disappeared from sight.

Canidy stuck two fingers in his mouth, and then raised them over his head to confirm his suspicion that the wind was coming from the direction of the stream and the cut-over area.

He ran to the pile of pine boughs. He could just make out a shining glint underneath that had to be the kerosene.

He dug it out. It was a five-gallon tin can, bearing a SHELL

[1]The C-47 series aircraft were powered with two 1200-hp Pratt & Whitney R-1830-92 "Twin Wasp" engines.

logotype. A sealed tin can, he saw when he unscrewed the cap. There was a seal over the hole he would have to pry out before he could pour the kerosene.

He changed his mind and threw the can atop the pile of boughs. And then he gestured to Alois.

"Shoot the sonofabitch, Alois!" he said.

Alois looked confused.

Canidy gestured.

"Bang! Bang!" Canidy shouted, as he mimed the action.

Alois looked confused, but he raised his shotgun, and looked to Canidy for approval.

"Right! Yes! Ja! Schiessen!"

The shotgun barked, and the can erupted. Canidy felt droplets of kerosene in the air.

Alois looked at Canidy, as if he was afraid he had misunderstood him and done the wrong thing.

Canidy smiled at him, then ran to him and reached for the shotgun. Alois debated for a moment parting with the shotgun, but finally handed it over. Canidy found a puddle of kerosene, put the barrel to it, and fired the other barrel.

There was a dull flicker of fire for a moment, and then the kerosene that had vaporized when the can had erupted ignited in a whoosh. A thick cloud of black smoke quickly formed.

Christ, I hope they just haven't given up! That somebody sees that!

The pine boughs were burning now, and noisily.

Canidy had just about decided that he could not hear the Twin Wasps at all any more, when the gooney bird appeared, flaps and wheels down, right on the edge of a stall.

And then very quickly, surprising him, something fell—five somethings fell—from the door. And then the first canopy opened and the second and then one at a time all the rest, and five parachutes floated toward the ground.

The gooney bird pulled up its flaps and its gear and was gone.

A gooney bird! How the hell did they get a gooney bird this far?

Canidy ran toward the first parachutist, who was just about to touch down. He heard Alois plodding behind him.

The parachutist, a big guy, landed badly. He screamed.

Canidy ran to him.

"I broke my fucking ankle again!" János said, furiously. "Jesus Christ!"

"Was hat ihr gesacht?" Alois asked, in rough German.

"I said I broke my fucking ankle," János said, in Hungarian.

Alois smiled sympathetically, and then stooped over and scooped János up in his arms like a baby. He looked at Canidy and nodded at the forest and then looked stone-faced at Canidy.

When there was no immediate response, he spoke to János, who translated:

"He wants to carry me into the woods, OK?"

Canidy nodded his head. "Ja!"

The other parachutists were on the ground now, and they ran over to Canidy. They were all armed, he saw, with .30 caliber carbines with folding stocks.

"Who are you?" one of them demanded.

"That's Major Canidy," another said, recognizing him.

"Pick up your chutes and put them on the fire," Canidy said. "And then . . ."

He interrupted himself. The sound of the Twin Wasps was back.

The equipment drop. Why the hell hadn't the jumpmaster kicked that crap out the door after he dropped the jumpers?

The gooney bird appeared again over the cut-down area, its flaps and gear down again. He was now even lower than he had been before, when he'd buzzed the meadow.

If you stall it, friend, you're going to land here in this meadow!

The gooney bird didn't stall. But the pilot chopped the engines, and the gooney bird touched down. He bounced once, and then stayed down, and Canidy saw smoke from the gear as the pilot braked it.

Dolan, you sonofabitch! If I had wanted you to land here, I would have said so. You're too fucking old to be a hot shot pilot!

Canidy ran down the meadow and to the rear door of the gooney bird, and looked in.

And Lt. Commander John Dolan, USNR, lying on the cabin floor, looked back at him out of sightless eyes.

2

Croydon Airfield
London, England
1130 Hours 21 February 1943

It was raining, and there had been fog, and there had been serious doubt that the Washington courier would be able to get in that day at all. Late the previous day, the ATC C-54 had managed to make it into Prestwick, Scotland, ahead of the front, but too late to try for London.

There had been a break in the weather, and an arctic blast of dry air moving down over Scotland had cleared the skies enough at 0930 for the C-54 to take off. But by then London had been socked in. The question had then been whether the break would close in again at Prestwick before the fog cleared at London.

It was decided in the end to take off and head for London in the hope that it would clear.

At Croydon, it had been necessary to "light the burners." The theory was—and damn the cost—that if enough gasoline were burned in devices set up alongside a runway, the heat generated would cause the air mass and the fog it contained to rise, clearing the runway. In practice, as now, what the burners did for pilots was serve as sort of a super beacon. If you could see the glow of the burners, you knew that the runway was somewhere down there, and with a little bit of luck, when you went down low enough, you could find the runway.

The C-54, flown by a commissioned TWA pilot who had lots of experience finding San Francisco in the fog, came in low and slow toward the glow on his horizon over London and found the Croydon runway on his second pass.

As he taxied toward the terminal, it was raining so hard that he had trouble seeing out the windshield. The ground crew who came out to meet them were wearing yellow rubber coats, hats and trousers, and looked, the pilot thought, like so many misplaced sailboat sailors.

The first passenger to come down the ladder was a Chief Petty Officer of the U.S. Navy. He had a Valv-Pak in each hand and smaller pieces of luggage under his arms.

As he came down the stairs, an Austin Princess limousine drove up close to him. The Chief opened the front door and tossed the luggage inside, and then backed out and held the rear door open.

"Get in, Ellis!" Colonel William Donovan said, as he came down the stairs from the C-54.

"In here, Ellis," Lt. Colonel Edmund T. Stevens said, motioning with his hand. "You're getting soaked."

Ellis got in the back seat, and a moment later Donovan got in beside him and closed the door.

Donovan gave Stevens his hand.

"Well, Ed," he said, "how are you?"

"Just fine, thank you, Bill," Stevens said. "David said he hopes you will understand that he would have met you if he could."

Donovan's reply surprised Stevens. Donovan was usually not only polite, but manifested the lawyer's ability to say the unpleasant in the nicest possible way.

Donovan said, "I didn't want to see him anyway. Not just now."

And then Donovan leaned forward and cranked down the divider separating the back seat from the chauffeur's compartment.

"Young lady, would you drive up to the terminal and get out, please? I'm sorry, but you're about to be put out in the rain."

"Yes, Sir," the driver, a WRAC sergeant, said.

"You call the office and have them send a car for you," Stevens said.

"There's a bus, Sir," the WRAC sergeant replied. "I can take that."

"Do what Colonel Stevens said," Donovan said. "The bus doesn't go near Berkeley Square."

The WRAC pulled the nose of the Princess close to a door of the terminal, pulled on the parking brake, jumped out, and ran into the building. Ellis climbed over Donovan and got in the front seat behind the wheel.

"She forgot her purse," Ellis announced.

"No problem," Donovan said. "We'll probably be at Berkeley Square before she gets there. Get us off the field and drive in wide circles."

"Yes, Sir," Ellis said, and backed the Princess away from the terminal building. "Colonel, you put the window down."

"It's all right, I want you to hear this anyway," Donovan said.

But then he didn't say anything else until they had left the field and were driving through Thorton Heath toward the Thames on Highway A235.

"Get off the highway, Ellis," he ordered.

Ellis made the next right turn.

"The ostensible purpose of my visit," Donovan said, "is to smooth things over between you and SOE. 'Representations have been made at the highest levels' to the effect that you are not only being uncooperative but are interfering with their smooth operation. All of which proves that you are doing what I told you to do."

"Anything specific, Colonel?" Stevens asked.

"No, just general allegations about your being uncooperative, which I interpret to mean you have both locked them out of our cupboard and have turned a deaf ear to the pronouncements of the professionals," Donovan said. "But you'll have to arrange for me to see them, as soon as you can."

"This afternoon?"

"Fine," Donovan said. "And let's do it on our turf. Either at Berkeley Square or at Whitbey House. I don't want to give them the impression that I have been summoned for a dressing down on their carpet."

"What about the apartment in the Dorchester?"

"Fine," Donovan said. "And let's do it over drinks and hors d'oeuvres. As fancy as we can manage."

"I'll get Helene Dancy to set it up," Stevens said. "Better yet, Charity. She's at Berkeley Square."

Donovan grunted approval.

"Ellis," Stevens said, "there's a radio up there."

"I can hear it, Sir."

"We're Birddog," Stevens said. "Call Foxhunt, Captain Dancy's monitoring it, and tell her to have Charity set up a fancy do for half past five at the Dorchester, details to follow."

"Aye, aye, Sir," Ellis said, and reached for the microphone.

"Napoleon said," Donovan said, "that an army marches on its stomach. This one marches on hors d'oeuvres."

Stevens chuckled.

"My real purpose, of course," Donovan said, still conversationally, but very seriously, "is to be near what's happening in Hungary. So you better start by telling me what *is* happening, Ed."

"You got the message where Canidy asked for a team?"

Donovan nodded.

"It went in at 0500 this morning, or thereabouts," Stevens said. "We've had no word how that went."

"This morning? God, that was fast! How did you arrange that?"

"We flew the team . . . specifically Stan Fine and young Douglass flew . . . the team to Cairo in one of the new B-17s we got for Operation Aphrodite."

"And then used Canidy's B-25 to drop the team? That's why you involved young Douglass, to fly the B-25?"

"That was the idea, but something went wrong. The last radio from Wilkins said that the team was being dropped by a C-47, flown by Dolan and a C-47 pilot we borrowed from the Air Corps, and that the B-25 with Douglass and Fine in it was going to Vis."

"Where'd you get the C-47?" Donovan asked. And then went on without waiting for a reply, "I didn't know a C-47 had that kind of range."

"It doesn't," Stevens said. "I called Joe Kennedy and asked him about that, and he said that it's possible to refill the main tanks of a C-47 from barrels of fuel carried in the cabin. He also said that it's dangerous as hell, but apparently that's what they have done. Wilkins borrowed the C-47 at Cairo."

Donovan grunted.

"It's time we thought of the worst possible scenario," he said. "That should be plural. The first thing that can go badly wrong—and I am frankly surprised this hasn't already happened—is that they will find out who Fulmar and the Professor really are . . ."

"Colonel," Stevens began.

"Let me finish, please, Ed," Donovan said. "The best we

could hope for in that situation would be that the Germans would decide we wanted Dyer for what he knows about jet- and rocket-engine metallurgy. That they would not suspect that what we're really after is getting nuclear-useful people out of Germany."

"Yes, Sir," Stevens said.

"The second thing that could go wrong would be for Canidy to be captured. Quite aside from what else he knows, I think we have to consider that the Germans know full well who he is . . . that he's the number three here . . . and would decide that we are either very interested in Professor Dyer, or, I'm afraid, that there is more to all this activity than is immediately apparent."

Stevens didn't reply.

"I think I have to say this, Ed," Donovan said. "On reflection, I think I made an error in judgment. I think what I should have ordered—to cut our losses to the minimum—was to give the Germans Fulmar and the professor."

Stevens didn't reply.

"Or alternatively, to arrange for them to be eliminated. On reflection, that's what should have been done. There are two ways to do that. The first would be to message Canidy to do it. I don't know if that would work. If he went in there without orders, in direct defiance of orders, I don't think we can expect him to obey any other order he doesn't like."

"Canidy is not a fool," Stevens said, loyally.

"Sometimes I wonder about that," Donovan said. "The second way to insure that the Germans don't get to question Fulmar and the professor is to bomb St. Gertrud's prison."

"Canidy's thought of that. He asked for Composition C-2."

"I meant by aircraft," Donovan said. "A raid on Budapest. Failing to reach the target, a squadron of B-17s would bomb an alternative target. A target of opportunity. Pécs. That happens all the time."

"That's a little far-fetched, isn't it?" Stevens said.

"It's laid on for tomorrow," Donovan said. "Presuming the weather permits. If not tomorrow, the day after. I have been assured . . . there is only minimal antiaircraft around Pécs, they can go in low . . . that there is a seventy-five percent chance that the prison can be taken out completely. Totally destroyed."

"My God!"

"You know what's involved with this," Donovan said. "I don't see I have any alternative. Do you?"

"No, Sir," Stevens said, after a moment.

"With that scenario," Donovan said, "there is the possibility that the team, and Canidy, can get out."

"Yes, Sir."

"If he does," Donovan said, "by the time I've finished with him, he may wish he was still in Hungary."

"Sir," Stevens said. "From his perspective, I'm sure he thought he was doing the right thing."

After a moment, Donovan said, "I'm surprised to hear you say that, Ed. I thought by now you would have figured out that 'the right thing' has absolutely no meaning for the OSS. We do what has to be done, and 'right' has absolutely nothing to do with that."

He raised his voice.

"You can take us to Berkeley Square now, please, Ellis."

When they got there, Captain Helene Dancy was waiting for them with a just-decrypted message:

TOP SECRET

OPERATIONAL IMMEDIATE FROM STATION VIII FOR OSS LONDON

C47 THREE HOURS OVERDUE HERE STOP TOTAL FUEL EXPENDITURE OCCURRED NOT LATER THAN 0800 LONDON TIME STOP MUST PRESUME AIRCRAFT LOST STOP INASMUCH AS SUCCESSFUL DROP SIGNAL UNRECEIVED MUST PRESUME FAILURE STOP UNABLE ESTABLISH CONTACT YACHTSMAN OR PHARMACIST STOP ADVISE STOP PHARMACIST II"

Donovan read it, and then handed it to Stevens.

The C-47 with Dolan and Darmstadter was lost. And the worst possible scenario: before they had been able to drop the OSS team.

"I think you'd better radio him to come home," Donovan said. "And message Wilkins to arrange for a ferry crew for the B-17. I don't want to lose that, too."

3

127 Degrees 20 Minutes West Longitude
07 Degrees 35 Minutes North Latitude
0600 Hours 21 February 1943

The *Drum* was on the surface. In these waters, off the eastern shore of Mindanao, the risk of a submarine on the surface being spotted by Japanese aircraft and patrol boats was almost unacceptable. But surfacing had been necessary. There was no way to attempt to contact the American guerrilla radio station from a submerged boat.

In these circumstances, when the life of his boat was literally at stake, Lt. Commander Edwin R. Lennox ordinarily would have exercised command from the bridge on the conning tower, where he could make the decisions (including the ultimate decision: to dive and run or stay and fight). But Lt. Bill Rutherford, the *Drum*'s exec, was on the bridge and had the conn, and Lennox was below leaning against the bulkhead. He, Captain Whittaker, and Lt. Hammersmith were watching as Radioman Second Joe Garvey tried to establish contact with U.S. Forces in the Philippines.

Once he had learned that Joe Garvey was not really a motion-picture photographer, Lennox had wondered how good a radioman Garvey could be (he looked to be about seventeen years old) and how the boyish sailor was going to fare when they put him ashore on Mindanao.

The first question had been answered when they had been under way only a few days. The *Drum*'s Chief Radioman, into whose care Garvey had been entrusted, a salty old submariner not given to complimenting his peers, had volunteered the information that "Garvey really knows his stuff." From the Chief Radioman, that was tantamount to comparing Garvey to Marconi.

Lennox had noticed the two of them together frequently after that, with the innards of a radio spread out in front of them, and he had overheard several of their conversations, of which he had understood very little.

But he understood the problem Garvey and his Chief Radioman were trying to solve. The first part of it was that the American guerrillas were operating a homemade radio, and establishing contact with it using the radios available on the *Drum* might prove difficult.

And then once—if—they made it safely ashore, the next problem was the radio Garvey was carrying. They intended to replace the guerrillas' homemade radio with equipment capable of reliable communications to Australia, Hawaii, and the States. What they had was a new, apparently not fully tested "transceiver,"[2] a device weighing only sixty pounds, including an electrical generation system that was pedaled like a stationary bicycle.

But that was several steps away. What had to be done now was to let the guerrillas know, and to keep the Japanese from learning, that Whittaker and his team were coming ashore—and where, and when.

Solving that problem had nothing to do with the esoterics of radio-wave propagation in the twenty-meter band.

Joe Garvey had been sending a short message twice, and then listening for a response, and then sending twice again, and then listening again:

KFH FOR WYZB FOR GENERAL FERTIG
RELAY WRISTWATCH QUOTE POLO COMING FOR NORTH PUERTO RICAN COCKTAILS TODAY UNQUOTE ACKNOWLEDGE KFH BY

The message, Captain Jim Whittaker had explained, would be delivered to Master Sergeant George Withers, whom he had left on Bataan, and who was now with Fertig on Mindanao. "Wristwatch" made reference to the watch Whittaker had taken from his wrist and given to Withers just before he had left him.

"Polo" was simple. Jim Whittaker had been a polo player, and was known by that nickname.

Whittaker was sure that Withers and Fertig would understand that "cocktails" meant "at the cocktail hour." Whether they interpreted that to mean five P.M., or any hour up to eight or nine didn't matter. If they were on the beach where

[2]An integrated transmitter and receiver.

Polo was coming at the cocktail hour, they would wait until the last hope he was coming was gone.

The tricky part of the message was "Puerto Rican cocktails." Whittaker said he was banking on Whithers being initially baffled by that, saying aloud to find a meaning.

Puerto Rico? Puerto Rico? Puerto Rico?

"Word association, Skipper," Whittaker had said. "What's the first thing that pops into your mind when you think 'Puerto Rico'?"

"Rum," Commander Lennox said, immediately.

"Think geographically," Whittaker said.

"San Juan, I guess," Lennox had said. "But I knew about San Juan."

It was Whittaker's intention to go ashore north of the small city of San Juan on the eastern shore of Mindanao at six, just before darkness fell.

"They will be thinking geographically," Whittaker said, firmly. "They'll get it, all right. The message isn't what's bothering me."

"Something is bothering you?" Lennox asked, sarcastically. "I can't imagine what that would be."

"Well, for one thing, we don't seem to be getting any reply," Whittaker said drily, "which could mean that either Garvey's radio isn't working; or that Fertig's radio isn't working; or that Fertig's people just aren't listening; or if you insist on taking counsel of your fears, that they have been killed or captured by the Japanese."

"And what if they have been, Jim?" Lennox asked, very seriously. "What are you going to do if you can't raise them on the radio? Try again tomorrow?"

"I've thought about that," Whittaker said, now as serious as Lennox. "Garvey tells me that the signal he is sending is strong enough to be picked up all over the island. That means that other Americans, or at least Filipinos friendly to him, have heard the message and will get it to him. And so, of course, have the Japanese. I don't want to give the Japanese any more time to play word association than I already have. I want to go ashore at six tonight."

Lennox nodded.

It was, he realized, the first order Whittaker had given him that was not open to suggestion or argument.

"I think I'm going to go up to the bridge," he said, and then added without thinking about it, "if you don't need me?"

"No, go ahead," Whittaker said, absently.

Commander Lennox had just reached the ladder to the conning tower when the Klaxon sounded, and the speaker's voice came over the loudspeakers:

"Japanese aircraft ninety degrees three miles! Dive! Dive!"

4

Drop Zone Aspirin near Pécs, Hungary 0535 Hours 21 February 1943

Lt. Hank Darmstadter walked down the slanting floor of the C-47 to where Canidy knelt, with his ear to the chest of Lt. Commander John Dolan, USNR.

"Is he dead?" he asked, softly.

Canidy straightened, still on his knees, and nodded.

"What the hell were you thinking of, sitting down?" Canidy asked.

"He had an attack just before we landed at Cairo from Vis," Darmstadter said, and then answered Canidy's question: "I couldn't kick the equipment bags out myself."

Two of the parachutists appeared at the door of the aircraft. They had stripped out of their black coveralls and except for the carbines they held in their hands looked like civilians.

"Jesus!" one of them said, when he saw Dolan.

Canidy got off his knees and looked around the cabin for something to put over Dolan's body. He saw nothing.

"Give them the equipment bags," Canidy said to Darmstadter, and then turned to the team. "Take them into the woods. I don't suppose there's an axe in there?"

"Whole fucking kit of engineer tools. Even a power saw," one of them replied as Darmstadter lowered one of the long, padded bags onto his shoulders.

"And C-2?" Canidy asked.

"Hundred pounds of C-2, in two pound blocks," the

parachutist said, as he headed for the cover of the pine forest staggering under the weight.

The second parachutist took a bag as the other two members of the team trotted up.

"The lieutenant's in pain," he said. "Pretty bad. Should we give him morphine?"

"Not yet," Canidy said.

The parachutist gave Canidy a dirty look.

"Christ, he hurts! They never should have made him make this fucking jump!"

"He's not dead," Canidy said. "We'll be, if we don't get this airplane out of here before it's spotted."

Then he looked at Darmstadter.

"You *can* get it out of here?"

"No problem," Darmstadter said immediately, confidently.

A wild thought popped into Canidy's mind, and he asked the question:

"Loaded?"

"With what?"

"People. The team. Three others."

"Yeah," Darmstadter said, and then anticipated the next question: "I've got about two hours' fuel aboard. If I can find Vis, that gives me a thirty-minute reserve."

"What do you mean, if you can find it?"

Darmstadter pointed out the door. Canidy looked. It had begun to snow: large, soft-looking flakes.

"Dolan was navigating by reference to the ground," Darmstadter said. "Roads and railroads. I won't be able to see the ground. And I'm not sure I can find Vis just using a compass."

"That kind of snow won't last long," Canidy said, reassuringly.

But, he thought angrily, *that fucking snow is just what we don't need!*

And then he realized that exactly the opposite was true. The snow was just what he *did* need. It would obscure the tracks the landing gear had made on the meadow. And, if he was right, and it left just a dusting of fresh snow atop the inch or two on the ground, it wouldn't interfere with a takeoff.

"Start it up," he ordered. "I'm going to find a place to hide this big sonofabitch."

As he ran into the center of the meadow, looking for a break in the trees, someplace where the C-47 could be taxied to, he wondered whether his decision to use the gooney bird to get out of here was based on sound military reason (Darmstadter couldn't find Vis—he could; it was an available asset and should be used) or whether he subconsciously saw it as a lifeboat with himself as a drowning sailor, and was irrationally refusing to let it go, as drowning sailors will fight to get into an already loaded lifeboat, not caring that their weight will swamp it.

He snapped out of that by telling himself the decision had been made, and there was no going back on it now.

He found no place to hide the airplane, now sitting where it had stopped with engines idling and Darmstadter looking out the window, waiting for instructions.

Canidy ran back to it and signaled Darmstadter to turn it around, and then guided him to the edge of the forest, stopping him only when the nose was in the trees and the propeller on the right engine was spinning two feet from a thick pine trunk.

Three of the team members were watching him. He wondered if they were simply curious or had already decided he was crazy.

"You said there was a power saw," he said. "Get it. Cover as much of this thing as you can with the largest boughs you can."

"Why don't you just blow it?" one of them, the one who was so concerned about János being in pain, said. "You already got one fire."

"Everybody gets one question," Canidy said. "That was yours. I don't want to hear another. The answer to your question is we're going to get out of here on that gooney bird."

"You'll never get that off the ground in that short a distance," the parachutist said.

"That was an opinion," Canidy said, icily. "You get one, only, of those, too. The next time I want to see your mouth open is when I ask you a question."

The parachutist glared at him but said nothing.

"Get going!" Canidy said. "I want the snow to cover the boughs."

"There's an auxiliary fuel system," Darmstadter said. "A 55-gallon barrel connected to the main tanks. You want me to try to get it out?"

"That and anything else heavy we don't absolutely need."

"You're not talking about Commander Dolan?" Darmstadter flared.

"No," Canidy said. "We'll take Dolan with us."

The Countess's housekeeper appeared in the main room of the lodge when Canidy, Alois, and Freddy János, white-faced, his arms around their shoulders, walked into it.

She put a balled fist to her mouth. Canidy could not tell whether she was manifesting sympathy or fear.

"Major," János said, embarrassed, "I think I'm going to pass out."

"I'm going to give you something for pain just as soon as I get you in bed," Canidy said. "Tell him to tell her to keep her mouth shut."

They half carried János to the bed in which Canidy had slept and laid him flat on it. Canidy, as gently as he could, cut the boot from his leg, and then pulled a coarsely woven cotton sock—Hungarian, rather than GI wool-cushion-soled—from it. Somewhere in János's gear was a pair of Hungarian shoes which the plan called for him to put on once he was on the ground. The notion that jump boots might protect his ankle hadn't worked.

The ankle was blue and swollen, but there didn't seem to be any bones threatening to break through the skin.

Canidy opened a flat metal can, sealed with tape, and took a morphine syringe from it. He pushed János's trouser leg up as far as he could and shoved the needle into his calf. It would take a little longer for the morphine to take effect that way, but it would be less painful for János than moving his body around to get at his upper arm or buttock.

"That'll take a minute or two," Canidy said. "I'll be back."

"I'm getting sick to my stomach," János said.

"Tell him," Canidy said, nodding at Alois. "He'll get you something to throw up in."

Then he went looking for the Countess and von Heurten-Mitnitz.

It was not necessary under the circumstances, he decided, to bother knocking on doors and politely waiting for permission to enter.

He found them behind the third door he opened, nearly hidden under a goosedown comforter.

"Good morning," he said.

Helmut von Heurten-Mitnitz suddenly erupted from under the comforter, reaching for his Walther pistol as his eyes swept around the room.

The movement took the comforter off both of them. They were both naked.

The Countess, as Canidy had thought she might be, was a baroque work of art. His Excellency was a white-skinned, skinny man, from whose chest sprouted no more than a dozen long black hairs.

"What's all this?" von Heurten-Mitnitz demanded in outrage as he put the pistol down and pulled the comforter over himself and the Countess.

"The team is here," Canidy said.

"I presume you mean Ferniany," von Heurten-Mitnitz said.

"No, I mean the team," Canidy said. "They were dropped about thirty minutes ago. I think you ought to get dressed and get out of here right away."

I have just decided, Canidy realized, *that I am not going to tell them about the gooney bird.*

"Did everything go all right?" the Countess Batthyany asked.

"One of them has a broken ankle," Canidy said. "I brought him here."

"Where did you put him?" she asked.

"In my bed," Canidy said.

The Countess slid out from under the comforter, modestly turned her back to Canidy, and wrapped herself in a dressing gown. She found shoes, worked her feet into them, and brushing her magnificent mop of red hair off her face, walked out of the room.

Helmut von Heurten-Mitnitz got out the other side of the bed and started to dress. Naked, Canidy thought, and in his underwear (a sleeveless undershirt and baggy drawers, plus stockings held up by rubber suspenders on his skinny calves), von Heurten-Mitnitz was not at all impressive.

"We have one dead man, too," Canidy said.

"What happened?" von Heurten-Mitnitz asked.

"Natural causes," Canidy said. "A heart attack."

Von Heurten-Mitnitz didn't seem at all surprised by that announcement, which surprised Canidy.

"What are you going to do with the body?" von Heurten-Mitnitz asked. "Or the man with the injured . . . leg, you said?"

"Ankle," Canidy said. "I haven't made up my mind yet. The first priority, I think, is for you and the Countess to get back to Budapest."

"I think you're right," von Heurten-Mitnitz said.

Canidy returned to his room.

"You landed the airplane," the Countess greeted him, looking up from the bed, where she was prodding and pulling on the ankle of the now unconscious János.

Alois had apparently told her, and she would now certainly tell von Heurten-Mitnitz.

"Yes," Canidy said.

"I will remain here while Herr von Heurten-Mitnitz returns to Budapest," she said. "It would be better, if I were here when . . . if . . . the authorities come."

"I think it would be better if you went to Budapest," Canidy said. "Just as soon as you can."

She ignored him.

"I have sent for rubber bandage," she said. "I'm sure there's some here. I think about all we can do for this man is to wrap the ankle tightly, and then stiffen the ankle. You take my meaning?"

"Splint it," Canidy said, nodding. "Thank you."

Alois came into the room with von Heurten-Mitnitz on his heels.

"Their airplane landed," the Countess said.

Von Heurten-Mitnitz looked at Canidy, surprised.

"Intact?" he asked.

"Yes," Canidy said.

"And you plan to use it to leave?" von Heurten-Mitnitz asked.

Canidy nodded. "If we can."

"I think it would be best if you took Beatrice with you," von Heurten-Mitnitz said.

"No," the Countess said. "I am staying here to do what I can while you go to Budapest. But I am not leaving with them."

"I don't see any way that what has happened here can be hidden," von Heurten-Mitnitz said.

"Then you leave, too," the Countess said.

"There is a good chance that no one knows about either the drop or the plane landing," Canidy said.

"I think that is highly unlikely," von Heurten-Mitnitz said.

"You and the Countess slept through two passes and the landing itself," Canidy said.

Von Heurten-Mitnitz grunted, reluctantly granting the point.

"I don't want to have to worry about you, Countess," Canidy said, "while we're getting Eric and the professor out of St. Gertrud's. I want you to go to Budapest, and now."

She met his eyes for a moment.

"All right," she said finally. "Just let me do what I can for him."

Twenty minutes later, the Opel Admiral drove away from the lodge. By then, it had stopped snowing. Canidy wondered if enough snow had fallen to conceal the tracks the C-47 had made on the meadow, or to obscure the outline of the aircraft under the pine boughs.

Since Ferniany hadn't shown up, there was nothing else to do, so he went to see.

5

1715 Hours 21 February 1943

Ferniany drove up to the hunting lodge at the wheel of a small, canvas-bodied Tatra truck about the size of an American pickup. Canidy, summoned from the kitchen by Alois, went out to meet him. Ferniany had three men from the Hungarian underground with him, but that was about all.

There had been "a little trouble," he told Canidy. The Germans, or maybe even the Hungarians, he didn't know which, had had radio direction-finding trucks in operation, and they had located the radio transmitter from which he had radioed the drop zone coordinates.

There had been enough warning that the trucks were moving around, together with cars full of police, for him to get away before the police got to the hidden transmitter, but he had had to leave everything behind.

The police by now had found the signal panels, the radio, and the weapons, including the Sten submachine gun Captain Hughson had loaned Canidy on Vis.

"Where did the truck come from?"

"We stole it," Ferniany replied, just a little smugly.

"How do you plan to get rid of it?" Canidy asked.

Ferniany looked at him, making it clear he didn't think much of the question.

"Abandon it, when we're through with it."

"How many trucks do you think are stolen in Budapest and then abandoned in Pécs?" Canidy asked. "Did it occur to you that the police might find that curious? Or that the SS, now that they're aware there are people in here with transmitters and signal panels and English weapons, might be absolutely fascinated to learn that a truck had been stolen in Budapest and abandoned here?"

"We'll hide it in the forest," Ferniany said, lamely. "Bury it, even."

"The damage is done," Canidy said. "As soon as the team has gotten our people out of St. Gertrud's, you do whatever you can about the truck. Either, preferably, get it back to Budapest and abandon it there or take it someplace else. But get it away from here."

Ferniany did not seem to understand that stealing the truck had been a stupid thing to do. If they had been caught in the act of stealing it, or once they had it in their possession, even the dumbest Hungarian cop would have made the connection between someone barely escaping from the radio-detection operation, and someone heading out of town in a stolen truck.

And if he sensed that Canidy was furious, he showed no sign of it.

"You said, 'as soon as the team' gets our people out . . ." Ferniany challenged.

"Yes, I did."

"Major," Ferniany explained patiently, almost tolerantly, "without the signal panels and the radio, there's no way we can expect the team to get in here," Ferniany said. "We're going to have to do this ourselves."

"You've got some kind of a plan?" Canidy asked. It was all he trusted himself to say.

"Prisons are designed to keep people *in,*" Ferniany said, solemnly announcing a great philosophical truth.

"And?"

"From seven o'clock at night until five o'clock in the morning, there are on duty only six people: five guards and a sort of clerk. *And,* there is only one guard on the motor pool where they keep the trucks and motorcycles."

"You mean the mine trucks, the ones they carry the prisoners back and forth to the mine in?"

"Right," Ferniany said.

"So what you're going to do is knock over the guard at the motor pool, steal a mine truck, and drive it to the prison. You'll be a little early, but they'll recognize the truck and pass you inside, whereupon you and your three men will take on the five guards and the clerk, grab Fulmar and Professor Dyer, and make your escape?"

"I detect a little sarcasm," Ferniany said.

"Not a little," Canidy said.

He let that sink in, and waited for an angry response. He was surprised when none came.

"Right up there in importance with getting Fulmar and Dyer out," Canidy said, "is getting them out without calling anybody's attention to the fact that they are anything but what they were—thanks to your stupidity, we should keep that in mind—arrested for: black marketeers. Don't you think the Germans would be goddamned curious to learn why two people—who just happen to fit the descriptions of two men the whole goddamned SS is looking for—were busted out of an obscure Hungarian prison with more shooting and dead bodies strewn all over than in a Jimmy Cagney gangster movie?"

Ferniany's face colored with anger.

"I'm right on the edge of telling you to go fuck yourself, Canidy," Ferniany said.

"You really wouldn't want to do that, would you?" Canidy asked primly.

"Why wouldn't I?" Ferniany said. "According to you, I don't do anything right." He paused, but then was carried along by his momentum: "Fuck you, Canidy. Stick this whole operation up your ass. I'd like to hear how you plan to get them out, you wiseass sonofabitch."

"Now you've gone and done it," Canidy said, even more primly.

"Done what?" Ferniany said, curiously, a smile forming on his face.

"Used naughty words in front of the enlisted men," Canidy said, gesturing to Alois and the men from the underground, who had been fascinated by the angry exchange, not a word of which they understood. "Whatever will they think?"

Ferniany looked at the four Hungarians. Then, although he tried not to, the innocent curiosity on their faces made him laugh.

That seemed to reassure the Hungarians. The looks of puzzlement were replaced by broad smiles.

"I would be fascinated, Major Canidy, Sir," Ferniany said, "to learn precisely how the Major plans to carry out this mission."

Fourteen

1

Near San Juan, Island of Mindanao
Commonwealth of the Philippines
1815 Hours 21 February 1943

THE COMMANDING GENERAL of United States Forces in the Philippines had climbed a tree. It wasn't a very tall tree, and he hadn't been able to climb very far up it, but it was on the highest point he could find on a bluff thirty feet above a narrow sandy beach, and he was sure that it was giving him the best possible view of the sea.

It was growing dark. In fifteen minutes, it would be completely dark. Moving through the jungle at any time was difficult, and when it was dark, damned near impossible.

He knew he had made a bad decision coming here at all. What he should have done was send Withers and one or two of his men down here to see what happened, not come himself.

But he had wanted so desperately to believe that something would happen. So he had come himself, and brought an unnecessarily large force with him. He knew it was because he wanted witnesses that his hopes had come true. But what else was there for him to do?

He put the one and only pair of binoculars in the hands of U.S. Forces in the Philippines to his eyes.

He would search the open sea one more time, until his eyes started to tear from fatigue, he decided, and then he would order the withdrawal of this force by night to the mountains, and on the way maybe he'd think of one more credible excuse why "the aid" hadn't come this night either, one more reason to hope that maybe tomorrow . . .

There wasn't one miserable fucking thing on the surface of the water.

Somebody tugged on his shoe. He looked down in annoyance.

It was Master Sergeant Withers. He was pointing down at the beach, his hand shaking, and with tears running down his cheeks.

There was a submarine down there, in far closer to the beach than Fertig would have believed it possible for a submarine to maneuver. Torrents of water still gushed from ports in its side, but there were people on the conning tower, and then the colors went up on a mast over the conning tower.

Fertig's eyes filled with tears.

"I'll be a sonofabitch, there they are!" Withers said.

There was all sorts of activity on the submarine now. Sailors ran purposefully about the narrow decks, objects were handed up through hatches.

The commanding general of USFIP slid down the tree trunk, and slid down the bluff to the beach.

They had to wait for what seemed like an hour, but what was really not more than five minutes, before a rubber boat appeared close to the surf.

Half a dozen of his men ran out in water to their shoulders to reach it, to help it ashore.

Fertig thought, idly, that they seemed to be having a hell of a hard time pulling it.

And then somebody jumped out of the rubber boat, and Fertig walked into the receding surf to meet him, although he had told himself he would not, the salt water would be hell on already deteriorating boots.

He was a tall, and good-looking young man in khakis.

He splashed through the surf to Fertig.

And then he stopped, still in water to his knees and came to attention and saluted.

"Captain Whittaker, General," he said. "United States Army Air Corps."

"Welcome to Mindanao, Captain," Fertig said, returning the salute crisply, controlling his voice with a massive effort, glad now that it was dark enough that Whittaker wouldn't be able to see the tears on his cheeks.

"Sir . . . Sergeant Withers?"

Fertig pointed to the second rubber boat coming through the surf. With the same apparent difficulty that those helping the first boat had had, Withers was trying to hurry it ashore.

"Excuse me, Sir," Whittaker said, and ran into the surf. He returned with a very small sailor riding on his shoulders.

"Send 'B'," Whittaker ordered, as he set the small sailor onto the beach.

Joe Garvey flashed the Morse code signal for 'B', a dash and three dots, from a flashlight with an angled head.

There was an immediate response from a signaling light on the conning tower of the submarine. Garvey hurriedly took a pad from his pocket and wrote it down.

"What was that?" Fertig asked.

"Garvey sent them 'B'," Whittaker explained. "'B' is 'safely ashore, with equipment, in contact with U.S. Forces in the Philippines.'"

"Sir," Radioman Second Joe Garvey reported, "*Drum* messages, 'Aloha. God Bless.'"

Fertig looked out at the submarine. It was under way. The colors had already been hauled down. Its deck was already awash. It was going back under.

It didn't matter. If one came, others could. Others *would.*

"My men seem to be having a time getting your boats ashore, Captain," General Fertig said, trying valiantly to sound nonchalant.

"We've got medicine for you, General," Whittaker said. "And some small arms and ammunition. And a million dollars in gold coins. You wouldn't believe how much a million dollars weighs until you try to tow it around in a rubber boat with a 5-horse outboard motor."

2

St. Gertrud's Prison
Pécs, Hungary
0630 Hours 22 February 1943

The Tatra dump truck scraped the stones in the tunnel between the courtyard and the street with the left edge of its bumper.

A little harder than usual, Eric Fulmar, riding against the cab in the bed of the truck, thought idly. And then there was immediately another proof that it was going a little harder than usual. Instead of squeaking on through, the truck jerked to a stop, and with a clash of gears, backed up.

Oh, Christ, now what?

Then the gears clashed again, and the truck moved forward, and they were through the tunnel and onto the street.

It had snowed again overnight, not much, just a white dusting over the slush. Fulmar had hoped for freezing rain. That made the ride to the mine more interesting. He had concluded that all the truck drivers he had met since they had been locked up shared one quality: they had all learned how to drive last week and tried to hide this by driving as fast as the trucks would go.

On the slippery cobblestone streets on the way to the mines, they often skidded the truck into a ditch or into something hard enough to bend the fenders into the tires. This was routinely followed by marvelous displays of Hungarian temper and absolutely marvelous attempts to get the trucks out of the ditches by doing precisely the wrong thing.

Sometimes, as much as two hours would be lost. It was more pleasant than handling a donkey in the mines, and Fulmar looked forward to icy road conditions. He was disappointed this morning when the driver managed to negotiate a turn that had several times seen the truck skid into a ditch so steep that the rear wheels of the truck left the ground.

They were maybe a kilometer away from the mine when he felt the brakes lock, and the truck skid, and then jolt to a halt.

He could not see over the cab, so he had no idea what they'd hit.

A moment later, there was a call in Hungarian for everybody to get out.

Getting everybody out to push was routine, too. And while it wasn't as interesting as watching the Hungarians try to get the wheels of a dump truck back on the ground by swearing and throwing stones at it, it would still delay the journey into the mines.

It wasn't until he had slid from the truck bed and turned around that Eric saw that whatever was happening was not routine.

There were men behind the truck, Hungarian civilians with pistols; and the two Keystone Cops on the motorcycle who trailed the truck were on the ground, spread-eagled. As Fulmar watched, the driver and his assistant were brought to the rear of the truck and forced onto the ground beside the cops.

One of the men with pistols motioned the prisoners into a line, and then into two lines, then three, prodding the slow ones with the barrel of his pistol. And then another man came down the line and rudely jerked people out of line by grabbing their shoulders.

If I wasn't so afraid, this would be funny.

The man reached him, jerked Fulmar out of line, and marched him toward the front of the truck. Fulmar saw what had stopped the truck. A tree lay across the road. At first, he thought it had been sawed, but then he saw that it had been taken down by somebody who knew how to use Primacord.[1]

Standing near the cab of the truck were more Hungarians. One of them, in a large soft black woolen hat, looked somehow familiar.

"You do not recognize me," Canidy ordered quietly when Fulmar was dragged before him.

Fulmar shook his head in wonderment and smiled, but said nothing.

---

[1]Explosive formed in the shape of rope.

"We don't have much time," Canidy said. "Just tell me which of the others would escape if they had half a chance?"

Fulmar looked confused.

"You heard me," Canidy said. "I need to know who are the serious criminals."

Fulmar was as much confused by the question as he was surprised to see Canidy. But he finally understood that the question was important for reasons he could not imagine.

"These guys are petty criminals," Fulmar said. "If they weren't in jail, they'd probably starve. No real criminals, if that's what you're asking."

"Damn," Canidy said. "Now, is Professor Dyer one of the people we pulled out of there?"

Fulmar looked.

"Second from the end," he said, "with the glasses."

Canidy waved another of the Hungarians over and spoke softly to him in English.

"No gangsters," he said. "We'll just have to take half a dozen of them with us, that's all there is to it. You saw Dyer?"

"Yeah, but I don't think he recognized me."

"Let's try to keep it that way for the time being," Canidy said. "You go ahead and get them to uncover the plane."

"The plane?" Fulmar blurted. "You've got an *airplane?*"

"Take Loudmouth here with you," Canidy said. "He insists on talking English."

There was a sharp cracking noise, followed a moment later by a creaking, tearing noise, and finally a great crashing sound.

Fulmar realized that another tree, its trunk severed by Primacord, had been dropped across the road.

"Let's go, Lieutenant," the man Canidy had spoken to said softly, and Fulmar followed him off the road and into the forest.

It was a long way across steep, heavily forested hills from where the prison truck had been stopped to the meadow; and when they got there, Fulmar was sweat-soaked and panting from the exertion.

He didn't see an airplane. All he saw was a Hungarian standing at the far end of the meadow beside two of the largest horses he had ever seen. The horses wore whatever horses used so they could pull a wagon or a plow, but there was nothing around for them to pull.

And then, as they crossed the meadow, he saw a round red light sticking out of a snow-covered mound. And he understood that he was looking at the top of an aircraft vertical stabilizer.

An American pilot wearing a leather A2 jacket and with a Thompson submachine gun in his hands came out of the woods.

"This is Fulmar," Ferniany told Darmstadter. "Canidy's bringing the other one."

Darmstadter looked with unabashed curiosity at Fulmar.

This young guy in blue work clothes was the purpose of this whole operation?

"Hello," Fulmar said.

That shocked Darmstadter into action.

He looked around for someplace to put the Thompson down and finally hung it from a brass horn on the harness of one of the horses. Ferniany watched him, then shrugged and put his pistol in his pocket and went to the mound of snow-covered brush.

When the branches were off the tail section, Alois hitched a stout rope to the tail wheel and the huge horses pulled the C-47 far enough out of the forest to turn the airplane around.

It took half an hour to remove all the branches from the C-47. Some of them had frozen to the wings and fuselage, and small branches had wedged into the openings of the movable control surfaces.

Darmstadter started the engines, to make sure they would start. The engines started without difficulty, but when he tried to run the controls through their operating range, he found that snow had melted and then frozen the controls cables.

He let the engines run until they had reached operating temperature, then shut them down. Then he went after the ice in the ailerons and other movable control surfaces while Fulmar and Ferniany hammered at the ice on the wings. They quickly learned the best way to get it off was to stamp on it with their feet or slam it with their fists. The aluminum would then flex enough to free the ice, which could then be pushed or kicked out of the way.

They were still working on the airplane when the team, the Hungarian underground, Canidy, Dyer, and six wholly confused and terrified petty criminals from St. Gertrud's prison arrived.

"Wind it up," Canidy ordered. "We're going. Get those people aboard."

"We're taking them?" Fulmar asked, incredulously.

"Instant immigration," Canidy said. "Get them aboard."

Canidy stood by the door of the airplane as the Hungarians and the team and Professor Dyer got aboard. He collected the weapons and passed them to the Hungarians. Darmstadter started one engine and then the other.

"Get on, Eric," Canidy ordered.

Ferniany and Canidy looked at each other a moment, wordlessly.

"You aren't really such a horse's ass after all," Canidy finally said. "Take care."

"You are," Ferniany said with a smile. "A horse's ass, I mean."

Then he slapped Canidy on the back, and ran to get out of the prop blast.

Canidy climbed into the gooney bird. As he closed the door, Darmstadter started to taxi to the absolute end of the meadow.

Canidy slid into the co-pilot's seat as Darmstadter turned the gooney bird around.

Darmstadter locked the brakes, checked the mags, and then ran both engines up to takeoff power. The gooney bird trembled and bounced. He took the brakes off, and the airplane began to roll. First with maddening slowness, and then picking up speed. But not quite enough to get it off the ground.

As they reached the end of the meadow, Darmstadter pulled it into the air. There was not enough velocity to maintain flight, and it started to stall. Darmstadter pushed the nose down, getting it out of the incipient stall; and the gooney bird now followed the contour of the cut-over hillside down toward the stream. It was flying, but only barely.

And then he pulled back on the wheel again, and this time, having picked up just enough speed, the gooney bird was willing to fly for real.

"Very impressive," Canidy's voice came over the earphones. Thinking it was sarcasm, Darmstadter snapped his head toward him.

Canidy was beaming and making an "OK" sign of approval with his left hand.

And then Canidy's face registered genuine surprise, and the "OK" sign changed into a finger pointing out the windshield. Darmstadter followed it.

There were sixteen B-17 aircraft flying in five staggered Vs at what was probably eight thousand feet. Their bomb bays were open, and as Darmstadter and Canidy watched, streams of 500-pound bombs began to drop.

"They're bombing Pécs," Darmstadter said. "What the hell is there in Pécs worth bombing with a squadron of B-17s?"

Canidy didn't respond to that.

"I think you had better get back on the deck," he said. "Steer one nine zero."

3

OSS London Station Berkeley Square
London, England
1630 Hours 22 February 1943

Lieutenant Joseph P. Kennedy, Jr., came into David Bruce's office. Kennedy looked, Colonel Wild Bill Donovan thought, not unlike his father as a young man.

"Hello, Joe," Donovan said. "How are you?"

"Not very cheerful, Colonel," Kennedy said, raising a package in his hand. "Dolan's personal items. I didn't know what to do with them."

"I'll take them, Mr. Kennedy," Chief Ellis said. "I'll see that they get to his next of kin."

"Does he have any?" Kennedy asked. "I never heard him talk about a family."

"I'm sure there's a brother or a sister or somebody," Donovan said.

"And what do I do about Darmstadter?" Kennedy said.

"Write the letter myself, or let his old outfit do it? He was on TDY to the composite squadron, officially."

He was, Donovan thought, approvingly, already assuming the responsibilities of command.

"You write it, Joe," Donovan ordered. "Be vague. But let them know he went in as a volunteer doing something important." He thought about saying something else, realized that he shouldn't, but said it anyway: "I wish we could report them KIA (Killed in Action). Until we have positive word, of course, they'll have to be carried as MIA (Missing in Action). But I don't think there's any real hope."

"Yes, Sir," Kennedy said.

Donovan had been avoiding making the decision what to do about taking the necessary action about Dick Canidy and Ferniany. At the very least, they were missing in action. It might even be better to hope that they were dead. Just before it went off the air, interrupting a code block, the OSS radio station had sent the code for "Station discovered, in immediate danger of being captured."

It was reasonable to presume that Ferniany had been captured in Budapest. If that was true, and he was lucky, he would be dead. If that was true, and he was unlucky, he was alive and in the hands of the SS; and it might be some time before they were through with him and shot him. Or hanged him with a length of piano wire.

If they had caught him alive, it had to be presumed that he had given them Canidy's location and told them what he knew. No matter how little that was, it was certain to be damaging to von Heurten-Mitnitz, the Countess Batthyany, and the whole Hungarian pipeline.

There seemed to be little doubt that Fulmar and Professor Dyer were dead. The last B-17 had carried photographers, and there was proof beyond question that St. Gertrud's prison and three square blocks around it had been bombed into rubble.

Canidy, to be sure, might still be alive, on the run somewhere in the forests near Pécs. He had as many lives as a cat.

It was the particularly obscene nature of this business, Donovan thought, that I am forced to hope that he is dead. If he is dead, what he knows will not become known to the Germans.

He had decided that when he made up his mind to do it, he would personally write to the Reverend Doctor George Crater Canidy. He knew that it would be important, that Canidy would really want his father to believe he had died saving lives, not taking them. In a sense that was true, and maybe, Donovan decided, he would be able to make that point.

A more immediate problem was telling Ann Chambers. She had no legal right to know, of course. But legality had nothing to do with it. Donovan wanted her to hear it from him, and that meant he would have to tell her in the next couple of hours, before he got on the Washington plane.

"Joe," he said, "you understand, of course, that Operation Aphrodite is now your responsibility?"

"Yes, Sir."

"When Stan Fine gets back, he will fill the role Canidy had. You will report to him."

"Yes, Sir."

"There's more to it than the sub pens at Saint-Lazare," Donovan said.

"I assumed there was," Kennedy said, matter-of-factly.

Donovan's eyebrows rose.

"I'll have Colonel Stevens fill you in," Donovan said.

"Yes, Sir."

"We have to expect setbacks, Joe," Donovan said, wondering if he was talking as much to himself as he was to Kennedy. "And not everything has gone wrong. Just before you came, there was word that Jimmy Whittaker is safely ashore in the Philippines."

"Sir?" Kennedy asked, confused.

I am more emotionally upset by all this than I like to think I am; there was no reason for me to tell Kennedy that, and I should have known that he didn't know what was planned for Whittaker.

"That's out of school, Joe," Donovan said. "You don't have the Need-to-Know."

"You sent Jimmy *back* to the Philippines?" Kennedy asked, incredulously.

"He volunteered to go," Donovan said.

That's pretty lame, Donovan, and you know it. You did indeed send Jimmy back, knowing full well the risks.

The door opened. Capt. Helene Dancy walked in.

"I asked not to be disturbed," Donovan said, coldly angry. "Do I have to lock the door to keep from being interrupted?"

Just because you don't like yourself right now is no reason to jump all over her.

Capt. Dancy did not reply. White-faced, obviously hurt and angry, she marched to his desk, laid a TOP SECRET cover sheet on it, and marched back out of the office.

TOP SECRET

OPERATIONAL IMMEDIATE FROM STATION VII TO OSS LONDON EYES ONLY BRUCE AND STEVENS

EXLAX AND TINCAN ONE ALIVE AND WELL STATION VII STOP GOONEYBIRDING STATION VIII STOP WILL REQUIRE IMMEDIATE AIR TRANSPORTATION STATION VIII DASH LONDON SIX HUNGARIAN CRIMINALS AND REMAINS LT CMDR JOHN DOLAN STOP CANIDY

It took Donovan a moment before he trusted his voice.

"I think, Joe," he said finally, handing him the message, "that you had better hold off on writing Lieutenant Darmstadter's family until we can get this sorted out."

As Kennedy read the message, Donovan added, "Let Chief Ellis see it when you're finished."

"'Hungarian criminals?'" Kennedy asked. "Is that some kind of a code?"

"Not as far as I know," Donovan said.

"I wonder what happened to Dolan," Ellis said.

"You were friends, Ellis?" Donovan asked.

"Not really *friends,*" Ellis said. "Yeah, well, maybe. A couple of old sailors. I liked him."

The door opened again.

"Yes, Sir?" Capt. Helene Dancy asked.

"First, Helene, I'm sorry I jumped on you," Donovan said.

"That's perfectly all right, Sir," she said.

She's still mad.

"I think you had better message Wilkins, over my signature, and tell him to give Canidy whatever he wants when he gets there. You don't know what 'Hungarian Criminals' means, do you?"

"No, Sir. I presumably do not have the Need-to-Know."

"Neither do I, apparently, Helene," Donovan said. He smiled at her, and finally she cracked and smiled back.

"In that case, Sir," she said. "I think we have to presume that Major Canidy, for reasons he will certainly explain to us, is going to have six Hungarian criminals with him."

Donovan chuckled.

"Will that be all, Colonel?"

"Lieutenant Kennedy has Commander Dolan's personal effects," Donovan said. "Will you see if you can come up with a next of kin name and address?"

"I've already inquired. Nothing yet. I'll keep trying. Anything else?"

"You might tell Ann Chambers that Canidy is on his way home. If you think she'd be interested."

4

The National Institute of Health Building
Washington, D.C.
1830 24 February 1943

Chief Ellis was tired, unshaven, and mussed. It had been almost forty hours before the ATC C-54 from London had touched down at Anacostia. But he had ignored Colonel Donovan's orders to "go home and get some sleep, there's nothing that won't wait until tomorrow."

There was always something that wouldn't wait.

"You look like shit, Ellis," Staley greeted him.

"I feel like shit," Ellis said. "How come you aren't all dressed up in new Chief's blues?"

"Captain Douglass said he thought it would be nice if the Colonel made it official," Staley said.

"Yeah, hell, why not?" Ellis said.

"But you done it, Ellis," Staley said. "Thank you."

"We old China sailors got to stick together," Ellis

said. "And you're at the age where you look silly in bell-bottoms."

He tossed his overcoat on a chair, pushed his cap back on his head, sat down at the desk, and slid the stack of classified documents in front of him.

"Anything interesting in here?"

"Yachtsman is alive and well," Staley said. "That came operational immediately from London yesterday. What's it mean?"

"It's damned good news," Ellis said. "You don't have to know why. The Colonel will be happy as hell."

"Whittaker's ashore in the Philippines," Staley said.

"We heard that," Ellis said.

"And the radio works," Staley said. "There's a whole bunch of messages from Fertig."

"And anything else?"

"Two things for you," Staley said, uncomfortably. "I opened the telegram. I figured it might be important. It's on the bottom."

Ellis lifted the stack of cover sheets and found the Western Union telegram envelope.

US GOVT WASHINGTON DC 4 PM FEB 23
CHIEF PETTY OFFICER JOHN R ELLIS
C/O THE NATIONAL INSTITUTE OF HEALTH WASHINGTON DC

THE SECRETARY OF THE NAVY REGRETS TO INFORM YOU THAT YOUR FRIEND LIEUT COMMANDER JOHN DOLAN USNR DIED FEBRUARY 21 WHILE ON OVERSEAS SERVICE. FULL DETAILS WILL BE FURNISHED TO YOU WHEN AVAILABLE. YOU WILL BE SHORTLY CONTACTED BY NAVY OFFICIALS WITH REGARD TO YOUR SURVIVORS BENEFITS.

FRANK KNOX, JR
SECRETARY OF THE NAVY

"Jesus H. Christ!" Ellis said. "I guess he didn't have a family."

"It means you get the ten thousand insurance," Staley said.

Ellis gave him a look of disgust.

"There's a letter for you, too. Where the Western Union was."

The white envelope bore the neatly typewritten message, "To Be Delivered to Chief Ellis in the Event of My Demise. Lt. Commander J.R. Dolan, USNR."

Ellis tore it open. It was undated and short.

Dear Chief Ellis:

It's my professional judgment that one of these Torpex-filled airplanes is going to sooner or later blow up with me in it.

If you get this, I was right.

No complaints. It's a lot better way to go than sitting around the Old Sailors' Home waiting for it.

I have a cousin. I never could stand the sonofabitch. Unless I named you as my beneficiary, he would have gotten the insurance.

Hoist one for me, if you think about it some time.

Regards,

John R. Dolan
Chief Aviation Pilot, USN, Retired
(Temporary Lt. Commander, USNR)

Ellis folded the letter and put it back in the envelope.

"What's it say?" Staley asked.

"I'm going to catch a shave and put on a fresh uniform," Ellis said. "Then I'm going to go to the Chiefs' Club at the Navy Yard and tie one on. You want to come along?"

MEN AT WAR

"For those of us who were on war fronts in the early 1940's, it is fascinating to read this well-told story of the brave men and women who built the O.S.S. into the world's most effective intelligence organization. Heartening and thrilling."

—William Bradford Huie, author of THE EXECUTION OF PRIVATE SLOVICK

MEN AT WAR

"(Baldwin) captures the essence of the lure of clandestine operations which brought about the creation of the O.S.S. and the filling of its ranks with men and women of extraordinary courage whose exploits, even today, are best revealed in a book of historical/fact—fiction. Baldwin's 'heroes' are accurate, compelling prototypes of those in the O.S.S/CIA who have fought the hot and cold wars of the past four decades."

—William R. Corson, author of THE NEW KGB

"Secrecy, heroic deeds and seduction played out against a world at war."

—Publishers Weekly

"A WINNING COMBINATION OF HISTORY AND FICTION, FOCUSING ON THE FORMATION AND EARLY YEARS OF THE O.S.S., THE PRECURSOR OF THE C.I.A."
—Publishers Weekly

BUDAPEST, HUNGARY
An O.S.S. agent and a German scientist fall into enemy hands. The O.S.S. has to bring them out—or eliminate them.

MINDANAO, THE PHILIPPINES
MacArthur is gone, but an American guerilla army fights on—and the O.S.S. is about to join the war against the Japanese.

ENGLAND
America's best pilots are turning B25s into deadly flying bombs, in an all-out strike against the Nazis.

WASHINGTON
Roosevelt and Donovan dispatch their young fighters, fliers and spies to the four corners of the globe—in a sweeping assault on the Axis powers!

PRINTED IN CANADA

ISBN 0-671-60758-8